The Twilight Garden

Sara Nisha Adams is a writer and editor. She lives in London and was born in Hertfordshire to Indian and English parents. Her debut novel, *The Reading List*, was a finalist in the Goodreads Choice Awards for Fiction. Sara finished writing her second novel, *The Twilight Garden*, in her garden shed while foxes dug up the flowerbeds outside.

@saranishaadams
@saranishaadamsbooks

Also by Sara Nisha Adams

The Reading List

The Twilight Garden

Sara Nisha Adams

HarperCollins*Publishers*

HarperCollins*Publishers*
1 London Bridge Street
London SE1 9GF

www.harpercollins.co.uk

HarperCollins*Publishers*
Macken House, 39/40 Mayor Street Upper,
Dublin 1, D01 C9W8, Ireland

Published by HarperCollins*Publishers* 2023

1

Copyright © Sara Nisha Adams 2023

Sara Nisha Adams asserts the moral right to
be identified as the author of this work

A catalogue record for this book
is available from the British Library

ISBN:
HB: 978-0-00-839137-9
Export TPB: 978-0-00-839138-6

This novel is entirely a work of fiction.
The names, characters and incidents portrayed in it are
the work of the author's imagination. Any resemblance to
actual persons, living or dead, events or localities is
entirely coincidental.

Typeset in Adobe Caslon Pro by Palimpsest Book Production Ltd,
Falkirk, Stirlingshire

Printed and Bound in the UK using 100% Renewable Electricity
at CPI Group (UK) Ltd

All rights reserved. No part of this publication may be
reproduced, stored in a retrieval system, or transmitted,
in any form or by any means, electronic, mechanical,
photocopying, recording or otherwise, without the prior
permission of the publishers.

This book is produced from independently certified FSC™ paper
to ensure responsible forest management.

For more information visit: www.harpercollins.co.uk/green

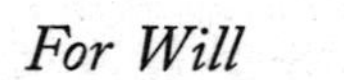
For Will

Part I

AUTUMN

Friday, 21 September 2018

You'll be pleased to know the garden is already tucking itself up for the autumn. The hazel is losing its leaves and looks rather spindly: the shadows of its corkscrew branches sometimes catch the corner of my eye and for a second, I imagine it as something otherworldly. We've always adored that tree, haven't we? Morris used to love curling up under there after a hard day's work, chasing birds or falling leaves. Though, in his ripe old age, his mind was a little more ambitious than his legs allowed him to be.

Our bed of dahlias is still going strong – café au lait, this year. The lad at the garden centre recommended them to me. I'm glad I followed his recommendation. They're quite something! Very luscious. But with all the heavy rain we've had, their heads are heavy, and I can barely cut the stalk without the flower dropping off with a splat. And if I do manage to pop any into a vase, I'll often spot a little snail who has snuck deep into the petals. One morning, I found three or four tiny snails creeping their way out of the cut flowers, sliding over my kitchen counters to the sink.

I'm afraid I don't have much gossip to share from Eastbourne Road. But do you remember me telling you about the red-trouser man who lives across the street from me? The one who is always pressing his belly up to his second-floor window whenever there's a commotion outside? Well, he's been at it again. Today, on a wander to Clissold Park, I spotted his bare stomach up against the glass, his phone sticking out of the top sash, taking photographs of a traffic jam. I passed those warring neighbours too . . . They're still banging on each other's doors, demanding they both 'keep the noise down!', but in the process, they manage to make more noise than there was in the first place!

There must have been something in the air today, putting everyone on edge. September is still bright and fairly warm, so perhaps the leftover heat is frazzling our neighbours' brains. You used to feel it at this time of year, too. Do you remember? Always snapping at those foxes, especially *when it was hot.*

Anyway, this new neighbour – one of the warring ones – well, she looks 'rather fancy', as you'd say. She's been here several months now, but she's new in the sense that she hasn't tried to get to know any of us. (But that's more common these days, I suppose.) Ever since she moved in, she's had the builders round – thankfully, they left the other day. For good. I breathed a sigh of relief when they packed up their skip. It was all so noisy. All that banter, the clattering of rubble. If Fraser had still been here, he'd have been yapping out the window at them every morning, trying to join in with their out-of-key singing, I reckon.

The house itself is almost unrecognizable. It's painted navy with a duck-egg blue door, which apparently is very 'on-trend' according to Jenny. In fact, I suppose the whole of Stoke Newington is starting to look more and more 'trendy'. Everything is manicured, too. Front gardens are all 'minimalist', decorated with little olive trees and bay trees in pots. Polished tiles, painted doors, and bin stores – yes, little sheds for the bins! I know we kept it nice when it was our time, but it was different, wasn't it? We were always sweeping, painting and tidying. We did what we could. And Prem loved making things, practical things. That chair! He was so proud of it. I imagine he'd have made a fantastic bin store if that was in vogue at the time.

The main difference between now and then, however, is the fact that I barely know a soul who lives behind those perfectly painted doors. I should start to chat more, invite people into the garden, I guess. It's what I promised. Things are different these days though, no one is quite as friendly as they used to be. Stepping out the door or saying hello to a stranger feels harder than ever. While this place will always be home, nothing is quite as familiar any more. All the old faces are making their way out of the city, or out of the world entirely.

Still, at least there's the garden. Every year it changes, but it always feels as magical as ever.

Love always,

Your friend,

Maya x

Chapter 1

Winston

September 2018

'Excuse me!' A voice, pinched and painful, pierced through the music flooding his headphones. 'Mr Winston, isn't it?'

He kept his eyes squeezed shut, trying to keep the calm of the morning going. The air still held the warmth of summer, but the breeze was all autumn. Winston was already missing the long, languorous days of August and early September, even if his usual sunbathing plans had been ruined by his charming new neighbour, who had turned every waking moment of this summer into a headache.

Since she'd moved into the house next door, which had been empty ever since Winston had lived here, everything had been chaos.

The two neighbouring houses had an unusual feature: a shared back garden. It had once been Winston's silent, scrubby smoking spot – his place for a moment of peace. But now it was their battleground.

For weeks, Winston and the Queen of Sheba (as his mother would call her, though he gathered from the builders that she was called Bernice) had been storming over to each other's houses to complain about something or other. First, it was because her builders began every working day at 8 a.m., sticking on an obnoxiously loud radio station, before drilling away, causing Winston's walls to vibrate ominously. They were friendly guys, and Winston would always stop to have a chat with them when he walked past, but when he learned that the Queen of Sheba had requested they work as many Sundays as they could manage, Winston couldn't bear it any more. Sundays were the only day he had off work. Without that day to lounge about and do nothing, he was a zombie all week long.

'What am I supposed to do? Live in a building site for the rest of my life?' she'd said to him one day, when he'd hammered on her door to ask if the builders could start at a more respectable time. 'I honestly don't care what you do with your life,' he'd muttered under his breath, 'As long as you don't keep ruining mine!'

Just a few days ago, he'd had to pound his fists against the adjoining wall between their terraced houses because when the builders weren't making a commotion, her young son was. Winston couldn't fathom how one small child could make so much noise, especially one who publicly appeared so angelic and polite. The kid had taken to charging up and down the stairs. But it sounded like a whole herd of rhinos. After six years living at Number 79, at the end of the terrace, with an empty house on the other side, Winston was used to peace and tranquillity. Bernice was a shock to the system.

In order to block out the noise of her child, he'd begun to play his music at a ridiculously loud volume (sometimes it was drum and bass, sometimes old school R&B, sometimes Kate Bush – he had eclectic taste). Naturally, the cacophony caused the Queen of Sheebz to come hammering on *his* door in return.

'Turn that blasted racket down!'

He could tell she wanted to use something stronger than 'blasted racket', but the peachy face of her son was poking out from behind her.

'Sebastian is trying to do his homework,' she said, more softly, and the Sebastian in question nodded his head in confirmation, no sign of the charging rhino that lived within.

And now here she was once again, disturbing Winston's repose in the garden. His heartbeat picked up a notch in frustration as her shadow loomed over him.

'Mr Winston?' she repeated loudly, clearing her throat.

He removed his headphones fiercely. 'I've told you, it's just *Winston*,' he said, sharp. What on earth was he doing wrong this time? He was sitting on the old wooden chair that had lived in this garden long before Winston arrived. His feet were resting on the ugly, grey cladding of the raised beds, with its decades-old paint peeling off. He hated these raised beds, overgrown with brambles and bindweed, the tangled mess accentuated only by the spicy tang of fox poo.

'Excuse me!' she said again, as though he hadn't spoken at all.

He opened his eyes. '*What* do you want?'

'Please don't smoke around my son,' she said to him plainly.

Of course. He should have known. Whenever he was smoking in the garden, Queen of Sheba would bang on her kitchen window, miming the action of stubbing out a cigarette, her face scrunched up in a grimace.

'I don't want him inhaling second-hand smoke.'

He sat up at that, his eyes searched for her son.

'He's not even out here!' Winston said. But as soon as the words left his mouth, he caught a glimpse of the boy, his face pushed up against the glass from a first-floor window, hands covering his mouth, doing his best to hold back the giggles threatening to burst out of his eyes, ears, nose and mouth.

Winston's cigarette fizzed away at his fingertips. He leaned back to take one last long drag, blowing the smoke upwards in the direction of her glaring gaze. If his mother could see him right now, she'd be both appalled and delighted at his attitude.

'Of *course*, honey, you should have said,' he replied, ice in his voice. The Queen of Sheba winced at the word 'honey', as he'd hoped, but her reflex, the drop in her eyes . . . it made him wonder if it hit deeper. If someone else she despised had called her that, once upon a time.

Within seconds, that look on her face, the darkness and distance in her stare, was gone. Her disdain was back. 'That's disgusting,' she muttered. Then she turned round and headed into her kitchen, the door swinging shut behind her. Their two terraced houses looked back at Winston. The structures were mirror images of each other – Victorian brickwork, pitched roofs, tall chimneys. But her house was modernized; the large crittal kitchen windows were brand new and spotless, fitted by the builder who thought he was the next James Blunt. Winston's sash windows, however, were clearly years old, the glass water-stained and grubby from the rain, sitting within ancient, rotting frames.

Winston allowed himself a deep breath to soak in the peace. Finally. Until—

'Hey!' Sal's voice called over the garden wall from the street running alongside the garden. First, all Winston could see was Sal's bobble hat, which, he assumed, belonged to Sal's wife, Angela. He hated to stereotype, but pink and white stripes and a rainbow bobble weren't really Sal's vibe.

'All right, Sal?' Winston said, as Sal's thick eyebrows and green eyes made their way over the top of the wall. He was instantly cheered by the sight of his boss and friend.

'Winston, my son, would you be able to cover the shop for me? I know you're on your day off but it's only for a few hours. I've got to pick Angela up from Pilates.'

'Of course.' Winston tried to hide his immediate disappointment. He'd been looking forward to a day off work, pissing off the neighbour, lazing about on the sofa listening to old CDs that reminded him of his family, and batch-cooking food he'd always forget to eat. He'd planned a whole day of activities to forget the fact that he was spending his and Lewis's five-year anniversary alone. Lewis was at the office, again, for the tenth day in a row. He'd barely been home at all in that time, and the anniversary present Winston had wrapped up earlier in the week was now sitting on the kitchen counter, untouched. He'd managed to find an original Little Eva vinyl – a record Lewis's dad had always played for him as a kid but had long since lost. The envelope on top was adorned with a decorative 'L' and five stars, one for each year they'd been together. Winston felt silly now, paying that much attention to the detail.

Maybe working in the shop would be a more fitting way to celebrate their anniversary anyway. He spent more time with the customers than he did with Lewis these days.

He glanced down at his phone. Lewis hadn't even sent a 'Happy Anniversary' message yet. There was just one text from Winston's elder sister Ruth, who lived in Canada with her family: *Little Winston, missing you. FaceTime soon?*

She sent the same message every week or so, sending photos of her two children, who had grown so much since he'd last seen them: they were eight and nine now. He'd last seen them when they were toddlers.

No matter how regularly she messaged or tried to call, Winston never seemed to find the right time to ring her back.

As Sal's bobble hat bobbed off along the wall, Winston headed through to the hallway to put his proper shoes on. 'Shit!' he cursed, slipping on a batch of junk mail littering the doormat. He bent over to pick up another envelope full of pamphlets about some local gardening scheme; photos of frilly flowers adorned the pages.

'Who on earth thinks I have the energy for gardening?' he muttered, shoving it onto the telephone stand along with all the other post. Handyman business cards. Palm reader leaflets. Takeaway menus. And envelopes addressed to 'The Occupants of Number 79' with scrawled comp slips from estate agents asking, 'Have you thought about selling your house?'

He slammed the door loudly behind him, in honour of the Queen of Sheba.

'Funny to see you here on a Sunday,' said Jenny, one of the most memorable and long-standing locals at Sal's shop. Winston instinctively reached up to get her two packs of twenty Marlboro reds, complete with a rather unappetizing photograph of someone's blackened lungs. Jenny must be over eighty now, though Winston had never asked her age, and rumour had it that she'd bought forty Marlboros from Sal's shop three times a week since records began.

'Come on, Vincent, hand them over,' Jenny chuckled. Winston admired her loyalty and consistency, and her dress sense. Today she was sporting a vintage-looking fur coat, and some wet-look leggings. He *wasn't* such a fan of her getting his name wrong. Though at least she was consistent there too.

He always heard his mother's voice in these moments: 'I gave you an English name so no one could get it wrong.' Winston had tried correcting Jenny about his name, but every time he did, she simply said: 'I *know*. Like the painter. Lovely name.' The only thing that stopped him from correcting her further was the thought of having to say: 'No, Winston like Churchill.'

Sal, however, got the roughest deal. Jenny still called him 'chubby cheeks', the nickname his father lovingly used when Sal was a boy, spending all his time reading picture books behind the counter. The shop had been in Sal's family for decades – it was something of an institution on Stoke Newington Road.

'How come you're here today, Vince?' Jenny repeated.

'I'm covering Sal – he's picking Angela up from Pilates,' he said, maintaining a smile.

Jenny nodded, handing over her cash and wandering off with a wink. Her hands held firmly onto her Zimmer frame, waiting for the sea of queueing customers to part for her: they always parted for Jenny. Word had got round that there were consequences if you didn't oblige. Someone's big toe had once fallen victim to Jenny's Zimmer. 'An honest accident,' she'd said, but her cheeky smile told a different story.

Winston loved the sense of belonging at the shop. The everyday quirks, the snapshot of other people's lives, the familiar faces. He even liked people like 'Howard the Complainer' who enjoyed moaning about the state of the world for half an hour before proceeding to buy a lonely pack of Sesame Snaps for his goddaughter. Winston liked chatting to the woman who came in every so often to buy mung beans, usually when her father was popping over: 'He only eats mung beans, sometimes with okra,' she'd say, and the two would laugh and share recipe tips. 'Tell me he at least has the mung with badh and kadhi?' Winston asked, and Vritti, the customer, would nod. 'If I'm making it, that's the only way. My mother would be appalled otherwise.' And finally, there was the anonymous customer, who'd pop in now and then simply to remark on the weather. 'Cold today, isn't it?' he'd say, if he saw Winston in his fingerless gloves. Or 'Rather hot, isn't it!?' if the gloves were off.

Together, they were a community. And among them, he could be completely himself.

Well, usually.

That's when he spotted her. Queen of Sheba. Cradling a bottle of wine in each arm, like twin babies. She was chatting obnoxiously loudly to a little Bluetooth headset.

Why was she here? He'd *never* seen her in the shop before.

'Complete nightmare,' she tutted away. 'He's unbelievably *rude*. He has no respect at all . . . No, Clemmie. It *is* true.' Her eyes were darting around the shop, flicking from the cabinet housing seventeen different types of rice, to the artisan beers in the refrigerator, and the aisle displaying every kind of olive imaginable.

'It's like he's been raised by savages . . . No, Clemmie, I don't mean that in a racist way . . .' she whispered the last sentence, still loud enough for several heads in the shop to turn towards her. 'He's always wandering around,' she continued, 'puffing away on vile cigarettes, lounging about all the time on a chair that looks like it was eaten up and spat out by wolves. Sometimes I wonder if he's got a job at all, because he always seems to be bumming around. How does he afford the rent? This is a *nice* area on the whole. No, Clemmie, it's not how it was in the nineties, it's *actually* nice now.'

Winston's face burned. He did not 'bum' around, his only day off was Sunday! And she could talk – he'd seen her spend hours in front of the television watching endless repeats of *Homes Under the Hammer*.

As the teenager at the counter packed away three Pot Noodles into a 'War on Plastic' canvas bag, the Queen of Sheba stepped forward. 'I've been thinking of calling his landlord. Get him booted out. I at least want him to be forced to tidy up after himself,' she said, at the precise moment her gaze fell on Winston. She didn't register him at first; her eyes lazily roving over him, uninterested in the invisible person behind the counter.

And then . . .

Her expression.

Priceless.

She stopped speaking, mouth hanging open, eyes wide, disbelieving.

'Hello again, neighbour,' Winston smiled sweetly, as she plonked her bottles on the counter.

She made her excuses to her friend, her tone instantly shifting from exasperated and outraged, to something more saccharine. 'Anyway, better go. Love to you and the family, darling Clemmie . . .'

As he rung each bottle up, Bernice kept her eyes on the cash register – flashing up £11 and then £14 and then TOTAL: £25.

'Nice wines,' was all he said. He didn't know why. 'Some kind of wine connoisseur, are you?' He tried to maintain the tone he used with the other customers, but it came out sharper.

'Sommelier,' she said bluntly.

'What?' He kept his eyes on his hands, bagging up the bottles.

'The word you're looking for is *sommelier*,' she said again, the French accent even more pronounced this time.

'Right,' he said. He hadn't been looking for any word, but now 'knob' came to mind. 'Twenty-five pounds, please,' he said.

Winston focused his eyes on the floor-to-ceiling stacks of cereal in the far-right corner, the beaming face of Tony the Tiger taunting him in his frustration. On the security monitor in front of him, he noticed how far away from the desk she was standing. Most people leaned up against his counter, gesturing wildly with their arms as they told stories of their grandchildren, work dramas, or cheating partners.

'Cash or card?' Winston asked.

'Card.'

No 'please'. But why would the Queen of Sheba say please?

Before he could ask if she wanted a receipt, she was out the door. And in her wake was Jenny with her fur coat and her Zimmer frame, pushing her way back to the counter. He watched as the queue of grumpy faces melted away to amused smiles, as she chorused: 'Thanks, pet,' and 'Move out my way please, love.'

'Vince!'

Winston gritted his teeth behind his smile.

'Vince!' she repeated.

'All right, Jenny?'

'You gave me *menthols*. I haven't got my glasses on, but I'm pretty sure they're menthols, Vince.'

She popped the unopened packets back on the desk. Those dark, blackened lungs looked up at him. They *were* menthols. If she didn't have her glasses on, how did she realize?

'Felt different to me,' Jenny said, reading his mind.

'Sorry, Jenny.' Winston swiftly handed over the correct packs of Marlboro reds. 'Really sorry.'

'No stress, love,' Jenny pocketed them. 'You've never done that before. Everything okay? Who was *that*, anyway?' She nodded her head in the direction of the door.

'Who was who?' he said, conscious of the customers now tutting behind her.

'That woman. Bag of bottles. Your girlfriend or something?' She squeezed her face into a teasing smile. 'What's happened to your fella?'

'No, no, that's my new neighbour. Moved in a few months ago. We're not the best of friends.'

'Ha!' Jenny laughed, throwing her head back. 'I thought the sexual chemistry was sizzling,' she joked, throwing a theatrical look at the customers behind her, who obliged with a giggle at Winston's expense.

'Thanks, Jenny,' Winston groaned. 'Always the charmer!'

Winston took a quick glance at his phone, wondering if Lewis had messaged yet. But there was nothing – only his phone background, a photo of Lewis and Winston arm in arm on the beach, silhouetted by the sun. It felt like another life.

'Next, please,' he said, trying to hide the croak of disappointment in his voice.

Chapter 2

Winston

September 2018

After being shepherded away from the shop on Sal's return, Winston wandered slowly down Stoke Newington Road. He passed couples laughing together, or pulling each other close, braced against the autumn breeze. Groups of friends sat outside the pub putting the world to rights, sloshing their pints to punctuate their points, cackling at their silliness. He kept his head down, observing as one foot moved in front of the other. He tried to ignore the darkness of the evening creeping into his chest, making it harder to breathe. The cold turned his lungs to blocks of ice.

After his shift, usually Winston would sit himself in front of the TV and wait for sleep to catch him there. It meant that when Lewis came in after work, no matter how late, he would wake Winston up, and they could head upstairs together – so going to bed was a little less lonely at least. But since Bernice and her son had moved in next door, falling asleep on the sofa was harder. Their laughter, their happiness, and sometimes their shouting matches, kept him alert, awake. As much as he despised the Queen of Sheba, he envied her too. A constant reminder that she had a life, a family, a son to keep her company.

Here, Winston was alone more often than not.

He turned the corner off Stoke Newington Road onto Eastbourne Road, and allowed himself to look up. His gaze washed over the identical architecture of the Victorian terraces on his street. Some houses were newly painted, front doors shining with their brass knockers and bold numbers. He wondered what went on behind those doors. There were so many people here he'd never met. He was always chatting to customers in the shop, but when it came to the neighbours on his road, he barely knew faces, let alone names. Most curtains were closed now. Though some living-room lights exposed silhouettes of cheese plants and fig trees, creating an impressive urban menagerie. These were the only clues he had to work out who lived beside him, what their lives might be like.

Halfway down the road, he could already hear the television playing from Number 68 several doors away. The first-floor flat at Number 68 *always* had the TV on. A British sitcom and its tinny backing track drifted out of the eternally open window to welcome Winston home to his house across the road: Number 79.

As his front door came into view, he pictured himself six years ago walking down this same street to view the house for the very first time. Lewis, who was only a colleague of Winston's back then, had a spare room going after one of his flatmates moved out.

'You don't want to be living with your aunt forever, do you?' he'd said.

Winston really didn't. His 'aunt' was a distant cousin of his mum's in Harrow. At her house, Winston had to abide by her curfew, her restricted diet, and a dull commute. He'd already lived there for five years at that point. Enough was enough.

Lewis and Winston had got to know each other while working at the same bank in the City. Lewis seemed to belong there.

Winston never had. Despite their many differences, there was something that drew Winston to Lewis. He was playful, yet he rarely made jokes at the expense of others, and he never took himself too seriously, which couldn't be said for all Winston's colleagues.

A year or so into his new life, after spending a lunchtime with Lewis, talking about anything and everything from TV shows they loved and their dream celebrity dinner party guests to moaning about their bosses and debating the pros and cons of the capitalist system, Winston called his mother up and said confidently: 'Ma, I've made a friend.' On the other end of the phone, he could hear his mother in her garden in Ahmedabad, the parakeets squawking loudly. He felt the warmth of the wind as though he was there with her. 'Beta,' she replied. 'I knew you would. It's impossible not to be friends with you. I'm proud of you.'

But Winston hadn't expected to fall in love with his friend just a few months later.

'Welcome,' Lewis had said, opening the door of Number 79 to Winston all those years ago. 'This could be your new home!' he bellowed, in a dramatic TV-estate-agent kind of way. Winston's cheeks hurt so much from the laughter that followed.

The house had been a typical bachelor pad: video games piled up next to the television; tacky soft furnishings from TK Maxx or Primark; brown fluffy cushions and leatherette sofas, wearing away at the arms. The shelves were lined with rows upon rows of beer bottles on one side of the chimney breast, and bottles of port on the other.

'You like port?' Winston said, thinking of it as an old man's drink.

'My flatmate's a trainee lawyer,' Lewis answered, as if that explained it.

When Lewis showed him the third bedroom, with a window overlooking the large garden, Winston took a sharp breath. There were rose bushes in peachy-whites and bright reds, out in full bloom. Large dusky lilac and deep purple buddleias were popping up in all four corners of the garden. It was beautiful, if a little neglected. And it wouldn't be long until the bindweed swallowed them whole – tell-tale tendrils were already climbing up the stems.

'Garden's huge, isn't it?' Lewis said. 'I asked why there wasn't a fence . . . we can get right up to next door's kitchen door. Landlord said the garden is shared. Some weird clause in the deeds or something, but no one lives in that house at the moment. I think it's for sale. But for now, it means the garden is basically all ours. We've not done anything out there, but we're going to get some sort of picnic table so we can have parties or something. Haven't got round to it yet.'

Winston took in the room once more – the white walls and large window made it airy and bright. The shelves were bare, ready to be filled. It felt like an opportunity to live a new life. 'I love it,' Winston had said, and it was decided. Winston was moving in.

They lived like that in separate rooms with Justin, Lewis's lawyer friend from uni, until he moved out to live with his girlfriend a few months later.

'What do you think about . . . maybe . . . not getting anyone else in? I can't be bothered to interview any more flatmates,' Lewis said one day when they were hanging out in his attic bedroom, squeezed side by side under the Velux window, drinking wine from mugs.

'Really?' Winston replied, looking at Lewis. 'Just us two?'

'Just us,' Lewis nodded.

'I guess we can see how it goes,' Winston replied, a flutter of nerves in his stomach.

Over the next two months, they only got closer. He spent fewer evenings in his own room, and more time in Lewis's top-floor bedroom. From Lewis's window, he could see the whole city. The whole world.

Eventually, after a year living together, Winston found Lewis in the kitchen, chopping onions for his special spaghetti Bolognese recipe. 'I'm going to quit,' he'd said, and Lewis looked at him, knife held on the chopping board, eyes panicked.

'Us?' His voice quivered.

Winston's breath caught in his throat. *Us.* They had never discussed the concept of 'us' – they'd seamlessly become an 'us' without ever vocalizing it. Hearing Lewis utter the word, he realized for the first time that he hadn't dreamt it all up.

'No,' Winston smiled. 'My job.'

Lewis nodded. Resumed his chopping. A smile curled his lips, and his shoulders relaxed. Lewis had recently been promoted and was firmly on the banking career path. Winston, on the other hand, had been looking for any excuse to jump, trying to find another role, another opportunity, that might suit him better.

'Do you know what you want to do?'

'Not yet,' Winston gulped. He didn't have a plan – his mother told him to *always* have a plan. 'But I hate it there. You know I hate it. It's not my dream . . . it's what my dad wanted.' Winston's hairs stood on end at the thought of all the money his father had paid to get him here, to provide his son with the opportunity to live the life he'd mapped out for him, in the City of London. 'I'll get a part-time job, until I figure something out.'

'That's okay,' Lewis nodded, smiling at Winston. 'You've got to do what's right for you. Life is too short, Winston. My new salary can cover most of our rent, and Dad's helping me too, so we'll split it based on income. We'll work it out.'

Winston had heard his mother's warning in his mind, telling him to 'never rely on someone else for money'. And he knew it was too much: a three-bedroom house, for the two of them. It was extravagant. They were in their mid-twenties: everyone else he knew was living in a boxroom, or renting a huge house with a mice infestation and strangers they'd never hope to be friends with. His mother was right, but this was Lewis. This was *us*.

When he first applied to work at Sal's shop, it was a stopgap. Convenient. Only two minutes away. A chance to earn some money while he worked out what his 'next step' would be. But working with Sal and Angela created a new family for him and he began to feel that he could belong here, in this city, beyond his life with Lewis.

The work was hard and tiring. His feet ached after long shifts, and he'd collapse into bed at the end of the day. But he felt closer to people. He was no longer in an office twelve floors up, looking down at his city, unable to interact with or understand the people with whom he shared it.

But as Winston perfected his work-life balance, in a job he loved, a job he was privileged to be able to choose, Lewis's began to slip. He worked longer and longer hours, and Winston realized that while he had more time, he had no one to spend it with.

'You've sold your soul,' Winston wanted to say. But Lewis's job meant Winston could live the life he did, and so he never said a thing.

He put his key in the door, illuminating the keyhole with his phone torch and pushing the door open. 'Hello? Lewis?' he called, more in hope than expectation. There was no reply within the dark, silent house.

Once upon a time, in those early days of love, opening the front door sparked joy. Stepping inside, Winston felt safe in the world he and Lewis had created for each other, with the collection of silly magnets on the fridge, the shoes spilling out of the hallway cupboard, the photos adorning the mantelpiece from trips to Rome, Florence, Paris. He'd wander into the kitchen to find Lewis pouring a glass of wine for them both, his famous Bolognese (the only thing he could cook!) bubbling away on the stove. It was everything he hadn't realized he'd so desperately wanted.

Today, on their anniversary, he wanted to relive those moments. He wanted Lewis. But as he stepped forward, his foot collided with a box on the front step: *DEAL WITH ASAP* was scrawled messily across the side. The previous address hastily scribbled out.

This was the closest he'd get to Lewis today.

He picked the box up and brought it to the kitchen counter, placing it next to his own gift for Lewis.

Inside was a selection of Yankee candles, a bottle of Veuve Clicquot and a note ripped out from a lined notebook.

W, it read, in Lewis's scribbled, spidery handwriting. *Happy Anniversary, my love! Am working late today. Sorry I can't be with you this evening, but here's something so you can enjoy our night. Love, your L xxx*

Winston opened the bottle of Veuve immediately, barely registering the thrill of that 'pop'. He gulped straight from the neck, waiting to feel something.

He wandered into the living room, where light from the streetlamps outside cast a ghostly golden glow over the empty room and the furniture. He stared out at the pristine hedge of Number 80 opposite, with its polished red-and-cream tiles leading up to the lollipop-red front door. Even from here, he could hear the piercing voices from Number 68's television. Would that be his life one day too? Sitting in front of the TV, all day, every day, the sliver of air through the open window his only contact with the outside world?

Then he spotted two people from the four-generation family that lived at Number 78: a house the same size as his and Lewis's. Mother and adult daughter unlocked their front door, their arms laden with shopping bags and big five-litre bottles of cooking oil: they were regulars at Sal's, though he didn't know their names. Often he could hear the baby wailing, followed unfailingly by the great-grandma calling out in patois, demanding someone calm the child down. Winston always smiled when he heard them, because it reminded him of his own childhood, living with his grandmother back in India.

There were people like the red-trousered man at Number 80, whose pristine hedge kept his perfect, expensive life shielded from the rest of the world. It shouted, 'my life is so perfect, I have time to trim this hedge every week, or I'll pay someone to do it for me.' Then there were families like the one at Number 78, who he imagined had lived here for generations, their neighbourhood changing around them constantly. And then there were people like him, who lived in other people's houses, holding onto a lifestyle he might never really be able to afford.

With the bubbles tickling the back of his throat, Winston left the window and wandered through the empty house, the bottle held at his side. In the garden, he trudged to the far right-hand corner where Queen of Sheebz had tucked his wooden chair behind the eucalyptus tree, blocking 'the eyesore' from her view. Since Bernice had arrived here, he was no longer at peace in this mess of a garden. He was as unwanted and unwelcome as the rats and foxes that ran through. He yanked the rickety wooden chair away from the tree and carried it to the very centre of the garden, like an act of rebellion. His eyes ran over the words *Handmade by Prem* inelegantly engraved into the wood on the back of the crossbar. He sat down heavily, a slosh of champagne spilling over the lip of the bottle, trickling stickily down his hand.

Winston loved his job. And there were so many things he loved about this city, and this neighbourhood. But why did it feel like there was something missing? As the chill of the night clawed under his jacket, biting at his ankles, he wondered whether that feeling of home would come back any time soon.

He listened to the medley of sirens and cars tooting along Stoke Newington Road in the distance, punctuated by chatter as people wandered past the garden wall, and he took in the smells of his neighbours frying onions and garlic for dinner. With his bottle of Veuve Clicquot held tightly in his hand, Winston was surrounded by signs of life.

So how come he felt lonelier than ever before?

Chapter 3

Winston

September 2018

Winston woke early after a fitful sleep. He'd jumped at the slightest noise on the street during the night, hoping it meant Lewis was home. But there was no key turning in the door, no creaking of floorboards or rustling of covers to signal Lewis's arrival. He'd stayed at work all night. And Winston tried to ignore the lead settling in the pit of his stomach.

He leaned his arms on the windowsill. The city was waking up beneath him, the night sky making way for the new day. In the foreground, rectangles of warm, yellow light spilled out of windows: bedrooms, landings, living rooms. Chimneys and pitched roofs demarcated areas of home from the rest of the city: towers, and offices, lights in the Shard, cranes ready to create more buildings. Winston felt tiny in comparison. A dot on the landscape of this life.

He was taking a deep breath and a slurp of his hot tea, the taste of morning bitter in his mouth, when he caught sight of a bright pink splodge moving around in the garden, clattering and stomping.

'Oh, for shit's sake,' he heard from the Splodge of Sheba. She was muttering expletives loudly, her frustration punctuated by dull wooden thuds and metallic clanging as she wrestled inanimate objects in the garden.

'Oi!' he shouted down, forgetting the sleeping neighbours surrounding them. 'What the hell do you think you're doing?'

Wearing yellow rubber gloves, a pink towelling dressing gown and beige fur-lined mules, the Queen of Sheba started to lift his wooden garden chair, holding it as far away from herself as possible.

Winston slammed the window shut and catapulted his way down the stairs as quickly as he could, the calm of the morning over.

Pausing in the kitchen doorway, tea in his hands, he took a breath, trying to keep his face as neutral as possible, tilting his head to the side. It was the pose his mother employed whenever he was caught prising open metal tins of leftover dhokri, or trays of handvo cooling on the counter, or sneaking handfuls of lovingly rolled khandvi from the fridge.

'My son was playing with it!' Bernice said sharply as he threw the door open wide, stepping into his sliders. 'It looks like it might rot to nothing at any moment.' She looked Winston up and down. 'Hazardous,' she finished.

'It's *my* chair,' he said tersely, picturing the words *Handmade by Prem*, whoever he was, engraved on the back. He felt his hands squeeze tight around his mug, the heat burning into his skin.

'Clearly,' she paused, for dramatic effect, placing the chair down for a moment. 'But this is our *shared* garden . . . as much as I hate that fact . . . so anything rotting or dangerous of yours affects me and my son. This needs to be a safe space for him, and I won't let you come in the way of that.'

Heaving the chair up once again, she marched towards her kitchen door, forcing Winston to step onto the patio to keep sight of her.

'Where do you think you're going now?'

'I'm dumping it in the bin,' she replied, wrestling the chair into her house, slamming the door behind her. The panes of glass in Winston's kitchen window rattled in their frames. Her windows, on the other hand, were as still as anything.

'What the hell,' Winston hissed under his breath. With a soft rage bubbling up, he strode towards his front door, opening it wide. As threatened, the Queen of Sheba was depositing his wooden chair into her black bin, the frame barely squeezing inside. She strode back inside while throwing a smug look over her shoulder.

Winston waited for a moment or two, silently seething, before stomping into Bernice's front garden and promptly pulling the chair out of her bin. The twitching of her living-room curtains told him she was watching his every move. But if he could get back inside with the chair before she had time to unlock the twenty latches on her front door, he'd be fine.

As he quick-stepped it back into his house, the weight of the chair demanded the use of all the muscles in his core. He headed back into the garden. Crunching through the fallen leaves, expertly weaving through the mounds of mud and cat shit, he stormed towards the rotting shed in the left-hand corner and placed the chair safely under its awning.

He paused then, peering through the shed's only window, licked with a dusty green residue. A weathered sign hung above the door. He remembered it from his first week in the house. While it had been faded then too, the words *The Potting Shed* had been legible in flaking yellow and blue paint. Someone, a long time ago, had clearly taken care over that sign, this shed. Who had it been? Was it Prem? The person who made the chair?

His mother had a shed like this one in her garden, painted a bright orange to offset the lush greens of the baby banyan beside it, the ornamental grasses sailing in the wind, and her banana trees. Inside, she had built shelves with hooks and pegs across the length of the shed, so all her tools were organized. She even had an index sheet.

He imagined his mother, selecting her tools for the day, as he peered back through the green-fogged window of the shed. In all the time he'd lived here, he'd never set foot inside, though the rusty padlock was hanging off. He could see tools, watering cans, gloves, old-fashioned secateurs. He imagined Prem, or whoever had lived here, taking care over their instruments, potting up plants, nurturing the garden that Bernice and Winston used as their battleground. And once more he saw his mother stepping out of her own shed with a basket full of equipment, ready for her day, a smile on her face. A lump rose in Winston's throat.

Back inside a few hours later, Winston's phone buzzed on the coffee table. He woke with a jolt, taking a moment to realize where he was. He must have dozed off. The faces of his sister, mother and father beamed at him, clutching each other at a family wedding, outfits glowing like the sun. But it was only a photograph on the living-room mantelpiece in front of him. Outside, cars were bombing it down the road, kids on bikes were yelling at each other, young women shouting down the phone at friends, saying things like: 'What the fuck does he think he's up to? I know!' and 'Babe, you look gorgeous in that outfit, wear that. He'll be so jealous.'

Another buzz, and Winston pushed himself up from the sofa and grabbed for his phone. It was ten o'clock already. His heart skipped a beat. But it wasn't Lewis messaging him. It was another text from his sister, Ruth.

Are you free for a video call? The kids would love to see you. They keep asking about Winston Uncle xxx

He started typing. Something ordinary at first – like *yes, of course!* – but the thought of seeing her face, her children, people he loved, he couldn't work out what he'd say. And if Ruth asked him three simple words, 'How are you?', how would he reply? If he was with her, he could pull her close, tell her everything he needed to in one hug. If he could see her properly, maybe he could in some way communicate what was going on with him. But how could he put into words what he was thinking, feeling, when they were thousands of miles from each other – and when he barely understood it himself?

He turned his phone face down on the table, trying his best to ignore the tangled knot in his gut.

Slap, thud. Winston heard the post fall onto the doormat, and a figure skated past his living-room window a few seconds later. The proper post wasn't due for another few hours, he was sure of that. It was probably more junk mail – one of those envelopes stuffed full of useless gardening leaflets.

Feeling a heat rise to his face again, he got up and headed to the front door. He was right. But this time, the envelope had split open, and photographs of foxgloves and flowers in vibrant greens, pinks and oranges lay all over the mat. He gathered the scraps of paper in his hand and pulled one close to his face.

Weird. *No.* This wasn't your run-of-the-mill junk mail.

The photos depicted people milling around, chatting, laughing, dressed in old-fashioned clothes that made them look like something out of the 1980s. Some of the leaflets were even cut out to look like newspaper headings. *Eastbourne Road Community Garden*, one headline read.

Was this a smart marketing ploy, or something else? He stared at the photograph, the faces, searching for a clue. For one moment his eye caught on a face he was sure he recognized – a woman in the crowd.

The pinpricks of ink made out a face so familiar.

Was it his mum?

No. How could it be? This was nothing more than his imagination.

He hastily gathered the leaflets into a pile and shoved them onto the telephone stand with the rest. Then he threw himself out the front door to see if the junk-mailer was still there. There was no one in sight but an old lady with her hair in a net bun, quite a way down the road. Not a youngster employed to dump pamphlets through letterboxes.

He looked left, then right again, before bellowing: 'Stop putting spam through my fucking door!' just as he caught sight of the red-trouser man at Number 80, peering through his first-floor window, stomach pressed against the glass, phone at the ready. Winston could see the complaint now: 'Angry young brown man, early thirties, from Number 79 with grubby green door and uncared-for front garden in dressing gown shouting at nobody. Possibly unhinged. Needs investigation now.'

Without a second glance, the faces in the photographs still in his mind's eye, Winston grabbed his keys and shut the door dramatically behind him.

Chapter 4

Winston

September 2018

'Vince!' Jenny was wheeling her Zimmer frame out of Sal's shop. Her long grey hair was tied up with a leopard print scrunchie, sitting in a bun on top of her head, and she wore a smart leather jacket with a red and green patterned silk scarf tied around her neck. 'Having a lazy morning, are we?'

Winston remembered his dressing gown and sliders. 'Oh, for God's sake.'

'Don't worry, darling,' she said. 'We've all done it . . . Well, I haven't. I never leave the house looking anything less than a million dollars, but—'

Before Jenny could finish, Winston rushed into the shop and headed to the miscellaneous aisle where Sal kept plastic cups, Turkish coffeepots, Tupperware, bumper stickers and, most importantly, the misspelt passive-aggressive letterbox stickers: NO JUNK MAILE OR PAMPLETS PLEASE.

He grabbed the first one he saw. At the till, Sal considered him with the same look of curiosity as the curtain-twitcher at Number 80, only with a sprinkle more kindness in his eyes.

'Everything okay, son?'

'Yes, I've been getting a load of annoying junk mail,' Winston said with a sigh, staring at the sticker sitting on the counter.

'These signs are a *very* good deterrent,' Sal nodded. 'My cousin's best friend's son-in-law's brother designs them, you know? They're very smart. Nice to help out a family business. You've got to do something, after all! We're all tired of people telling us we'll be "cured" of all our worries if we dial this number, or telling us to book a silly, ugly venue for a party for 50 per cent off. I haven't had a party in years, and if I do, I'll have it here, of course!' Sal said. 'In fact, Angela wants to have a fifty-fifth birthday for herself next year . . .'

'Yes,' Winston said, though he didn't really care about party venue pamphlets. He just didn't want to be faced with photographs of luscious gardens, when his own looked like crap, and the only place he really wanted to be was in his mum's garden, with her. But that was impossible.

'Look at me rambling on,' Sal said, laughing at himself. 'Do you want to come round for dinner later, son?' Sal put his hand out to grab Winston's. It would have felt like a strange gesture from anyone else, but Sal was like a father to him.

While Winston never told his mother that he'd quit his job at the bank, worried she'd be disappointed in him, disappointed that he stopped living the life his father had laid out for him . . . at least he'd never lied to her when she'd ask, 'Are you with people who care about you?'

He could say, in all honesty, 'yes'. Because over the years, Sal had become Winston's family.

'Not today, Sal,' he said, softening under the warmth of Sal's rough palm, trying to keep the self-pity out of his voice. 'But thank you!' he called back.

He rushed back down Eastbourne Road, sticker in hand, before the Queen of Sheba, of all people, could catch him outside in his dressing gown.

'Hey.'

Winston stopped in his tracks, looking over the road to where the voice had come from.

It wasn't the Queen of Sheba. It was Lewis. Dressed in smart jeans and a crisp white T-shirt, a thick cardigan flung over the top.

'You're back,' Winston said, trying hard to keep the disbelief out of his voice. He'd been out at work all night, the night of their anniversary, and all he could say was 'Hey'?

Then Winston spotted the duffel bag in Lewis's hand.

'I . . .' Lewis looked back in the direction of the house. 'I just got back from work – long night again, you know? Picked up my stuff. I've been looking for you. I was on my way to the shop to see if you'd be there. I booked a few days off, remember. Our anniversary trip.'

Winston looked at him blankly, then back down at the duffel bag. Had Lewis even noticed his present sitting on the kitchen table?

'We said we'd visit Therese? Spend a few days in Oxford together. You said you'd book time off with Sal?'

Winston shut his eyes in frustration, squeezing them tight so all he could see was the black of his eyelids. They'd discussed the trip vaguely a few weeks ago, but Winston hadn't done anything about it, unable to believe that Lewis would manage to take any time off when it came to it.

'You coming?' Lewis looked at him hopefully, his smile soft. Winston felt a pang in his gut – that smile, it won him over every time. But why did Lewis expect Winston to drop everything at a moment's notice to see Therese, when he couldn't even be bothered to turn up last night?

'I'm sorry,' Winston said.

He meant it. He was sorry because he knew Sal would give him the time off in a heartbeat, but he couldn't even bring himself to ask. As much as he wanted to say yes, to throw himself into

Lewis's arms and pretend everything was suddenly okay, to sit on the train playing I spy as fields rushed past them, chilling with Therese and Lewis in the pub, trying his best to keep up with all their in-jokes, and telling quips about his work and the customers at the shop purely to entertain them, the only words that came out were: 'Send Therese my love, I completely forgot to ask Sal and I really can't let him down now.'

Lewis nodded, and pulled him close, without saying a word. In the silence between them, Lewis's disappointment rang out, and Winston wondered why it was always so much louder than his own. He breathed in Lewis's cologne for the first time in a long time. Usually, he caught no more than a sprinkle of scent lingering in Lewis's wake as he rushed out the door.

'See you when I'm back, and we'll celebrate properly, I miss you,' Lewis said, and kissed him.

'Happy Anniversary,' Winston whispered, his voice fading to nothing.

Back inside the house, with NO JUNK MAILE stuck firmly on the letterbox, Winston returned to his spot in the kitchen doorway and looked out at the garden. He pictured his mother there, in amongst the weeds and the leaves and the mud, and his heart ached for her.

Suddenly, with a resounding *thwaaack*, a bird, a thrush or a starling – he didn't know what – flew straight into next-door's window. The newly fitted glass so clean and clear, it was almost invisible. His heart began to thud, and he felt the throb in his temples, the thoughts of his mother and surprise at the bird compounding behind his eyes. He threw the kitchen door open to see. And there, on the ground, the delicate brown bird lay, lifeless.

'Oh God, oh God,' he muttered. The same thing had happened when he was a small boy. Ruth had screamed, thrown her hands in the air, unable to catch her breath. Her face a picture of terror. Their mum had run outside immediately, scooping the little bird into her hands. 'Winston, beta,' she said calmly, her tone soothing. 'Go into my shed and take out a small shovel. Dig a hole, somewhere nice and tucked away. Somewhere this poor bird might want to sleep.'

The air began to feel claggy, sticking in his throat, but without wasting a moment, Winston followed his mother's instructions from all those years ago, and ran towards the back of the garden, jumping into the shed, forgetting the rats and mice and God knows what else might be in there, grabbing the first tool he could find. A huge, red-rusted shovel.

'We'll wrap her up in a small handkerchief and make sure she has a quiet place to rest.' His mother's voice, like a song on the wind.

Just as boy-Winston had, adult-Winston ran into the kitchen for a tea towel to swaddle the bird. It weighed no more than a feather, its body rigid but beautiful. He took in the gentle wave of its wings, as feather lay across feather, the intricate patterns and fluffy down of its chest creating a tapestry of loveliness. 'It's okay,' he said. He left the bird, wrapped up, near the shed as he began to dig a few feet away.

Winston felt the weight of the shovel strike the heavy, clay soil. Each shovel of earth pulled at the muscles in his arms, his shoulders, but the pain of the effort was welcome. He heard every scrape of the metal shovel as though it was colliding with his own bones. As he dumped each mound of soil a foot to his left, the thud rang in his ears, like he was burying himself alive, obscuring himself from the world around him. With every movement, he felt himself disappear. With every movement, he embraced an unexpected relief.

As he got deeper and deeper, he was falling into the earth, into the hole, diving right through to the centre of the world.

Never to be seen again.

Standing up straight, wiping his brow with his muddied hand, he stepped back, looking at the sky, reminding himself he was still here. He turned to the spot where he'd left the bird.

But there was nothing there.

His eyes darted around, searching hurriedly for a fleck of white among the golden yellows and reds of the autumnal garden. Looking for an answer.

And then he found one. In the tea towel left forgotten beside the trunk of the eucalyptus tree, and in the tail of a fox disappearing over the garden wall, with, he imagined, the little bird clamped in its jaw.

Winston collapsed onto the bare earth, resting his arm on the mountain of soil, worms wriggling among the rubble and stones beside him. From this spot on the floor, the mess of bindweed, comfrey and brambles overwhelmed him, submerged by their height and density. And as his first tear fell, it made way for the others, for a wash of grief he hadn't allowed himself to feel for years.

'Are you okay?' A quiet murmur, somewhere in front of him.

Winston looked up, spotting the face of Sebastian through the tangle of weeds.

Winston cleared his throat. 'I'm okay.'

'Are you upset?' The boy's voice was insistent now. Curious.

'A bird died,' he said, matter-of-fact. 'And a fox took it. I guess I'm missing my mum a bit, you know.' He shrugged. 'She could always make things better.'

Seb nodded sagely. 'It'll get better,' he said. 'That's what *my* mum says anyway.'

For once, Winston hoped the Queen of Sheba was right.

Chapter 5

Bernice

October 2018

'Come on, you'll see Mummy next week!'

Simon was bellowing, trying to sound calm while growing steadily more impatient. He was standing on the other side of the road, the door of his black cab wide open. Suddenly, Bernice was back in their penthouse apartment in Marylebone, watching her then-husband clamber out of a cab at three in the morning, stumbling over his own feet in the process. The tell-tale signs that Simon had been out schmoozing clients over cocktails and tumblers of 'delightfully peaty' whisky.

'Come *on* now, Seb,' Simon snapped, bringing Bernice back to the moment. Sebastian was holding onto Bernice as tightly as he could. This time last week, he'd tucked himself in the back seat quite happily, clutching Simon's personal iPhone. The ultimate bribe. Today, even the iPhone wasn't enough. Every week was different when Simon picked him up, but today was proving particularly challenging. He'd already said to Bernice that morning: 'Does Daddy have to work over half-term?'

Simon had supposedly taken the week off to spend the school break with Seb, but she could see his hand was already hovering over his left-hand jeans pocket where his work phone lived, as though anxious to check it.

Seb's little arms wrapped tighter around her. In between semi-growls of frustration and cooing sounds at Seb, Simon kept glancing at his watch.

When Bernice had last dared to broach the topic of Simon's perpetual busyness, after he'd banged on the door three hours late one weekend, he'd simply said: 'I'm a *good* dad, Bernice. I love spending time with him.' And he *was* a good dad. He bought Seb things, he took him out on trips, he listened to Seb babble on about whatever he was obsessed with at that point in time. But still, when he was with his family, it seemed as though he was always waiting for the next thing to happen, waiting for *something*, usually work, to come along and take his attention away.

When Simon and Bernice had been together, she'd never had the privilege of *waiting* for the next thing to come along. Her pressures were non-stop from her own work as an architect – demanding clients, last-minute adjustments to plans and designs, and urgent site visits – combined with all the pressures from her family life too. Her friends always told her about their partners who'd take on the task of making weeknight dinners, shepherding the kids to and fro if they needed time away or to catch up on work. Why was her life so different? As soon as she picked Seb up from school, her work had to fit around him. And it was the balance she wanted, but Simon made no changes to his own schedule to help. All the while, she spent most evenings after a long day at work making Seb dinner, before watching TV with him or reading a book, or finishing a jigsaw puzzle or a craft thing for school, and making sure he got to bed on time.

Sometimes, she'd take him to Regent's Park or Hyde Park, close to their old flat, but it always felt like a whole expedition.

Packing a bag of snacks in case he got hungry, and clean shoes in case his got muddy, bottles of fruit juice, in case he refused to drink water . . . But it was worth it, because Seb's favourite place was the park.

When she'd been growing up, *her* favourite place was her grandparents' garden. Her safe space. She'd loved spending weekends there or visiting in the evenings after school when her mother had to work. She'd play outside for as long as she wanted, splashing about, making mud pies, chasing washing-up liquid bubbles blown by her grandfather, without a worry about how mucky she got. It was a freedom her son didn't have. It was a freedom she so desperately wished he could experience – and, if she was honest, she wished it for herself too. As if she was trying to reclaim something that had been lost . . .

She'd pestered Simon for years about moving out of the city, getting somewhere bigger, somewhere – importantly – with a garden their son could enjoy. 'We don't have to go very far to get some decent outside space, Simon,' she'd said. But he'd put a stop to it. 'Bernice, you know I need to be close to work. It means I get to spend more time with you both.'

After the divorce was finalized, while she was renting a flat next to her mum in Hampstead, she searched Rightmove for 'houses with gardens' almost every single day. Until, eventually, she stumbled across Number 77 Eastbourne Road. The house needed work, the retro-orange textured wallpaper was ancient, the marbled shag carpet thick with dirt and grime. And where there wasn't shag carpet, there was even uglier lino, plus a kitchen that looked like it belonged to an old lady with no sense of style.

But the size of the garden amazed her.

When she saw the place in real life, she fell in love with it. It had been empty for years, mouldy and damp, and she saw it as an opportunity to make it all her own. When the estate agent flagged the slight quirk in the contract – the shared garden – she hadn't worried. In her desperation for a home all to herself, and a garden for her son to play in, she hadn't considered it would really be a problem. In London, most people kept themselves to themselves, didn't they? She doubted the person next door would bother her.

'Come *on*, Sebastian, this is getting silly now,' Simon said sternly, his brow furrowed. 'Grandma is expecting you. She hasn't seen you since the summer holidays and she's so excited. She has all sorts of fun things planned, let me tell you!'

One of the best things about the divorce was that Bernice no longer had to see her ex-mother-in-law (gosh, the *ex* was so refreshing) except for very rare occasions, like nativity plays or sports days. Helene was your stereotypical monster-in-law, if ever there were one. Harsh. Overly critical. Scarily obsessed with her own son. Bernice could have given up her life to care for Simon, waiting on him hand and foot, and it wouldn't have been enough for Helene. As far as Helene was concerned, Bernice wasn't intelligent or beautiful or accomplished enough for her incredibly clever and 'deservedly' successful son. After slogging her guts out through years of training and devotion to the job, Bernice's career in architecture registered only as a 'silly little hobby' to Helene. But Simon, whose *gift* for schmoozing flush financiers to attract them to his law firm, that was '*real* talent, and *real* work, darling'.

'Sebastian!'

'Come on, sweetie,' Bernice whispered. 'You'll see me in a few days – you'll have such a wonderful time with Grandma Helene and your daddy!'

'I want *you* to come,' Seb muttered into Bernice's jumper, his fists clutching at the wool, his auburn hair blending into the fabric.

'I know, sweetheart.' Bernice's heart fell like a rock. She felt the hollow it left in her chest. 'But you'll have a wonderful time. And I'll call you every day.'

'Oh, this is ridiculous,' Simon said. Taking a deep breath to steady himself, he slammed the cab door shut and marched over, gently prising Seb's fingers from Bernice's jumper. Bernice couldn't look at him – she kept her hand on the fluffy crown of the little boy at her side.

'Come on, my love,' Simon said, trying to catch his son's now beating fists. Seb only cried louder.

Simon looked at Bernice then, his face dropping, and on the waterline of his eyes she could see the reflection of the streetlamps flashing on. His cheeks were reddening, and she wondered if he might cry at any moment. He wore an expression of utmost despair.

'What should we do?' he said, searching for help. 'Should he stay here with you?'

Bernice shook her head sadly. 'No, Simon. You know that's not fair – he should be with you,' she said. 'He does *want* to be with you, he's just tired.'

Simon nodded, looking at the floor, his hands holding onto Seb's fists gently.

And, as his parents went quiet, Seb eventually calmed himself down too, letting Simon carry him on his shoulder in a fireman's lift. 'There we go, sweetie,' Simon said, lowering a deflated Seb into the back seat, his sobs and banshee wail dying off.

'Next week,' Simon said to Bernice. 'See you next week.' He said it like a question; unsure, uncertain.

Bernice tried to settle herself, a hot cup of tea warming her hands, as she looked over some building plans she'd been finalizing, spread all across the kitchen table. She tried to concentrate. Her heart wasn't hammering quite so violently now, but she could still picture Seb's anguished face, his fists pounding, Simon's look of despair. Her forehead tightened and she pulled her eyes away from her work to roam over the garden, distracting herself, focusing on the stillness and the beauty in the burnt oranges and pinks of the autumn leaves.

Then she saw it.

Practically in the middle of the garden.

A bloody hole, with half a shovel sticking out of it, a mound of dirt a foot away.

What on earth had the nightmare neighbour next door done now?

She shot up and stormed out of her front door barefoot. The cold of the paving slabs on the soles of her feet gave her a primal sense of power. She began to pound his front door. When no one answered, she battered the door harder. 'Excuse me!' Even the ridiculous misspelling of NO JUNK MAILE wasn't enough to shatter the fury on her face.

She continued to pelt the door as hard as she could. And suddenly, she heard someone turn music on, the bass belting the ground.

Irresponsible and inconsiderate. That's what this man was.

'Open the door!' she shouted.

'Can I help you?'

His face appeared at the bay window, the blind pulled halfway up, music slipping out through a narrow gap in the sash, open at the top. 'It's a Sunday afternoon. People on this street want some peace and quiet. You don't mind, do you?' Winston said, nodding over Bernice's shoulder towards – lo and behold – nosy parker at Number 80. 'Unless you want to make it into his "neighbours from hell" documentary, I'd recommend shutting up.'

'I don't care,' she said, yet she could still feel the warmth of embarrassment spreading across the back of her neck, her hair lifting up in pinpricks. 'You've f-fucked the garden up!' She was so used to saying 'fudge' instead of 'fuck' when Sebastian was around, the word sizzled on her tongue, burning on her lips and at the back of her throat. 'That hole. It's a hazard for my son. You need to sort it out. Immediately.'

'I'll put something around it,' Winston shrugged, hands driving to shut the window, but she reached forward to hold the frame still.

'No,' she said insistently. 'You'll fill it in. Now.'

'There's not much point filling it in,' he said, looking directly in her eyes. He straightened up, standing tall – she was grateful for the window, a barrier between them. Usually, he looked small, curling into himself as though he was trying to disappear. But she realized now how much he must slouch, because in that moment, he seemed to tower over her, confident and proud.

'Why?'

He looked down at his hands for a second, and she saw he was clutching a mess of papers, or letters.

'I was just—' he started, but Bernice's rage bubbled up again.

'I don't *care* what you "just". Anything you do in that garden needs to be run past me, do you understand? It is a space for my son. It needs to be safe. You don't get to make the decisions. I do,' she snapped.

It only took a moment for the guilt to creep into Bernice's conscience. She heard Simon, bellowing at her across the kitchen one evening when he'd come home to find paint splashed all over the dining table, after a particularly enjoyable art session with Seb. 'If you want to paint, take it *outside*. This is our *home*, not a playschool!' He'd pulled out a bottle of beer and retreated to his office, a room in the flat she'd asked over and over again to be a playroom for Seb, so he had a place to be a messy little kid without having to worry about ruining the furniture. He'd said no every time.

Winston sighed heavily, bringing Bernice back to herself, to her anger, her guilt, winding themselves around each other like two vines suffocating one another.

'I live here too,' Winston said plainly. 'You can't control everything.'

She wrung her fingers together, tried to stand tall. 'And neither can you. You don't own the place. I refuse to let you turn that garden into a danger zone.'

'A *danger* zone?' Winston scoffed.

'Yes. A hole in the middle of the garden is *dangerous*. If anything happens in that garden to make it worse, I'll be calling your landlord.'

'Right,' Winston shrugged. 'Call away.'

And with that, he shut the window in her face, drawing the curtains closed.

Chapter 6

Winston

October 2018

Anything you do in that garden needs to be run past me, do you understand?

The Queen of Sheba's spiteful words were still drumming in his ears.

He did understand. He understood she was an utter control freak.

But if that's how she was going to be, he was prepared to make life as frustrating for her as she made it for him.

As Winston's anger grew, he saw his mother standing in front of him. He hadn't seen her in so long. How could his imagination conjure her so accurately? Holding up her gardening gloves in one hand, she pulled her sunhat onto her head with the other, and then there she was, in the midst of her garden, hiding from the heat in the shade of her beloved and ancient banyan tree, the sunlight bouncing off the cool water of the pond, full of lily pads, and shimmering onto her face. The call and chatter of larks, plum-headed parakeets and thrushes in the trees, the soundtrack to her day. It was a comforting image. A reminder of the past. A reminder of what he loved.

Bernice didn't get to control the garden. No matter how much she insisted. Maybe Winston needed to *insist* right back. And if he were to do up the garden a bit, to make it workable if not as beautiful as his mum's – while making a good old racket in the process, then so be it. Pissing off Queen of Sheba would be an added bonus.

Winston wandered through the hallway and picked up the gardening leaflets he'd chucked on the side. He was flicking through them, the shape of an idea coming into view, when another envelope fell through the door, landing heavily – *splat!* He picked it up and spotted something curious, something he hadn't noticed before. The envelopes: they were all addressed to 'The Young Man at Number 79' in elegant but scrawled handwriting. He'd seen junk mail arrive impersonally for 'Neighbour, Number 79' or 'Occupant, Number 79'. But this . . . it was different.

It wasn't simply *generic* junk mail.

Did this person know him? Clearly they didn't know him well enough to include his name – but they knew who lived here?

Poring over the contents at the kitchen table, Winston realized that the leaflets weren't advertising anything. They were photocopies of real photographs and newspaper cuttings, flyers for events years in the past. It wasn't clever marketing. They were a collection of memories.

In one of the sharper photographs, he spotted a familiar scene: a raised bed. A garden chair. A shed in the corner. A eucalyptus tree. A wall on the right-hand side, a fence on the other . . .

He held the piece of paper up to his kitchen window. It matched. The wall, the shed too. Except in the photo, it wasn't crumbling or falling apart. The roof was solid, not dipping dangerously in the middle. It was a bright blue, standing out in sharp contrast to the greens and reds of the flowers in the foreground.

Winston's eyes flitted between the picture and his garden stretching out in front of him, like a spot-the-difference puzzle.

Judging by the dates on the various newspaper clippings and the flyers, these photos were from decades ago. Dates popped up from the 80s and 90s. A time when this garden was lived in, loved.

Who had sent them?

Words from the flyers and newspaper clippings barked at him, blurring into one in his mind. *Stoke Newington Community Garden! Garden Open Day Times this Sunday! Come join the fun on Eastbourne Road – tea and samosas provided! Bonfire Night celebration!* Jolly messages in speech bubbles showcased comments from neighbours: *'Alma and Maya host the best garden party there is – great garden and nice cups of tea too!' Erol, local shopkeeper.*

Erol, did that name ring a bell?

He turned the envelopes over, searching for a return address. Why was there no note?

His gaze then fell to another photograph, and he began to trace his fingers over the flower beds, following their shape. Standing among the foliage were two women, arm in arm, trowels raised in opposite hands, waving to the camera. Winston didn't recognize them, though the photo was clearly very old. One had light-coloured, short hair, cropped a little like his own; the other woman reminded him of his mother, she had a long plait hanging over her shoulder, neatly tied with a ribbon at the end, her nose pierced with a stud identical to the one his mother used to wear. Winston pictured her, then, in the hospital, the photo his sister had sent years ago, the breathing tube she'd used after her operation taped to the spot her piercing had once been.

He focused his eyes once more on the picture in front of him. He presumed these women were Alma and Maya.

He racked his brain, trying to conjure the residents he met in the shop, the old-timers Sal was always chatting to as though they were family. He often called them Auntie or Uncle, rarely by their first name, but Winston hadn't met these women, had he?

Then again . . . he hadn't been looking for them before.

He grabbed another photograph, dated 1979, with a black-and-white picture of a group standing around a small bonfire, contained within an incinerator. In a garden. In *his* garden. What with the dark surroundings and the poor-quality printing, their faces were made up of nothing more than a cluster of dots, and he couldn't make out any clear details. He wondered if there was anyone he recognized. Jenny, perhaps? But no matter how hard he looked, squinting, he couldn't be sure.

He did, however, spot a bed of dahlias, growing in neat rows. The flowerheads heavy, leaning on their stems with the weight of their beauty. He looked outside now, where there was nothing but weeds. He'd never seen this garden teeming with people or plants. For Winston, it had always been a place to be alone. Until Bernice had come along, of course.

He spotted another picture on the pamphlet: the two women again, standing either side of the gate that led out onto the street – the gate that had never been opened. Above it was a sign: *Eastbourne Road Guy Fawkes' Night* – hand-painted, by the looks of it, with a flourish of a child's handprint on either side.

He thought about texting Lewis, sending him photos of what he'd spotted. Maybe Lewis would come home from work to sit with him, pore over the details, make up stories of the lives lived here before them. But since Lewis had got back from Oxford a few days ago, he'd barely been around – catching up on work after his time off. Lewis didn't have time for such *frivolity*, did he? Not with all the serious 'I've got a big deal in the works' work he had at the bank.

Winston flipped the Guy Fawkes pamphlet over – there he found a handwritten note. It wasn't addressed to him, though. It wasn't an answer to the mystery. All it said was: *Forward planning: spring bulbs to plant in late October/November.* A gardener's reminder. Or, was it a nudge intended for him?

He looked at the women in the photograph. Best of friends, by the looks of it. Eastbourne Road neighbours.

'I hope you don't mind that I'm about to start working on the garden specifically to piss my neighbour off,' he said to them, hearing how stupid he sounded. 'I guess it goes against the spirit of it all a bit . . .'

But, Winston thought to himself, holding up the photograph of the beautiful garden to obscure the view of the messy scene outside, *if I end up making the garden nice, surely that's a good thing* . . .

And, thanks to whoever had put those envelopes through the door for *the Young Man at Number 79*, it looked like a seed had been planted.

Chapter 7

Maya

1972–1973

'This is useless,' Maya's husband Prem said, waving the piece of paper in the air, despairing. Maya took the scrap from him. 'I wish Bina had been able to pick us up.' Before their flight at Nairobi airport, she'd jotted down instructions from her elder sister on how to get to her house in London. But in her panic, the detail had turned to hieroglyphs. Scanning her hurried handwriting, Maya did her best to decipher it all, hoping to connect with the part of her brain that had written it down. But her inner monologue simply replied with: *What are you doing? Why did you leave your life, your parents and Mombasa for this?*

The hope that Maya had felt as she boarded the flight, dressed in her linen blouse and stirrup trousers, handmade by her mother, had dissipated as soon as the doors of the plane flew open and they were greeted by rain and cold winds. Immediately, Maya had put on two knitted cardigans, though they were useless against the rain. She knew she should have packed their coats in the hand luggage.

From Heathrow, they'd managed to catch a coach to a bustling Paddington station, but the remainder of the journey proved the biggest challenge yet. People were running everywhere, weaving in and out, barely looking where they were going. She could see very little sky from where she stood, only buildings and a blanket of cloud. She always looked up at the sky in Mombasa, enjoying the blues, dark purples, reds and oranges sometimes too. It was notably grey here. In Mombasa, it was often humid even along the coast. Here, the water in the air made it cold and damp.

Everything felt different here. The cold was just the start of it.

Once Maya had gathered the address from the recesses of her memory and rewritten it onto the reverse of her useless instructions in her neatest English handwriting, she showed the piece of paper to every bus driver on the way, pointing to the words 'Number 79 Eastbourne Road, Stoke Newington, London, N16' in the hope they might be able to help. More often than not, her enquiries were returned with a look of disdain or annoyance. Eventually, someone had pointed them in the right direction. And in their shock and gratitude, Maya and Prem promptly forgot which stop the person had told them to get off at, and which bus to get next, and the expedition from the airport to Stoke Newington ended up taking three times longer than Bina said it would.

Hours later, they alighted not far from Eastbourne Road and wandered up the high street. It was quieter here, with bright shop fronts greeting them, people wandering up and down a little more casually. The road was wide, with a steady stream of traffic. When she saw the sign for Eastbourne Road plastered to a building on the corner, Maya clutched Prem's hand in glee.

'It's here!' she said. Her husband looked at her, his smile bright against the dark, foreboding sky. The houses on the road were all neat, terraced brick houses, with chimneys and large sash windows, frames painted white. She admired the uniformity. Bina had tried to describe it to her in a few letters, but Maya still hadn't known what to imagine. Prem, who had watched TV programmes set in London, had some idea of what to expect. But Maya, who only ever got to watch her neighbours' TV (and they only watched wildlife programmes), hadn't a clue.

There was life everywhere. Children played in the street. Mothers chatted over walls, hair tied up with cloth. As Maya and Prem wandered down the road, they felt all eyes on them and the huge, heavy bag that Prem was moving from hand to hand. His dark hair that had been neatly combed to one side before their flight now looked notably dishevelled, and his suitcase-carrying-arm was clearly straining. His suit jacket was crumpled, his glasses slightly wonky on his face, perhaps knocked by some commuter on their journey. With their suitcase banging between them, dusty from the trip, rags of sari tied around the handles to identify it as theirs, they looked at every house, checking the numbers one by one.

'Is this it?' Prem turned to Maya, his forehead licked with sweat, the top button of his linen shirt undone, despite the bracing autumnal air in London, misty with cold and smog. She looked down at herself. She didn't look any better. Today was the first time in four years she'd see her sister, and here she was turning up as a drowned rat.

'Yes, Number 79 Eastbourne Road, this is it.' She checked the piece of paper three times before confirming. A bubble of anticipation rose in her chest.

Bina and her husband Sanjay had moved here from Kenya shortly after they married, and were currently in the process of buying a house in north west London. They'd arranged for Maya and Prem to take over their tenancy as soon as they left. 'Until you can buy a house of your own, once you're settled and have saved up,' Bina said. Maya's mother had been the instigator, convincing her to go to London. 'Be with your sister,' she'd said. 'You are a British citizen, and things will be good over there for your children. Lots of opportunities. You'll be happy there. Bina is so happy.' Prem had agreed it'd be an adventure. But it took a year or two for Maya to come round to the idea. Then, thankfully, Maya had been offered a job as a sales and admin assistant at a pharmacy for a family friend in London: there were signs of hope for this new life of hers. Yet still, it was a wrench leaving. She loved her home, she loved being close to her family.

Now here they were. Standing in this spot, the tangle of emotions hit Maya again. She was scared. A fizzing in her gut told her she was excited too. But right now, she only wanted to be at home, somewhere familiar, somewhere at least a little bit warm.

The door swung open, and Maya came face to face with her brother-in-law, who she hadn't seen since his wedding. Sanjay looked like a rabbit in headlights at first. She nodded to him shyly, and Sanjaykumar, a smiley but reserved man, beamed, waving his family inside. 'Maya, Prem! You made it, here, come on in.'

Maya held her breath, not knowing what to expect as he led them inside, and pointed to where they could leave their shoes and coats. The house was big and clean, though she spotted black spots of damp in the corners. Bina was sitting in the front room with bowls and saucers of homemade chai, her smile as infectious as it had always been. Her skin was luminous, but her eyes looked tired. Everyone she'd met so far seemed tired, in fact. Maya wondered if that's what this city did to people.

'Come, come, sit! You must be exhausted,' Bina said at a hundred miles an hour, holding her sister tight, clutching her face in her hands, landing a kiss on her forehead. 'Marriage looks good on you, Mayaben,' Bina said, but there was a hint of sadness in her tone. Bina hadn't been there for the wedding. Maya looked down at her socks, shy, sad too.

'I thought you'd need this.' Bina nodded to the glass bowls and saucers of chai on the table, taking in Maya and Prem's frazzled faces. 'Drink this down, then I'll show you around. I can introduce you to the neighbour. She's home today. She sort of comes with the house. We share a garden, you see.'

Prem and Maya looked at each other then. They hadn't anticipated sharing anything with anyone. After living with Prem's parents after their wedding, they'd been excited to start afresh just the two of them.

'Comes with the house?' Prem asked tentatively, his brow furrowing as he wiped it with a handkerchief in his pocket.

'You'll see what I mean,' Bina said. 'Don't worry, you'll love her. She's a real character. We celebrated her fifty-first birthday at the beginning of this month, but she's young at heart.'

Maya gulped. At twenty-six years of age, she knew she'd need to pay utmost respect to her neighbour, and hoped she'd do Bina proud. Part of her wondered if this person was a mother figure to Bina.

Hurriedly slurping down their chai, they caught up on everything that had happened in the intervening years, filling each other in on the gossip from back home, the life Bina and Sanjaykumar were living here, while pushing bowls of homemade chakri and ghatiya between each other. 'There are some really good Afro-Caribbean shops, and stalls on Ridley Road market, so lots of the vegetables and ingredients and spices we had in Kenya, they are here too,' Bina said, as Maya marvelled at the homemade chakri. Seeing the joy in Bina's smile, Maya was excited now. Excited for the rest of her life to begin. Excited to explore a new place. Excited to look at every room in the house.

'Right,' Bina said, piling up the empty bowls onto a bright orange metal tray. Each pot landed with a clang. 'Let me show you.'

Bina led the tour, Sanjaykumar settling into the background.

'Bina,' Maya asked quietly. 'When are you moving?'

'Hopefully in a fortnight.'

'You haven't started packing yet?' Maya asked, concerned. Bina's stuff was *everywhere*. It was quite typical of her big sister to leave the mammoth tasks to the last minute.

'It's okay, it's okay – your room has been cleared out, so you'll have a place for your things.'

Maya gulped. The rest of their stuff was being shipped over next week . . . it wouldn't be much, but would there be room?

'A *Velux* window,' Bina said in English now, as they stepped into Maya and Prem's new bedroom. The roof was vaulted, a sloping window on one side, a large sash window on the other. The walls were white, and despite the dark skies outside, it was bright in here, the light caught in all corners. From here, Maya could see everything. Rows of houses, gardens, church spires, and—

'See that,' Bina said. 'The Post Office Tower, you can just about see it past Alma's eucalyptus tree. Tallest building in London!' Bina raised her eyebrows, doing her best to sell her city to her bone-weary family.

Maya nodded and stepped onto the high bed, her bare feet sinking into the soft mattress as she craned her neck to get a good view through the window. Below, she spotted the shared garden Bina mentioned, and a woman with fairly short hair, predominantly grey, with some flecks of brown. She wore large glasses – clear, with a slightly pink tint – and was wrapped up in dark brown trousers, concealing the mud caking them, and a thick green fisherman's jumper.

She was knee-deep in compost, raking through soil in a central flower bed.

'Come, let me introduce you,' Bina said. She led them back down the three flights of stairs, her chundri flowing behind her.

'Alma!' Bina called, opening the kitchen door wide, voice loud and chirpy. Sanjay was quietly chopping some vegetables in the corner. Maya smiled at him, pleased to see he took charge of the cooking. Bina didn't have the best track record there.

'What?' Alma grunted back.

'Come meet my sister and her husband, they're taking over the tenancy on the house. They flew in from Nairobi today.'

'Right you are,' Alma replied flatly, continuing to rake through her compost.

Prem and Maya looked at each other. Maya's husband grabbed her hand, squeezing it tight, as if to say: *Don't worry, not everyone gets on with their neighbours. It won't matter*. Maya's brief hope about a mother figure vanished in a puff of smoke.

'Alma,' Bina repeated.

She looked up, taking Prem and Maya in. Static, unsmiling, she merely nodded, uttered a quick, 'Hello there' and got back to her task.

'She's like this sometimes but I promise, she's an angel,' Bina whispered, as Maya watched the woman now kneeling in the soil, searching for something amongst the compost with her bare hands.

'No, I'm not!' Alma snapped back. 'I'm a nightmare neighbour.' Bina rolled her eyes and chuckled, but Maya couldn't see what was funny.

A few days later, Maya was making breakfast for the four of them – batata puwa, Bina's favourite – as a thank you. She'd seen Bina or Sanjay pop out to the back of the garden to dump dregs of food on the compost heap, so, to be helpful, she did the same, picking up the potato peelings, stalks of coriander, and the tops of the chillies, and she trotted over to the eucalyptus tree in the corner, the direction Bina usually travelled. She couldn't see a pile, but perhaps it had already rotted away . . . she wasn't quite sure how compost heaps worked. Her mother dealt with that sort of thing at home. So, at the bottom of the tree, she emptied her palms of the scraps, when suddenly—

'Oi!' a voice boomed behind her. 'What on earth are you playing at?' Though the anger and sense was clear, it took Maya a second to fully register the words, too rattled by the shock. Maya knew English fluently. She'd grown up speaking it, her school lessons had been exclusively in English, but since she'd arrived here, it felt like everyone was speaking more quickly, in a range of accents, some quite different from Maya's own. It would take some getting used to.

Alma appeared over her shoulder. In a pair of wellington boots and muddy denim trousers. For someone fairly short, she had a thundering presence.

'I'm sorry! I'm using the compost heap,' Maya babbled, panicked, heart beating fast.

'That is no bloody compost heap!' Alma's palms grabbed roughly for the rubbish on the floor. She dumped it into Maya's palms, and stormed back inside.

'Oh no,' she said to herself. 'Well done, Maya, good start.'

She added 'where is the compost heap' as well as 'what are you able to put on the compost heap' to her mental list of things to ask Bina before they moved out. And, out of fear of doing anything else wrong, Maya made sure to ask Bina before she touched, moved or did *anything* in the garden. From now on, if Maya saw Alma outside, she vowed to keep out of her way . . .

Months later, once the cold gave way to spring, Maya wanted more than anything to sit outside in the shared garden. She didn't dare intrude on Alma's space. She'd noticed, however, that the garden gate was often ajar, letting in neighbours from the street adjacent to Eastbourne Road. She recognized people she'd sat next to on the bus on her way to the pharmacy.

There was the man with a perfectly round tummy like a football, his dark hair always blowing every which way in the wind. Bob, apparently. He reminded her, in the way he looked, his age, and in his laugh, of her father. There was Patrick, a colleague and now-firm-friend of Prem's who lived a few roads away. He would often join them in the garden, sharing the ackee his mother made. Then there was Isha – Maya had heard Alma greet her several times – who would come to the garden to pick fresh herbs and produce now and then, while regaling Alma with tales of her day. Maya had been too nervous to pick herbs herself, despite looking longingly at the chimney pots teeming with coriander and mint metres away from her kitchen door.

'Alma knows everyone,' Bina commented when Maya had enquired about the mystery garden visitors. 'She invites her friends to the garden to sit and enjoy, help themselves to herbs and vegetables. Not everyone round here has a garden to grow things in, and Alma loves sharing it.'

'That's lovely,' Maya said, her eyes lighting up at the prospect. If she eventually built up the courage to spend any time in the garden, would she meet people too? She'd struggled to make friends so far. The team at the pharmacy lived in East London, and they weren't the friendliest. She was so exhausted from trying to get used to a new way of life, a new home, she didn't know where else to look. Maya missed her family, her friends and neighbours back home, the women and children she'd grown up with.

Every night after work, sitting in bed listening to the radio before turning off the light, Maya would cry in Prem's arms as he whispered promises that it wouldn't feel like this for ever. 'Soon, Maya,' he'd say, his words gentle and comforting, his breath warm on her forehead, 'soon this will feel like our home. Look at Bina,' he reminded her. 'She's happy, and she had *no one* here. We have them, and we will get there too.' Hearing Prem's words always grounded her, knowing she had her husband by her side. He rarely spoke about how difficult he was finding things, struggling to fit in at his new job as a bank clerk, but she knew his words of comfort were sometimes as much for him as they were for her. She could hear it in his heartbeat, see it in the droop of his eyes.

'Look, Alma is lovely, really she is,' Bina continued. 'She takes a while to warm up to people, but she wouldn't have so many friends if she were horrible, now, would she?' Maya was tempted to agree, but she wondered whether London had simply turned her sister soft.

As the summer months approached, Maya eventually found the courage to venture into the garden on her days off from the pharmacy. She'd learned from Bina that Alma worked for the council doing something or other, and whenever Alma wasn't working, she was in the garden – digging or weeding, picking or pruning. So, if Alma was around, Maya made sure to keep herself in a corner, so as not to annoy her. When the sun moved from the one spot Maya allowed herself to occupy, she'd watch it with envy as it worked its way across the rest of the garden, dubbed by Maya as 'Alma's territory'. As evening set in, there was always one spot beside Alma's kitchen window that held onto the last of the sunshine.

One day, after weeks of silence and avoidance, Alma said gruffly: 'Do you want to move your chair there for warmth, then?'

Maya looked up from her book. Had she imagined her neighbour's words? Wished them into existence? But when she saw Alma was looking right at her, she felt heat rush to her face. She nodded hurriedly, desperate not to miss the opportunity after all this tension. Clumsily, Maya dragged her chair to the sunny spot, tentatively sitting back down. She smiled shyly at her neighbour, still a stranger to her, embarrassed. A newcomer all over again.

A few moments later, Alma sighed: 'This garden is a mess.' She started wandering around the flowerbeds with her mud-splattered, dog-eared leather-bound notebook in hand, presumably listing all the things that needed doing.

Maya looked around the garden. She couldn't understand. Apart from a few piles of upturned earth around some buried fox poo (she'd spotted the culprit the evening before), some empty flowerpots, and a watering can that had a film of brown sludge swimming on top of the water, it was utterly idyllic. A twisty hazel tree was lush and leafy, and a plant she didn't recognize created a frothy foam of green, like a cloud. Roses popped up all over the place in full bloom, the scent filling the air. Life was bursting out everywhere.

When everything felt precarious, and lonely, the garden seemed to be the one place where Maya could feel at peace, when Alma wasn't around anyway. It returned to her a sense of hope; something she had lost since that plane journey over.

'You know,' Alma said, addressing Maya directly now. 'This garden needs constant attention in summer – there's almost too much to do for one person. I've already got to thin these carrots out' – Alma nodded to a vegetable bed in front of her. 'Isha loves these carrots, but if I get too many in there, they'll get too crowded and won't take.'

'Do you want some help?' Maya said, standing up from her chair.

Alma looked at her as though Maya had said something in a foreign language.

'I mean . . .' Maya continued, her voice gentle. 'I'd be happy to help, if I can. But your . . . your friends,' Maya pictured the neighbours she'd seen, chatting away to Alma, picking the vegetables and herbs, feet up on the patio, a cup of tea in hand, 'I'm sure they'd be happy to help you sometimes too. Make things easier.'

Alma shrugged.

'Maybe I can help you now?' Maya picked up a rake resting against the wall, standing there in her sandals and socks, a necessity thanks to the draughty floorboards in the house.

'I don't think you'd know where to start, love.'

'You could tell me what to do,' Maya shrugged. Alma shook her head, her wispy hair lifting in the breeze. 'Or maybe you could share your list . . .' Maya nodded to Alma's notebook. 'If people pop round, they can do something. Even five minutes of their time will help you out, won't it?'

'I suppose,' Alma shrugged, as a little black kitten wandered out of Alma's kitchen and wound around her legs.

Maya took a step back – she didn't really like animals but, sensing she was on the cusp of a breakthrough with her neighbour, she tried to keep the smile on her face as Alma picked up the kitten (who was admittedly very cute – her meow no more than a squeak) and placed her on her shoulder.

'And, my husband, Prem, he used to do carpentry – he's not professional, but he loves to make things – so if we need anything built.' Maya gestured to a pile of wooden basket-like things in the corner. 'Like those things.'

'Trugs?' Alma said.

'Yes, trugs. Or new blocks around the . . .' she pointed to the flower beds.

'The raised beds?' Alma offered.

'Yes, exactly. Or garden furniture, he can help. We can all do a little.'

'All right, that might be an idea.' Alma nodded stoically. 'I like things in a certain way, but . . . if they follow the list . . . maybe that'd be fine. I know I can be a sourpuss . . . but I do love seeing people enjoy the garden.' She looked around her, then back down at her list. 'Thanks. Maya, isn't it?'

'It is.'

'Good to have you on board. I suppose this is your garden as much as mine . . . Bina just left me to it. Helped herself to the pots of coriander, sage and thyme, though, didn't she? This is Susie by the way,' she said, nodding to the ball of fur on her shoulder. Maya nodded. She wasn't about to say hello to a cat. 'Well, first thing's first . . .' Alma continued, stretching. 'Someone's got to scoop up that fox poo. Could you help with that? That's always a job I bloody hate.'

Maya kept the smile on her face, her teeth gritted. 'No problem.'

It might not have been the smoothest start to a budding friendship, but it was a start, nonetheless.

Chapter 8

Maya

October 1974

Maya woke early, at just gone six thirty.

It was her favourite time of day.

First, she opened the blind covering the sash window overlooking Eastbourne Road. The bright, garish curtain made way for the autumn light. She looked across the road towards Bob's flat, Number 68. His window was open, letting the fresh air in. Now, she felt she could call Bob a friend. He worked as a computer systems analyst – he'd tried to explain it to her, but she still had no idea what it involved. She caught a glimpse of Number 80, too, with the cracked red and white tiles leading up to the front door. She loved those tiles, and so wanted to wander over to Mrs Graham's and clean them up for her, but she knew her help would be unwelcome. Mrs Graham, in her mid-eighties, had come over with a cottage pie the week she and Prem had moved in. She didn't talk very much, and generally kept herself to herself, but she was generous and never accepted anything in return. Unfortunately, as far as the cottage pie went, neither Prem nor Maya ate beef, and Bina said Alma was a vegetarian, so it was donated to Sanjay's colleagues instead. Delicious, apparently.

In the past couple of years, Alma had taken it upon herself to introduce Maya to everyone – Bob, Isha, Erol, Jenny and anyone who wandered past the open gate. She'd often introduce Maya, before running off so Maya had to fend for herself, building her friendships bit by bit. Alma was weaving her into the fabric of her life.

The breeze hit Maya's bare arms, now resting on the Velux window frame on the other side of the bedroom. The sky brightened as the sun fought its way out of bed, burning through the haze. Her eyes danced over the gardens of Eastbourne Road, lingering for a while on her shared garden below, its central bed appeared like a painting. As autumn was setting in, the bright colours and swathes of greenery were gradually thinning out, dulling down. The bright reds softened to ripened maroons and ochre, the blues and pinks dying to a greyish white, elegant in their twilight days. Branches shed their clothes.

For this brief and silent moment, she was the only person alive; this wonderful world was all for her.

She pulled on her dressing gown and hopped over the creaky step so as not to wake Prem. Downstairs, at the kitchen door, she slipped her shoes on and fumbled with the keys. She wanted to smell the wet, dewy grass, the newly fallen leaves.

If you'd asked Maya a year ago whether she could imagine herself lighting up at the thought of waking early to sit in a freezing cold garden in London, with her gruff, unfriendly neighbour, she'd have said you were crazy. She could hardly believe that the frosty Alma finally thawed, let alone that they were as close as family now.

But little by little, afternoon after afternoon, working on the garden together, in companionable silence or shared laughter or exhaustion, they had warmed to each other. It helped that Maya had slipped over one icy morning, early in their friendship, to land slap bang on her backside on the frozen ground, triggering a deep, full cackle from Alma. The noise itself had been enough to shock Maya's pain away, sending her into fits of giggles herself. 'Cup of tea?' Alma had said, tears in her eyes. 'And an ice pack for the arse?'

Swinging the door open, Maya stood on the step and breathed it all in.

'Peaceful, isn't it?'

Maya gave a start, clutching her hand to her heart instinctively. Sitting in the far corner of the garden, sheltering under the eucalyptus tree, was Alma, her cropped hair spiky and unkempt from sleep, a mug of coffee clutched between her hands: Maya could smell it from here, smoky and sharp. Usually, she loved the smell. Today it turned her stomach.

Alma was already in her slouchy gardening trousers and her trusty quilted jacket, worn out at the elbows and sleeves, tufts of padding dribbling out.

'Morning, Alma,' Maya said, a smile illuminating her face. A cup of coffee for Maya was steaming in the brisk air on the trestle table beside her.

'I got a letter from Bina,' Maya continued, her voice soft, wanting to retain the peace of the morning.

'Oh, Bina!' Alma exclaimed loudly, with more emotion in her expression than she'd shown Maya in the first year they'd known one another. She turned away from scrutinizing a patch of bare earth that had been fiercely dug by foxes right next to her newly planted onions, their little noses peeking up above the surface of the soil. 'How is she? How are her twins?'

'She's doing very well – back to work now! She's got a new job, processing photofilm at a factory. Grunwick, I think it's called – she seems happy,' Maya said hurriedly. Her sister Bina was a keen photographer and seamstress. Since she'd had her twin boys a year ago, she'd been making outfits, lehengas and blouses for local women who struggled to find a tailor they could trust. But with the competition from the tailors on Ealing Road, it had become harder to find regular work, so this new role seemed like a step in the right direction.

Sanjay was a conductor on London buses, and he adored his job – and while he worked long hours, he'd recently started to prioritize shifts that allowed him to help out with their two baby boys at bedtime. In north west London, they'd found a community of friends and family who had also moved from Kenya, and though Maya was only a short train ride away, they had both been so busy with their own lives, trying to keep on top of things, they didn't see each other as often as they'd like to.

'That's good, I know she's been looking for something for ages,' Alma said. 'Let me know when you reply. I'd like to post her some more bay leaves. I know she wanted some. Could give her some onions and garlic in a few months.' Alma waved her arms around the space, pointing out the onion nubbins, trying to ignore the unsightly divot beside them, and the garlic, which Maya had insisted on. Alma wasn't too keen on garlic. 'I'm not a vampire, I just don't like the stuff,' she'd said.

'Those bloody flowers she made us plant were looking nice this year, weren't they? I only wish the fox would do his business there, rather than on my veg,' Alma said, disappointed. 'You know, when I was younger, if me and my pa saw them in the garden, we were delighted. Rare they were then. Not now . . . now they're menaces! Rotten.'

'Some extra nutrients,' Maya joked. Alma gave her a stern look. This war was firmly between Alma and the fox, and each generation of fox cubs that came after. Maya knew it was better not to get involved.'

'You look tired,' Alma said then, matter-of-factly, as though seeing her for the first time that morning. 'Are you feeling all right?'

'Yes, I'm fine,' Maya said, noticing her own voice rising a notch, alien to her own ears. She gulped down her embarrassment, wondering if the lie was written all over her face.

'Maya,' Alma said again, softening. She placed her cup of coffee down on the edge of the raised bed. 'The other day you were feeling sick, and I know you haven't been sleeping . . .'

'Okay,' Maya said, a smile creeping onto her face. 'It's early days so don't go shouting your head off, okay? We only found out a week ago . . . And Prem and I were planning to tell you together, but well . . .'

Alma looked back at her, confusion crinkling her forehead. Behind Alma's eyes, she could also sense a tinge of fear.

'Alma, it's *good* news, you don't have to look so worried,' Maya giggled, and Alma visibly relaxed, her brow loosening.

'Go on then, put me out of my misery if it's such good news,' Alma responded sternly.

'We're going to have a baby.'

As the words left Maya's mouth, she saw Prem's face in her mind's eye, the moment they found out. Ever since Bina had had the twins, they'd been excited to start a family of their own. At first, every month came with a sinking sense of disappointment, but Prem, ever the optimist, told Maya all would be okay. All would be fine. God had a plan for them. And eventually, when the first signs arrived, she told herself not to hope too fiercely, not until she'd gone to the doctor's to check for sure. The moment the doctor had confirmed it, Prem had swept her up in his arms, almost knocking over the doctor's chair, before setting her gently back down, eyes budding with tears. 'Sorry, sorry . . .' he'd said, voice breaking, mouth bursting into the wide smile she loved so much, his cheeks instantly reddening.

'Oh Maya . . .' Alma lifted herself up, removing all trace of a hunch. While Maya hadn't told Alma everything the past few months, her next-door neighbour would turn up with a bland cup of tea whenever she found her crying in the garden. Alma had seen how much Maya had been praying for this news. She knew how much it meant.

Alma raised her arms, exposing the stuffing dribbling out of her jacket under her armpits, and began shaking her hands, her mouth open in an elated, silent scream. 'This is the best news I've heard for years! Congratulations you two!' Alma cupped her hands around her mouth, directing her whisper up to the attic window.

Maya rarely saw Alma so animated, so full of joy.

'You know,' Alma said, counting something on her fingers, brow furrowed, mouth puckered in concentration. 'Yes, this means the tot will arrive when the garden is in full swing. In the middle of summer. You can't have asked for better timing, could you?'

The last thing Maya wanted, really, was to be heavily pregnant in the London heat she'd come to hate. Yet looking at Alma's face, her brown eyes twinkling, smile radiant, a lump formed in Maya's throat.

Then Alma's smile twisted into a frown. 'What are you doing up so *early*, you daft bat? You should be taking it easy now! And come inside, let's get you out of this chill.'

Alma ushered her through her kitchen door, ignoring her protestations of 'I'm fine! Honestly!' With Alma's arm wrapped around her, Maya took one more glance at the garden. Then she looked down at herself and her middle – no signs of life yet, but it wouldn't be long.

'Don't fuss, Alma!' Maya cackled.

'No more working in the garden for you. You must rest. Prem can get Erol and Patrick to fill in where we need it,' Alma said firmly. 'And I'll see if Bob can help a bit more too.'

'Oh, Bob, eh?' Maya said cheekily. 'I'm sure he'd love to spend more time around here, Alma.'

Bob was already a regular visitor to the garden. And when he inevitably started regaling them with stories of work and office life, Alma would close her eyes, rest her head back and leave Maya to nod and 'ooh' and 'ah' at all the right points. But Bob wasn't too interested in Maya's approval . . . He was too busy battling fox damage and garden jobs for Alma's attention. He only ever wanted Alma to notice him.

'Stop it, you daft mare,' Alma laughed. 'And you, get up lazy gal,' she said to Susie the cat, who was curled up on the Formica kitchen table. Alma scooped her up and the cat dangled sleepily from her hands, before allowing herself to be plonked onto the lino floor. Alma wiped some stray cat hairs off the table and set down Maya's coffee mug. 'Here,' Alma nodded to the kitchen stool, as though Maya had never sat in Alma's kitchen before.

Maya considered the thick, brown liquid. The smell crawled up her nose, lodging in her throat, and she gently pushed the mug away from her without Alma noticing.

'You know, I haven't spent much time with a baby since our Kate was one,' Alma said. Kate was Alma's niece. She was Maya's age, in her late twenties. They saw each other rarely as she lived in Derby, but Alma's eyes lit up whenever she spoke of her. According to Alma, Kate embodied the spirit of Alma's pa. She'd been searching for her father's spirit, his kindness, his heart in other people for years. It wasn't until she met Kate that she finally found it.

Tentatively, Maya cooed at the cat until Susie decided she had better ideas and headed out through the cat flap.

'Where's that bloody cat off to,' Alma said, jumping up from the chair to open the kitchen door for a better look. The windows were steamed up from the warmth of the coffee pot; the garden outside was almost completely obscured.

As Maya suspected, Susie was heading straight to the onion patch. She began to dig, in precisely the same spot the fox had, while the two women watched absently, still basking in Maya and Prem's news and the quiet of the morning. There were no cars on the roads yet, no sirens either. Only the bird song to keep them company.

Until . . .

'No!' They chorused.

'Susie, please!' Alma called out, her voice loud enough to wake up the whole street.

Their arms flew up, coffee sloshed, they ran into the garden and over to the cat, who was enjoying her new toilet among the expensive compost of the onion bed. At that moment, Prem popped his head through the attic window, the orange sunrise illuminating his face, dark hair like a bird's nest, eyes half-closed from sleep. He called down: 'What on earth is going on?' Then he registered the scene: 'Susie! Don't go there!'

Susie continued with the matter in hand, brushing some soil over when she was done. In response to the horror on their faces, she made a small meow as if to say 'Come on, what do you expect. I'm not a *savage*!'

The two friends looked at each other, despair in their eyes, as Susie trotted back into the house, brushing up against Alma on her way. Angelic as always.

'That cat! She'll be the death of me. In cahoots with those foxes, isn't she?' Alma shook her head, staring at the soil and the dislodged onions in despair. 'I better get rid of all that before Erol pops in – he said he was going to help plant the fritillaries before his shift at the shop begins. And you know how squeamish he is.' She made a face, as if to say, *What a wimp*. 'And Jenny will be here with little George, I don't want him finding any nasty surprises when he's playing about in the beds. You know he's at that age when he loves to put *every*thing in his mouth.'

Maya shuddered in disgust. 'You know, I'll sit this one out, I think. Because of the baby.' She patted her stomach.

'Prem, want to help?' Alma called up to Prem, still poking his head out of the window, taking in the view.

'You know I would,' Prem called down. 'But I've got a big day at work . . . best get a little more sleep.' And with that he slinked away from the window, closing it behind him.

'Oh yes, very convenient . . .' Alma laughed, grabbing a shovel and a paper bag from 'The Potting Shed' and pinching her nose to prepare herself for the job ahead.

As Maya sat back down, giggling at Alma, she pictured how much her life had changed already, and she thought about what was to come. She couldn't imagine it, not yet – *a baby* – but it was something she'd always dreamed of. She was terrified. But, with Prem, and Alma, and the garden . . . she was sure they'd be okay.

Chapter 9

Winston

October 2018

'Winston, what you really need are some tulips,' Sal said, as they wandered around the plant shop next door to Sal's. 'I always have tulips in my allotment this time of year – nice and easy to plant and a lovely treat when they come up!'

'These ones?' Winston picked up the packet closest to him, holding it up briefly for Sal to see before throwing it into the basket.

'No!' Sal called, putting his hand up in front of Winston's face. 'You must *look* and *read* and work out what goes nicely together, Winston. Goodness me. If you want to start doing nice things in your garden, you should put a little extra effort in to make sure all is okay.'

Sal shook his head in semi-despair and wandered around the shop picking up several packs of bulbs, arranging them in all sorts of combinations. 'You see? These colours' – he held up a pink and a yellow – 'they go nicely. These colours' – a red and a purple – 'a bit horrible.'

Winston quite liked the red and the purple together, but he kept his mouth shut. This trip had already taken an hour longer than he'd intended it to. He was starting to regret getting Sal's help.

'How come you're suddenly so interested in gardening anyway?' Sal asked curiously, piling more packs of bulbs into the basket.

'No reason,' Winston shrugged, keeping his own vengeful gardening motives a secret, knowing Sal wouldn't condone them. He remembered the mystery post and pictured the two women from the photographs, arm in arm, and felt a pang of guilt almost as strong as his vendetta against the Queen of Sheba. 'Need something to keep me occupied.'

'That's good,' Sal said. 'My dad got me into gardening, so now it's like I'm passing it down to you! You should visit the allotment soon – you've barely spent any time there, have you?' Sal clapped Winston on the shoulder, causing the bulbs in both their baskets to jump in surprise.

Winston smiled. 'Yes . . . sounds nice, Sal, one day. But next time I'm buying bulbs or whatever, don't be offended if I don't ask you to join me . . . I didn't expect to be here for two hours.'

'Oh, my son, you can't rush this! You must have a *vision* for the garden. Although once things are planted, you must simply hope for the best. And with gardens there are always mistakes, but we always get another chance to try and fix them the next year!' Sal nodded sagely, proud of his unsolicited, riddle-like wisdom . . .

'What's all this?' Lewis said, strolling into the kitchen.

It was a Sunday, and after a week's worth of working overtime to make up for his time off in Oxford, it seemed he was finally coming up for air. Winston wanted to ask, 'How was Oxford?' but he couldn't bear to acknowledge that they'd hardly spoken since. They'd barely seen each other, except for the odd kiss goodnight after a late shift at the shop and a kiss good morning before Lewis left early for work the next day.

Winston was sitting on the kitchen floor surrounded by five packs of bulbs. At Sal's insistence, Winston had also invested in a notebook, which he was scribbling and re-scribbling all over, trying to plot out some kind of planting scheme. 'Throw them haphazardly and then plant them where they land!' had always been his mother's tactic. She liked the 'natural' look, but that method felt far too risky for someone with no gardening experience. He kept one eye on the decades-old picture of the women in the shared garden for inspiration, even though the image had already embedded itself in his mind. He'd been staring at it for the last few days.

'Wins?' Lewis shuffled a bulb around with his shoe. 'What's all this?' he repeated.

'I'm planting some bulbs!'

Lewis smiled tenderly. 'They look great! But, how come you're gardening?'

Winston could tell him about Bernice, always nagging him. He could tell him about his mum, how much she loved to garden. He could tell Lewis how much he missed her, how maybe gardening might bring him closer to her. He could tell Lewis about the pamphlets and flyers posted through the door, the garden that it used to be. He could tell Lewis how lonely he felt, here, at home, on his own all the time. 'I thought it'd be a fun thing to do,' he shrugged, unable to reveal any more. 'I spend so much time out there chilling, it'd be nicer if it looked cared for.'

'But is there any need? Gardening's expensive and it's not even our place. Futile spending your own money on it. We're not going to be here forever.' Lewis's tone was gentle, but pointed.

'Isn't it about time we made it nice?' He was about to tell Lewis about the whopping great hole in the garden. Winston remembered the weight of the shovel, the satisfying crash every time it carved into the soil, the heft of it as he piled the earth beside him. Bernice, in her own fury, had since chucked a flowerpot into it, smashing it to pieces. 'We get nice stuff for the house, why can't we make the garden look good too?'

'It's not the same,' Lewis countered. 'We can take stuff in the house away with us when we move out; we can't take bulbs you've planted out of the ground.' He picked up one of the packs, his hand skimming past the newspaper clipping, unseeing. 'These *are* really gorgeous though,' he conceded, turning the packet over in his hands. 'My auntie loves tulips like this, feathery petals.'

'I love them!' Winston said, trying to drum up his energy again. 'I've bought enough so we can cut a few flowers for vases and things when they bloom.' He pointed to the list of bulbs in his new notebook, the scribbles and scrawls meaning nothing to anyone but him. Even to Winston, it seemed hilarious that he was getting his own back on his neighbour by planting beautiful flowers that, hopefully, they'd all enjoy. And yet, she'd made it crystal clear: he was not to do anything there without her 'permission'. Even the sight of him digging up the garden, planting the bulbs while playing his loud music, would set her teeth on edge.

'They come out in spring, right?' Lewis said, his eyes reading the pack.

'Yeah,' Winston nodded, picking up a stray bulb, uselessly trying to match it up with the correct pack.

'Long game . . .' Lewis said to himself.

'Not really, it's only a few months.' Winston felt his energy deflate. 'You want to help?'

'I'm really sorry, Wins, I have to go back to the office.'

It was only then that Winston noticed Lewis was wearing a full suit, with two homemade sandwiches, probably ham and mustard mayo, in a Tupperware tucked under his arm.

'It's Sunday.' Winston's voice was bland.

'I know, but it's okay, it's good really. I'm so close to securing this new deal . . . it'll be great for me. For us. Just a little longer, a few weeks I think, and it'll be done.'

Lewis kissed Winston on the forehead, as though he were a child or elderly relative.

'Lewis, your tie,' Winston called as he turned to head out. 'You need to fix it.' His voice cracked.

'Thanks.' Lewis paused in front of the hallway mirror, hands fumbling over one another.

'Here,' Winston stood up, knees cracking from sitting cross-legged too long. 'Let me. How are you still so rubbish at this?'

Winston felt a flutter in his gut as he drew closer to the man he'd been with for so many years. Breaking the silence, Winston's phone started buzzing on the counter; they both glanced over.

Ruth. Her name flashed up for a FaceTime call.

'It's okay, get it. I can sort this.' Lewis's hands brushed Winston's as he grabbed for the tie.

'No, no,' Winston held on. 'I'll call her back later. We caught up the other day,' he lied. 'I was thinking,' he said, trying to talk over the sound of the buzzing, 'what do you think of hosting a Diwali party? Nothing big, but we could invite Sal and Angela.' Winston's eyes remained focused on the tie, unable to look directly at Lewis. He had the image of the photograph in his mind again: the crowd of neighbours huddled around the incinerator for their own Guy Fawkes' Night. And, maybe more importantly, he could also envisage Bernice, arms crossed in her kitchen doorway, as she watched a fire blazing in the middle of *her* garden. Winston and his guests drinking mulled wine, mugs clinking in celebration, laughing and joking. 'Probably worth doing a bonfire to get rid of some of the green waste, before I get started properly on the garden. We'll have loads to burn . . .

and my mum always loved a Diwali night party. We could do a Guy Fawkes-Diwali mash-up.'

'I like that idea,' Lewis beamed, eyes glinting. 'Yeah, let's do it. Tell me when and I'll make sure I'm home.'

'Really?' Winston heard the hope, the desperation, in his voice, ringing loud and clear in that single word.

'Definitely.' Lewis kissed Winston hurriedly on the lips. 'See you soon. Happy gardening – don't work too hard!'

The door shut behind him, and Winston was left alone again, with nothing but his bulbs, a plan to annoy his neighbour, and photographs of people he'd never met held in his hands.

An hour later, Winston was in the garden muttering, 'Three times their length?' like a mantra. At the beginning of October, there had been days as hot as twenty degrees, but now it was bitterly cold and it was clear November was right around the corner. Leaves were slushy and wet on pavements, yellows and oranges turning to browns, and Winston could see his breath as mist in the air. However, after an hour of repeatedly kneeling down and standing up, checking and re-checking his planting plan, he was hot and bothered in his jacket and beanie.

He stuck his hand trowel into the ground to mark the spot for some Queensland tulips. They looked like one of Jenny's pink, ruffly blouses. He continued to dig, shovelling out small mounds of soil until his metal trowel collided with something rocky. The piercing noise scraped through his ears into his brain. 'For shit's sake,' he growled through gritted teeth. 'I'm not made for this.'

He yanked Sal's green-and-white gardening gloves on, instantly cutting out the sharpness of the autumn morning and he got to work, squeezing his hand into the hole, pulling out a rock, followed by handful after handful of earth.

'Mum, you proud?' Winston said into the cold air, keeping one eye on Bernice's kitchen door, waiting for her to come storming out in frustration. The sheer *audacity* of him to plant some *beautiful bulbs* in their shared garden.

'Oh crap,' Winston swore again, as he shoved his hand too hard into the ditch, smashing his fingers against another rock at the bottom.

'*Ummm*,' came a chiding voice from behind him.

Seb was sitting on the kitchen step again, holding his knees tight, as though trying to curl up and vanish. Winston was tempted to ignore him, but something about the boy's face gave him pause: cheeks red with cold, eyes red with the shadow of tears.

'You all right?' Winston placed his hands on his knees, his fingers still throbbing from the collision.

The boy shrugged.

Winston wasn't sure what he was getting himself in for, but the boy had been kind to him last time, so he decided to be kind back. 'Do you want to help me?'

The boy's face brightened slightly, eyes widening. He nodded furiously. His auburn hair was sticking out in tufts at the top of his head, like he'd waged war with a hairbrush.

'I suppose I could. You don't look like you're getting anywhere very quickly . . .' Seb said, in a voice that was trying to be a grown-up's, pulling his shoulders back, gesturing to the bulbs littered all around the ground. Seb wiped his runny nose with the back of his coat.

'It's hard work. Reckon you can keep up?' Winston teased gently, pushing himself up, his hands leaving brown splodges on his already dirty trousers.

'Yes! Look,' Seb ran up to a bulb, knelt on the ground, and ploughed straight into the earth with his bare hands.

'Hold on, hold on. Use this.' Winston handed him the trowel.

'Thanks, Mr . . .'

'It's just Winston,' he replied gently.

Seb grabbed it with gusto, and a smile broke across his face. His wonky front teeth reminded Winston of his own as a kid – the crooked, imperfect smile his mother loved so much.

After a few minutes of working in silence, Winston mustered up the courage to ask, 'Are you okay?'

The little boy shrugged, not looking up.

'If you're upset, we can talk about it,' he continued, unsure. He didn't have a clue how to talk to a child. 'I'm not very good at much, but I'm all right at listening.' It sounded like the kind of thing a character on kids TV might say.

Winston watched as the boy continued, so focused on digging with all his might, getting out the frustration or sadness he'd seen in the kid's eyes, sitting lonely on that kitchen step. In stark contrast to Seb's childlike, unwavering energy, Winston felt his back beginning to ache from all the leaning over. His calves were burning from squatting.

'I . . . I think I upset my mum. She . . .'

Winston looked up at him, nodded to encourage him to go on, confirming he was listening.

'She was shouting at my dad on the phone, about me. It makes me sad when she's alone. When I'm with my dad, I think she gets lonely because of me.'

'Oh, mate,' Winston said quietly. He couldn't quite work out the details of the boy's distress from his disjointed explanation, but the sense was loud and clear. This boy, who was barely older than ten, was already worrying about his mum, thinking about her feelings, feeling responsible for her too. 'I'm sure she's okay. And it's definitely not your fault.' He had barely stopped to think what else was going on in the Queen of

Sheba's life. He'd only pictured her angry, disgruntled. 'Look,' Winston continued, feeling like he had to say something more helpful to the kid. 'Grown-ups get upset. Sometimes we know why, sometimes we don't, but you don't need to be worried. I'm sure when you're not around, she has lots of fun things to do too!'

'Sebastian!'

Winston and Seb's faces shot towards the kitchen, where Bernice stood outlined in the doorway.

'Look at you!' she said. 'You're all grubby! It's going to get all over the house.'

Seb had big, brown hand marks all up the sleeves of his shirt where he'd tried and failed to roll his sleeves up. There were patches of mud on his face, highlighting his cheekbones like a mismatched bronzer.

Seb stood up, glanced at Winston, and his lip started to quiver. Winston tried to whisper to the boy: 'Don't worry, it'll clean off!' but he wasn't sure if it was the dirt he was sad about.

'I'm sorry, Mummy,' Seb said, his mouth dramatically upturned in the way only children can manage.

'Hey,' Winston whispered again, hoping to stem Seb's imminent stream of tears. 'I was thinking of throwing a little party to celebrate Diwali and Bonfire Night next week. Do you think you'd like to come? It'll be here, in our garden.'

'Yes!' The boy's eyes opened wide in excitement, no tears in sight. Winston half-wondered if the boy had ever been invited to a party before. 'What's Diwali?'

'It's erm . . .' Winston wondered how he could explain it as quickly and simply as possible. 'It's . . . like the Hindu Christmas . . .' he said finally, cringing at his abysmal description, but the boy seemed to understand immediately. 'Do you think your mum would like it?'

'I don't think so,' Seb said, from behind a muddied hand – half worried, half mischievous. Winston winked, and Seb giggled, his worries forgotten.

'Sebastian! I won't ask again,' Bernice called. 'Your lunch will be on the table in a minute and you need clean hands for that!'

'Got to go!' Seb dropped the trowel like a lead weight, and charged towards his mother. She brushed him down outside, before slapping her hands together into the garden to get off any extra dirt, her gaze firing through Winston.

Moments later, Winston felt the cold creep back into his bones. He looked at the kitchen door – the lights were all off inside so he couldn't see a thing. He pictured Seb's worried face, how he'd opened up about his mum, and wondered if Bernice, his nightmare of a neighbour, was okay after all. Maybe her life wasn't as perfect as he'd imagined it.

Chapter 10

Bernice

November 2018

BERNICE SLUNG ON HER oven gloves, yanking a tray of Waitrose sausage rolls out of the oven. Simon was meant to be picking Seb up – it was Sunday, *his* day – but he'd called to cancel two hours ago. He was late last week, so she'd thought he'd try hard to make up for it this time. But sadly not. Now Bernice's plans to see her friend Clemmie for lunch at a new gourmet restaurant were out the window, and she'd be left with a disappointed Seb to entertain. She hadn't been surprised when Simon's name popped up on her phone, but she hated that not only did she have to cancel her own plans, she was the one who had to tell Seb, because her charming ex-husband didn't have the guts to do it himself.

'Bernice, darling,' Simon had chimed down the phone, his voice slick with sweetness. 'This case is taking longer than expected. We're going to need a couple more days to prepare, and I can't really have Seb here with me. I can take him one day during the week instead.'

She'd had years of this. 'Bernie, they need me here. I know it's the weekend but—' or 'Bernie, my love, you know I'd much rather be at home with you two.'

Piling anaemic sausage rolls onto a plate, Bernice's stomach clenched. She hadn't bothered to eggwash them, as Simon always used to insist: 'If we're going to have some frozen sausage rolls, at least make it look like you've put some effort in,' he would laugh, trying to make his insult sound like nothing more than an innocent joke.

'Mum!' Seb ran in from the garden, cheeks pink from the cold, his woolly hat riding up over his ears. 'Mum! It's Winston's early Diwali party tonight! Do you think I can stay here this evening? Please? Daddy won't mind, will he?' His voice was buzzing with energy, and she tried not to roll her eyes. Seb told her about this so-called invitation last week after she'd discovered him covered in mud in the garden, chatting to their nightmare neighbour. She'd been sure then, and was still sure now, that it would likely be more young people like Winston with no responsibilities and no morals getting very drunk and lairy.

But part of her was relieved. Relieved that staying home, unable to spend the day with his dad, wouldn't break Seb's heart this time.

Bernice pictured herself sitting across the table from her friend Clemmie, sipping a small but expensive and delicious glass of wine, while devouring plate after plate of tiny food. She'd hoped, if she'd been with Clemmie, she might have been able to linger a little longer in central London after their lunch to try to catch some fireworks displays. The last thing she wanted was to be home with fireworks exploding in her back garden, threatening to break through one of her windows.

Each morning, for the last week, Winston could be seen storming his way through the garden, pulling up weeds, creating a huge pile of garden waste in the corner, which had become a new hiding place for the foxes and cats of the neighbourhood. If she dared to open the windows, Bernice could smell the evidence of them, mingled with the stench of rotting leaves. With Seb running about outside, it would only be a matter of time until he brought cat poo into the house, leaving brown splodges on her white tiled floor.

She'd spotted Seb planting bulbs with Winston a couple more times since last Sunday, digging up little trenches here and there. She loved that Seb was out there having fun, but she couldn't help feeling Winston was a bad influence. Would Seb start swearing profusely at the dinner table? Or smoking . . . what if he started smoking at the age of ten?

To add to all that stress, Winston had been digging on *her* side of the garden too. There was no rule as to which part belonged to whom, but she thought it was common sense that everything from the boundary of her house to the fence could be safely declared 'hers', and everything from his house boundary to the garden wall was 'his'.

She'd spent the week making a list on her iPhone of the date, time and context of all his small but infuriating acts of rebellion, ready to send to his landlord when things got too much to bear.

'Oh, goodness gracious,' she muttered under her breath now, looking out of her window.

There he was again, dressed in a maroon gilet that looked about a hundred years old. Mud-caked gardening gloves covered half his forearms. His face was flushed red and his nose was running. Whenever he stood up to allow himself a breather from pulling up weeds and brambles roughly with both hands, he would wipe his nose on his bare arm. Bernice had to look away, for fear it would put her off their lunch.

'Mum?'

'Oh, sorry, Seb, sweetie,' she said, placing an oven-mitted hand on her son's head. 'I'm a bit annoyed about what he's doing to the garden.'

Seb followed her gaze, standing on tiptoes to see more clearly. Winston was once again kneeling over, wrestling with weeds, balling them up into something more manageable, then throwing it onto his waste heap.

'Mum! He's *tidying* it. That's what he said,' he continued, defiant, when Bernice gave him a disbelieving look. 'He said he was going to burn all the garden waste to celebrate Diwali and he has two friends coming round for some fireworks. He also said *we're* invited, remember? It'd be nice for you to make some more friends!'

Bernice laughed at that. Seb stepping into the role of parent. How many times had she said, 'It'd be nice for you to make some more friends' to him? Seb, like Bernice in many ways, struggled to connect with people. They were both a little too used to their own company.

But . . . two friends? Unlikely. She'd expected hordes of people, trampling all over the garden, littering cans of beer, cigarette butts, those canisters of laughing gas that ended up all over the pavements and in gutters. Dozens of Winstons let loose on the garden – 'tidying' it up. And maybe there'd even be that cloying, fruity scent of marijuana she'd got so familiar with as she wandered around the streets, wafting out of windows and around corners as she took Seb to Clissold Park. To be fair, she hadn't smelled it on Winston yet, but she had the measure of him. That was for sure.

'Well,' Bernice said sharply, eyes still on Winston. 'You can stay here and watch any fireworks from upstairs. But we won't be joining them this evening. The last thing I need is for you to smell like smoke at school tomorrow. It'll be safer from upstairs.'

'Muuum!' Seb whined.

Later, as dusk was setting in, the autumn sky glowed pink and orange over the rooftops, the branches of the trees clawing at the colour. Bernice paused to look out of the window, take in how beautiful the dusky sky looked. Until she heard a commotion outside.

'Oh my *goodness*!' came a woman's voice, sharp and shrill.

'And so it begins,' Bernice muttered. She picked up Seb's empty dinner plate and began to wash it by hand in order to peek outside again. At first, she saw nothing but her own curious and irritated face reflected back at her. When her eyes adjusted, and the warm light from a bonfire outside cut through, she saw a couple huddled together. Winston handed them something out of a cardboard box. The man, maybe mid-fifties, was dressed respectably. No ripped jeans, nor totems decorating his neck. And no giant spliff hanging from his lips. The woman also looked rather nice in a lovely puffer coat. Next to Winston was a man she thought could be his partner. *Lewis, was it?* He was wrapped up in a cable-knit jumper. It looked expensive. His blonde hair flickered red in the flames.

'These are *delicious*, Winston,' the woman said.

'They're my mum's favourite sweets for Diwali,' Winston said, tucking into a round orange ball.

There was a crackle from the ancient incinerator, followed by a billow of smoke. All four of them stepped back, exclaiming 'whoa' as they went.

'We haven't seen you for ages, Lewis,' the man said.

'Oh, it's been so busy, you know. I've barely been home.'

'He's got a big deal in the works,' Winston said, an arm resting on Lewis. Bernice recognized a bit of herself in the forced lightness in his voice, the smile plastered on his face, eyes focusing on the curling flames. She felt an unexpected pang of sympathy for Winston.

'Let's hope.' Lewis pulled Winston close. 'Right, who's for more mulled wine? We've got a whole vat in the kitchen, so don't be shy. And we've got some non-alcoholic punch for Sal, and if the wine gets a bit much for you, Ange.'

There was a raucous giggle from the woman, muffled by her gloved hand.

'I'll have some punch, but I'll get it,' the older man said to Lewis, collecting everyone's glasses and heading inside. Bernice recognized him, she was sure of it.

'What's this in aid of anyway?' the woman – Ange – said, when it was only her, Lewis and Winston in the garden.

'Diwali,' Winston replied plainly.

'I know, but you've never invited us over like this. When have you ever hosted a party?'

Winston shrugged. 'It's not a big thing – we've only invited you two.'

'Is it . . . do you have some news?' Ange's face was bright, excitable.

'No, no,' Winston said hurriedly.

Bernice thought she caught a small look of disappointment from Lewis – his eyes turned down, lips tightening. But maybe she was reading too much into it.

'I've been doing up the garden, so I needed to burn some stuff,' Winston continued, before lowering his voice further. 'You know what,' Bernice could just about make out his words over the snapping of the fire, 'this neighbour of mine, she seems to think I can't do anything in my garden, despite the fact we've lived here for *years*. So . . . I thought I'd . . . I don't know . . . have some friends round, have some fun, and show her I'm not going to let her take over everything.'

'Oh Winston,' Ange shook her head. 'That's silly. You should have invited her! I expect she's grateful for you sorting the garden out, no? Saves her a job!'

Winston shook his head. 'If only. She doesn't want me to have anything to do with it. I didn't invite her, but I invited her son – he's a sweet kid, nine or ten, I think. He's been helping me out now and then. I think he wants a friend, really. Someone to talk to.'

Bernice's stomach dropped. She looked over at Seb, his eyes glued to the TV.

'I suppose I've been spoilt so far,' Winston continued. 'Having you guys, people who actually welcomed me here. But this Queen of Sheba, I'm nothing to her – an inconvenience. She wants this garden to be a *private* space for her and her family.'

'Oh Winston, I'm sure that's not the case. Everyone wants to know their neighbours, I'm sure she'll come round eventually.' Ange kept her voice low, but Bernice had popped the window open slightly so she could hear better. 'You know, Sal used to know the people who lived in your house and the one next door.'

Winston looked up, curious, turning to face Ange.

'Sal's dad used to help out in the garden from time to time. The two women who lived here kept it open for their friends and their neighbours, generally, I think. I didn't know them very well, met them once or twice . . . Lovely ladies.'

'Mum!' Seb called from the living room. 'What's that smell?'

Bernice pulled her attention away from the strangers outside to find smoke floating up to the white ceiling.

The incinerator? She checked the kitchen door. It was closed. And there was nothing coming through the window, still ajar.

She followed the trail of smoke to its source: the oven.

'Oh, damn!' Bernice shouted.

'Mum!'

Suddenly, the kitchen was alive with chaos. The smoke alarm was screeching, Sebastian was squealing, and smoke was curling out of the oven in waves. Bernice pulled out her charcoaled cheese on toast and threw it into the sink, the cheese blackened and bubbling. It sizzled in the washing-up water, before sinking slowly under the frothy surface.

'Bloody hell.' She eventually threw open the kitchen door, wafting smoke away from the alarm with a kitchen towel, as Sebastian burst into laughter.

'Oh, goodness!' the woman outside called in her direction. Her face was round, kind, her nose moist from the cold, cheeks rosy from the fire. 'I hope that wasn't us! Winston, Lewis, should you move the incinerator back?'

'Ange,' Winston replied coolly. 'There's no way we can move it when it's alight.'

'No,' Bernice shook her head, trying not to let the embarrassment show on her face. 'My fault – a toastal disaster.'

Toastal disaster? What's wrong with you, Bernice!

Sebastian appeared beside her in the doorway, calling out unusually confidently: 'What are you eating?'

'Indian sweets!' the older man said warmly. 'Would you like some? There's barfi, ladoo, and is this one jalebi, my son?' Winston nodded.

'Sure!' Seb called before even looking to his mother for permission – because he knew she wouldn't grant it. Seb ran outside to take his pick from the proffered box, smiling up at his new friend.

'Mulled wine?' Lewis asked, turning to Bernice. 'Looks like you might need it. I'm Lewis, by the way. I'm not sure we've properly met. I'm Winston's partner.'

'Come join us, dear!' the other man called again. 'The more the merrier!'

She watched Seb, tucking into a sweet, chatting to Winston and spraying crumbs as he spoke. Bernice looked around her for an excuse, but it was clear Seb wasn't going to come in any time soon.

'Oh, all right,' she mumbled, slipping on her crocs and a jacket. 'I'll stay for one.' She left the door open, letting the smoke waft itself out.

'I'm Angela and this is my husband, Sal. We run one of the convenience shops on Stoke Newington Road.'

Ah, that's where she recognized him from, though she'd only been in there a handful of times.

Sal smiled brightly, wrapping his coat more tightly around him as a gust of wind blew a chill and a plume of garden-waste-smoke towards them. 'Technically I'm Winston's boss,' he explained, 'but really he's more like a son to me.'

Bernice gave a tight-lipped smile. 'Nice to meet you. I'm afraid I don't really know anyone round here, I'm quite new.'

'Winston said you've been here for several months?'

Yes,' Bernice choked on her voice. 'But, well, I still *feel* new. Haven't really . . . met many people around here. Busy, you know.' Seb looked up at her, nodding encouragingly, as though he was the parent here.

'Here's some winter punch for the young man.' Lewis handed a small mug of steaming red juice to Seb, who wrapped his cold hands around it. 'And a mulled wine for you.'

'I've got sparklers!' Angela said, whipping a packet out of her leather tote. 'Bernice, is your son allowed to play with them?'

'Yes, I suppose so.' A smile broke through Bernice's awkwardness. 'You'll be careful, won't you, Seb?'

Seb nodded with his whole body, splashing his drink in the process. Within moments, he was writing his name in the air with crackling lights, and Lewis, Winston, Bernice, Angela and Sal whooped and cheered like it was the most magical thing they'd seen.

'You're having a party and didn't invite me?'

Bernice spun round, to see Simon standing in her kitchen doorway.

'We finished earlier than we expected, so I thought I'd surprise you with fireworks.' He held up a blue plastic bag, rockets sticking out. 'Bonfire Night, isn't it?'

'Hello there,' Lewis called, the perfect host. 'Come and join, we were about to get started on the fireworks ourselves, so you've timed it perfectly. We're having an early Diwali celebration . . .'

Simon's smile was forced, his black wool coat buttoned up to his neck, navy wool scarf neat under his chin. He looked like an undertaker.

Bernice glanced at Winston, his face stony. Seb ran up to his dad, shrieking 'Daddy!' at the top of his voice. He turned back to look at Bernice, his beaming face telling her what she knew already. This was all he wanted, a Bonfire Night party with his garden-pal neighbour, his mum *and* dad.

She doesn't want me to have anything to do with this garden. That's what Winston had said to Angela, and here she was, taking over his party, ex-husband and all.

'Be careful, okay?' Bernice said, as Simon made his way through the garden to set up his fireworks, grabbing ones Lewis handed to him as he passed.

'I'm sorry he's taking over,' Bernice whispered to Winston. It was the first time she'd spoken to him since their last falling out through his bay window.

Winston looked at her. She expected to be met with the expression she knew so well from him: anger, hidden behind a mask of nonchalance. But his eyes were soft, warm even. 'Don't worry,' his voice was almost friendly. 'Makes life easier for Lewis. He's been trying so hard to avoid setting his new jumper alight.'

As Bernice turned back to look at Simon, she noticed all the potential hazards: the wonky planks of wood demarcating the ancient flower beds, the sparks from the fire. Despite all the space, it still felt too close, too cramped. She wondered if her nightmare of fireworks cascading through her window was about to become a reality.

As Simon lit the string, the flicker of light crackled and hissed its way to the firework. Sal and Angela pulled Seb back gently, noticing him straying too close in his anticipation. Bernice felt a tug on her heart, of gratitude and relief. For once, she didn't have to do it alone.

Seb clapped his hands together in delight as the first firework whizzed into the sky, twisting over and over before exploding into a bloom of noise and light.

'That was AMAZING!' he said, gleeful. Bernice heard pops and bangs of fireworks all around them, neighbours watching their own displays in awe and excitement. Then she caught a glint of worry in Seb's next phrase: 'Look what we've done!'

The burnt-out rocket had landed in one of Winston's freshly planted pots. The force of the impact had caused the pot to topple and break in two, spilling its innards of soil and bulbs, smoke swelling above it.

For a second, everything went silent – fireworks in the distance seemed to pause mid-air, the bonfire stopped spitting. They held their breath.

Bernice looked over to Winston, her body tense.

But her neighbour was smiling, shaking his head at Seb as if to say, 'Please don't worry,' while Simon declared, 'Stay back, guys!' Over-dramatic. Bernice knew this Simon well. When he felt out of place, or unwanted, he did his best to take over, to be the one in charge. It was what he did best.

'Dad,' Seb said, as Simon trudged his way towards the far end of the garden to set up the Catherine Wheel. 'We need to be careful of these areas.' He gestured towards the newly dug trenches, planted up with yet more bulbs. 'Aliens,' Seb had called them, when describing them to Bernice earlier that week. She could only assume they were 'alliums'. 'Winston has been doing the gardening so these are all delicate. Things are growing here.'

'Yes, son,' Simon barked confidently. When he was like this, in 'in-charge mode', he never took notice of anyone else.

The Catherine Wheel whizzed on its post, and everyone ooh-ed and aah-ed. Simon took several steps back, and Bernice caught a glimpse of Winston wincing as Simon's brogue crunched into the soil and, presumably, the bulbs Seb had just pointed out.

'Mum!' Seb nudged Bernice in the ribs. 'He's stepping in it.'

'I know, sweetie, I'm sorry,' Bernice said, used to apologizing for Simon's mistakes. 'He doesn't mean to.'

'But I told him.'

'I know, my love,' Bernice whispered, keeping one eye on Simon, who was now making his way back to them, as the Catherine Wheel whirred itself out.

'Dad, stop!' Seb said, growing visibly upset. 'You're treading everywhere I told you not to.'

Simon looked down at his feet, his brow furrowed. A thin layer of sweat formed at the top of his forehead. In his face, Bernice saw the man she'd gone on a first date with, who'd spilled ice cream down his top as they'd been walking along the beach in Brighton. Eyes wide, mortified. Back then, with her, he would have laughed it off, gone shy. Now, years later, he'd developed a strong sense of pride, refusing ever to admit if he was embarrassed, upset, *wrong*.

'Sebastian. Do not speak to me like that, okay? It's easily fixed. Not a problem.'

'Dad! This *isn't* your garden. You should apologize!' Seb shouted, holding Bernice's finger in his hand tight.

Simon looked at Bernice, waiting for her to say something. To stand up for him. 'I'm not going to apologize,' he said harshly – looking directly at Winston. 'It's not *his* garden. We own it. He only rents. We can do what we like.'

The air in the garden hung heavy with cold, the smoke drifting silently.

Bernice let out a sigh of disbelief. But she could believe it, couldn't she? Simon, the master of defensiveness. The master of the illogical comeback, anything to make him the 'bigger' man. Despite the fact the person he was arguing against was his ten-year-old son, who only wanted to look after the garden he'd been working on. Bernice couldn't look at Winston. She realized, then, that in everything she'd said to him about the garden, she'd become more like Simon than she thought.

Simon kept moving, too awkward to stay still, and Bernice heard a crunch as he stood on a bulb that had escaped from the rocket-blasted pot.

'Dad!' Seb said, sobbing now, his face scrunched up in anger. 'I helped with it too. It's my hard work as well!'

Simon looked down, his mouth opening then closing – silent, gormless. In the past, Bernice might have helped him out. She might have seen the insecure, worried soul that lived deep down inside and spoken up for him, made excuses for him, tried to explain him to everyone.

But he'd taken it too far this time.

'Can you move please?' Lewis cut in, sharply, but not rudely. 'Let me get this out of the way.' Simon reluctantly did as he was told and Lewis scooped up the earth into the pot, carefully taking the rocket out and carrying it safely to the back of the garden, before returning to collect up the bulbs, trying to rescue them all.

'Well,' Winston spoke eventually. Beside him, Sal and Angela looked thoroughly perplexed about what had just occurred. 'Have a nice night!' Winston called, his voice tight. 'We'll, er, get out of your way . . . Simon.'

'Thanks so much for joining us, lovelies,' Angela said, looking deliberately at Bernice and Seb. 'You made our evening.'

Seb kept his head down, eyes on the floor, his shoulders shaking almost imperceptibly with frustrated little sobs.

'Thank you for inviting us,' Bernice said softly, while Simon sulked by the kitchen door, a petulant child.

'Yeah, thanks for coming,' Lewis said plainly. 'And Seb, thank you for being such a great help in the garden. Winston told me!'

Sal nodded goodbye, a smile stuck on his face. 'And son, don't worry about all of this, plants are sturdy things, they'll be okay.'

Seb nodded, eyes remaining on the ground, kicking blades of grass under his trainers.

When the door had closed gently behind them all, Simon said, 'That's better, peace at last. Darn nightmare sharing a garden with people like that, isn't it?'

'That's enough, Simon,' Bernice whispered, shepherding their son inside. 'Seb, sweetie, will you go up and brush your teeth? I need a quick word with Dad.'

Seb nodded, she imagined he was relieved to escape.

'Simon,' Bernice said cautiously, 'this is my house, my home, and they're my neighbours. I—'

'Bernie,' Simon said sweetly, 'I know – I thought it'd be nice for Seb to feel like we were there as a family. He always says how much he likes it when we're all together.'

Silence hung between them. They both knew that hadn't been the case today. She sighed, she couldn't bear to challenge him further, so she took the simple route out: 'Anyway, come see Seb during the week, to make up for not taking him today.'

'Okay, see you, Bernie,' Simon said, nodding at her on the doorstep. For a moment, she imagined he might say, 'Sorry', but he simply turned away and walked off.

As he wandered down the road, she felt her disappointment lodge in her chest. She thought of what she might say to Seb in the morning, when the dust had settled, and finally she thought of Winston. She'd ruined his night. She'd been so angry with him for trying to intrude upon her family life, her garden, her happiness . . . but, this evening, she'd been the intruder. *She'd* been the one to ruin his night, plain and simple.

Closing the door behind her ex-husband, Bernice looked down to find an envelope on the doormat.

There was no stamp.

It was addressed simply: *The Lady at Number 77.*

Chapter 11

Maya

October–November 1975

'You sure you fancy a party?' Alma said, looking at Maya resting on the sofa.

At that moment, baby Hiral opened her eyes, her little hands, all wrinkly and soft, reaching outside of the blanket, her tiny mouth yawning in delight. Maya and Prem's little girl had been born in the height of the summer of 1975. A July baby meant a long, sweaty final trimester for Maya, and she'd taken a short break from her job in the pharmacy to take up some seamstressing with the companies that her neighbour Isha worked for, so she could work at home and avoid the bus. In reality, this meant she could sit in the cool of the living room, all day every day. Prem had taken on extra evening shifts after his day at the bank finished, working at a factory close by, so Alma had taken on the responsibility of providing Maya with ice packs whenever she was home.

Hiral was now only a few months old. She spent most of her time bundled up in the arms of Maya, Prem or, most commonly, Alma. In the few months they'd known and loved her so far, she'd proven herself to be a peaceful, easy baby. 'All right for some!' Jenny had said, nudging George, who had apparently been a loud baby but had turned into a quiet and polite toddler.

When Maya and Prem were able to take Hiral home from the hospital, she was wrapped in a crocheted blanket gifted by Jenny, yellow ribbon decorating the ends. They'd opened the door to the familiar smells of home – of morning coffee made by Prem, cumin and jaggery from dinner a few days ago, and freshly cut flowers from the garden, picked by Alma. They were home. They knew it now. This was home.

'I . . .' Maya replayed Alma's question about the party over and over in her head. Over the past few months, getting used to looking after Hiral, Maya had seen less of her friends. Her heart swelled at that word. Friends. She knew now that Alma's friends had firmly welcomed them in. It had been her idea to host a Bonfire Night party. They'd done one last year, and it had been so much fun. Maya had been desperate to do so again; to invite friends, and friends of friends, more neighbours, into the garden they all loved so much.

Maya was a natural host. She'd missed that part of herself recently.

Usually, whenever they had people round in the garden, a regular occurrence, Maya was constantly running around, making sure everyone had something to drink while they were turning soil, or propagating, or just milling about. Alma, on the other hand, was much more focused on the garden itself. 'No one comes here for your snacks and the tea. They're here to dig in,' she'd say. But wasn't that what friendship was all about? Maya reflected. Feeding people, making people feel at home. Her mother would never forgive her if she let people leave her home under-fed and under-watered.

She'd missed being around her friends, seeing them enjoying the space they'd created. At first the garden was all Alma's domain, but Isha, Bob and Erol often liked to help with odd jobs here and there, sometimes Jenny and Patrick joined in too, so now it felt like a space they'd all created together. Alma still gave the orders, of course. But even she seemed to enjoy the help and the company. 'Sometimes,' she said one day, 'it reminds me of working here alongside my pa.'

Hiral was now at the stage where she seemed to be able to take in the world around her. And Maya was desperate to show her the world and the people she and Prem loved so much.

Sure you fancy a party? Alma's question repeated in her mind.

'Yes,' Maya said, noticing her voice rising in pitch, her eyes searching for Prem's. He nodded, his cheeks lifting in a smile. She immediately felt herself relax. 'Yes, it'll be Bonfire Night, we should do it – I'd love to.'

'All right, then,' Alma said, clearing her throat, whipping out the gardening notebook that was never far away. She began to list all the things they'd need to get done.

'We really need more seating,' Maya said to Prem then, rocking Hiral in her lap.

'Oh, we'll bring out some chairs from our houses, don't fuss, Maya,' Alma said.

'No, Alma, your dad's garden furniture is all a bit worse for wear. We've been making do with fold-up chairs or our kitchen furniture. Why don't we get some furniture to keep out here? It'd make sense . . . don't you think?'

Alma frowned, assessing the state of her pa's picnic bench outside, the seat hollow with rot. It was at least fifteen years old. 'I guess so . . .' she shrugged.

Maya looked imploringly at Prem, sipping his third coffee of the day on the kitchen doorstep, his eyes searching for the birds as they always did.

He'd promised to build benches last summer, but had always found an excuse not to. Usually, the excuse involved some kind of social occasion with Erol, Bob or Patrick.

'Okay, okay,' Prem said eventually, Alma and Maya's eyes burning into the side of his face. 'I'll pick up some wood. Erol can help me, maybe.'

And so, after a few more nags from Maya and Alma later that week, he finally got to work. Erol and Prem spent a couple of days lugging reclaimed slats of wood into the garden, and at every waking moment the two men could be found drawing, measuring, sawing, with Alma close by collecting the sawdust for mulch. 'Waste not want not.'

A couple of days before the party, Prem called Maya and Alma down to the garden, with Hiral bundled in his arms. His face beamed with pride, his eyes glinting.

'What do you think?'

Maya looked around, searching.

'Here,' Prem said, nodding with his head towards the chair at his side: a single chair, perfectly crafted, with arms wide enough to rest a cup of tea on.

'Wow,' Alma said, her eyebrows lifting in an expression that said, 'Mmm, not too shabby.'

It was praise enough for Prem. 'Very glad you like it, Alma. Wasn't sure if it was up to your father's standards.'

'He'd love it, I'm sure. Plenty of room to rest his whisky *and* his brew.'

Maya hadn't taken her eye off the chair. 'Prem,' she said slowly, *carefully*. 'It's *one* chair . . . we're having a whole party of people here!'

'Yes, they'll love it . . . Won't they?' He furrowed his eyebrows, eyes still hopeful. He wiped his brow with a rag from an old underskirt of Maya's, hands grubby with wood oil.

'Where will everyone else sit? I presume *you'll* sit here.'

'No, my darling, *you* can sit here – put your feet up,' he said, one hand holding a lightly snoring Hiral, the other pulling out a matching footstool from under the chair.

'Prem!' Maya shook her head, unable to keep the smile off her face. 'We need a bench for *lots* of people! Maybe even a picnic table, to replace Alma's father's!'

'The party is in *three* days,' Prem said. He eyed the huge pile of wood in the corner guiltily. It was his Everest.

'Well . . . you and Erol better get working then,' she said, peeling Hiral from Prem's arms.

After three more days of sawdust flurries, effing and blinding, and cigarette breaks (Erol was a very bad influence on Prem), plus constant advice from Alma ('No not like that, like *this*, chaps!'), they finally finished the picnic bench, large enough to seat eight people.

'Prem,' Alma said, 'this is blooming marvellous. Well done you.'

A day later, that same picnic bench was laden with food from neighbours up and down the street. Erol and his ten-year-old son Sal had come earlier that day to pile the table with home-made vegetable samosas as big as a face, patties of falafel, filo pies, and a pool of red sauce with haricot beans luxuriating in it, topped with fresh herbs. Maya's mouth was watering just looking at it.

Jenny had sewn a tablecloth made from her old curtains – once fraying around the edges, now as good as new, not a stain or a fray in sight. And even Mrs Graham had brought over a potato and leek pie for the occasion. 'Care to join us?' Alma had asked, but Mrs Graham put her hands up. 'Oh no, I can't be dealing with the noise of you youngsters.' She nodded gravely.

'Haven't been called a youngster in a long time,' Alma said, ruffling her short grey hair with pride.

And with that, Mrs Graham trotted off.

'Welcome!' Maya stood beside the open gate, the *Eastbourne Road Guy Fawkes' Night* sign welcoming in a line of friends and neighbours dressed head to toe in knitwear, trench and duffel coats. Jenny, who never looked anything less than fabulous, was in a fur coat, with little George wrapping himself around her legs, sporting a slightly threadbare diamond jumper, on top of a flannel shirt that was far too big for him.

'Give us one of those,' Jenny said, gripping a Marlboro in one hand and grabbing a mug of mulled wine from the wicker tray Maya was holding with the other.

'All yours,' Maya said, winking at George, who looked too shy to be there.

Maya admired the handiwork that had gone into the sign, Hiral's baby handprints adding the final magic touch.

Then, remembering, Maya glanced around in a panic. Hiral, where was she?

As if reading her mind, Prem appeared at her side. In his arms was a sleeping Hiral, nothing but a ball of blankets, being jiggled up and down by her father. Maya's face broke into a smile. Alma marched over and planted a kiss on her littlest neighbour's blanket ball of a head. It was only in these moments, the quiet snatches between the hustle and bustle when no one was looking, that Alma let her brusque guard down. Hiral had proved herself to be Alma's Achilles heel.

'Oi,' Alma yelped over to Maya. 'Watch out, that tray's slipping!'

Breaking back to reality, she watched as one mug went splat onto the floor, an errant splash of mulled wine settling into the fur on Jenny's fluffy coat.

'Fantastic,' Jenny sighed, despondent. 'Now it looks like I killed the bloody thing myself.'

Grimacing, Maya caught sight of four-year-old George, who had cleverly avoided the splash and the smashing mug, and seemed completely unfazed by his mother's almost-swearing. Without a second thought, he left the disaster zone and ran straight into the garden, where he spotted a few of his little chums, running around in circles not too far from the bonfire, their anxious mothers taking turns to draw them away: 'Children, be careful!'

'What you acting like some kind of hostess for, Maya?' Alma asked, sniffing at the broken mug on the floor, grabbing the orange handle and shards of ceramic. 'We know these people – they're not strangers to us. And you,' Alma said to Jenny. 'What on earth are you wearing that poor dead animal for?'

'You know she's a vegetarian,' Maya said to Jenny playfully.

'Of course, why else do you think I wore it?'

'Are you teasing us, Jenny?' Prem chimed in, a cheeky grin back on his face, Hiral stirring in his arms. 'That must be polyester.'

'Polyester?' Jenny cawed. 'How dare you!'

'Stay away from the flames, Jen,' Alma said. 'We'd hate to find out.'

The four of them collapsed into laughter, clinked their mugs together in the air, and then made their way into the heart of the garden.

Erol, Bob and Patrick had placed themselves strategically beside the snacks, each holding a cigarette in one hand and a toothpick in the other. Maya noticed Bob's gaze scanning the garden, before finding Alma, his eyebrows raising in hope, trying to catch her eye. Isha had brought her mum along, who was sitting down on one of Alma's kitchen chairs, enjoying the food. Alma pointed out Isha's son, Yusuf, who was hanging out by the fire with a friend. Here there were neighbours Maya hadn't met properly too, though she'd seen them around; watching her neighbours congregate in a space she'd helped create set a fire glowing in her heart. She only wished that Bina could have been here – but she was working, and was having trouble taking time off because of her bosses.

Alma's niece Kate had driven down from Derby specially, arriving a smidge before six o'clock, a small holdall in hand rattling away with baby toys for Hiral.

'Ladies,' Kate said. 'Let me take a picture of you in front of that sign! It's delightful.'

'Go on then,' Alma grunted. 'Prem, take Hiral, will you?'

Prem trotted over from the other side of the garden and scooped her up.

'Oh God.' Alma stretched her arms and grabbed her mug of mulled wine from Maya's hand. 'That girl is getting heavy.'

Realizing she was no longer with her Auntie Alma, Hiral instantly began to stir and her mouth gaped open, ready to scream at the top of her lungs.

'We better make this quick, Kate,' Alma said, plastering a smile over her gritted teeth, her mug raised in her hands, wrapping her free arm around Maya, who mimicked her pose.

The camera flashed bright, once – Kate wound on the film – twice – she wound on the film again – then three times, before Alma said: 'Oh come on now, Kate, that's more than enough.'

'Okay,' Kate acquiesced. And Alma's arms were held wide for Hiral to return. The baby's face settled into its usual docile expression as soon as she was nestled back in her favourite person's arms.

When Maya glanced back at the table, she spotted the only things left were the dishes Alma was in charge of: a scattering of devilled eggs, some crackers with Tartex on (it tasted like salty mush), two broken vol-au-vents, and one lonely cube of cheese and pineapple on a stick.

'I better get some more of those canapés from the kitchen. People might be hungry,' Maya muttered under her breath, her eyes scanning the groups of friends and neighbours clustered around the garden, like little pockets of crocuses sprouting from the grass.

'Calm down,' Alma said, taking a glug of her mulled wine. 'You really are a very stressy host. Everyone's having a lovely time, it's not about what people eat, it's about the fact of them *being* here, together.'

'What's in these?' Jenny said, pointing to a few dollops of cream cheese on a cracker.

'Cheese and dill,' Maya said, and Jenny smiled, '*Deeeel*,' she said, imitating Maya's accent and chuckling. 'I love the way you say it. Makes it sound so special.'

'Stop it, Jenny, don't be daft,' Alma said, firmly but not unkindly.

'All right, Al,' Jenny said, grimacing at Maya jokingly, before picking up some cream cheese and dill and shoving it in her mouth.

Maya barely registered Jenny imitating her voice. She knew Jenny wouldn't have done it mean-spiritedly, plus she'd heard so much worse whispered about her behind her back on the bus; she'd caught the sneers and glances as she and Isha walked down Church Street to do some grocery shopping. She'd heard stories from Patrick, who was born here – his parents had lived here since the fifties, and yet he was always being told to 'go back home', knowing full well they didn't mean Hackney. She'd learned to glaze over, ignore things, in order to keep going, in order to keep her head up. She hoped when Hiral was older, when she was at school, things might be better. She prayed for it every day.

'Sorry, Maya, she puts her foot in it sometimes,' Alma said quietly, ever protective. 'Are you okay?'

Before Maya could reply, Erol shuffled over, a tray of canapés in one hand, a cheese and pineapple cocktail stick in the other.

'Oh, thanks, Mr Waiter! That's where they'd got to,' Maya said, pleased to move on from the moment as Erol pulled out a bag of chilli flakes and handed them to Alma. 'For the foxes,' he said. 'Remember?' he continued when she looked confused, 'I said it might help keep them away?'

Alma nodded, looking a little unsure.

Then Erol placed a used cocktail stick on a little pile, pulling it from his teeth, before helping himself to one more.

'Erol!' Maya groaned, snatching the plate off him. 'I thought you were serving these, not eating them all yourself!'

'I'm a sucker for cheese and pineapple on sticks, okay? And technically it's *my* cheese and *my* pineapple. Anyway . . . excuse me for changing the subject, but who's bringing the guy?' Erol asked, winking cheekily at Maya.

'The guy?' Maya asked, unsure, cheese sticks still on her mind. She looked at Alma for a clue. Alma rolled her eyes.

'You didn't even get a *guy*?' Erol asked again, aghast. 'I thought the English Bonfire Nights always had *guys*. How can it be Guy Fawkes' Night without one?'

'Erol,' Alma said sternly. 'We've only got that minuscule incinerator.' She nodded to the fire, burning their latest crop of weeds and old shrubs. Sadly, Alma's pa's rotten bench was also keeping them warm this evening. 'At least it's being put to good use,' Alma said, shrugging, but every time someone threw a broken plank onto the blaze, Maya could sense it gave her a sting of sadness.

As Prem placed more wood into the incinerator, they all crowded around the fire, in a desperate attempt to keep warm . . .

'Next year,' Prem said, 'maybe we should get a proper bonfire going? We can make this a tradition, ne?'

As their breath fogged in front of them, they nodded hurriedly.

'You know, I think that's a really good idea,' Alma said.

* * *

For the rest of the evening, groups of people came and went, popping in to say hello en route to their nightshifts, or on their way home after a day's work. Some came and stayed until the very end, but there remained a constant flow of faces, old and new.

Once the fire had worked its way through most of Maya and Alma's garden waste (it made for a rather smelly, smoggy fire, which they hadn't anticipated), Prem and Erol popped to the shop for firewood, and Bob ran around both Maya and Alma's houses in search of chairs for the stragglers.

'That was a success, wasn't it?' Bob said, two chairs in his arms. 'Prem's been banging on about how proud he is of you . . . for setting it up. And Hiral's first party!'

Maya nodded, smiling. Her eyes were roving around the kitchen, flicking back out to the garden. 'Hold on,' she said suddenly, heart pounding in her sternum. 'Bob? Did Prem take Hiral to the shop with him? I . . . I haven't put her to bed yet but . . .'

'It's okay,' Bob said softly. 'He didn't take her, no, but . . . she'll be here somewhere.'

'She's not a hamster, Bob!' Maya snapped, unable to calm her rage.

'No, I know, but she has to be.'

'Could someone have—'

Kate, who had been poking the incinerator, jumped into the kitchen then, her red hair illuminated by the fire behind her. 'Everything all right in here?'

'Hiral . . .' Bob said, his face sombre, his words light. Maya could tell he was doing his best not to worry her. 'Have you seen the baby?'

'She was with Prem,' Maya said, shaking her head. 'She was in his arms.'

'Hold on,' Kate said, trudging through the kitchen.

Maya's mind was running at a million miles an hour. Despite the cold flooding in from outside, sweat was trickling down her brow, heat filling her cheeks. What had she done? Where was Hiral? She hadn't put her to bed. She could be anywhere . . . anything could have happened to her. There were so many people in the garden. People she didn't know. People Alma didn't know. They wanted to open the garden up, but how could they have been so irresponsible?

Bob passed her a glass of water, without saying anything else. She took it, clutching it between both hands, unable to stop them from shaking.

'We'll find her,' he said, 'she'll be safe. She's surrounded by people who love her.'

Maya nodded, but threw herself into her own house. They'd left all the doors open. So careless, wasn't it? Anyone could have come in here. She checked the sofa, where Hiral sometimes enjoyed her afternoon nap when Maya was reading. But Prem and Maya wouldn't have put her there on her own. They wouldn't have left her. She ran up to their bedroom, expecting to see Hiral in her cot next to Maya's side of the bed, knowing that the moment she set eyes on her little girl she'd burst into tears and her heart would stop beating so fast. When she opened the door, she'd see her, she'd realize she'd been overreacting.

But as she pushed the door open, she saw nothing but the teddy bear Alma had given her. Big embroidered eyes, innocent, unknowing.

Charging back down the stairs, she headed straight into Alma's house again where she came face to face with Kate.

'Come,' Kate said. Her voice was calm, giving nothing away. She led her through to Alma's living room.

The first thing Maya saw was the back of Alma's green chair. Her pride and joy: green upholstery, teak arms. Perfectly cared for.

It was her dad's chair from the fifties, and had some dingy-looking fabric on it, but Prem had reupholstered it for her in a bright green, to perfectly clash with the bold orange patterns decorating her living-room walls.

Maya wandered around the chair, and saw Alma slumped there, fast asleep, with Hiral nestled tightly in her arms, cushions propping them up for support.

Maya's hand clutched her heart.

She let out a breath. She wanted to reach for Hiral, but couldn't bear to wake her up.

'See,' Bob said softly. 'She's always going to be okay. She's got a village to look after her.' He passed her the cup of tea, rubbed her arm gently, and Maya nodded, her eyes stinging.

They had a village to look after them all.

Chapter 12

Maya

November 1975

Later that night, Maya found herself waking up in the pitch black. Her eyes shot to the cot beside her. Immediately, her heart was with Hiral, replaying the worry and fear she'd experienced earlier.

When she glanced at the clock on her bedside table, the radium-green hands glared through the dark at her. It was only 11.15 p.m. They'd all been exhausted after the party, collapsing into bed as soon as everyone had cleared off.

A clatter out in the garden pulled at her attention. That's what had woken her up. Probably a fox, she thought, but when she heard some hurried calls from the garden below, she shot up in bed, peering out of the Velux window.

'Prem?' she said, shaking her husband by the shoulders, in an attempt to wake him. Finally, he grumbled to life.

'What is happening?' he said softly, his eyes adjusting to the sight in front of him as Maya peered out of the window. She heard urgent shouting on the street beside them – she could make out three distinct voices creating a melee of sound – and for the second time that day, her pulse was racing, sweat prickling her forehead and under her arms.

'Prem, something's going on,' she said.

He pulled himself up to the window, squeezing beside her.

'Can you see?' Maya said, feeling the shake in her voice.

'Yes,' Prem said. 'There are people in the garden.' He pointed to a movement beside the potting shed. 'I thought Alma kicked everyone out at ten?'

Before Maya could reply, he ran to their chest of drawers, pulling on trousers and a shirt, then headed down the stairs. Taking herself back to the window, Maya could feel the gusts of wind outside forcing the ice-cold air into the room, the blind billowing behind her. She heard the tell-tale squeak of the kitchen door, and spotted that Alma and Kate were down in the garden now too, following behind Prem, heading towards the shed. Prem was purposeful. He didn't look afraid.

She looked over at Hiral, her face visible now Maya's eyes had adjusted to the dark, the yellow light from the streetlamps trickling in through the open window, and the gaps in the curtains on the other side of the room. 'I'm going to go and see if Daddy is all right,' Maya said softly. She sounded calm. But she was scared. Terrified.

She closed the door behind her. If someone was about to break into her house, maybe a closed door would slow them down. She swallowed down her lump of regret at leaving Hiral behind, and trod carefully down the stairs. When she reached the kitchen door, she saw that Prem had left it wide open, the breeze causing the flowers left on the counter to spill over. The ceramic vase close to rolling off and smashing on the floor. She shivered.

Stepping outside, she watched Alma and Prem standing beside two men. Kate was walking towards the gate, turning the latch to lock it. Why was Kate locking these men in with them all?

The men had their backs to her, hunched over. Something about them seemed small, but she couldn't help her imagination running away. Maya's mind flashed with horrible scenarios, and in an instant she pictured Prem, Alma, Kate, Hiral . . . gone.

Maya inched forward cautiously. Then one of the men turned round. With the weak glow from the garden light illuminating his features, she recognized him instantly.

This was Isha's son. Yusuf.

They weren't men at all, they were boys. Prem put his arm around Yusuf. From the crease in his forehead, the flash of his eyes, she could tell he was frightened. The shouting, the anger . . . it had been on the street. Not from these boys. She didn't recognize the other boy next to Yusuf, but he was looking over his shoulder, as though expecting someone to rush into the garden.

'Come inside,' Maya heard Prem's voice, soft, encouraging. Yusuf nodded.

'Thank you, Uncle,' he said.

After the two boys had drunk a mug of hot water each, their breathing quietened. Alma, fierce, took the role of investigator. But she was gentle with her interrogation.

'Boys, can you tell me what that was all about?'

They exchanged a look with each other, as if asking one another for permission to tell their story. Yusuf's friend – Ade – nodded, before slurping on his water.

'There's these boys,' Yusuf said. 'They told us to meet them by the tinned-up house, a few streets away. They've been . . .' he swallowed, took a deep breath, keeping his eyes on the table, 'they've been bullying Ade, teasing him at school and stuff. They said to meet them there to sort it all out, so we could make it stop, but they didn't turn up.'

Yusuf looked at Ade, and paused. His lip was quivering when he continued, and Maya realized just how young these boys were.

No more than thirteen, she was sure. Too young to be out this late at night. Too young to be this scared.

'Yusuf,' Alma said. 'Does your mum know where you are?'

'She thinks I'm at Ade's. I said I'd go there after the bonfire party,' he shrugged, not making eye contact.

'And I presume your mum thinks you're at Yusuf's?' she asked Ade. He nodded, eyes on his water.

'But what was the shouting?' Maya cut in then, unable to stop herself. She could still feel the ripples of fear coursing through her veins.

'It's okay, Maya,' Prem said. 'Stay calm,' he whispered to her. 'They need us to stay calm.'

'It was . . .' Yusuf started to reply. 'The police. They . . . they chased us away from the house. They thought,' Yusuf's voice caught. 'They thought we were sus.'

'Sus?' Maya asked, eyes to Prem.

'They followed you here?' Alma asked firmly.

'They chased us to the end of the road . . . I don't think they saw us come in here. I . . . I didn't think we'd be able to get back, so I thought we should come to the garden. To hide. I thought they wouldn't find us here.'

Maya watched Alma's face turn from stern to furious, her blood boiling. But behind the anger, she saw something else: heartache. For these two boys. Barely teenagers, and already fearful to just live their lives.

For years, Bina had warned Maya of stories about police picking on young Black men, stopping them, treating them like criminals for nothing. For *living*. She'd heard stories of police who'd turned their nose up at attacks on Black and Asian men, looking the other way, ignoring the reports, refusing to follow up on any evidence, making excuses. A year after they'd moved to London, she'd told Prem to be careful. 'They'll see me as the Indian keep-quiet-and-get-on-with-it kind of foreigner. But they will always want us to feel different – they want anyone who doesn't look like them to feel as though we don't belong,' he'd said. 'And we have to keep alert. We always have to look out for each other.' It seemed like he was repeating something he'd heard on TV. The words were awkward, stern, serious. They didn't seem to fit in gentle Prem's mouth. As though he'd only just learned how to articulate the silent threat so many people had been living with for a long time.

And here she was, digesting the words all over again, realizing, understanding that those words and that fear – it had become these boys' reality.

'Look,' Prem said, putting a hand on each of their shoulders. He pulled a chair up to sit next to them, talking softly. Maya could barely hear him. 'You can come here whenever you need to. If you want somewhere to go to get away from those boys, you come here, or if the police do anything again, you tell me. Have you told your mothers?'

They shook their heads hurriedly. 'No,' Ade said, the first word he'd spoken. 'She'd be . . . I don't want her to be angry.'

'Ade, she won't be angry.' He looked at both the boys then, and continued: 'Your mothers just want the best for you, they want to protect you.'

Ade and Yusuf looked down at their hands, and when Prem realized he couldn't convince them right now, he said, 'Okay.' The lines in his forehead softened. His hands tapped both the boys on the shoulders again. 'You come here whenever you need. Will you promise me that? The garden is always open for you.' They nodded. 'And if anything happens again, I'm here to talk about it. Even if you don't want to mention it to your parents for now. But if you're in danger, I'm going to have to say something.'

'Yes, Uncle.'

'Let's wait half an hour or so, okay? Then I'll take you both to Isha's. Do you want some cake?' Prem said, pointing to the leftovers from the party, now packaged up on the counter.

They nodded, eyes immediately brightening.

Maya smiled, watching her husband hand cake out to Yusuf and his friend Ade. In that small moment, things almost felt normal . . . The boys almost seemed like boys again. Not teenagers forced to grow up too soon.

'Prem,' Maya whispered to him while they were eating their cake, 'we should tell Isha, shouldn't we?'

Prem pondered for a moment, before shaking his head almost imperceptibly. 'I think that would be the wrong thing. We should encourage them to tell their parents . . . it should come from them, not us.'

When Prem walked them out of the front door half an hour later, she noticed the boys' shoulders hunching over, as if they were trying to shrink into the background. Trying not to stand out.

She hated it – she felt her pulse pick up again, this time with rage not fear, and she wanted to storm the police station, she wanted to find the bullies, she wanted to tell them to leave those boys alone.

Maya wandered through the house and stepped out silently to the back garden. At first, all she could think about was Isha, how worried she'd be, how much she loved her son, how angry she'd be to know what he was going through. She wanted to tell her, but she realized Prem was probably right.

The night was quiet now, no signs of what had happened only an hour earlier. As she took a deep breath, feeling the cold enter her lungs, she hoped if ever the boys needed it again, that they'd come back. She hoped they could find sanctuary here if they needed it.

Chapter 13

Winston

November 2018

To the Young Man *at Number 79.*

There was another letter . . . sitting on his doormat. Winston slung his coat on, stuffed his keys in his pocket along with the envelope and headed to his evening shift at Sal's. When he was tucked behind the counter, the evening passing slowly, he allowed himself to sneak a look at what was inside.

Once more, it was an assortment of memories from the past: a few roughly photocopied flyers, headed *Seed swap day* and *Any suggestions for the garden at Eastbourne Road very welcome!*

Angela had mentioned the garden – all those years ago – at the Diwali party, hadn't she? He focused on the envelope once again. Could these be from her? If it was, why would she call him 'the Young Man' . . . she knew his name. Unless she wanted it to be a mystery. A strange, gardening treasure hunt of some kind. But no . . . that couldn't be right. This handwriting, it wasn't hers. Or Sal's. He saw their handwriting all the time on the wholesaler order list. It couldn't be them. And mystery really wasn't their style.

Seed swap day. He smiled. His mother was always collecting seeds from her garden or from half-used packets she'd bought to share with her friends and neighbours. She'd line them up in little packets or envelopes, paperclipped closed, in a cardboard box on their front wall for people to help themselves. 'Gardens aren't something you can keep all to yourself,' she said. 'It's about enjoying it, in all the big and small ways. Together.'

Well . . . whoever was posting these notes through the door, they were sending a very clear message. The garden was for sharing. And judging from the flyers and the photographs, there had once been a whole community sharing it.

Maybe he could change things. Welcome people back into the garden, so it wasn't just him sitting there alone, waiting for the day to end, for his life to start. Waiting for Bernice to come out and complain about him being there at all.

'Winston!' A voice pulled him from his thoughts, and he scrabbled to put the pieces of paper back in the envelope, tucking them under the counter.

There was Lewis, standing on the shop floor.

'What's wrong?' Winston asked. 'What are you doing here?'

Lewis shrugged, dumping a huge packet of pasta on the counter. They both looked at it as though it were a bomb they weren't sure how to defuse.

'I got back from work a bit earlier and wanted to see you. Check you were okay. Are you okay? After last night?' Lewis asked.

Winston felt as though all eyes in the shop (someone choosing their wine for the evening, and someone else selecting toilet roll) were on them. Exposed, uncomfortable.

Looking at Lewis, it was as though they were strangers, working each other out.

'No, I'm okay,' Winston nodded. He pictured Simon at the Diwali party: his stern face, his patronizing tone, marking his territory on the garden with every stamp of his shoes. He and

Lewis hadn't spoken about it when they'd got in. They'd both brushed their teeth, Winston nagged him about the state of the bathroom sink, cluttered with Lewis's beautifying products, and they'd gone to bed. Why would he come to the shop specially to ask if he was okay? Why couldn't Lewis just *be* there more often? If they were around each other more, he wouldn't have to go out of his way to understand how Winston was feeling. He would *get* it.

'It was uncalled for . . .' Lewis said diplomatically. 'I'm sorry. One day, when we have a place of our own, we won't have to put up with that. We can do whatever we want to the house, the garden. It'll be ours.' Lewis's voice was formal, as though he'd rehearsed this strange speech of his.

Winston frowned at him. 'Lewis, we *have* a place of our own . . . We've lived there for years.'

'Come on, Wins,' he sighed. 'You know what I mean. A place we *own*.'

'Spaghetti?' Winston said, keeping his voice even, feeling his bubble of annoyance grow. He did not want to be lectured about owning a property, investing in bricks and mortar right now. He looked Lewis in the eyes, and Simon's face stared back. 'We've already got loads in the cupboard.'

'Oh,' Lewis shrugged. 'I . . . I didn't look in the cupboards. Fancied my famous Bolognese,' he said. 'I thought we could have dinner together – after your shift ends. I've got some wine and everything. What else do I need?' Lewis made a quick sweep of the shop, fumbling about, indecisive, before finally picking up some tinned tomatoes and vegetarian mince, along with some olives.

'Lewis,' Winston sighed, feeling an edge of impatience creep into his voice. 'We've got all this stuff.'

'Have we?'

'Yes.' Winston's reply was harsh. Lewis didn't even know what they had in the cupboards. It was a stupid thing to get annoyed about, but it said it all to him. Lewis swept in, then swept out, barely leaving a mark on the place he called his home these days. And this famous Bolognese he used to make *all* the time – now, he could barely remember the recipe.

'Well. No harm getting some more. They keep,' Lewis said, nudging the items forward.

Winston rang them up and put them into a blue bag.

'Oh wait, I've got this . . .' Lewis waved a scrunched-up canvas bag at him.

Winston inhaled sharply, mainly for Lewis's benefit, and repacked the items.

'Thanks!' Lewis chirruped. 'I'll see you soon, yeah? Dinner will be on the table.'

Winston simply nodded in reply.

'Ruth has been texting me too, by the way – she says she's been struggling to get through to speak to you. Wondered if there was something wrong with your phone.' Winston looked away, down at the cash register. 'Maybe we could video call her together later? She misses you.' He turned away before Winston could reply.

He watched Lewis walk out of the shop. He wanted to reach out, to call him back, to grab him and pull him close. To tell him he didn't know what was up with him, why he kept pushing Lewis away, why he couldn't tell Lewis everything he was frustrated about, about how achingly lonely Lewis's absence made him, how he couldn't pick up the phone to Ruth. He wasn't even giving Lewis a chance to make it better.

All because he didn't know the answers himself. And he was too afraid to find out what they might be.

'Winston?' Sal asked, bringing him back to the moment. 'How are you, my son?' It was a greeting more than a question.

'Yesterday, that party – it was Diwali, but we were not celebrating.' Sal's face was sombre. 'Have you been sad?'

Winston looked away then – Sal was well known for being embarrassingly direct. But he didn't want to answer the question. A crack in his voice would expose his lies. And the truth would force too much emotion to the surface.

He took a breath. 'Has Ange done something with the receipts from this morning? There are so few in the till?'

Sal wandered over to him, looking him square in the face. He was a foot shorter than Winston and, with Winston behind the desk, raised by another foot at least, Sal seemed miniature.

Sal looked as though he was trying to sear into Winston's soul, searching for the secrets buried within. 'I worry about you, Winston,' he said. 'You seem sad.'

Winston pictured himself in the garden, alone, the cold biting at his nose. The sound of his shovel scraping rocks underneath. The hairs on his arm standing on end. The ache in his muscles. He felt alive then, didn't he? In the garden, he felt alive.

Sitting at home, waiting for Lewis to text. Sometimes, when customers looked through him, too busy talking on the phone, he was invisible. Half his time, he was just waiting to disappear.

'Winston, talk to me,' Sal said, his voice stronger now. 'Come on, my son,' he slapped his hand on the desk.

Winston was elsewhere, he'd left his body behind. 'It's useless,' Winston shook his head. 'Lewis and me . . . we fucked it up, I don't know—'

'Winston!' Sal scolded. 'Your language, please. I do not like it!'

'Sorry, Sal. I'm sorry, I . . . he came in to buy a bloody packet of spaghetti. I know it's only pasta, but for God's sake . . . it says it all really.'

Sal's expression was one of almost complete befuddlement, but he tried to cover it with a soft smile. 'Yes, the spaghetti,' he said, after a moment, shaking his head as though in on the outrage. 'Winston, go home. See Lewis. He was kind, generous last night. It was obvious he wanted to be there with you. It is you who was quiet, standing away from him. But, my son, it is very normal – you've both been busy, love takes work sometimes. It is not always easy.' Sal stepped up onto Winston's platform. 'Look, I'll take over here.'

Winston shook his head. The thought of sitting opposite Lewis, eating the same Bolognese they used to eat years ago, back when they spent almost every waking moment together. It didn't feel right. He didn't know what he'd say. And what if he said something he'd regret?

'No, Sal, I can't.'

'Okay,' Sal nodded. 'Look son, go upstairs, have a rest in the spare room. Sleep here for the night, eh? And make sure you tell Lewis where you are, otherwise he'll worry. Angela will make the spare bed.'

'I'm fine, it's fine.'

'That's enough, Winston,' Sal said, his face stern. He clapped a hand on Winston's shoulder. 'You do as you're told. You will stay with us.'

Winston woke with a throbbing forehead, a layer of sweat coating his body. The noise from the main road was loud and clear up here, the heave and sigh of bus engines stopping and starting at the traffic lights right outside. Police or ambulance sirens had already been blaring for hours.

He glanced at his phone, sitting on the doily-covered bedside table next to him. Two missed calls from Lewis: 10.30 p.m. He must have already been asleep by then. He'd texted Lewis to say he wasn't feeling well, and it was easier to stay at Sal's than try to make it home. But Lewis hadn't believed him. His reply: *Are you avoiding me?*

And who could blame him – the walk home was five minutes, max.

'Did you sleep?' Sal's head poked through the door.

'I'm all right, yeah,' Winston yawned, rubbing his hands over his eyes. Grateful to be waking up somewhere else. Away from the memories, and silence, of his own home.

'I didn't ask if you were all right,' Sal said frankly. 'I asked, did you sleep?'

'Yes, Sal,' Winston laughed. 'I did.'

'Very good. Now, Angela's made you some breakfast. Only eggs. It's what we have on Tuesday mornings,' Sal said proudly, lingering in the doorway.

In the kitchen, looking out of the window on to Stoke Newington High Street and a brand-new hipster-run coffee shop, painted entirely black with elegant white lettering on the large window, Angela was shuffling a frying pan on the hob. The sweetness of onions and garlic and the sharp tang of chilli dominated the room, hitting the back of Winston's throat.

'I thought we were having eggs, Ange?' Winston said, coughing.

'We are, my boy,' she said, voice thick from sleep. 'I don't cook without onions, dear. You should know that.'

Without needing to respond, Winston sat himself down at the small wooden table, tucked into the corner of the room. A place was already set for him. Sal hovered in and out of the kitchen, pecking Angela on the cheek every time he came in, making a detour to get to her.

'Oh, stop it!' Angela chastised. 'He never leaves me alone, this one. Can't keep his hands off.' Angela rolled her eyes at Winston, nudging her head in Sal's direction, and they laughed. Winston felt his spirit lift as the warmth of Angela's eyes, her smile, caught his.

Sal and Angela had known each other for nearly thirty years. Angela's favourite story to tell, over and over again, was the one of how they first met. In the shop, apparently. She'd been a customer, buying crunchy nut cornflakes. Every time the topic came up, and sometimes, even when it didn't, she'd say, wistfully, 'As soon as he handed me my change, I knew . . .'

Winston wasn't even sure if he believed the story. He thought it could be manufactured to be good advertising for the shop. But it was lovely nonetheless.

'Come say goodbye to me before you go,' Sal said. 'I've got to go to the butcher's so I could walk out with you. The new boy is on shift at the moment, so I don't want to hover round too much!'

Angela's nephew was working in the shop, and had been for the past few months, helping out with a few shifts here and there. Sal still called him 'the new boy', and never seemed to let him out of his sight.

Winston nodded vacantly, distracted by Angela slopping chillied, garlicky, oniony eggs onto his plate. It didn't look great, but it smelled delicious.

'Of course,' he said. 'I've got to walk past you anyway.'

'Hey . . . you, cheeky!' Sal mock-punched him. 'You say goodbye to me because you want to, not because it is easy.'

'He's a man of love,' Angela said as he wandered out. Winston didn't really have a clue what that meant, but he nodded in agreement. He'd come to mindlessly accept Sal and Angela's moments of profundity even if he had no idea what they were going on about. They were romantics, after all.

In the early days of Lewis and Winston, he'd wondered whether they'd end up like Sal and Angela, inseparable, keeping their spark of love alive through all the little things.

It was those little moments that mattered.

Angela plonked herself down next to Winston, lifting his chin up to look at her. 'You're sad, Winston.' She had the tone of a kindly schoolteacher telling him he had potential, if only he were to work harder.

'Oh God, not you too. But thanks, Angela.' Winston pulled a laugh into his response.

'Okay, maybe not sad then. Depressed. That is more than an emotion, isn't it? My sister had it.'

Winston turned away then, eyes on the sloppy eggs.

'No,' Angela continued. 'I don't mean to *upset* you, I mean to ask you what's going on?'

'Honestly, Angela, I'm fine. A bit exhausted, that's all.' Winston shovelled the last of his eggs in.

'And why did you stay here last night?'

'Like I said. Tired.'

'You live so close, I could have *carried* you home.'

'Sal offered,' Winston said assertively, hoping this would be enough.

She pulled out a cigarette from her purse. 'Don't tell Sal. But look what you're driving me to, dear! You don't mind, do you? Oh, heck . . . why do I need to ask you anyway. This is my home.'

Angela let out a mouthful of smoke. 'I never see Lewis in here any more. He used to spend time with you when you were working. Do you remember? Very annoying, I found it. But I miss it. It seemed different at yours the other night. No? You two, together, hosting this party. But you weren't there, Winston. You weren't there with us.'

'What are you talking about, Angela?' Winston said, gritting his teeth together. Winston imagined Sal whispering to her, their heads resting on pillows, rehearsing their line of enquiry. *Ask Winston about Lewis tomorrow, okay? That boy needs someone to talk to.*

'You were there physically,' Angela said, as though trying to work out a shared conundrum. 'But your *mind* was elsewhere. Lewis was hugging you, holding you, hosting for you – and you weren't there with any of us.'

'Look, it's complicated. We don't spend as much time together as we used to. It's not like those early days when we were love-sick, joined at the hip.'

'So you're missing him?'

'Sometimes,' Winston shrugged. 'I don't really remember what *not* missing him is like. It's hard to compare.' He remembered walks round Abney Park, coffee cups in hand, arms wrapped so tightly around one another they could be the same person. Lying entangled on a picnic blanket in Clissold Park, reading out snippets from the paper together, finishing each other's cigarettes and each other's sentences. He shrugged again. Trying to remain composed. But the feeling of lead in the back of his throat clogged his windpipe.

Angela said nothing but clapped her hand on to his shoulder. She thought she was being comforting.

Winston thought he might bruise from the strength of her compassion.

'You two make a lovely couple,' she said eventually. 'I know he's a banker wanker as you used to say . . . and we all hate those,' Angela winked at him, 'but he's a good boy. He has so much love to give. I know it's you he wants to give it to if you'll let him. If you'll just talk to him, tell him what's wrong.'

'Thanks for breakfast, Ange,' he said gruffly, standing up sharply to wash up his plate, despite Angela's protestations of, 'No, no, Winston, I'll do that, lovely one.'

On his way out, he picked up Sal, who was very indiscreetly keeping an eye on everything 'the new boy' was doing (perfectly, as far as Winston could see). The poor kid was currently stuck in conversation with Howard the Complainer, who looked like he was just getting started on his rant of the day. He hadn't even picked up his Sesame Snaps yet.

Without stopping to help, Winston ushered Sal out and they walked in silence, side by side. Sal had to hurry every other step to keep up.

They paused when they reached Aziziye Mosque, which had a butcher's and a Turkish restaurant at the front. In the sunshine, the turquoise, royal blue and white tiles looked even more beautiful than usual, inviting you inside.

'Son,' Sal said, both hands reaching up to Winston's shoulders. 'You can always talk to me. Okay?'

Winston nodded. And he watched Sal walk inside the butcher's, greeted energetically by the customers already there, Sal's friends from mosque. He watched Sal consumed by hugs, camaraderie, and turned to continue his walk home, alone.

Unlocking his front door, Winston imagined Lewis sitting in the living room, reading. Putting his arms round him, embracing him, telling him he'd missed him, that he wanted to spend the day together. Maybe Lewis could bunk off work, and they could go somewhere. Like they used to.

But the house was silent. Empty. And Lewis's work shoes were gone.

Winston wandered through the kitchen; everything looked spotless. Lewis must have cleaned up. The only evidence of anyone having been here last night was a pot on the stove, half full of Bolognese.

He flicked the kettle on, letting the click-click of a limescaled heating element fill the void in the room, and his eyes went immediately to the back garden. The charred remnants underneath the incinerator. The broken pot, smashed neatly in two. In the daylight, everything looked worse. More miserable. Like a house party once everyone had gone home, when there was only the hungover cleaning up left to do.

A scraggedy fox crept through a small trench under the fence, his fur both rust-red and grey in patches, tail fluffy at the end. He made a beeline for the pot's upset soil.

'Great,' Winston muttered. Within seconds, the fox was furiously digging with his front paws – glancing from side to side for fear of getting caught in the act.

'Eh!' Winston banged on the window. The fox looked at him, dead on. Paused. Paws still in the ground. Then he continued.

Scrabbling around for the key, Winston flung the kitchen door open as soon as he could, and the fox bolted, leaving nothing but a divot in the soil.

'You knobhead,' Winston said. He would have used a harsher word, but it felt unfair to use a *proper* swear word on a fox, who couldn't swear back.

'Hello!'

Winston turned round, half expecting to see Lewis. But it was Mr James, his landlord. Mr James was probably in his late seventies, and looked ridiculously good for it. His grey hair was neatly slicked back, as always, and though he was now walking more slowly than he used to, with the help of a stick from time to time, especially when the weather was cold, he never seemed fazed by doing some small DIY in the house if he needed to. He preferred to fix something himself rather than call someone in. 'Make do and mend,' he used to say. 'That's what I was brought up with. Need to keep my hand in. I was born a smidge before the Second World War, you see, and that's how we kept going afterwards. Fix, fix, fix. My daughter is always telling me to start letting someone else deal with everything,' he'd say. 'But I enjoy it!'

He'd introduced himself as Charlie James, and insisted they call him Charlie, but his seniority made the first name sound so awkward, and it had simply been Mr James ever since.

'Winston! I'm so sorry,' he said now, looking mildly alarmed. 'Lewis said you'd probably both be out. I was in the area, seeing an old friend across the road, and thought I'd pop in to make a start on the admin, I suppose. I rang the bell, but there was no answer. Did you get my message?'

The doorbell had been broken for months. Winston shook his head.

'Oh, sorry – must have messaged Lewis. Thought he'd let you know,' Mr James said, trying not to look around. Whenever he visited, he always seemed to keep his eyes focused straight ahead, determined to maintain his tenants' privacy.

'Well,' he said, spotting the garden and stepping out onto the patio, giving a low whistle. Winston followed him outside, investigating the broken pot. 'This is looking much less scruffy, all in all,' Mr James continued. 'The weeds and those blasted brambles, they're gone?!'

'Yeah,' Winston nodded.

'You know,' Mr James said wistfully. 'My neighbour, from back when I lived here as a boy, she used to garden here. She kept it so nice, her and her dad. And my mum loved it so much too,' he paused then, wistful. 'Lots of vegetables, flowers. A bit of everything. My dad never much cared for it . . . thought my mum was wasting her time on it, with the neighbours, but they really made it something. I used to help out myself sometimes.' He laughed, a smile on his face. 'Nice that you've been tidying it up. Or is that the woman next door?'

Winston wanted to ask more – when Mr James was a boy? This house, it had been in Mr James's family for years. Did he know the two women in the photographs in the mystery post, or did he live here long before their time? Before Winston could ask anything, Mr James said: 'Bonfire?'

Winston shrugged.

'Your new neighbour,' Mr James whispered. 'She's been a nightmare on the garden side of things. Kept complaining about it being shared – but it's in the deeds. Nothing I can do. Nothing I *want* to do. How's she been with you, Bernice?'

'Hmm,' Winston murmured. He could tell Mr James everything, but there was no point, was there. 'Not bad.'

'That's good to hear. Though, won't be your problem for very long now, will it!'

'What do you mean?'

'I mean, congratulations are in order! I'm here to take some photos to send to my estate agent. Won't be easy getting tenants as good as you lads.'

'Mr James,' Winston said slowly, wondering if the man had confused himself, though Mr James had always possessed a particularly sharp memory. 'What are you talking about?'

'Look, I've got this for you,' he said, pulling out a bottle of champagne from his rucksack. 'I thought I'd leave it here for you both and you can toast your new home. How long until you move into your new place then? Homeowners, eh?!'

Winston took the bottle from Mr James's hand, holding onto it as tightly as he could, his stomach twisting into knots. His landlord's face started to blur into nothingness, and he forced himself to sit down on his wooden chair, *Handmade by Prem*.

Chapter 14

Maya

October 1976

'Alma?' Maya tiptoed into the garden, where she saw Alma asleep with one-year-old Hiral snoring quietly on her tummy, both wrapped in woollies and blankets on the newly laid lawn. Prem and Maya had managed to convince Alma to put some turf down to replace the bark chips they'd had before. Jenny had been complaining about there being no soft landings for accident-prone George, and Maya and Prem were keen for Hiral to have some grass now she was starting to walk.

'But it's wasted space!' Alma had complained. 'It's Jenny, isn't it? She's put you up to this.'

'Alma,' Maya sighed, taking on the role of peacekeeper. 'Let's do it. Besides, that little bit of bark chip stuff does look rather mucky. And the foxes love doing their business in it.'

Doing their business. It was an Alma phrase, one of the many things Maya had picked up from her friend. She was always talking about Susie's *business*, the foxes' *business*. How quintessentially *English* it sounded in her mouth.

Alma had sighed. 'Fine. We better make use of it then.' It was almost a threat.

And now here she was, sprawled out on the lawn holding Maya's daughter close, in the depths of autumn, the edges of the lawn scattered with ash leaves from the garden next door, the corkscrew hazel naked in all its twistiness, the air cold but the sky still bright, setting a warmth on their skin. The roses were still going strong, on their second or third bloom of the year, and the Virginia creeper running along the length of the wall was turning a ruby red. Maya couldn't believe it was nearly the end of October. But she felt like this every year now, when the seasons each revealed their beauty layer by layer. Prem had recently taken to sitting out in the garden early every morning, in his chair, with a cup of coffee or a chai in hand. No matter the weather. He'd sit and listen to the birds – sometimes he'd talk back to them, tell them about the day ahead, and he'd simply watch as time changed the garden little by little. 'I'm addicted to it,' Prem said. 'I didn't know I would be.'

Maya wandered over the rickety cobblestone path Prem had laid last summer, cutting through some mind-your-own-business in her wicker sandals and socks.

'Alma?' Maya whispered loudly.

She opened one eye, landing on Maya, then shut it again quickly, snoring in time with Hiral, pretending she hadn't heard at all.

'Alma!' Maya spoke louder now, a laugh creeping into her voice.

'All right, all right!' Alma stage-whispered back. Hiral didn't move an inch. 'I'm just exhausted.' Alma rolled her eyes back in her head dramatically. She wasn't usually one for theatrics.

'You do *look* tired,' Maya pushed a step further.

'It's probably how much that little one of yours cries at night. Shouldn't she be growing out of that by now?' Alma tapped Hiral's be-hatted head gently.

'She's still a baby.'

'But she's got her own room now. Only big girls have their own rooms. Doesn't she like her room?'

Maya and Prem had spent the last few weeks decorating the spare room to become Hiral's bedroom. They'd got permission from their landlord, providing they 'did it well' or painted over it when they left. The suggestion, however benign, of them leaving at some point in the future instilled a sliver of fear into Maya. She couldn't bear the thought of leaving this house that had become her home, or leaving Alma behind, the person who had become as close as family.

They'd painted the room a brilliant blue with fluffy white clouds – perfect, like something from a dream. Prem should have been an artist, not a bank clerk. But Alma was right about the bedroom. Hiral *hated* it. That sky was *too* perfect, the clouds *too* pristine . . . No sky in the world looked like the one in Hiral's room. Nothing *real* could ever compare. Maybe that's what had ruined it for her little girl. Maya and Prem had set the standards too high – real life would never be good enough.

'If only you could tell the little lady to be grateful, eh?' Alma chuckled warmly. 'Doesn't she know, only very spoilt girls get their own decorated rooms like that – and at her age, too! I'm still using the eiderdown my father had when I was a child – fifty years ago, Maya, and my feet stick out at the ends. What does Hiral make of that?'

'Alma, she's not spoilt,' Maya said, hurt. 'Spoilt' – the one thing she'd spent her parenting life trying to rally against. Her mother's last words before she left were, 'If you and Prem have children there, do not let them come back spoilt. Let them have our values, none of those English ones.' Maya hadn't known for sure what these English values were – but she had been told that spoiling children was one of the worst of them.

'Right Alma,' Maya continued seriously, 'we said we'd paint those signs for Bina before she got here.' Earlier that week, Prem had gone to the local DIY shop and bought all sorts of paints and fabrics and offcuts of cardboard and wood to make signs for Bina's upcoming protest.

'I wasn't sure what the most powerful colours would be,' he'd said, 'but I hope these will work.' He unloaded cartons of big bold reds, yellows, oranges, blues – and purple, of course. 'I know it's Bina's favourite colour,' Prem explained, as Maya paused with her hand on the container.

'All right,' Alma said, pushing herself up from the ground with one hand, straining to hold onto Hiral's sleeping form with the other. Hiral was heavier than she looked. 'Let's get you into your room for a snooze before your bathtime, while your ma and I start painting.' Maya felt a smile creep onto her face at Alma's tone, speaking to Hiral as she would to any adult.

'Hey, Auntie Alma, hey Auntie Maya!' The garden gate was thrust open and the two boys, fourteen now, Yusuf and Ade, came bursting in. School bags slung over their shoulders, their jumpers tied around their waists. 'We're back. Can we help with anything? Is Prem here?'

'Boys!' Prem stepped out of the kitchen on cue, carrying several cups of tea. Since Guy Fawkes' Night last year, Yusuf and Ade had become regular faces in the garden. At first, Yusuf came along with his mum Isha, helping her out, picking vegetables for their supper. If Isha was working on a complicated tailoring project in their living room, Yusuf would bring Ade here to hang out after school. 'It's nicer to be here than hanging about in the park,' Ade said. Prem was sure the boys at school were still causing them trouble, though they hadn't told him as much. Initially, they'd simply drink a cup of tea with Prem, chatting, but then, as they watched the garden growing, week after week, fascinated by the process of it all, they'd begun to get stuck in. Now they came every Thursday, and Prem was always back from work in time to keep them company.

'Got some chilli pickle and cheese sandwiches to keep us going. Fancy them?' Prem asked.

'Yes please!' Yusuf said, his eyes already searching the garden, ready to make a start.

As the boys tucked into the sandwiches, Prem shepherded them over to the first gardening tasks. Somehow it was easier for the boys to talk to Prem when they were all occupied: in summer, they deadheaded plants together, in early spring they dug up the old and started planting the new. When they were all getting on with something, they didn't have to keep everything to themselves. It was easier to talk when it felt like you weren't talking at all.

'When you're done with that, fancy helping us paint these signs?' Maya asked. 'We're painting some banners for my sister – she's protesting.'

The boys looked at each other, then at Prem, eyebrows raised. They were already well aware of the importance of protesting. It was something Maya had never had to think about when she was growing up. But these boys had likely already been on protests in their young lives, and they'd witnessed many more, minutes from their front doors, up and down the high street. People fighting urgently for their lives, their neighbours' lives, their rights, their parents' rights.

'Want to help?' Maya continued, and they nodded.

Maya's sister, Bina, had been protesting since August in an industrial dispute that almost every one of Bina's friends and colleagues at the film factory in Brent was involved with. They were fighting to be paid a fair wage, fighting for working rights. They were afraid of being dismissed without a moment's notice.

Maya felt so proud. Proud that her sister and her friends had held onto their own power. The women involved in the strikes were predominantly Asian women from East Africa – she'd heard them called 'strikers in saris'. Bina wore that name like a badge of honour. The strikers included people they'd grown up with in Kenya, as well as friends Bina and her family had made in London. Her exciting new job at the factory ended up being one she wrote home about for all the wrong reasons.

Maya had heard stories of the picket line – the cold getting to their fingers and toes, protesters wrapped up in layers to keep the warmth in. They'd had support from all over. She'd even heard that a member of Bina's bookclub, Naina, had come to deliver food to the strikers every lunchtime. Maya, Alma and Prem had already made one lot of signs for Bina and her friends that summer, but after so much use, days and days of standing on the picket line, the signs were now weathered and flimsy.

'Maya,' Bina had pleaded, calling up a few days ago. 'I'm going back to the picket line. I need this to be over. We need to win.' Bina's voice caught in her throat, but Maya just let her talk. 'Will you do some more signs? There's no space here, and the landlady upstairs is insistent I can't paint indoors. Can you help?'

'Yes,' Maya had said, picturing the last time they'd painted the signs, laid out in the garden. 'Yes, we'll do it in the garden.'

And she knew that the garden's chief tender, Alma, would be on board. Alma was constantly, all-consumingly enraged about the injustices in her own community, at the way Yusuf and Ade were treated by school bullies, and by policemen twice their age. At the discrimination both Patrick and Prem faced from customers and management in their bank clerk jobs. At the ignorance and venom in the words people muttered under their breath about Maya and Prem when they were on a walk, the insults shouted behind their backs. At Erol's constant fear of having to prove he 'belonged' here as much as anyone else.

And she was also furious at Bina's situation; the bosses treating these women like they deserved less than everyone else.

Alma relished the opportunity to paint the signs – but she wanted to do more. While Bina refused to let her stand on the picket line in the cold months, Alma called up a few friends instead who worked for trade unions. But they were already well aware of the dispute, and there was nothing more she could do for them. They were working as hard as they could.

In the early days of the strike, when Alma could do nothing but share words of encouragement with Bina, she'd sat at home alone, turning her hands over and over, popping around to Maya's every day, adding to her list of grievances, bemoaning her uselessness. It was this frustration that had eventually been expressed in a whole host of signs littered with swear words, painted in the dead of night ('Goodness me, what's that noise?' Prem had said at two in the morning. 'Probably foxes,' Maya had replied).

Fuck you, bosses! Fuck the oppression!

We demand bloody respect and our workers' rights!

Greedy! Evil! Awful Bosses! Damn the lot of them!

Maya had woken the next morning to find signs hung all around the garden, from the shed, the fences and the garden wall, roses and clematis popping up behind them; their space transformed into a protest site.

Alma had then taken them on the Tube all the way to the picket line where she'd seen Bina with her more modest, targeted sign of *Cut Grunwick off now* and proudly handed her the new ones.

'Alma!' Bina had greeted her with delight. 'Thank you. But I need less of the eff word, okay? I have never used the eff word in my life.'

Alma had shrugged. 'If you want to be noticed . . .' she nodded towards her signs. '*This* is how you do it.'

'I'll take them!' interjected a woman next to Bina, dressed in a pink cardigan and a pale blue sari, launching herself towards the signs and passing them around. There was a ripple of amusement from the women on the front line. She wasn't sure if they'd be used, but she was glad to put a smile on their faces.

When Maya dumped the painting materials on the garden table, Ade's eyes widened. 'Paint,' he said, under his breath, analysing the risk. 'Maya, Alma,' he said, looking between them both. 'I can't get paint on my clothes. Mum will be furious.'

'Do you want to wear one of my aprons?' Alma said, immediately dragging out a flowery, frilly apron from her gardening shed. Maya was certain Alma had never worn such a thing in her life.

Ade looked to Yusuf, eyes wide. Mortified. Maya could see he wanted to be polite. Prem and Yusuf burst into laughter, clapping Ade on the back.

'Now,' Maya cut in, conjuring the air of a schoolmistress, waiting for her class to pay attention. 'Would your mothers mind if you had some orange juice and biscuits? I know you've already had a sandwich and I don't want to spoil your appetites.'

Yusuf gave nothing away, while Ade nodded eagerly.

'I'll take your word for it,' Maya said.

Alma looked at Yusuf, who turned away awkwardly. 'I know Isha's been checking your bag for contraband sugar, Yus! Fourteen-year-olds still need to think about their teeth.'

Maya went in to help Alma with the drinks, enjoying listening to Prem, Ade and Yusuf chatting away – laughing about school, neighbours, Alma's potty mouth. She watched as Prem laughed with them, encouraging them to talk more, listening when they had something to share. He cared deeply about those boys; they were as much his friends as Patrick, Bob and Erol were.

Alma pulled out her battered Romary's Cocktail Assortment tin, decorated with a rather pallid photograph of wine in crystal glasses and cracker biscuits. Once she'd teased the tin-lid off, it revealed a mound of chocolate digestives.

'How many biscuits each, do you think?' Alma asked, grabbing handfuls of ten and twelve biscuits at a time, putting them onto individual plates.

'Alma no! No more than two each?' Maya said, horrified.

'All right, they can come back for more. Isha doesn't stop telling me about Yusuf's sugar intake, and I never ask. But one day, I spotted him outside Erol's shop with a big bag of sweets. Let him live, though, of course – what Isha doesn't know won't hurt her.'

Maya nudged her friend playfully. 'I'm sure Isha will be fine with Yusuf having a *couple* of digestives, especially as they've both been working so hard.'

Alma turned to the kitchen door. 'Juice and biscuits – sorry if they're a bit stale, boys, don't judge me for it,' her voice boomed across the garden.

'Oh, God!' Yusuf said, before swiftly covering his mouth with a half-painted hand. Everyone turned to look at him. On the white fabric of the banner, there was a brand-new orange splodge that resembled . . . well, an orange. He looked down at the fabric, and then to his hand with the paintbrush, lifting his arm above his head. His sleeves had dipped themselves into the paint.

'Don't think Mum's going to care about sugar, Alma,' Yusuf said, a cheeky smile spreading across his face as he rolled his sleeves up again, despite the fact that this was likely to make it all worse.

Ade, biscuit in his mouth, burst into laughter.

'Wow!'

Everyone turned around, and there was Bina, standing in the kitchen doorway. She was wearing a yellow sari, with orange paisley patterns, covered with a cardigan with pearl and gold-style buttons. Maya looked between her sister and the signs dotted all around the garden. Yusuf held his up proudly to show her: *You can get lost! We demand our rights!*

'Boys!' Bina said, covering her mouth with her hands. Maya had never heard her voice that squeaky; her sister was always the epitome of composure.

She moved over to the signs, painted with big bold lettering. Yusuf looked up, as though waiting for a teacher to mark his work. Maya noticed that her handwriting seemed to have less confidence than Yusuf's. Her letters started big but then petered out to almost nothing, whereas Yusuf's remained bold, defiant, demanding to be noticed, to be heard.

'I love them,' Bina said, addressing the boys.

Stop the oppression!

Workers united! We won't be defeated!

'I hope it works,' Ade offered, from the shed. 'I'm sorry for what you're going through.'

Bina smiled at him, nodded. 'Thank you,' she said, after a moment. 'This is one small thing in a sea of many other injustices in this world,' she said. Maya noticed in Bina their mother's love of sharing cryptic words of wisdom. It seemed time away from their mother had turned Bina into her. 'But here' – Bina looked around the garden – 'here we all have each other to look after one another. These are . . . they are wonderful.'

'Erm . . .' Ade and Yusuf looked at each other awkwardly, as Bina started to well up. 'We better head off now. Thanks for the company and the biscuits!' Yusuf called, wrapping his painted sleeve into itself, before traipsing out of the gate.

'Miss,' Ade said, turning to Bina once more. 'It's good that you're sticking up for yourself. Mum always tells me that's what you've got to do.'

Prem shot Maya a look then, and smiled. Maybe Ade had told his parents what was going on after all.

After Alma had disappeared to the kitchen, and Bina had bagged up the banners ready for tomorrow's picket line, Maya and Prem sat in the garden, listening to the sounds of Stoke Newington around them, their hands wrapped around one another. Sirens blared in the distance, chatter drifted over as people wandered past the gate, the sizzle of cooking. The smell of garlic and onion filtered through the air.

'That smells like Isha's signature lamb stew, I reckon,' Prem said, and Maya smiled. 'You're not going to tell Isha about Yusuf's digestives, are you?' he asked, when Alma came out to join them with a beer in her hand.

'I'll leave that up to Yusuf,' she said, taking a sip.

'It's always lovely to have them in the garden,' Maya said, the boys on her mind.

'You know, I think they really like it here too,' Prem said, putting his arm around her. 'Yusuf is coming up with so many ideas for the space, new things we can plant. I saw Isha the other day, and she said he'd drawn a few planting plans, Alma. Maybe he could share them?'

Maya and Prem looked at Alma then, who nodded. 'Well, Yusuf and Ade are definitely part of our team now. Happy to take a look, but my planting plans haven't changed in decades . . . so you know.'

Maya and Prem exchanged a knowing look then, smiling.

'Look,' Maya said suddenly, pointing to a little trail of orange paint on the garden table. It had a neat row of paw prints running from the top corner to the bottom.

'Susie?' Maya asked, and Alma turned her head sharply to look at the cat, languorously grooming her paws, her back leg held high over her head. There was no sign of any paint on her at all.

'Can't imagine that madam ever getting her paws mucky . . . She's too much of a snob.' Susie gave Alma a dirty look.

'Foxes?' Prem said.

'Oh, bloody hell, it must be.' And at that moment, Prem, Alma and Maya caught sight of a little fox slinking out of the garden under the fence, leaving a fading trail of orange blobs.

Maya pulled her bottom lip down as if to say, 'Oh dear, oh dear.'

Alma took another gulp of her beer. 'I'd rather have them painting signs than digging up my beds. They only want to get involved after all. We need all hands on deck at times like these,' she said with a wink.

Chapter 15

Bernice

November 2018

Missing you, Mummy

Seb would always send a voice note from Simon's phone whenever his dad picked him up. The same every week. It was always the moment that made Bernice feel loved and lonely, all at once. She'd look forward to having the day to herself, but when it arrived, when Seb sent that message, she had to pull herself up from the sofa, force herself to do something nice, to take her mind off things.

Missing you too, sweetie – she replied – *have a lovely day with Daddy! I'll see you tomorrow after school. Risotto for dinner!*

Until then, it was just her. She cradled her coffee in her hands, placing her phone face down on the counter. She didn't want to think about missing Seb today, even though he occupied every spot in her mind; the happy spots, the sad spots, and the worried spots too.

It was only 9 a.m., and mist lay low over the garden. She could see the sun trying hard to burn its way through. From this point at the top of the house she could see the Shard in the distance, Canary Wharf too, with the light blinking on top of the pyramid roof. It was a reminder of a previous life. Here, she could look down and see row upon row of houses, gardens, *homes*. When she'd lived in the apartment in central London for all those years, and Simon left at six to start work, she'd sit at the kitchen table looking out of a window that stared into a personality-less office block or half-empty apartments; people rarely stayed there for long. She'd felt lonely then. Sometimes it felt like she was the only person around.

But, she thought to herself, as she took in the garden below, she was still alone, wasn't she?

That curious envelope, addressed to *The Lady at Number 77*, had shown her photos of the shared garden decades ago, when it was full of people. It felt like her worst nightmare. Having her own space, space she'd worked so hard for, space she'd yearned for for so long, suddenly invaded by people around her. But in those photos, people were smiling. They had their arms around each other, singing, dancing.

If she called out, would anyone hear her? No, except maybe for Winston. He had become a silent, constant and, dare she say it, comforting presence of late.

She'd usually spot him out in the garden if he wasn't at work, enjoying a moment of calm, sitting in his disgusting, rotting chair, with a cup of tea or glass of wine. A few times, she'd seen him digging, or raking soil over the beds, 'aerating' it with an ancient garden fork.

If Seb saw him after school, he'd run up to his new friend, excited, asking for tales of the garden even if there was nothing new for Winston to say. She'd noticed yesterday that, when Seb ran up to him, Winston moved his cigarette out of Seb's view, making sure the smoke didn't go anywhere near him. Bernice wanted to say thank you, but her embarrassment at how she'd behaved previously held her back.

Now, as she looked out at the freshly planted beds, she realized she was looking for him too. No matter how much she hated the noise from his music, he was another person living life close by. She didn't detest his presence, not really. Seeing him, with the city and homes sprawled out in front of her, it helped her feel connected . . . to someone at least.

And while she might not admit it to Winston, she felt guilty for calling his landlord, demanding that a fence be erected in the middle of the garden. The landlord flat out refused. Said he couldn't even if he wanted to. But Bernice now recognized Winston had put so much work into the space, and it was slowly becoming somewhere she might actually want to spend time. And he'd been able to get through to Seb. When Seb was quiet, Winston was the person he'd still want to talk to. She was grateful for that too.

Slipping down the stairs a few hours later, Bernice ventured into the garden herself for the first time in a while. The air was cold, and her breath formed icy clouds.

She followed the half-formed paths Winston had been working on – the grass had been trimmed away and he was in the process of laying down some cardboard. 'A weed super present,' Seb had told her confidently. It didn't look great now, but she was sure it'd come into its own when finished. As she got to the far end of the garden, the path petered away, leaving a scrubby bit of de-weeded land, and she watched her step to avoid any poo. That was her overwhelming experience of having a garden in London. She hadn't dreamed of it when staring lovingly at photographs on Rightmove, yearning for a space of her own.

She trudged straight over to the shed. She'd seen it in one of the photos slipped through her letterbox, looking almost brand new. At first, she'd wondered if Winston had put them through her door . . . Maybe to rile her. A coded 'fuck you' to the fact she'd pushed for a fence. But seeing those photos, with neighbours arm in arm, garden open days and community bake sales . . . it seemed a funny way to annoy someone.

She had no idea what was in the shed, she'd never taken a proper look, but Seb was always running in and out of there collecting tools. She figured she should check if it was safe. The door was unlocked, and as she pulled it towards her, she was greeted by the damp smell of soggy wood, cobwebs and dust, and a space chock-a-block with ancient tools: disintegrating rakes, trowels in every state of disrepair, some snapped clean in half, others with their handles hanging off. There were dozens of pairs of gloves too, in all sizes. There were watering cans – plastic ones, tin ones dented all over – and buckets. Old, dusty rolls of tarpaulin, seed trays and stacks upon stacks of plastic flowerpots. Some cracked, others decorated in fossilized mud.

Below one of the hooks, Bernice could make out scratches in the wooden walls – *I ♡ Susie, love Hiral xx*

The handwriting was young, childlike – Bernice couldn't help but smile. The edges of the scratches were smooth, worn down by time.

She took a breath, and turned her attention back to the contents, and crucially, the hazards of the shed. 'This is *definitely* a danger zone . . .' Bernice muttered, horrified at the thought Seb had been running in and out of here. She needed to get rid of anything that he could impale himself on, and ensure there were no more hidden dangers. She grabbed a pair of gloves that looked around her size, wincing a bit as she shoved her hand into them, praying no slugs, snails or spiders called them home.

As she started to work her way through the junk and detritus of whoever had lived here before her, she felt frustration bubble up inside her, with every yank and clatter of metal. Why hadn't Winston done anything about this? It was so obviously dangerous for a young boy, and yet he'd let Seb wander in and out freely? As she pulled a stepladder away from a wall, an old brittle ice-cream box of Allen keys fell onto the floor, tinkling like wind chimes. 'Oh, for God's sake,' she muttered, wiping her brow with the glove.

'Look, please, let me talk!' A shout cut through the silence of the garden, coming from Winston's house.

Instinctively, Bernice stepped back and slowly pulled the shed door closed behind her, shutting herself in with all the mud-encrusted tools and creepy crawlies. Panicking there could be mice or rats in there with her too, she nearly screamed out loud when her leg brushed against something. But it turned out to be an old-fashioned feather duster, clammy from the cold.

She peered through the grimy window to see Lewis and Winston stepping out into the garden. Lewis was in a roll-neck jumper and smart trousers, Winston in his Sunday attire, dressing gown, jogging bottoms and a cigarette dangling from his fingers. He was pacing up and down the patio, looking anywhere but at Lewis.

'Listen to me, Winston! Listen to me,' Lewis said. His words were bold, sharp, but Bernice sensed a sadness behind them. It sounded like Lewis could burst into tears at any moment. 'I've . . . I wanted to tell you. I've been trying to talk to you for ages, Winston. I've been making all these plans for *us*. But it's felt like you've not been there at all.' Lewis paused, waiting for a reply, but Winston, his back to his partner, took a drag of his cigarette, his eyes squeezed tightly shut. 'I thought you'd be happy,' Lewis continued. 'I kept trying to tell you. I waited for you, called you. On Monday. I wanted to make dinner for us. I told you *please* come back. I was going to tell you then. But you never came home.'

Winston opened his eyes at that, but stared towards the back of the garden. Bernice ducked, hoping he hadn't seen her face, haloed in the dusty shed window.

'Maybe I wasn't home that day, Lewis, but I think this is the sort of thing you should have told me *months* ago. Maybe this was something we should have decided together.'

His tone was flat. Emotionless. Giving nothing away.

'I know . . . But, I wanted . . . I didn't want to put the stress on you.'

'Don't you even try to play the martyr when *you* have bought a fucking house in Oxford that I haven't even seen! And you tell our landlord without even talking to me? Are you crazy?'

'What!' Bernice gasped, as though watching a soap on TV. She looked at Winston: still, stony, eyes closed.

Lewis paused, his eyes searching the back of Winston's head for a clue. 'I haven't handed our notice in . . . I mentioned it to Mr James. I was excited I . . . I wanted to tell you. I've been *trying* to tell you . . . I saw it months ago, put an offer in . . . because, because it seemed ridiculous to miss the opportunity. I *wanted* to show it to you, Winston, but you never came. To Oxford, remember? I wanted to surprise you.'

'Lewis,' Winston growled. 'Buying a house is not the same as a surprise trip away. It's a decision you make with your partner, not *for* them. All your little hints about "not renting forever" and the "sensible idea to invest in property", I thought you were simply leading up to a conversation about us considering it in the future. Maybe *I'm* the idiot for not realizing that meant you were in the process of buying us a house all by yourself.'

Bernice remembered when Simon bought the Marylebone penthouse for some ridiculous price, when she'd spent ages bookmarking all these houses further out with outdoor space, communities and neighbours who might even pop round for a drink. When the offer had been accepted, she'd simply deleted the tabs from her internet browser while Simon popped out for some champagne to celebrate.

If she listened carefully, she was sure she'd be able to hear Winston's heart plummet to the ground, knocking heavily on the paving slabs, broken and dirty from weeks of gardening and muddy boots. The feeling so familiar to her.

'I've wanted this for a long time, Winston. I wanted you to be a part of it too, but,' he took a deep breath here, 'I'm not putting my life on hold for you, waiting for you to suddenly be ready for this. At some point I had to be the responsible one. Neither of us wants to be renting for the rest of our lives, putting money in someone else's pocket.'

'Don't we?'

'Of course not,' Lewis said. 'I know your mother would be horrified if she knew you'd been renting all these years. You know that too. You were always lying to her – pretending you still worked in the City, that you were saving for a house . . . I thought we both wanted to make something real.'

'Don't bring my mother into this,' Winston snapped. 'This is not what I want, Lewis. This is what *you* want. What you've always wanted. You've said "I want" a million times . . . over and over again. Did you ever consider me? Like, really?'

'Winston,' Lewis softened, his voice soothing. 'Trust me. You'll love this place. You will!' He took a step towards Winston, but wasn't brave enough to move any closer. 'Remember those country hotels we used to visit years ago for fun? And we'd drive past those houses in the villages . . . You always loved those cottages. I wanted that life for us, Winston.'

'I can't afford a house, Lewis. And I like where we live. I like it here.'

'You don't need to pay me anything. I've bought it, Winston.' Lewis said it as though it was a gift, a huge privilege. But Bernice's stomach twisted. Suddenly it was as though they had been put on mute. She couldn't hear anything, she could just see Winston waving his arms around, Lewis stepping backwards. She heard nothing but the pounding of the blood in her ears. There were no cars, no planes flying overhead, no birds, no children playing in the small park across the road.

Then finally Winston shepherded Lewis into the house, pulling his dressing gown tight around him. He bellowed: 'It's *your* house, Lewis. Not mine. This is your life, not ours. Your decisions. Your house. Leave me out of it. I want to be here. I want to *stay here*.'

And with that, he shut the door behind Lewis, before sitting down in his rickety chair. He looked out at the garden for a few minutes. Would Bernice ever be able to come out of the shed? She couldn't bear the thought of Winston realizing she'd seen it all unfold.

Eventually, Winston pulled himself up to inspect some newly planted pots and patches of earth. Searching for shoots, even though it was far too early. But as he turned his attention to the garden, she saw his shoulders drop, relax, the muscles in his face that had previously been pulled tight now loosened as he ran his fingers through the soil.

When it became clear Winston wasn't heading inside anytime soon, and she could no longer stand the smell of damp, mouldy old wood, Bernice let herself out of the shed, brushing herself down as quietly as she could manage. Tiptoeing across the garden, she averted her gaze from Winston.

'Saw it all, did you?'

Bernice stopped in her tracks, reaching out for her kitchen door.

'I'm really sorry,' she said, trying to make it sound as genuine as she intended it to be. Stepping inside the house, her eyes landed on two limes in her fruit basket. It was only 9.30 a.m., but it might be just what he needed . . .

A few minutes later, she returned to the patio: Winston hadn't moved at all.

'Here,' she passed him a cocktail glass, complete with cocktail umbrella, handmade by Seb at school. 'A margarita, not frozen. Though it might be in a few minutes,' she said, nodding towards the delicate frost crusting the tips of the grass.

Winston looked at the glass – and he smiled weakly. 'I knew having swanky neighbours would come in handy.'

'You want to talk?'

'Not sure,' Winston took a sip, grimacing at the sharpness of the limes.

Bernice brought out a chair from her kitchen, and sat opposite him, cocktail in hand.

'Well,' she said quietly. 'I'll be here, in case you change your mind.'

Part II

WINTER

Friday, 21 December 2018

It's getting brisk out, these days. We had a mild autumn, though I saw so many people wrapped up in layer upon layer of knitwear. Clearly they never experienced the autumns and winters we had to endure back in the seventies and eighties. Those morning fogs we used to get. They were a nightmare! Thank goodness for the crochet blankets Jenny used to make us every Christmas. Prem hated them – she always made his in pink and yellow, just to tease him, and he always ended up using them as a rag to oil the bench or his wooden chair. Thankfully, Jenny never found out. I've not told her to this day!

It's funny, no matter what the temperature is, I keep the living-room window open a smidge still, because Fraser and Morris used to like getting some fresh air when they were sitting along the windowsill. Even now, even though they've gone, those little creatures still have me wrapped around their paws. They also enjoyed having the television on all the time too . . . and now it's a routine I can't break. The voices keep me company, playing along in the distance.

I've been putting out some bird feed in the garden, you know, as you always recommended at this time of year: piles and piles of it, especially when it's frosty. I always used to be anxious to avoid creating a hunting spot for Morris, though, so I would put out only a little bit, right at the top of the feeder so the birds could swoop down and away as quickly as possible.

The garden is all planted up with bulbs, ready for spring. Do you remember we used to work our fingers raw planting them out in the coldest of Novembers? You never used to wear gloves . . . And then somehow, I picked up your terrible habit. Until Prem got me those lovely ones.

I miss everyone at this time of year. Well, I miss you all the time, but I'm always thinking of the Christmases we were lucky enough to have together. How different everything was back then. I get the feeling, these days, that everyone deserts this road when it's Christmas time. It's like I'm the only one left alive! All the youngsters seem to head off to their parents and families, somewhere with more space, more greenery, I expect. I never see anyone popping down the road on Christmas Day to say hello to their neighbours like they used to. I do sometimes spot George and Jenny going for their traditional Boxing Day walk, though. They always call in on their way back, which is nice. Sometimes I do envy Jenny, with George living with her still. What I would give to have Hiral here with me. She visits when she can. But her Christmases in Italy are often very hectic with work, so she comes a few months after. Which is lovely in its own way.

At least I still take my Christmas Day walk. It used to be me and Frase. It's that much lonelier on my own, but it gets me out of the house.

That reminds me. I tootled along to de Beauvoir Town the other day. It was a longer walk than I'm used to, but I've always loved that little neighbourhood, and I was curious. I haven't left Stoke Newington in months, it can sometimes feel like a bubble. But it's changed an awful lot down there. Like everything, I suppose. But while I was there, I had this feeling of stepping into another world. The shops, the greengrocer's, the pub, it's all a bit different. Polished. Lovely, yes – but it almost felt like a film set. It doesn't quite fit with the reality of the city surrounding it, the tower blocks right next door. That de Beauvoir . . . it feels impossibly perfect, like something youngsters might want to photograph, or put on the 'net'. Remember you, me, Bob and Prem had a few mulled wines outside the pub there years ago. I miss that. I miss you.

The garden is hibernating now, as it should. There's not much to see, but it's the anticipation I enjoy so much. I can't wait to see those irises and tulips in just a few weeks!

Thinking of you this Christmas.

Love always,

Your friend,

Maya x

Chapter 16

Winston

December 2018

WINSTON WOKE EARLY. SIX o'clock and he was sitting up in bed. Today, Lewis was moving out. He was going to his mum's for Christmas. After which, he'd be in his new house in Oxford. He was due to complete before New Year. Winston was sure his iPhone knew, because it had created a bunch of video reels from his photos entitled '2015 with Lewis', '2016 with Lewis' – jolly, joyful photographs of them huddled together, unflattering photos of Lewis trying to eat a forkful of food in a fancy restaurant, evenings at the pub playing cards. But his phone had chosen a soundtrack that was mournful, slow, fragile, as though echoing the precise sound Winston's gut had been playing on a loop for weeks. Every so often, there'd come a cacophony of rage. But for the most part, his rage had gone. He was left simply with sadness.

Smartphones were creepy.

Downstairs, he could hear Lewis packing up the last of his things. There were metallic clatters from the kitchen, pans stacked roughly on top of each other. Winston had promised to help, but his heart was racing too fast right now. Seeing Lewis might actually snap it audibly in two.

He scrolled away from the photos and searched Google for: *What can you plant in December?* Desperate for distraction.

Flowers to plant in winter

What to do in the garden in winter

He needed to occupy his mind.

Almost every page began with: *Midwinter is a quiet time in the garden*

There's not a lot going on in December

Spend winter protecting your plans, pruning your trees and feeding the birds

It wasn't what he'd been looking for. He was hoping to see something like *This is your opportunity to dig huge great trenches, you know how much you love that, slamming your shovel into the ground to work out all your frustration and sadness because your partner has bought a house without telling you and it's over! Five years . . . all done. And now you have to help him pack.*

But sadly, no such luck.

His finger hovered over Ruth's name in his call log – seven missed calls over the last few weeks.

He wanted to tell her. To talk to her about everything. But with everything happening with Lewis, with him, it had been easier to sit and tell Bernice bits and pieces over a margarita, freezing his fingers off in the garden. Because Bernice didn't know him, she didn't have hopes or dreams for him. Talking to Ruth only ever made him realize how far away his life was from the one his family had imagined for him.

They pictured the big boss job in finance, big garden, huge house, the car, a spouse who'd be with him no matter what. Ruth had never met Lewis in real life, but she'd been in touch with him for years, and as far as she was aware they were both city bankers, working their way to the life his family had always dreamed of.

He'd always told his mum he was still at the bank, even after he'd started working in the shop. He couldn't ever bring himself to let her down with the truth. Break her heart. She'd encouraged him to move to London, to pursue his dreams. *That's where you'll be happy*, she'd told him. Only now, he wasn't, was he?

He'd been running from Ruth because he was too ashamed to tell her how sad he was feeling. It was in this moment he realized just how unhappy he was.

'I want you to come with me,' Lewis had said, the night of the margaritas. Winston could do nothing but shake his head, his insides churning.

'I think you need to go,' Winston replied. 'Move out, live this life you've built for yourself—'

'For us,' Lewis cut in.

'No, Lewis, if it was for us, you'd have spoken to me about it. You go, I'll need to tell Mr James that I'm staying on.'

'Will you at least come to see it?' Lewis's knees were curled up to his chest on a kitchen chair. Winston was perched against the counter, his back straight, eyes staring out of the window.

'I don't think that's a good idea,' he'd said, and they hadn't spoken about it again.

He'd managed to call Mr James to let him know that he'd be staying: 'But I think,' Winston's voice cracked, 'you might need to rent out the other bedrooms as I can't pay rent on the whole place.' Mr James was gentle about it, kind, as though he could read between the lines of Winston's request. Like he knew he was eating peanut butter from the jar, watching his fiftieth episode of *Friends* in a row, stuck in his room to avoid running into Lewis, who'd been sleeping in the spare room.

'Winston,' Mr James called loudly down the phone when he'd rung back later, 'don't rush on finding flatmates. Pay me your share of the rent for one bedroom if you can, and we'll take it from there. I'll line up some viewings, but you take your time for now.'

Winston couldn't quite believe it. Mr James was nice but he wasn't a fool. He knew that this house could earn him a good monthly rate, and he'd been a landlord for literally decades, he wasn't new to the game. Winston would barely cover half of that on his own. He wished he could call up his mum, ask her if he was somehow being ripped off, if there was going to be a nasty scare further down the line. But he pictured her in her hammock in the garden, reading a Jane Austen novel, as she so loved to do, and he thought she'd probably tell him to take him on his word, for now. That seemed like the least stressful thing to do.

'Loads of people have flatmates,' Bernice had said too on that fateful day in the garden, when practicality seemed to be the only thing Winston could focus on.

He'd glared at her. That meant she'd never had to do it herself, but had read *Guardian* articles about the housing crisis that young people were going through. A story in a paper. Never her reality.

A smash of crockery brought Winston back to the moment, and he threw himself down the stairs to see what was going on.

Lewis was on the kitchen floor, surrounded by a moat of half-filled boxes. He'd packed up cookbooks he'd barely used in the last few years, and almost every pot and pan they had. It was all Lewis's. All here before Winston arrived. The shelves that had once been full were now empty. He could see the splodges of mismatched paint covering imperfections in the wall previously hidden behind the stacks and stacks of mugs.

Lewis's eyes remained on the floor, where the source of the noise revealed itself. The tagine Lewis had brought back from Morocco on his gap year and had sat unused at the top of the kitchen cupboards was sitting in pieces on the tiled floor. In the first few months they'd started dating, Winston had suggested they cook something in there. Make use of it. They never had. And now, they never would.

'I . . .' Lewis looked down at the pot, despondent. Winston sprang into action, and began to wrap the beautifully decorated terracotta shards into some kitchen towel. Lewis watched on. 'Thank you. I'm sorry,' he said, eventually. The words hung there between them. Then he nodded towards the empty shelves. 'Most of the things are gifts from my mum . . . she'd be annoyed if I left them.'

'It's fine.'

'What's this?' Lewis asked.

Winston followed his gaze. Sitting on the corner of the kitchen table was the anniversary present, still wrapped. It had gradually been pushed further and further away, tucked behind pot plants and the random tins Winston had brought home from the shop that didn't quite fit in the kitchen cupboards. Dolmades, chickpeas, tomato soup.

'I'd forgotten about that . . . it was, it was for our anniversary. I don't think you saw it.'

Lewis turned it over to unwrap it. 'No,' Winston called. 'Don't. Take it with you. Open it for Christmas. I don't think I can bear to see you open it in front of me.'

Lewis nodded, and he tucked it carefully into a box.

'Now,' Winston cleared his throat. 'Where's all this stuff going to go? You won't get to move in for a couple of weeks. You can leave it here if you need?'

'My mum's got space in a spare room for it all – easier that way. Saves the back and forth,' he muttered.

Winston nodded. 'Yeah . . . makes sense.' He tried to hide the fact his heart was sinking. Lewis had no reason to come back. Taking a deep breath, he summoned the energy to ask: 'So, have you packed up all your clothes and things?'

Lewis shook his head. Winston laughed. 'I knew it – come on then. We can use some of your T-shirts to wrap the crockery.' He felt himself move into 'practical' mode. Lewis was useless at packing, always had been. It was usually down to Winston to sort things out for him.

In the room that now belonged only to Winston, Lewis tipped all of his clothes out of his drawers onto the floor, and brought up his suitcase and a few spare boxes. In silence, they worked together, choosing items from the pile and folding. Lewis kept looking up at Winston, to check what order he was doing things in, imitating him. Winston smiled.

'Look, hand any T-shirts to me, you do trousers and pants . . .' Winston said, and Lewis nodded. Grateful, it seemed, for the sense of order. And for a moment, it felt normal as they busied themselves with the task at hand. Working together as a team.

When Lewis's man-in-a-van arrived, they grabbed the boxes and carried them to the vehicle. Then they stood side by side, watching as the house that had been their home suddenly looked as dormant as the garden. Bare, empty, barely a trace of the love and care that had gone into it.

'Right, mate,' the man said. 'That's all sorted. Ready to go when you are.'

Lewis nodded. 'Give me a minute.'

But Winston had to turn away. He couldn't do it. He strode upstairs, unable to say goodbye, and watched as Lewis climbed into the passenger seat, his coat slung over his shoulder, his rucksack for the journey in his right hand. He looked up at the house, searching for Winston's face in the window. Even from this distance, he could see Lewis was crying. His eyes red.

This was it.

Winston clutched his hands together, holding on tight in order to keep his heart beating.

As soon as Lewis had gone, the van turning the corner at the end of the road, Winston closed the curtains and collapsed onto the bed, lying there for hours without moving an inch.

His mother had always told him change was a good thing. Change was welcome. But this wasn't the change he wanted, was it?

Chapter 17

Winston

December 2018

That afternoon, Winston forced himself out into the garden. In the freezing cold. But it was a relief to be out of a house that rattled with space, with the ghosts of the past and a future with Lewis that he'd never have.

The garden would be his new number one distraction, he decided; he pulled up his Google searches again.

Protect your plants – that was no use. He currently had nothing established, apart from an ancient climbing plant (a clematis, apparently) that he'd attempted to rescue behind loads of bindweed, and a few rose bushes that he was too scared to touch. They looked like they'd been there for decades, and he'd only kill them if he tried to do anything.

Prune your trees – the only trees in the garden were the massive eucalyptus that was probably far beyond pruning, and the corkscrew hazel that he had no clue about.

Feed the birds – now . . . this was one he could do.

A memory rose up of his mother holding bird feed in her hands, a parakeet flying towards her. When he heard the parakeets in London, their squawks early in the morning, the golden flash of lime green as they zoomed past in the sunshine . . . it always reminded him of her. For a moment, he imagined himself wandering through the banana plants she loved so much, creating a walkway towards the secluded section at the back of her garden, where fig trees and lemon trees and bold, green, brilliant plants shrouded you, kept you hidden, kept you safe. The smell of flowers, of pollen, mixed with the humidity. It was like losing yourself in the middle of a rainforest, never to be found again.

'Inside that house, I have to be your mother, your sister's mother, your father's wife,' she'd say. 'But out here, I can be me. Manjula.'

Winston pictured her wearing a huge smile and her pink salwar kameez. Two parakeets, perched on her hand, would peck away at the fruit held aloft, her expression one of glee, trying to suppress her laughter so as not to scare them away, tortured by the tickle of their beaks.

He laughed at the memory, and the thought of her joy at seeing the birds in the garden. It was the first time that day he felt his heart lift.

'Well,' he said to himself. 'Let's see.'

An hour later Winston was in Sal's shop. His boss's expression was instantly one of worry, his eyebrows curled in concern. He knew today was the day Lewis moved out. But when Winston smiled, he said: 'My son, you've got to stop coming here on your day off. I'll have to give you more shifts if you can't think of more interesting places to be!' Sal beamed back, but his eyes lingered on him longer than usual, before turning to serve George at the counter.

'You can use sunflower seeds for the birds. Very good,' Sal continued, when there was a free moment. 'We use them in the allotment. They love them!'

Winston nodded.

'We give Angela's parents a whole stash every Christmas. They have a bird feeder that sticks onto the window so they can watch from the living room.'

Winston turned the packet over in his hands, wondering if there was a catch, if Sal was trying to get rid of his old stock.

'There are some empty yoghurt pots in the kitchen upstairs,' Sal said. 'Pierce holes, put twine in, hang it up on a branch, poke holes throughout and you've got a bird feeder! Done!'

Winston tried to picture it in his mind. Would Bernice tolerate having some holey Sütdiyari- or Pakeeza-branded yoghurt pots hanging up around the garden? He thought not . . .

But, at home, it was clear there was nothing particularly 'aesthetic' he could make the feeders from, and he didn't want to waste the feed now. So he grabbed the empty one-litre-sized Pakeeza yoghurt pots from what was left in the Tupperware drawer, and he started to stab holes into them with a pen, being careful to smooth off the edges with a tiny nail file he'd got in a Christmas cracker years ago and had never used.

'For God's sake,' Winston muttered. 'Why is Sal *always* right?'

A moment later, there came a knock at his kitchen door. Winston glanced outside, discovering that the day had vanished. Twilight was firmly setting in, making way for night to take over. It was only four o'clock, though today felt like it could have lasted a week already.

As Winston's eyes adjusted to the dark, he saw a little face in the glass, illuminated by the kitchen lights. It was Sebastian, dressed in his Sunday best, ready for his dad to collect him, no doubt.

'Hello!' Winston said, opening the door, sounding chirpier than he felt. Without being invited to do so, Seb stepped straight inside. Winston suddenly felt awkward, thrown into the role of host, when all he wanted to do was dig himself a hole in the garden and jump into it, never to be seen again.

'Do you . . . want something to drink?' Winston asked, when Seb didn't say anything. What sort of thing were you meant to offer a kid? Seb remained silent and started snooping around.

Winston glanced up to the mug shelf. Lewis had left behind two chipped Sainsbury's mugs. Beside it was a mug with his name hand-painted in calligraphy. A present from Ruth, flown all the way here from Canada for his twenty-ninth birthday a few years ago. 'I'll give you your proper present when I see you, little brother!' the gift card had said. He hadn't seen her since.

'How come you only have three mugs?' Seb asked bluntly. This boy had got particularly brazen in recent weeks. He grimaced at the state of Winston's cupboards. 'In fact, where is all your stuff? How do you cook?'

Winston felt a punch to the gut, picturing the van full of Lewis's things driving off that morning. Lewis's face, looking up at him through the window.

'All my mugs and stuff were Lewis's,' Winston shrugged. 'He used to buy them all the time, from trips away, or Oliver Bonas if he wanted something a bit trendy. John Lewis sometimes too.'

'Erm . . . okay . . .' Seb said, confused, unsure if this answered the question at all. 'Well . . . anyway. Mum told me to come over. She said to check on how you were. She said today was a sad day for you, maybe. Is it because of all your stuff? It's gone?'

Bernice was now *checking up* on him? He really *must* be pathetic if that was the case. He'd spotted Bernice through her window watching *Dickinson's Real Deal* at two in the afternoon every day he'd been home this week; at first he thought she must be ill, but she'd seemed completely fine and said she was 'working from home' when he asked. Now he wondered if she'd been 'working from home' to keep an eye on him. She'd been out in the garden a bit too, wandering around, nodding at him if she caught his eye.

'No, I'm fine,' Winston said boldly.

Seb shrugged, satisfied with this answer. 'Did you know,' he continued excitedly, 'Mum is *planting* things.' His face lit up like the sun. 'I saw some packs of seeds on the counter. *Sweet peas* it said. Dark red and bright red ones too. She said to me she wants to start helping you out, to make this garden nice for us all.'

'Well,' Winston raised his eyebrows.

Sebastian nodded enthusiastically, and it seemed as though he was standing taller with every word he uttered. 'Mum always collects toilet tube rolls, because they're useful for school costumes and things,' he said, looking at Winston as if to say, 'you know how it is'. 'Now she's using them for planting! Like little pots for the seeds! And there's soil all over the kitchen table!'

Now *this* Winston couldn't believe. Bernice liked things spotless. That was his impression anyway.

'She's asked me to help look after a few.' He held up his hand to show off the soil under his fingernails, which had become a permanent fixture of his appearance recently. It was something Seb and Winston shared – their grimy fingernails a mark of their blossoming friendship. 'What you do,' Seb said, barely taking a breath, 'is you fill each tube with soil, and place one sweet pea seed in the centre about half an inch deep. That's like this much,' he pointed to a spot over halfway down his finger. 'Then we watered them and they're going to live on the kitchen table underneath our skylight until we can plant them out. What do you think? Good, isn't it? Mum's planting – like us! I think she felt left out.'

Winston's heart contracted at Sebastian's last words. 'That's great! You convinced her!' He held his hand up to be high-fived by the little boy. But, satisfied, Sebastian trotted out, leaving the door wide open behind him. The freezing cold December air flooded in, putting Winston's hairs on end.

'Mum!' Winston heard Sebastian squeal from next door. 'Look, we've got things growing on the kitchen table!'

'I know,' Bernice laughed. 'Let's hope they come to something. And did you do what I asked you to do?'

'Winston's good at looking after plants, isn't he?' Seb blundered on loudly, still so excited. Winston couldn't help but smile.

'Sebastian, did you see how he was?'

'Yes, Mum! He's *totally* fine,' Seb said confidently, before adding, 'I think' a little more cautiously. 'But he doesn't have all his stuff now, and maybe he was a bit sad. Yes, maybe.'

'Okay, thank you for checking for me. We need to keep an eye on him, okay? Make sure he feels that we can be there for him. Let's do our best to cheer him up. Okay?'

'Yes, Mum.'

Winston grinned to himself, and felt his temples start to thud with pain, trying to keep his feelings locked up inside. There'd been too many emotions for one day already.

'Now, have you finished all your homework, or do you need to take some with you to your dad's?'

Winston closed the kitchen door, pushing against a gust of wind, shutting out the sounds of the eucalyptus leaves rustling, the shouts from the neighbourhood, and the conversation next door. As he looked at the empty house around him, which felt cavernous now, he didn't feel alone. Because through the walls, he could hear Bernice and Seb's laughter. And he knew, if he needed them, they weren't too far away.

Chapter 18

Bernice

December 2018

'THAT'S A LOT OF veg – stockpiling for Christmas?'

Bernice looked up from her phone to see Sal behind the shop counter. That was his name, wasn't it? She hadn't seen him since the night of the Diwali party. Remembering Simon's behaviour that evening, and the impression her family must have left on Sal, she cringed. She stood up straight and replied: 'Something like that.'

'Are you doing the cooking?' Sal asked, friendly.

Bernice wasn't going to get away with one-line answers. 'Yes, I'm in charge of the cooking,' she nodded, pulling a grimace.

Sal laughed, deep and warm. 'Having family round?'

'We're going to my sister's house. In Somerset . . . and for some reason, I have to supply the food,' Bernice rolled her eyes.

'Families, eh?'

'Families,' she replied, smiling for the first time. 'Yeah, it's the first Christmas Seb is going to have without his dad, so I'm hoping to make everything extra special to make up for it.'

Sal looked at her then, not quite sure how to respond. 'Oh,' he said simply, though still kind, and he rang up the rest of her shopping.

Last year, Bernice and Simon had tried their best to keep Christmas as jolly as possible for Seb's benefit, despite the fact the divorce was nearly finalized. They tried to recreate the Christmases they'd loved in the past, the happier times. But, as expected, Bernice and Simon had spent the whole day bickering, barely able to be in the same room as one another. Sitting on the sofa, a glass of sherry in hand at the end of a tiresome day, Bernice had looked at her husband, to see the look of exhaustion on his face too, and said, 'Simon, next year, I think we should do it separately. One week Seb can be with me, the next with you.' Simon had looked at her fondly then and agreed. 'Yes, we'll make it work,' he said softly, more to himself than to her. It had been the only thing they'd agreed on all day.

'Do you have any nice plans?' Bernice asked Sal now as he continued to pack her endless piles of vegetables into blue plastic bags.

Sal looked up and grinned: 'Me and my wife will have a quiet one. I invited Winston,' he said. 'But you know . . . young ones, they always have plans. He says he might be busy. Do you know what he's doing?'

Bernice shook her head. 'I'm afraid I don't really know him that well,' she replied truthfully, though she'd been checking in on him almost every day, saying hi if she saw him in the garden. She'd not been able to stop thinking about Winston rattling around the house with nothing but the shop for company, and she felt herself softening towards him. She hadn't yet completely forgiven him for cutting her out of her own garden, but getting involved was the only way to deal with it. As her grandmother used to say, 'If you can't beat them, join them.' Nevertheless, Winston remained something of a mystery to her. She couldn't understand why he'd turn down the offer to spend the day with Sal and his wife. *Did* he have other plans? Did he want to spend the day alone? Christmas was about company and eating too much food.

While out gardening the other day, she'd noticed his phone flash up with several missed calls from someone called Ruth. Perhaps there were more people in his life than she'd first anticipated?

'Well,' Bernice said, picking up her bags of shopping. 'I hope you have a lovely day! Merry Christmas!'

'You too, dear,' Sal waved back. 'Jenny,' he called over her shoulder, as an older woman in a fluffy leopard print coat made her way in, pushing her Zimmer frame. Despite nearly running Bernice over, the woman didn't look at her once, her eyes firmly fixed on Sal.

'All right, chubby cheeks?' she croaked back affectionately. 'How's it going?'

Bernice watched for a moment, taking in the ease and familiarity between them as Jenny threw her head back in laughter, and Sal chuckled to himself at a joke she'd shared. Bernice had been so stiff standing there; despite Sal's kindness, his ability to chat, she'd felt out of place, awkward, her answers forced. This community – Winston's community – it was a world she wasn't part of.

The pictures in the envelope posted through her door a few weeks ago came back to her mind. The friendship she'd seen in those photographs turned the black-and-white images to colour. Would she find that here too?

When she returned home, Seb was waiting in his friend's mum's car on the drive – he'd spent the day at his new schoolfriend Alfie's. As soon as she unlocked the front door he ran straight through to the garden as Bernice unpacked the shopping.

When she wandered out into the bitterly cold garden, frost was still clinging to the leaves from the morning, and there was a sprinkling of ice on the grass. And there was Seb with Winston, already pouring seeds into old, empty yoghurt pots with holes in.

'We're feeding the birds, before things start freezing over,' Winston said, sensing her confusion. Bernice smiled, nodding.

'The cold is very bad for them if they haven't been fed!' Seb said, as though echoing a fact he'd learned. In one hand, he was holding a bowl of seeds, and with the other, he was rolling a fat ball between his jeans and the palm of his hand, leaving an oily residue on his trousers. The garden table was covered in dried mealworms. Bernice took a couple of steps back in disgust.

'They're dead, right?' she said, averting her gaze.

'Yes, Mum!' Seb laughed, exchanging a 'duh' glance with Winston. 'Imagine having a load of wriggly worms in these feeders! Writhing above your head as you walked around the garden! Gross!' Seb said, with the biggest look of glee, as though he couldn't imagine anything more disgustingly delightful.

Were those ugly yoghurt pots going to be hanging up? Bernice pictured her grandparents' garden – the sunlight glinting off the little pond, the elegant bird feeders hanging *neatly* from a tree, so her grandfather could watch from his office. The magical, wonderland of a place!

A few minutes later, Winston and Seb moved on from the mealworms and the fat balls. The feeders were hanging up, but Seb looked so happy about it, she couldn't bring herself to complain about how ugly they were.

'Anything I can help with?' Bernice asked.

'We've got a gardening list!' Seb said, and Winston nodded. For a few moments, Seb read the list out loud, barking instructions, before running inside for a 'TV break' and letting them get on with it.

'Oh bloody hell,' Bernice said. 'He's worn himself out bossing us about, hasn't he? This *is* hard work!'

Winston was in the process of mulching the beds to keep some recent additions warm over winter. He seemed to have a clear vision of what he wanted the garden to be like. Bernice would admire it, if it weren't for the fact he'd been making these decisions about *her* garden without her. But it was bringing Seb out of his shell, she reminded herself. This garden, this work, was as much a joy to him as it was to Winston.

'I think,' Bernice said, a moment later, 'we need to clear these pathways, so we can get through to the shed properly.' She was eager to take the opportunity to put her own opinion across. 'You know, my friend Clemmie is a garden designer. I can ask her about using some old slabs or gravel if she has any going.'

Winston nodded, not looking at her; she wasn't sure if it was an acknowledgement or not.

'And maybe we should grow something quite tall by that wall, so we have privacy, blocking off that gate,' she said, and Winston glared at her immediately.

'No,' he said. 'The gate stays. It's important. And there's an old clematis across that wall anyway – we just need to take care of it and it might actually come to something.'

'Okay . . . but why the gate?'

'Erm . . . It'd be useful if we want to carry manure or compost through, so we don't have to bring it through the house. And if people want to come in, if we want people in the garden, they could use the gate,' he said at top speed.

'But if we have people round, they'd come through our houses. They don't need to access the garden directly. I take your point about the manure, though,' she shrugged, and moved quickly onto sweeping the patio, pulling out any ugly weeds sprouting between the rickety paving slabs. She made a mental note to plant some thyme seeds in the gaps, so they could grow herbs and make something beautiful out of the cracks. It was something she'd seen on *Gardeners' World*.

As she focused on the smaller tasks, Bernice felt a sense of peace crawl over her. Looking around every so often to see Winston, thoroughly focused, was comforting; the two of them working in contented silence. The constant worries that were usually knotted together – worries about Seb, about Simon, how she could make sure he listened to her, worries about work, the stress of managing it all – they all seemed to crystallize. Solutions felt closer, if not fully formed. It was no longer a mass of tangled panic in her mind. She felt more in control, calmer.

'So,' Bernice said, when they both stood up for a breather. 'How come you started the gardening?'

Winston took a deep breath, stopped for a moment then said, 'My mum . . . she's got an amazing garden. It's . . . I just wanted this to be as nice. Feels important right now.'

'Do you see her much?'

'No, well . . .' Winston started to open the gardening notebook. 'My family are all in India. But . . . my mum, she passed away a couple of years ago. I haven't been back since.'

Bernice looked at the ground. Her heart dropped. 'I'm . . . I'm sorry to hear that.'

'It's okay,' Winston smiled, as a neighbourhood cat wormed its way in, perched on a tree stump, and started licking its paws regally. 'I can't afford to go back much,' Winston continued, eyes on the cat, pre-empting Bernice's next question, but she sensed it wasn't the whole answer. 'Not much point going back for only a few days and . . .' He sighed. 'I guess . . . I realized I missed her. I missed her space. Her garden was amazing – full of greenery, a little sanctuary. I reckon, since she passed away, my dad has probably left the garden to its own devices. I . . . I can't fix that garden for her, but I can fix this one.' He nodded, as though explaining the reasoning to himself.

Bernice went quiet.

'She used to have loads of banana trees. I've sort of been thinking of having one here too. I love the way they look. So many front gardens round here have them – London has the right climate.'

'I . . .' Bernice didn't know what to say. 'I'm not so sure . . . Maybe let's just put some nice, palmy things around the edges. In pots, maybe?' she said, as though striking a compromise. 'Give it that exotic feel . . . I'm sure your mum would be proud of that.'

Winston put the spade down, throwing a final handful of manure on the bed, and she caught him rolling his eyes. Finally, he said, 'Right, I'll get on with the gate then. Need to get some more manure this week and I'm not having it coming through the house. We're expecting some more prospective tenants round soon, so it's got to be neat. Can you chuck me those loppers?'

'I'll help you,' she said softly, realizing she'd been too quick to respond to his banana tree suggestion, and the walls that he'd been gradually bringing down brick by brick had suddenly shot back up.

The two began work in silence, hacking away at the Virginia creeper over the gate, throwing all their energy into it. When it became clear the loppers were too rusty to be much use, they pulled at it with their gloved hands. Eventually, when it got too hot, they discarded their gloves, yanking the vines away from the gate. Within half an hour, they could see what had once been a handle, peppered with the creeper's sticky little feet.

'It's rusted away,' Bernice groaned, wiping sweat from her forehead. 'What are we going to do with that?'

'It's all right,' he said immediately, as Bernice slouched onto Winston's wooden chair with such force she worried it might be the end of it. 'We can get a new one – Sal recently got a new back gate, we could probably take the handle off his old one.'

An hour went by, and Bernice busied herself around the rest of the garden – tidying up bits here and there, picking up weeds that probably weren't weeds at all ('Is this a weed?' she'd asked Winston. 'It depends on whether you like it or not,' he replied, pretending to be Monty Don or Alan Titchmarsh.)

Winston continued oiling the hinges, crowbarring the lock off the back of the gate. It practically crumbled away in his hands – and suddenly, the gate was open.

'Wow,' they both said, as it creaked on its rusty hinges towards them, revealing Grandville Road to them. A couple of passers-by on the other side of the street looked at them in surprise, a little sausage dog waddled along beside them, its tiny legs moving as fast as possible to keep up.

'Wow,' Winston repeated, out of breath from the crowbarring.

'Well done.' Bernice tapped him awkwardly on the shoulder. The bricks of the houses opposite glowed a pinky-red, their windows reflecting the pastel clouds back at them. She turned to look at the garden.

It looked better, but it was still a mess. Piles and piles of ivy and Virginia creeper dominated the view, and the handful of weeds Bernice had been picking up over the past hour hardly made a difference. The garden was still a mishmash of brambles, and big brown patches of dirt.

She tried not to feel disappointed, her grandparents' haven of a garden felt miles away right now. 'We can't expect it to be perfect right away,' Bernice said more to herself than to Winston.

'You sound like my mother,' he laughed.

'Mum! Winston!' Seb came to the kitchen door, his break clearly over. 'Have any parakeets been yet?'

Winston looked to the hanging yoghurt pots and shook his head. 'Not yet, buddy!'

'What did your mum used to put out for the parakeets, Winston?' Seb asked, his face dropping.

'Well,' he wiped his hands on his jacket. 'She had a whole bird-feeding table – because parakeets eat a huge amount. She'd put out lots of fresh fruit, oranges, apples, bananas.'

'Wow! Do you have photos of them on the table?'

Winston paused for a moment, pulled his phone out.

'You know, I've got some printed pictures in the house – hold on a minute.' He made strides towards the house.

'Winston, I'm sorry,' Bernice called. 'I think Seb and I need to start packing. We've got an early start tomorrow and I've got to cook loads tonight in preparation.'

'All right. Just one moment? Come in, I'll be a second,' Winston said, beckoning them both towards his kitchen door, and leaving it open for them to follow him in.

Bernice wanted to say no, but Seb looked so jubilant. If she dragged him away now, she'd not hear the end of it all the way to Somerset.

Inside, the house was dark and curiously cold. The kitchen was clean, empty. The open cupboards had only one or two plates, a handful of mugs, but the fridge door was covered in shopping lists and a chore checklist. Seb skipped his way through, following Winston.

'Seb, be polite – Winston hasn't said if we can go through,' she call-whispered.

'He says it's fine! If we don't mind the mess,' Seb called back.

Bernice admired the faded Persian rug lining the hallway, and as she reached the living room she braced herself for the smell of cigarette smoke, or beer. But it was well-decorated, and smelled like an artificial air freshener, which wasn't pleasant, but was at least better than the stale smoke fragrance she'd expected. She looked around for the 'mess' Winston was talking about, and she could see nothing but small, imperceptible signs of life – signs of Winston's life, at least. It seemed that almost any trace of Lewis was gone, though she didn't really have a clue what a sign of Lewis could be.

The floorboards were bare but polished to a dark sheen, and the furniture was a blue velvet, woven throws over the sofa. The bookshelves either side of the fireplace showcased a few books, but it was noticeably sparse – sprinkled with a few CDs, photo frames, and a selection of glass vases in various shapes and sizes. And, on a shelf about halfway up the chimney breast, there was a grainy portrait of a woman, a black-and-white passport photograph, enlarged to twenty times its size. A garland hanging from the top corners, framing the woman's face.

His mother. Winston's mother.

Winston was rustling in the cupboards underneath the shelves, shuffling through piles of post and papers.

'Is that your mum?' Seb asked, his eyes on the photograph too.

'Yes, Mummyji,' Winston nodded, still rifling.

'You look so much like her,' Bernice commented, unable to look away. The smile in the woman's eyes kept her transfixed.

'I think that's the nicest thing you've said to me.' Winston turned round and grinned. 'She was beautiful. She was the best.' Winston glanced at the photo of his mum, a small shoebox in his hands. He paused for a moment.

'Here,' he said, placing the box on the coffee table, switching on a large anglepoise lamp. She noticed the walls were bare too, photo frames sat on shelves, or rested on cabinets, leaning against the wall. Nothing here was permanent – it could all be plucked away, rewritten in an instant.

Seb was poking through the photographs with clumsy fingers. 'Careful, Seb,' Bernice scolded, 'only touch the edges.'

'Don't worry,' Winston shook his head.

Seb whispered 'okay' and did as he was told, like he was looking at important artefacts in a museum.

Underneath the photographs, Bernice caught a glimpse of a letter, written in a script she couldn't understand. The handwriting was neat, perfect.

'Wow,' Seb said, 'look at this parakeet!'

The photograph was almost sepia in tone, with a bright flash of green.

'My mum's favourite bird – some people think of them as pests, like pigeons. But I think they're magnificent.'

'And is this your mum's garden?' Seb turned to the next photograph full of vibrant flowers, red-hot pokers, a stunning backdrop of large banana trees. Bernice gulped down her guilt.

In the foreground was a man, shoes off, wearing a pale linen suit, reclining in a deckchair. 'My dad,' Winston pointed out. 'He loves to relax – he owns a string of health spas, so he makes it his business to chill out. Enjoying his third virgin martini of the day by the bananas.'

Bernice and Seb laughed. Winston looked away.

'It's so lovely,' Seb said, in awe. 'Mum, let's make our garden look like this?'

'We can try. Right young man, I'm going to start packing – have you done yours?'

'Where are you off to?' Winston asked then, but as Bernice was about to reply, she realized he was asking Seb, not her.

'To my Aunt Hannah's, in Somerset.' Seb rolled his head back on his neck and pulled a face.

'Eh, that's not very nice, Sebastian,' Bernice said, flicking him gently on the shoulder. 'Sorry, there was one of those *mealworms* on your shoulder,' she said, hiding a laugh as Seb wriggled away, shaking himself furiously.

'Really?' His face was one of pure terror, all glee and delight gone.

'No! I'm teaching you a lesson for being rude about your Auntie Hannah,' Bernice said, beaming.

'I didn't *say* anything,' Seb replied innocently.

'You know it's not about what you said,' she gave him the look that said *Don't push it, young man*.

Just then, Bernice spotted a photograph of two people in the shoebox. She couldn't get a proper look, but she was sure they were standing in front of a garden gate. The very same gate she and Winston had spent their afternoon unearthing from under the Virginia creeper. The picture was old – like something from the past. Her mind shot to the envelope that had fallen onto her doormat. *To The Lady at Number 77*. Could it be from the same person? *Was* it from Winston? Before she could get a proper look, Winston carefully prised the wad of photos from Seb's hand and tucked them back into the shoebox.

'Do you think the parakeets will come to our garden?' Seb said, hopeful. 'If we give them the right food?'

'Maybe, my friend. I have seen them all over the eucalyptus, watching over the city. So I think we just need to be patient.'

'I'll be patient!'

'It can be our New Year's goal,' Winston said.

'Deal.' Seb shook Winston's hand.

Bernice hadn't seen Seb – usually so shy and quiet – this comfortable and confident around other people in such a long time.

'Have a great Christmas, you guys,' Winston waved them out.

'Look after the birds!' Seb replied brightly.

'I will do, mate.' Winston ruffled Seb's hair affectionately.

* * *

'Okay, do you need a last-minute wee?' Bernice asked Seb the next morning, as he was buckling himself up in the car. He shook his head.

'Are you sure? This is your last chance. Have you been?'

'No,' Seb replied, face blooming red in embarrassment.

'Right, come on then.' Bernice threw herself out of the car and pulled open Seb's door.

Unlocking the front door, Seb ran straight upstairs to the loo, while Bernice trotted through to the kitchen to check she'd turned everything off. She opened the fridge once more. That's when she remembered it: the lasagne she'd prepared for Boxing Day. She'd left it sitting on the middle shelf, wrapped in foil. It was tradition in her family to have a Boxing Day vegetarian lasagne – her sister's favourite. She pulled it out of the fridge, placing it on her worktop. She heard Sal's words about Winston's lonely Christmas, she remembered the missed calls on Winston's phone, the emptiness of the shelves in his house, the photograph of his mum . . .

They could do without a lasagne for one year, couldn't they?

'Mum! I'm done.' Seb jumped from the last step to the hall floor.

'All right, sweetie. Go wait for me in the car. I'll be there in a second.'

As Seb ran out, she grabbed a Christmas card from the open box on the kitchen table, scribbling hurriedly, before popping the sealed envelope on top of the lasagne's tinfoil lid.

Outside, she locked the front door and wandered to Winston's front step, where she lay the lasagne and the Christmas card down, giving the doorbell a quick ring. She didn't want to embarrass him, so she trotted towards the car and slipped in. Buckling her seat belt, she saw Winston open the door, looking around to find no one there. Then his eyes settled on the tray.

For if you don't fancy cooking, she'd written in the card. *Don't spend Christmas alone if you can help it. Sending love, Bernice and Sebastian x*

When he closed the door, Bernice clicked her seat belt into place, a smile spreading across her face.

'Right, young man,' she looked at her passenger. 'You ready for Christmas to begin?'

'Yes!' he replied, and Bernice drove off, past the houses that were starting to feel more like home now, her mind still on her next-door neighbour.

Chapter 19

Maya

December 1980

'I'll look after her,' Alma said, 'you two have a lovely evening. Celebrate!'

It was Maya and Prem's wedding anniversary – just a few days before Christmas.

Prem looked at Maya closely. In the last few years, time had taken these small moments away from them – they were both on the go almost all the time between working and looking after an energetic Hiral. They were still hoping to save for a house of their own, eventually, though the reality seemed further and further away. And as time passed, they both admitted that they didn't really want to leave Eastbourne Road. They wanted to live their lives here, in this house, with this garden for ever. Hiral was five now, and Alma had finally retired, meaning she could help them out with babysitting when she had the energy to keep up. 'I'm convinced she gets her liveliness by sapping mine!' Alma joked.

'Do you think Hiral's going to bombard Alma with questions about Susie?' Maya asked.

Alma's beloved cat Susie had passed away a week ago. She'd been poorly for a while, and there seemed to be no clarity from the vets on what might be wrong. Then one morning, Maya watched as Alma trotted out to the garden for a non-festive cup of coffee, lingering under the eucalyptus tree as she always did. Maya had caught Alma staring at that tree so many times. She was protective over it. And that day, she'd discovered Susie asleep there, and began to stroke the cat, before realizing Susie wasn't breathing. Maya immediately saw the change in Alma's body language. Her arm suddenly going stiff, her hand hovering. Then Alma simply nodded. Her face dropped, but she gave nothing else away. She touched the bark of the eucalyptus tree, looking up through its leaves, before placing the same hand on her heart. To Alma, Susie would go on for ever. She'd always expected Susie to outlive her.

But neither of them had expected to lose her.

Now, Maya wasn't sure if they should leave Alma alone with Hiral in case their little girl sparked a fresh wave of sadness in Alma, forcing it all to come tumbling out while they were away.

'She won't find it upsetting,' Prem said softly. 'She'll understand. Hiral can do nothing wrong in Alma's eyes. She might enjoy the company, the distraction, of having to chase Hiral around all day.'

And so, they packed up an unseasonal picnic of sandwiches and a potato salad, and went for a wander around Stoke Newington. Heading up through Church Street, Maya could only remember the bitter cold of the last winter, and the binmen's strikes causing a build-up of bags of rubbish all around the town, littered outside tinned up or derelict houses, on the greens, on pavements, in street corners. Now that was all cleared, and it almost felt like a distant memory. As she ambled past some of the houses, still boarded up, she wondered if, one day, they might be repaired. She wondered which family might make it their home. And wandering past shops, the windows painted black, she couldn't help but imagine what might appear there in years to come.

'You sure you want a picnic in December?' Prem said, rubbing her hands in his to keep them warm.

'I like being outside. We'll sit on a bench, don't worry, I won't make you sit on the floor,' she teased, touching her cold hands to his warm cheeks, and he shuddered, clipping her nose playfully.

They settled down on a bench in Clissold Park, watching children running around kicking footballs, playing with their friends, their breath fogging up in front of them, the only evidence that they too might feel the icy cold.

'Did you know Bina's made a new tablecloth for Christmas Day?' Maya started, smiling at the story already.

'No?'

'She's sewn the protest banners we made together. Apparently it looks amazing!'

'Not the ones with Alma's swear words on, I hope?' Prem chuckled.

The strike had been called off two years after it began and the union remained unrecognized by Bina's employer. 'I feel as though I've wasted my time,' Bina had said, sobbing on the phone to Maya weeks later. 'It's like all the love and energy we put into it was for nothing.'

'Does everyone feel like that?' Maya had asked. 'Everyone on the strike?'

'No.'

'Exactly, because what you did – you should be proud of it.'

'But we lost, Maya,' she said. 'What does that say to me? About how much I and people like me deserve?'

'In some ways you lost,' Maya said. 'But in so many others you won. You showed people you should always stick up for yourself. You fought for something you believed in. And think of all the support you had, from around the country! You weren't just fighting for you – you were fighting for everyone, setting an example that you can demand what you deserve.' Prem had said the same thing to Maya. 'They won respect. They showed they wouldn't be taken advantage of.' Prem, with his large black glasses halfway down his nose, reading a book in bed, was wise. He was honest. He led with his heart. But even his words couldn't dim Maya's anger about the situation, anger that still burned now, years later.

'I'm glad she's proud of it,' Prem said to Maya then. 'To turn her history into a tablecloth . . . she better keep it forever!'

Maya nodded, reliving what Bina had gone through. 'I'm so glad she's proud of it too.' Maya pictured her sister on the picket line, weeks and weeks of shouting, standing up for her rights. She was working as an accounts assistant now, and she was happier, it was true. And at least she'd fought for her rights, her colleagues, her friends.

'Here,' Prem said, pulling something out of his pocket. 'For our anniversary.'

In the palm of his hand, he held out a small box, red velvet tied with a ribbon.

'Prem!' Maya said.

'Wait . . . before you tell me off about it, open it,' he said, hopeful.

Her cold fingers brushed the velvet, teasing the box open to see a gold heart-shaped locket. 'Prem,' she said, inhaling. She opened it up to see a photo of the four of them: Alma, Maya, Prem and Hiral. Scrunched together last Christmas Eve, gathered in the garden. Bina had insisted on taking the photo.

'Family,' he said, and that one word caused her lip to quiver. She nodded.

'It's so beautiful,' she said and reached for him, pulling his face to hers, warm lips and cold noses pressed together.

'I know things have been so busy recently,' he said, 'but whenever you wear this, remember family is always here with you. We're always doing things for each other.'

She grabbed his hand, squeezing it tight. She looked at Prem then. They'd been here for over eight years now. Nearly a decade.

She remembered Prem's face the moment they stepped off the plane; there was a light in his eyes. He was young. He'd been just twenty-nine then, she twenty-six, and now he was approaching his forties. She could see how exhausted he was all these years later, how hard he'd worked to build the life they had here. Dark circles under his eyes, eyes that still sparkled with hope. Prem never lost his hope. She squeezed his hand, tight, to tell him somehow how grateful she was for all of it. 'I know,' she said. 'I know.' Prem put the necklace on for her, and she felt the cold of the metal against her skin. It gave her a sense of hope too, reminding her of everything they'd created together.

'And,' Prem said, 'I didn't forget what was *actually* on your Christmas list. I thought I better give it to you here, rather than at Bina's . . . I'm sure she'd laugh at me.' He pulled out a present wrapped in robin wrapping paper.

Maya laughed, ripping the paper open straight away to reveal brand-new gardening gloves, her name embroidered rather clumsily on the front.

'Oh my goodness!' she exclaimed. 'These *are* something special,' she said, admiring the dodgy embroidery. 'Did Hiral do this at school?'

Prem shook his head, covering his eyes with his hand. 'No! I did,' he grimaced. 'I know . . . it's awful. I thought it might be easier than it was . . . Anyway. My cheesy line to go with this was . . . "This way I'm always there to give you a helping hand".'

'Oh Prem,' Maya laughed, unable to help herself, analysing the messy needlework. 'You're one of a kind.'

When they got back home, Alma and Hiral were in the garden, the lawn crunchy and sparkling with frost. Their little girl was skipping up and down the path, weaving in and out of the flower beds, hiding behind the yellow crispy stumps of asparagus, running away from Alma.

'Alma!' she called. 'Can you run?'

'Yes I can!' Alma grunted back, proceeding to walk rather slowly in pursuit.

Alma had put out a little picnic on the bench for them – shepherd's pie, Alma's winter favourite, and some green vegetables. 'Come on,' Alma said. 'Let's eat before your ma and pa get home. I told them I'd feed you!'

Prem and Maya held each other close in the warmth of the kitchen as they watched Hiral wriggle onto Alma's lap.

'You really want to sit out here, and on my lap, while we eat?'

'Yes! We can watch the birds like Daddy does.'

Hiral, who was wearing a bobble hat that Jenny had knitted for her, kept tickling Alma's chin with her multi-coloured pompom.

'That's why you wanted to sit there, you cheeky miss!' Alma laughed, trying to keep Hiral's bobble away from her.

'Not at all, Auntie Alma,' Hiral said sweetly. 'Can you pass me my cup?'

'Yes, chief.' Alma did as she was told.

She looked up at Alma then, horrified. 'Don't call me chief!'

'Yes boss.' Alma nodded curtly.

'Don't call me boss! Auntie Alma!'

'Yes, yes, sorry, Your Highness, but if you could stop moving for a moment, Hiral,' Alma said, 'at least while I'm eating. It's rather off-putting,' she repeated. Hiral continued to wiggle her head deliberately, at each mouthful, her face a picture of mischievous glee.

Prem chuckled. And watching Hiral, Maya couldn't help but return to the summer's day she was born, when she'd been snoozing in the sunshine while Alma and Prem replaced a few missing bricks from the wall, sweating buckets. The garden had been full of colour – hollyhocks and poppies floating in the wind, roses filling the garden with scent. Little did she know that because of Hiral, the garden would feel like that midsummer day for eternity whenever Maya stepped foot in it. So much so, she could barely tell when there was a nip of ice in the air.

'Alma! What are you doing at Christmas? Are you celebrating with us?' Hiral's voice was optimistic.

'Hiral, haven't your mum and dad told you how much I *hate* Christmas?'

In the darkness of their kitchen, Maya and Prem exchanged a knowing look. Alma took great pleasure in declaring this whenever Christmas songs started playing in Woolworths or Tesco's or, God forbid, Erol's. 'I don't celebrate Christmas, but I love the Christmas cheer,' Erol said, in his defence, when Alma complained about Christmas music in October. He'd often hang paper lanterns from the ceiling of the shop, dangling handmade paper angels from shelves, swapping the cardboard shelf talkers for snowflake-shaped ones instead. Like his father, as soon as November hit, Sal also bedecked himself in Christmas scarves, hats and novelty Father Christmas aprons.

'How different is it from any other time of the year?' was Alma's constant argument. 'Nothing more than a chance for them to make more money off us buying all this gumpf, like they don't make enough money as it is.' Maya never knew who the mysterious 'they' was.

'Auntie Alma,' Hiral said again, as Prem and Maya continued watching through the glass, misted up from their breath. 'Why *do* you hate Christmas so much?'

Alma shrugged. Neither Prem nor Maya knew the answer. Alma put it down to a hatred of capitalism or whatnot, but they'd both sensed there must be something more. Maya expected Alma to change the subject, but she poked Hiral's nose affectionately, and said, 'Well, when I was very little, about your age actually, and my father was out at work, I came downstairs, expecting to see my mother already chopping the vegetables for the Christmas lunch.' Alma was smiling. 'But instead it was just my auntie and my cousin there.' A tear reflected the amber light of the sunset. Her voice remained even. Prem and Maya didn't breathe at all as they stopped and watched. 'My mother had been poorly for a little while you see, and I'd known this day was coming, only I hadn't known what it really meant. She told me again and again that one day I wouldn't see her ever again, but I didn't know how on earth that could be. But that day did come. It was Christmas. I've hated Christmas Day ever since.'

'Did she die? Like Susie?'

Prem took a sharp inhale of breath at Hiral's innocent bluntness.

Alma nodded. 'She did. And you see that eucalyptus tree over there? Well . . . my mummy's ashes made that grow. There was a time when I lived away from the city for a little while, when the war was going on, and when I came back, the tree was still here. I couldn't believe it. It was my mum that had made it so strong. So, when I feel sad, I come out here and talk to that tree. It seems Susie used to come out and talk to it too. She was curled up here, you know? I think my mother was looking out for her as well, carrying her on her way. I'm not sentimental, but I'm sure she's looking after all of us.'

Maya remembered her very first week in Stoke Newington, all those years ago, when Alma had snapped at her for putting compost underneath the tree. Now, it all made sense.

Alma pulled Hiral in for a hug. Hiral's eyes were roving around, taking in the eucalyptus tree. Realizing the magic of it.

'Should we go out there yet?' Maya asked, and Prem shook his head, holding her hand. 'We'll leave them together for a little while. I think they're getting on just fine.'

Chapter 20

Maya

December 1985

DING DONG.

'Mum!' Hiral trotted in from her bedroom. At ten, she was more like a little lady than a child, dominating the house.

'Yes, beta,' Prem replied.

'Dad! You're not Mum,' Hiral chirruped back.

'Sorry, beta,' Maya pulled the quilt up to her chin, her breath visible.

'Who the f—' Hiral stopped herself. Her parents waited for her to replace the profanity she'd picked up from Alma. 'Who *on earth* is ringing the bell?'

Ding dong, the bell went again, right on cue.

'Not our bell, beti,' Prem croaked. 'It's Auntie Alma's.'

'Auntie Alma has *visitors*? On Christmas Eve?' Hiral and Maya replied in unison. Maya glanced at the brass carriage clock, ticking loudly on her bedside table – it had been a prize from a charity raffle Erol had run in his shop a year ago, and had replaced the garish green-glowing radium one they'd first bought. Alma had won it, but she'd hated it: 'Ugly bloody thing, like something my grandma might have,' she'd said, and dropped it into Maya's handbag so as not to cause Erol offence.

It was twenty to ten in the morning. Alma hated people ringing the doorbell before eleven. 'It's uncivilized,' she'd say. 'Before eleven, I'm in my dressing gown. And no one wants to see me with my bits hanging out.' Maya, in all the years she'd lived next to Alma, doubted Alma even owned a dressing gown.

Maya opened the front window, letting in a gush of winter air. Prem shuddered. 'Shut that window, Maya! Are you crazy?!' He buried his head under the quilt, book and all.

'Sorry!' She leaned over the window ledge. On the street, she could see multicoloured tinsel and Christmas trees in bay windows, coloured Christmas lights wearing flower-like plastic crowns, flashing reds, blues, greens, oranges and pinks in her neighbours' front windows, plastic statues of jolly-looking Father Christmases perched on doorsteps, and a sign hammered into a flower bed saying *Father Christmas, Stop Here!*

The sky was dull, overcast, the air crisp and cold, but the street, it carried its own warmth, its very own festive cheer.

Maya dropped her gaze to Alma's doorstep. Standing there were Ade and Yusuf, now full-grown men in their early twenties, their arms piled high with old ice-cream cartons in lieu of Tupperware, and flower-patterned Pyrex dishes covered with tinfoil.

'Boys!' Maya called down, and they looked up at her. 'How lovely to see you!'

'Hello, Auntie Maya.' They smiled and shrugged their shoulders instead of waving, their hands too full. 'Dropping some non-Christmas items round for you all . . . we thought we'd drop them with Alma, but . . . we're a bit early for her, aren't we?' Yusuf said, nodding towards the door, still firmly shut. 'It's before eleven . . .'

'Maybe a little . . .'

Alma's door finally creaked open wide. 'Merry Christmas Eve!' Ade and Yusuf's bright voices chorused, followed by Alma's telltale groan.

'What do you think you're doing?' Alma snapped, churlish as always in the face of affection. Maya, Prem and Hiral giggled.

'We wanted to thank you. And say Merry Christmas!' Yusuf said hurriedly. Even after all these years, and despite the fact he was almost twice her height now, he still sounded slightly frightened whenever Alma put on her gruff voice.

'Well, you can't come in, the house isn't ready for visitors. You know I don't do Christmas,' Alma said.

'No, no,' Yusuf said hurriedly. 'We know that. We thought we'd drop this off for you. Some mince pies Kelly made.' Kelly was Yusuf's girlfriend – they'd met at university and Maya, Prem and Alma had met her once or twice when she and Yusuf visited his mum Isha, but it was only ever a flying visit these days. 'And Ade's mum made egusi for you . . .' he continued.

'She said you all liked it last time!' Ade added. 'Are you having Christmas with Maya?'

'Sounds delicious. Thank your mum for me, Ade. And no, I'll be on my own. I don't *do* Christmas,' she repeated. 'And that lot make such a fuss of it.' She pointed up to Maya's house.

At that, Hiral called down playfully: 'Auntie Alma, don't be a killjoy!'

'Oh God, they're awake, are they? That blasted new Shakin' Stevens Christmas tune will start any second now,' Alma said with an eye-roll. 'It's been stuck in my head for the last month thanks to them. But thank you, boys.' The pile of ice-cream boxes was now in Alma's hands, the dish of egusi out of sight, carefully set down on her hall table. 'For whatever it's in aid of.'

'It's in aid of you,' Ade said. 'And the garden. For looking after it for all these years, for letting us be here when we needed it, and to say sorry that we're not around to help out quite as much.'

'Can't be avoided, you've got your own lives to live. That feels like thanks enough to me.'

'Well, enjoy it,' Ade nodded back, smiling. 'Or don't enjoy it, whatever you prefer at this time of year.'

Alma chuckled then, a deep, raucous laugh. 'Bloody hell, sorry, I'll wake the street up. This is really kind, thank you.'

'I might pop round tomorrow, with Kelly,' Yusuf called back as they headed off, closing Alma's front gate behind them. He addressed both Alma in her doorway, and Maya and Hiral at their front window. 'So we can introduce you to someone else, if you're free?'

'Okay, dear, but don't alter your plans for us. You know it's any other day for me,' Alma said, always the broken record.

'Come on,' Maya said, a few moments later. She shut the window behind her, and addressed the bundle of quilt that was Prem. 'Who's going to help me with some preparation? Lots to do.'

This year, Maya and Prem had hoped to take Hiral to Kenya to see Maya's mum and Prem's parents, but Maya's mum had insisted they keep saving their money for a house. 'Don't worry,' she'd said on the phone, businesslike as usual. 'There will be plenty of other times for us to see you and little Hiral, ne?'

So, while Maya had wanted nothing more than to sit in the front yard in Mombasa with her sister, her nephews and her mother, drinking chai from a saucer, chatting to the neighbours, she was wrapped in three jumpers to keep warm instead, preparing a full Gujarati meal for Christmas Day. Hiral had grown out of her love for her mother's Gujarati food quickly, and now preferred Turkish food, popping round to her Uncle Erol's for dinner when Sal was working on the shop floor. She had recently taken a shine to Sal, a handsome young man at twenty . . . always telling him about her favourite dishes in an attempt to impress him. Sal had no idea she was besotted, obviously seeing her as a little sister.

Maya had decided this Christmas she was going to remind Hiral what her favourite foods were: batata vada, grated paneer samosas, kachori made with fresh peas, mug badh kadhi, batata nu shaak, rotli, rus and shrikand too.

It meant, however, that there was lots to do, and her sous-chef Prem was a terrible cook with a strong tendency to burn things.

'Want to help?' Maya said again, as Hiral tucked herself into her mother's side of the bed, diving straight into a book.

'I'll help,' Prem said, sensing that Hiral was lost to them for now, and Maya gulped – picturing the kachori and samosas going up in flames. 'Chal.'

On Christmas Day, the kachori and samosas were all done, having survived Prem's arsonist tendencies. But now they were back in the kitchen to make the rest of the feast. 'I'll do anything you want me to, as long as I can wear this,' Prem said, holding up a brand-new novelty Father Christmas apron, still creased from the packet, though lewder than the ones she'd seen Erol and Sal wear. Father Christmas was showing a cheeky bit of chest hair.

'Prem! That's Saint Nicholas! A Saint!' Maya said, horrified, but Prem, whose face became Father Christmas's head, was grinning and she couldn't help but laugh at his joy.

'Chop this, just like this,' Maya began, wiping her tears of laughter away with the tip of her less offensive apron. 'Not too finely, not too chunky.'

'Got it,' he said, though he definitely hadn't.

A few minutes later, she chimed in with, 'Bas, now, stir this all the time. Don't let it boil. And bring the heat down before it gets too frothy, okay?'

Then, as she was about to show him how to sauté the hing, rai and jeera for her batata nu shaak, she saw two figures appear in the garden. It was Yusuf with Kelly, her smile so beautiful, her hair so magnificent Maya almost thought Whitney Houston had walked in. They were wandering around the garden – laughing and joking to themselves.

In Yusuf's arms was a baby, wrapped up warm, face poking out. Even from here Maya could tell he had the kindness of Yusuf's eyes. 'Prem!' she called. 'Yusuf! He's here. With his *baby*!'

'I used to plant stuff in here!' Yusuf exclaimed then.

'I don't believe you,' Kelly said, her voice light and lyrical, chuckling back.

'No, seriously! Ask Prem,' he said proudly. 'I used to sow the seeds for these. And I once planted the onions in that bed,' he continued, 'Mum used to use them to cook with.'

Then there was a knock on Alma's kitchen door and she threw the door open, rattling Maya's kitchen window in the process. 'What's going on now!'

But as she laid eyes on the pair, she sighed contentedly. 'Yusuf! And Kelly!' Even Alma couldn't keep her voice calm. 'And who is this?'

'This is Emmanuel,' Yusuf said. 'Emmanuel, meet Alma.'

Unable to contain her excitement, Maya popped her head out of her door, letting out the smells of frying spices. 'Yusuf, and Kelly, it's so lovely to see you again! Prem, keep an eye on that jeeru, okay? We'll swap in a second.'

'Auntie Maya,' Yusuf said back, and Kelly was grinning: 'Merry Christmas!'

'So,' Alma said, bringing her attention to the baby once more. 'Emmanuel. That's a very fancy name, isn't it?'

'It is, Kelly's choice . . . she's Catholic. Wouldn't let me choose anything with one syllable.'

'Oi,' Kelly nudged Yusuf in the ribs. 'You liked it.'

'Well, it's smart, very smart, if Isha likes it too! Suits you, little man,' Alma said to the baby, her face bright. 'How old is he?'

'A month old. He came a little bit early. We think he wanted to make sure he could see you!' Kelly said, locking eyes with Yusuf. Maya remembered Hiral at that age, everything she and Prem were going through. Sleepless nights, constant worry about whether they were doing the right things. But it was magical, it had felt like they were living in a dream at times too.

'Hello!' Prem popped his head out, and Maya's nostrils caught the scent of slightly burnt cumin seeds. She gritted her teeth, but said nothing. She watched as Prem took Emmanuel from Yusuf's arms, like a proud grandfather, briefly clapping Yusuf on the shoulder.

'Look at you,' Prem said, to both Yusuf and Kelly. And then, his eyes glazed over slightly, the emotion catching. 'You're a beautiful family,' he paused for a moment, taking a breath, pinching his lips together. 'What a beautiful boy. But I still think of this one as a teenager, you know!'

Yusuf and Prem laughed, and Maya wished she could pause this moment forever.

'Do you want to stay for a cup of tea?' Maya asked.

'Actually, I think we'd better be heading back.' Yusuf looked at Kelly, who nodded almost imperceptibly. 'Mum's nearly finished dinner. We just popped over to say hello. And show you this little one – last time you saw us, Kelly was pregnant, I think? But we'll come by again soon. We'll always come back for the garden – and you, of course,' he said with a chuckle.

Alma nodded curtly. 'Take some herbs for your mum!' she said, plucking bunches from the chimney pot planters. She was smiling, but Maya almost spotted a tear budding in her left eye. With a blink, it vanished, and Alma was her same sturdy self. 'Well, nice to see you both,' she said, her voice low and deep.

'You've got Christmas dinner plans, yeah?' Yusuf said, waving Emmanuel's wrinkly hand at Alma. 'You eating Auntie Funmi's egusi?'

'Oh, Yusuf, you know me. The egusi barely lasted the day yesterday – all gone. Didn't even share it with this lot. I'll have broth today.'

Yusuf chuckled. 'You haven't changed, Auntie.'

'I should hope not. I've spent my life avoiding that.'

'Auntie Maya,' Kelly said. 'You'll feed her something proper, won't you?'

'She's a stubborn one . . . I've offered.'

'Excuse me. I *am* right here,' Alma snapped, hiding a deep, throaty laugh behind her words.

Maya ran around stirring pots, adding sprinkles of salt, simmering stews, chopping vegetables. Alma sat in their kitchen, the windows steamed up with the smells of home, reminiscing about Yusuf in the garden, how she could barely believe he was a father himself now. How unexpected, and how lovely it had been, of them to pop by, to say hello.

Prem was taking a little breather in his chair just outside the kitchen door, trying to hide from Maya in case she bellowed more instructions at him.

'I do miss having them around. Reckon you do too, Prem,' Alma nodded her head, her hands wrapped around a mug of warm mulled juice. Alma had recently made the decision to stop drinking, worried it was affecting her memory. A few weeks ago, Prem had found Alma asleep in his garden chair one morning. When she'd woken up, she had no idea where she was. Days afterwards, Alma had no memory of the event at all and put it down to her large glass of port the night before. 'I'm sixty-four, Prem, you can't expect me to be as bright as a button these days! You youngsters, you wait . . .'

'Hiral!' Prem called suddenly. 'What on earth are you wearing?' Maya and Alma paused their nattering, eyed Hiral, who had floated in wearing an extravagant, glitzy jumper with shoulder pads.

In her new-found sassiness, she said: 'Shush! I'm reading!'

'Sorry, Hiral,' Alma whispered, her eyes screwed up to prevent herself from laughing. 'Can we address the bauble in the room? Why are you dressed like a Christmas decoration?'

Hiral looked down at her outfit, her cheeks blooming red. 'Auntie Alma,' she snapped. 'This is what *everyone's* wearing this year.' And off she went clutching her book, shutting the living-room door behind her.

'Don't worry, Alma,' Prem said. 'She's being a teenager – it's her prerogative.'

'She's only bloody ten, isn't she? Or have I lost a few years?'

'She's preparing. Wants to be an expert when the time finally comes,' Prem chuckled. 'Right,' he resumed his position by the stove and tapped his spoon on the pan. 'Are you going to eat with us?' He looked Alma directly in the eye.

She looked to the ceiling. 'You know . . . I've not had Christmas Day with anyone since my father passed away. Reminds me of . . . my mum. And then that Christmas, when Susie . . .' Alma paused. 'Well, you know. I know she was only a cat, but she felt like family to me.'

Maya nodded. While she'd never truly bonded with Susie, she could admit her house felt a little bit less like home without Susie wandering in, unwelcome, to the kitchen. Alma had been slower, a little vacant since Susie's death. 'They do say love and grief can cause you to lose your way,' Prem had said, explaining Alma's recent bouts of forgetfulness and her memory blanks. Grief resurfacing in those small moments.

Maya wondered if another cat might help keep Alma company. But she hadn't brought it up with her yet – she thought she might need to come to the decision herself.

'I have the odd phone call with Kate these days at Christmas or New Year,' Alma continued, ignoring the croak in her voice. 'She tells me how everything's going with her, but I only really spend the day on my own. You know that.'

'I know,' Maya responded softly. She looked at Prem, who was licking a spoon covered in spicy potato mush.

'It's too late for me to go and make broth, isn't it?' Alma said with an exaggerated eye-roll, slumping back into the chair.

It was only four thirty.

Prem nodded gently.

'In that case,' Alma looked from Prem to Maya, 'why don't I eat with you? It all smells delicious. I only hope it's not too spicy.'

'I made it extra mild, just in case . . .' Maya smiled, and beside her, Prem squeezed her hand. 'Do you want to set the table?'

Alma pushed herself up from her chair and hobbled, as though drunk, over to her friend. 'Thank you,' she said. 'Now, get out of my way, Prem, you oaf. I've got to get to the cutlery drawer.'

'All right, chief,' Prem joked.

'Don't call me chief!' Alma poked him in the ribs, cackling, repeating Hiral's catchphrase.

'Yes boss!' Prem and Maya responded in unison.

The evening went by without a hitch – Alma seemed to enjoy the food: nothing was too spicy. Hiral, however, remarked on how 'bland' everything was.

'It's because of me, Heer,' Alma said, her mouth full of food. 'I'll turn into a big ball of fire if I so much as look at a chilli pepper.'

And then Hiral laughed, her jumper glittering like her eyes. Maya observed her little family – Prem, Hiral and Alma squished round the kitchen table – and her hand flew to the locket round her neck.

The room was filled with warmth from the stove that would take hours to lose its heat, the steaming kadhi and rice left on the hob, and the joy and brightness from the people around her. The foxes giggled in the garden, but Alma was so relaxed, she let them have the time of their lives.

Prem, who had been a little worried about Alma ever since the incident with the chair, looked at Maya and smiled. 'Everything's going to be okay,' his grin said. And Maya agreed, clutching the locket in her hand. It had become a habit of late.

Together, they could do anything.

'To convincing Alma Christmas isn't all bad,' Prem said, raising his glass.

'To convincing Alma Christmas isn't all bad.' Hiral and Maya raised their glasses in turn.

'Oi!' Alma said, refusing to raise hers, slugging a gulp immediately. 'Jury's still out on that! Where's the pud?'

'Maya?' Prem's whisper came to her through the darkness, his face partly illuminated by the moon shining through their bedroom window.

'Hmm?' she grumbled back through her sleep.

'Can you hear that?'

'What?'

'That sound – it sounds like something is in the garden.'

'It's probably those foxes,' she said automatically. Used to being woken up by their shrieks.

'It's not foxes,' Prem said, serious.

'Go back to sleep, it's late.' Her eyes caught the new digital clock that Hiral had wrapped up for them that day to replace their carriage clock, now sadly relegated to the living-room mantelpiece. The lurid green numbers taunted her: 03:48.

Then she heard it for herself. A wailing.

It didn't sound like a fox, but they made all sorts of noises.

'What do you want us to do about it? It's probably an animal. Or someone drunk.' But Maya couldn't help her quickening heartbeat, her mind jumping back to the scene years ago, finding Ade and Yusuf, scared, hiding in the garden.

'Maya,' Prem turned on his bedside lamp. 'I think it's Alma . . . I'm sure I heard her voice.'

Without waiting for her to reply, he stood up. With his urgency and her pounding heart, Maya was instantly wide awake. She watched her husband grab his flannel dressing gown on the way out of the door and followed his lead, tumbling down the stairs.

'Dad?' Hiral said, poking her head out of her bedroom, her eyes scrunched up from sleep.

'It's all right, beta,' Prem said. 'Go back to sleep.'

But Hiral promptly ignored them and joined their convoy.

'Seriously, Hiral,' Prem whispered to her. 'Stay inside, okay?'

'What's going on?'

Prem and Maya didn't reply, they continued to stomp down the stairs, until they burst through the immaculate kitchen – it was impossible to believe it had been the site of an explosion of food and festivities only a few hours earlier. Opening the door into the garden, they could still hear the laughing and joking from kitchens further down the road, Christmas cheer continuing early into the morning.

On the patio, the biting December air nipped at every part of them.

But Maya could barely feel the cold, for the first thing she saw was Prem rushing towards Alma, sitting on the lawn, her legs crossed. She was rocking back and forth, her arms tucked around her.

'Alma,' Prem whispered, walking slowly and calmly towards their friend. For a moment, Maya stayed behind. Too scared to move closer.

Alma looked up at him, glancing behind, catching Maya's eye. She instantly shot to her feet, throwing herself two feet back.

'Keep away from me!' Alma's eyes were bloodshot. Fingers bright red with cold. She was wearing the same outfit as earlier. Had she even gone to bed at all?

'Where's my father!' She showed no hint of recognition, and within moments, Maya found a tear rolling down her own face, the heat of it burning her pores. 'What have you done with my father!'

Prem stepped back slightly, trying not to spook Alma.

Maya pushed past gently, taking it one step at a time. Trying desperately to keep the quiver of concern out of her voice, she said: 'It's me, Alma, it's Maya. Prem and Hiral are here too.'

'Where is my father? Why isn't he home yet?' She sounded so lost. Confused.

'Alma,' Prem's voice was soothing. Maya was more grateful than ever to have him by her side. 'Alma, you're safe, you're okay. We're here with you. I . . .' he paused, looking at Maya for reassurance. She nodded, gently. ' . . . your father hasn't lived here for many years.'

'No! No! I need to get into the house – he needs to let me in. I haven't got my key.'

Maya looked at Alma's cardigan. She usually kept them in her pockets. But now she saw they had been ripped off, two squares of fabric lying discarded on the onion patch.

Maya turned towards Hiral, still standing in the doorway, her arms hugging herself. Her face was inscribed with both fear and sadness. Maya tried to keep one eye on Alma as she said the words: 'Prem, please can you check the kitchen for Alma's keys?'

Alma didn't take her eyes away from Maya and Prem, her gaze flicking between the two, assessing the danger ahead. With Prem in the kitchen, Maya felt alone, exposed. A few moments later, he returned, Alma's spare set of keys jangling in his hand.

'Alma, I've got your keys here, okay?'

Alma began to cry, softly at first, and then big, hacking, child-like sobs. 'Where's my father?'

Prem tentatively took a step closer. Alma didn't move at all. She'd resigned herself to this stranger standing in front of her, dangling keys like a peace-offering.

'Alma, do you want to take your keys, or shall I unlock the door for you?'

She couldn't speak between her sobs, and Maya's gut clenched. She'd never seen her friend so vulnerable, so small and fragile.

Alma nodded her head towards the door, inviting Prem to open it. He did so, carefully, slowly, making sure to turn around every so often, narrating his every move. 'I'm going to step onto the kitchen step, okay? This may take me a little while as I can't see very much.'

A few feet back, Maya could hardly see a thing.

After what felt like hours of trying one key and then another, one way up and then the other, Prem eventually managed to turn the key. But nothing happened. And in that moment, Prem turned the handle . . .

The door had been unlocked. The door had been unlocked all this time. At the sight of the open door, Alma took her first step forward. Prem pushed it wide for her.

They felt the subtle wash of warmth from Alma's house escaping into the cold of the night.

Alma hurried up the step, grabbing her keys from Prem's hand and she slammed the door shut, turning the bolt from the inside. Maya ran forward now and pushed once. 'Alma!' she called, fear immediately taking over.

It was futile. She had locked herself in. Alma was frightened of them.

Prem held her tight. 'Maya, I think we should be calm, keep our voices quiet,' he said gently.

And she called again, softer this time, 'Alma, shall I keep you company?' She held her face up to the glass, cupping her hands around her eyes, trying to catch a glimpse of her friend inside. It was pitch black. Alma could be anywhere in the house.

She didn't know what to do. She ran straight into her house and called for Prem to follow her.

'Should we call the police?' Prem asked, serious.

'I don't want to call the police on her, Prem, I don't think she's dangerous.' Maya's voice became still again.

'But she didn't know who we were, Maya, she didn't know.'

'Yes, Prem, I know,' Maya whispered, her heart in her throat, 'but she knew where she was, she knew her house. I think, when she's in there, she'll be okay again. She'll be okay.'

'She could hurt herself, Maya.'

Without saying another word, she led him up the stairs and perched herself on a chair placed on the landing, halfway up. Alma always used to joke that if she sat in this same position in her house, she could hear everything that went on in Maya's. She could hear Hiral chatting when she had friends round, or Prem waffling on about the state of the world; sometimes she could even hear if Maya was frying something in the kitchen. Maya never believed her . . . but right now she desperately hoped Alma was right. She needed to hear Alma's house back. If she kept her house completely silent, would she be able to hear her friend if she called for help, if she cried out in pain?

'Prem,' Maya said, gesturing to the step in front of her. 'Get a cushion. Sit here. We can listen for her. We can make sure she's okay.'

Prem's words, '*Should we call the police?*' circled her mind like wasps buzzing around their hive. Maybe they should. Maybe that was the best thing to do.

But what if something happened?

What if they took Alma away from her?

What would she do then?

If Alma was in danger, she would know about it. She would feel something in her gut – a warning. She pictured them in the kitchen, laughing and joking, toasting that Christmas wasn't all bad. It felt like years ago now; she refused to believe it was only a few hours in the past. Everything had felt so calm then; now, everything was uncertain.

'Maya,' Prem said softly, one hand clutching his heart, pushing down hard. She wondered if his hurt like hers did. 'I think we need to start reminding ourselves that Alma might not be very well, and we can't be the only ones to look after her. Alma might need some proper help.'

Maya sat there, and shook her head, refusing to take in his words.

Chapter 21

Winston

December 2018

Ever since telling Bernice about his mum, after saying it out loud to someone new for the first time in years, everything had come back to Winston. And more than anything, he'd been desperate to call Lewis. Lewis was the one person who'd been there during the years his mum was unwell, when Winston kept making excuses not to travel home, because he'd been too scared to see her for the last time. He'd been too scared to travel to her. Superstition, maybe. Scared that if he turned up, then she'd let go. He should have known, he couldn't save her – nothing he did could save her. And now he had to live his life knowing he wasn't with her when she died.

Lewis had held his hand through it all. He'd listened. He'd been there.

'A standard procedure,' his mum had told him on the phone the day before she went into the hospital, two years ago. A heart bypass, he'd discovered later, from his sister. Video calls, phone calls, late at night. Lewis had been there to make Winston cups of coffee to keep him awake. He'd picked up calls at work, or in the middle of meetings, to listen to Winston repeat his worries over and over again. And he'd woken early in the morning to comfort Winston when he couldn't breathe through his tears.

Winston's mother died months later. The operation had gone well. But it was an infection that killed her. She was only sixty-five. She was too young. Too good.

'You should go,' Lewis had said, as soon as they'd heard the news. A matter-of-fact phone call from his father. 'Be with your family, Winston. I can come with you.'

But he hadn't. He couldn't. If he went, it meant it was real. He wanted to believe she was still there, living her life in India. If he saw it for himself, he couldn't believe any longer.

Now, after saying it all out loud, after telling Bernice, there was no escaping it. He'd been stuck alone with his grief, and the only person to blame was himself.

'No longer,' he said to himself. He'd spent years shutting people out. Even now. Barely listening to Lewis, not allowing him to explain anything. Turning down Sal's offer of spending Christmas with them. Ignoring Ruth's calls.

But today was New Year's Eve. His mother's favourite day. Winston gulped down his regret. When not in the shop, he'd spent the last week in bed, flicking through Netflix, searching endlessly for something to watch. Mr James had tried to arrange some interviews with new potential flatmates, but thankfully they'd all cancelled due to Christmas plans, and he was grateful to just be alone. So he didn't have to try to act like a real-life human for a while. He'd start watching a series and realize there was a happy couple or something in it and suddenly stop. He couldn't deal with that now. He'd been surrounded by other people's happiness recently – it was Christmas, after all. He saw couples in the shop, laughing, joking, arm in arm, and it stung. He felt stupid, childish. He should be tackling it like a grown-up. He and Lewis had just run their course, hadn't they?

This morning he'd forced himself up from the bed and down to the kitchen, where he spent twenty minutes staring out at the garden, a glass of water in his hands. He watched as a blue tit flew down to the bird feeders, attaching itself with both feet, pulling out seed after seed with its beak. It discarded the seeds it wasn't interested in, throwing them delicately down on the earth, before trying again. Winston's heart rate had slowed, the incessant, ever-present feeling of the vast, echoing house around him finally dissipated.

He kept his eyes on the bird.

As it flew away, he turned to the stove, opening his kitchen cupboards, pulling out potatoes, gram flour, and the last few spices Lewis had left behind, which were thankfully the ones Winston always needed: turmeric, mustard seeds, chilli powder and cumin. He pulled out some wilted coriander, and some fresh green chillies. He'd spent a week living off Bernice's lasagne and Super Noodles. He couldn't do it again.

'Wish me luck, Mum,' he said, seeing her face once again, as he started to chop and cook, turning his radio on to blast out Kate Bush. Bernice wasn't around, so he could happily sing at the top of his voice. When his voice croaked to life, he felt himself coming alive too – he pictured his mother dancing in her own kitchen when she thought no one was watching.

Once he'd mashed the potato, seasoned it, and rolled it into balls coated in gram flour paste, he was onto the deep frying. He remembered running around his mother's feet as a small boy while she yelled at him to move away. Now he knew why – as he plopped each vada into the pan, there was a sizzle and a splash, hot oil jumping around the kitchen. Every time the oil hissed, he shrieked, launching himself back, ridiculing his own silliness.

That evening at the shop, Sal battled his way through the Christmas decorations to get to Winston behind the counter. 'Son, what are you doing here? You can go home!' Sal said, patting a large Poundland plastic snowman holding his carrot nose and a snowball tummy. 'Angela and I will mill around on the floor in case anyone wants us.'

Almost before he could finish his sentence, a group of New Year revellers tumbled into the shop, hoovering up fizz and snacks from the displays Angela had spent ages putting together. Demolished in moments.

'I think I'll stay until the big crowds die down,' Winston nodded. Angela and Sal exchanged a glance with each other, one Winston couldn't decipher. 'I brought these.' Winston handed over a yoghurt pot full of batata vada. 'To say sorry, for not spending Christmas with you. It was a kind offer – and I think I should have taken you up on it.'

Sal was engaged in ringing through the ten bottles of prosecco at the counter, but Angela pulled Winston to her. 'Don't worry, we understand. Sometimes it's good to be alone.'

'I hope you like spice . . . I think I might have put too many chillies in,' Winston grimaced, nodding to the pot in Angela's hand, trying to change the conversation, to keep the spark of warmth alive in him before the grief and loneliness could tumble back in. 'How was your Christmas Day?'

Angela still held him close. If she let go, he'd be adrift at sea. 'Well,' she said, sighing deeply, happily. 'We took a few of Sal's father's friends from the area to see him. Jenny was there, so you can imagine, it was a bit of a raucous car ride. But it was a lovely day. Sal . . . he loves his dad so much. If we didn't have the shop, if we lived in a bungalow or something with a ground floor, Erol would be with us. It's what Sal would want . . . but Erol would also never allow us to give this shop up. Not now. It means too much to them all.'

Angela watched Sal, laughing with the already-merry customers, adding a free pack of Sesame Snaps in with each bottle of fizz.

'When he handed me the change,' Angela said, under her breath, nudging Winston gently.

He couldn't help but laugh, and then he noticed her eyes shoot to the shop doorway. He followed her gaze. Standing there, awkwardly waving, dressed in a glittery jumper declaring 'Happy New Year' with sharp, navy jeans, was Lewis.

Winston's heart was in his throat, and for a second he thought he heard his mother's giggle, but he knew it was only his imagination.

Lewis stepped forward, making his way into the shop, grabbing a bottle of champagne no less from the highest wine rack. Angela hadn't put the champagne on her special display: 'No one really gets champagne for New Year's, do they?' she'd asked Sal, who had said, emphatically, that actually people do. 'Well, we're not risking those bottles getting smashed if someone walks into it,' Angela had decided.

'Hey Sal,' Lewis said, taking the bottle up to the counter. Angela and Winston were rooted to the spot, a few feet away. Was it weird he hadn't come to say hello? Why on earth was he here?

'Hello, my son,' Sal said, baritone, welcoming, kind.

'I thought you said Winston would be at home,' Lewis whispered, but not quietly enough for Angela and Winston to miss it. Angela squeezed his hand, the warmth of her skin penetrated the cold armour Winston had spent time building up, and he felt his body relax slightly. The muscles let go just a touch.

Sal eyed Angela and Winston awkwardly before replying, 'You know . . . he never listens to us. We told him to go home, take the evening off.'

'Angela,' Winston nudged her beside him. 'What are you doing? What's going on?'

Angela pulled a face at him, grimacing, but a smile hid behind her eyes. 'Well . . . Lewis wanted to come and see you . . . after his day at work. He asked us if you'd be working.'

Winston rolled his eyes, but he couldn't hide the fact he was pleased to see him. It had been a fortnight since Lewis had left, but every day felt like a year. 'And you didn't think to ask me?'

Angela's face turned serious, a frown punctuating her forehead. 'Winston. You'd have said no. Sometimes you don't know what's good for you. I understand you think it's over between you two, but you need to talk.' She couldn't hold his gaze, and to avoid the awkwardness, she let go of his hand, and dug into the pot of batata vada, putting one straight into her mouth so she couldn't say any more.

Lewis wandered over, champagne held by the neck. Angela was still chomping her way through the spicy potato ball. He laughed, as Angela pointed to her hamster cheeks.

'Batata vada,' Lewis said, looking at Winston. He said the words so awkwardly and English, Winston's heart contracted with adoration, despite how cold and ungiving he was trying to be. 'You've not made that for ages.'

Winston nodded.

'I . . .' Lewis held the champagne up, as though that finished the sentence. When Winston said nothing, feeling his heart beating in his throat, Lewis continued: 'To say thank you, for the present. Little Eva.' Lewis paused. 'It's the most thoughtful gift. And . . . I wondered if maybe we could see the New Year in together. I know, I know it's still really soon. But I thought we could talk . . . I don't want—' He took a breath. 'I don't want to upset you, so tell me to go if you want. But . . .'

Lewis didn't try to finish his sentence.

Winston nodded. 'Okay.' He didn't know what else to say. He didn't want to be alone.

He looked to Angela and Sal, who quickly turned the other way, pretending not to have watched every second of Lewis and Winston's self-conscious reunion. Then they gave him the look of encouraging parents, setting their child at the school gates on the first day of term, telling them to go and make some friends.

Angela held a finger up. 'Hold on!' she said, before they could wander out of the door. She promptly flew to the snacks aisle, selecting packets and packets of crisps and popcorn. 'For New Year,' she said, not looking at Winston, as she put them into his arms.

Winston felt every second of the silent walk home, and when he opened the front door of Number 79, Lewis wandered in first automatically.

'Do you want to come through to the garden?' Winston asked.

'Sure. Crap, I didn't bring flutes,' Lewis said, more to himself, as he looked at the bottle in his hands.

'Don't worry, we can use two of the three mugs I have,' Winston laughed, before realizing it wasn't that funny. Lewis smiled apologetically.

'We'll wait until midnight though, right?'

'Sure,' Winston nodded, glancing at the clock on the wall. It was eleven now. What were they going to talk about for the next hour, waiting for the new year to start? That said, he wanted to know everything. How Lewis was. If his life had shrunk as much as Winston's had. He hadn't expected it, because Lewis had barely been around before, but the knowledge that it was over between them . . . it had made it all feel too real. He'd see things and want to message Lewis right away, but knowing he couldn't, knowing that was it . . . it felt like grief. All over again.

'Tidy in here,' Lewis said, like a stranger seeing a friend's new home.

'Yeah . . . Mr James tried to set up some viewings but everyone cancelled . . . Christmas, I guess. So, I'll have to keep it tidy for a bit longer.'

Lewis nodded. 'Is that okay? Are you okay sharing or are you going to . . .?'

Winston didn't know how to reply. 'Might be a good way to meet more people. I've . . . I've kept myself to myself for too long, I think.'

Lewis unlocked the kitchen door, on autopilot, before glancing at Winston for permission. Winston shrugged. He hated this. Lewis was acting both like a stranger in what used to be his home and like he still belonged here.

'Can't believe you still have that jumper,' Winston smiled as the glitter on Lewis's jumper caught the light.

Winston and Lewis had ordered matching jumpers online four years ago. A Christmas one, and a New Year one. A joke, more than anything. The next year, Winston had pulled his jumper out to discover it was moth-eaten, ruined. Lewis, on the other hand, had protected his in a special plastic sleeve, determined to keep it nice. He'd kept it safe ever since.

'Yeah . . . I love it,' Lewis said, locking eyes with Winston.

He felt his cheeks burning, his eyes stinging, wanting to look away, yet not wanting to break contact.

Lewis pulled a chair from the kitchen onto the patio, and Winston dragged his wooden chair – damp from the cold air – to sit beside him. And there they sat, facing the garden. Winston could feel the space between them like it was a stranger trying to keep them apart. He longed to reach across and grab his hand, so something could feel normal again. He just held his own hands tighter instead.

'You've cleared this *loads*,' Lewis said, voice barely a whisper. 'Has it been all right? How's the woman next door?'

'Bernice? No . . . she's all right. We've been working on it together.'

'I still don't get why you suddenly started gardening,' Lewis laughed. 'Good, though. If you enjoy it.'

Winston pictured the letters that had arrived through his door, the photograph of his mum in her garden, the red-hot pokers, as well as Seb's smiling face when he first plunged his bare hands into the soil, scooping out earth to plant some bulbs.

'I've had some prods along the way, I suppose,' Winston shrugged, smiling. 'And you know, my mum loved her garden. It's brought me closer to her, I guess.'

Lewis nodded then, looking at Winston, telling him he saw him, he remembered his pain.

'And like, it's allowed me to actually *do* something,' Winston started to babble. 'I've spent so much of my time sitting around doing nothing, and I know this is kind of nothing too, but at least it's creating something. There's not much to see for it yet, but there will be.'

Lewis smiled, eyes roaming the garden, lingering on the shed, the pots lining the patio, and the gate, now exposed for all to see.

'It's lovely,' Lewis whispered. 'Really lovely. Your mum . . . she'd love this, Wins.'

Winston held his breath, and they sat in silence once again. The air between them heavy with the words they were too scared to say.

'How was Christmas?' Winston asked eventually, hoping Lewis wouldn't ask the same question back.

'Loved it,' Lewis said flatly. He handed over his phone to show a photograph. Surrounded by his family at the large wooden dining table Winston remembered well. They were all wearing skew-whiff Christmas cracker crowns, arms round each other, faces varying degrees of 'ruddy' from the wine. 'They send their love.'

'And . . . how's the new place?'

'I . . . I haven't moved in yet. I should be completing next week. It really is beautiful, I'd love to show you one day. It's the place I always dreamed of.'

This was the first time Lewis had said *I* instead of *we*. The first time he'd admitted that this was his dream, not Winston's. Understanding that while they loved each other, they didn't necessarily love the same things. Share the same dreams.

'I do want to show you one day, Winston,' Lewis repeated. 'If you'll let me.'

Winston looked away, and Lewis got up, checking his watch, looking for a reason to leave the silence behind. 'I better get the mugs and champagne . . . nearly time.'

Seven minutes to midnight. Winston's phone flashed in his hand.

Happy new year, love from all of us xxxxx

A message from his dad. He never sent that many kisses, so Ruth must've had something to do with it. She'd messaged a few days ago to tell Winston she was back in India for the holidays – it was the first time her kids had seen their grandfather in two years. Though the kids would be asleep, their father, Ruth and her husband wouldn't have gone to bed. They'd be sitting around a fire in the garden, reminiscing, the hot sun starting to rise on the new year. It was a tradition his mother brought in, and he was sure they'd have continued it in her spirit. He scrolled through all the missed calls from Ruth – the odd one from his dad. One day, he could tell them about the garden. All Mum's tips he'd been using to bring it to life.

But he hadn't spoken to his father about his mum at all. His father couldn't bear anyone bringing her up, still so in denial, he'd probably live the rest of his life there. Winston understood he'd done the same. His own grief had shrunk to a stone buried deep in the core of him. By continuing with life, he was able to ignore it. But when he stopped to think about it for too long, he was forced to see how far he'd pushed it, how deep it had gone. How hard it was to reconcile with.

Then, like a whisper of affection from his mother herself, the first few fireworks launched themselves above his head from gardens far and near.

'Lewis!' Winston called a few seconds later, the thrill of the noise and sound coursing through him, pulling his attention away from his phone, his past. 'We should go upstairs, look out the Velux window. So we can see the ones over the city.'

'You got it!' Lewis called back, the mugs clattering together.

Upstairs, the two hung out of the Velux window, squished against each other, mugs clutched in hands. As more fireworks went off a few gardens down, Winston heard a cackle of laughter that sounded like Jenny.

And suddenly, the skyline erupted. The city was alight, pinks, blues, greens and golds. Winston glanced at Lewis, his eyes focused on the spectacle ahead of him, his mouth slightly open in a delighted smile, his skin glowing the colours of the rainbow. Eyes reflecting the sparkles ahead.

In this moment, Winston could almost forget everything that had happened.

They cheers-ed with their mugs, said a friendly 'Happy New Year', smiles on both their faces, and they watched as the fireworks continued with all the energy and vibrancy with which they'd started. And when it was over, they continued to look, pointing out single sparks in the sky from Londoners all around.

And, after fifteen minutes, not a word spoken between them, the air now silent, smoke drifting in the fireworks' wake, Lewis turned to Winston.

'Winston . . .' His voice was soft, quiet. Trying not to break the spell of the moment. 'I'm sorry. I know now how . . . how much you had to put up with. The fact I was never here. I'm sorry for pushing you away, Winston. I don't think I even realized I was doing it. I've been asking myself why I did that – why I kept myself so apart from you, focusing on this one thing. I thought I was doing it for us. But I didn't want you to say no to the house. I knew that if I did this, if I did what I really wanted to do, it might be the end of us. I didn't want to decide. I don't expect you to forgive me, but I wanted to tell you I *know* I made a mistake now. That house, it's not going to feel the same without you. And that's my fault, not yours. I'm so sorry.'

Winston simply nodded.

There was nothing else to say. He grabbed Lewis's hand, and continued to look out the window, letting the words, the apology float on the night sky, their arms touching, their bodies huddled together, staring out of the tiny window.

'My mum loved fireworks like this,' Winston whispered finally, and Lewis turned to him.

'I wish I'd met her,' he said. 'She sounded amazing. It's so clear how much she loved you, and how much you love her,' he finished, and Winston felt the muscles in his face pull tight, his eyes burning with sadness, and happiness, and everything in between.

'Thank you,' he whispered back.

Winston remembered Bernice's Christmas card, then, on the shelf beside his bed: *Don't spend Christmas alone.*

For now, as long as they stayed here, staring out of this window, welcoming the New Year in together, everything was okay.

Chapter 22

Maya

January 1987

'Happy New Year!' Bob peered over the gate on New Year's Day to see Prem, Maya, Bina and Alma huddled around the picnic bench. 'What are you thinking, sitting out in this temperature? Are you mad?'

They were all wrapped up in blankets, sporting Fair Isle scarves, hats, and bright red noses. Alma had on a flat cap over a woolly hat, two thick fisherman's jumpers, and a tartan scarf.

'I don't know what you mean, Bob. It's positively balmy,' she said.

'Didn't fancy the Lord Mayor's Parade then, down in town?' he asked.

'Course not!' Alma said, and Maya noticed Bob blush, his eyes dropping to the ground. Alma kept her eyes on the garden.

'Join us, Bob! We're keeping watch,' Prem said.

Bob hopped from foot to foot, trying to keep the blood circulating around his toes. 'Keeping watch?' he asked, unsure, his misty breath illuminated by the kitchen light shining through the glass.

'Foxes,' Alma half-growled. 'My New Year's resolution. Keep those foxes away. Going to do a daily lookout . . . I hate those fecking foxes almost as much as I hate Bina's old bosses,' Alma continued.

'Any New Year resolutions for you, Bob?' Prem asked, trying to lighten the mood.

'Erm,' Bob looked down at his feet, 'not really . . . said I'll spend more time with my sister, maybe. Down on the south coast.'

'That's a nice one,' Maya nodded encouragingly, anxious that Alma had barely acknowledged him at all, her eyes still searching the garden for signs of foxes.

'Fancy a beer, Bob?'

Bob nodded, and Prem hopped to the kitchen, returning moments later with an opened beer bottle. He dropped it into Bob's hand, before slumping back heavily onto the bench. Maya looked at him then, noticing his breathing was a little shallow, almost breathless.

'You all right?' Alma asked, her eyes on him. Prem nodded, waving their concern away. 'I'm fine, promise,' he said, snuggling up with Maya, who held his hand tighter as his breathing gradually returned to normal.

'You should pop to the doctors,' Bob said. 'You've been getting those funny turns for a little while now.'

'No, it's nothing . . . it's only when I've been sitting down too long, not moving enough.'

Bob's brow was furrowed, eyes on his friend.

Prem smiled at him. 'I'm okay,' the smile said. 'Seriously.'

After a few moments of silence, Bob turned to Alma again. 'What are you planning in the garden this spring then?'

'Well, Bob,' Alma said, looking at him finally. 'My niece, you know, Kate, she posted me some lovely lily bulbs, so I've popped those in already, give them a head start. But the squirrels are after them. Sniffing them out. Expensive, those lily bulbs, I reckon.'

Bob was gulping down his beer, but he could barely take his eyes off Alma.

'And then the usual – lots of tulips. Hiral's favourite,' Alma nodded to Hiral's usual spot on the bench, even though she was with a friend today. 'And Maya likes them too. Bit prissy for me. What do you reckon, Bina?'

'Tulips are *wonderful*, why are you so fussy, Alma?'

'Eh, you love them, Alma. What are you on about?' Maya tutted back.

'All right, they're okay I suppose.'

Maya winked at Bob, who rolled his eyes at Alma jovially.

'And I've worked up the soil over there for my hollyhocks. You remember my dad had loads of them?'

Bob nodded, but Maya was sure he hadn't a clue. Alma could recall things from decades ago as if they happened yesterday: her father's favourite flowers; his planting routine for the winter vegetables; his favourite kind of courgette – all sorts. Bob, who had run around and played in the same garden Alma had grown up in, remembered nothing of it. Maya was sure that in that garden all those years ago, Bob hadn't paid attention to Alma's father's planting plan, or his routine, or the quality of the courgettes and corn. The thing Bob was there for, the reason Bob kept returning all these years later, was Alma. It had always been Alma.

These days, however, ever since Alma's turn in the garden just over a year ago, Maya had noticed that everyday things had started slipping her mind. Where she'd put her keys, what she'd planted out only the day before, when her various appointments were, social or otherwise. There hadn't been anything quite as dramatic as that Christmas, but the smaller things were worrying Maya more. It made her wonder when the next big thing was coming, what was around the corner.

'I'm probably going to have my decennial argument with Charlie, or should I say your bloody landlord, *Mr James*,' she said, rolling her eyes at his name, mockingly, 'about me putting a fence up between the gardens,' Alma continued.

'What?' Maya asked, her eyes shooting to Prem.

'Yeah . . . he sent me a letter a couple of weeks ago. He's asking if we can discuss the boundary again – wants to erect a fence, *still*. Apparently as the owner of this terrace house, that boundary is my responsibility. Last time we did that, he called me an "old bat". Charming man. We used to be friends, you know,' Alma said. '*That old bat*. We're the same bloody age!'

'Alma,' Bob said. 'Isn't he fifteen years younger than us? You used to babysit him.'

Maya had been told stories of Alma babysitting young Mr James. She'd pick him up from school and they'd work on the garden together, running to and from the shops, popping into neighbours' houses to swap seeds of all kinds for the new vegetable season, lugging great bags of soil, digging and churning and planting. In the evenings, Mr James would pop over to Alma's house and help peel some homegrown vegetables for a stew – Alma's father made the best stew in Stoke Newington – and they'd sit together, eating, laughing, making plans for the garden.

'Why's he want a fence up?' Prem asked, his voice quieter than usual.

'Oh, I'm sure it's nothing. He just likes to make my life a pain sometimes. Has been arguing about it for years, ever since my dad was here – but we've always put our foot down. And I'll do it again. Probably preparing to sell one day in the future. Waiting for the right time. Make a fortune one day, he reckons.'

Maya's heart was in her throat as she took in the scene: her friends, her family, huddled around the bench. The fog in the garden cocooning them. Maya's stomach clenched; her mother had always told her to buy a place as soon as possible. 'That way, no one can really kick you out of your own home'. The fear of losing everything she loved felt closer than ever.

When Alma heard a rustle, she pointed her torch towards the vegetable and flower beds, searching for the fox, nicknamed 'Blasted Fox' – originating from little Hiral (luckily) mishearing Alma's constant refrain of 'Bastard Fox' years ago.

'He always seems so nice and chatty,' Maya said, her mind still on Mr James. 'He always asks about Bina and Sanjay still . . . it . . . it seems like he cares. How can he plan to sell and not even tell us?'

'Tell me about it,' Prem replied, looking down at the beer.

'That's what I'm doing,' Maya spun to face Prem instantly.

'No, I *know* that,' Prem said softly, a wheeze in his laugh. His hand shooting to his chest again in the cold of the air. 'It's that phrase that Alma uses,' he glanced at Alma for back-up, '*tell* me about it. Meaning "I know this already".'

'Well, if you know it all already, why didn't you stop me earlier,' Maya said, her frustration spilling over.

'Maya, my sweetie. I'm only agreeing with you.'

Bob and Bina, sensing the tension, turned towards the garden, which only served to enrage Maya more.

Everything was getting to her. Even the garden, once her happy place, was causing her stress. First there were the foxes, who seemed to gnaw their way in through the mesh surrounding all the fragile vegetables, destroying any newly dug area of soil, all year round. Then there was Alma: her health, the scares she'd given them, while refusing to talk to them about any of it. She'd simply dismiss her forgetfulness, saying, 'I'm old, Maya! That's what happens.' But Maya knew there was more to it. And now there was Mr James, who had the power to take her home, her security, away in a moment.

Later that evening, they retreated to Alma's sitting room, perched around her three-seater floral-fabric sofa, the electric fire blazing.

Maya searched for answers in Prem's face and found none. She saw only a sadness, a nervousness in his eyes, hidden behind his new thick-rimmed glasses. They were both scared. And while Alma was angry about the fence, she wanted to shake her, make her realize this might not be about a fence at all. She replayed Alma's words: 'waiting for the right time to sell'. Had she realized what that meant? Did she care?

'Don't worry about Mr James,' Prem said, holding himself up straight. 'I'll fight him off.'

At that, everyone's eyes shot to Prem: gentle, sweet Prem. Alma exchanged a confused glance with Maya. Bob tried to hold in a laugh, Bina looked away to hide the giggles taking over her cheeks. Within moments, Maya and Prem were laughing too, and Bob quickly followed suit.

'Bloody hell,' Alma said. 'I haven't heard you laugh in ages, you miserable lot.'

And Maya realized it was true. It was as though she'd been holding her breath ever since that Christmas and Alma's turn. She'd been waiting for something else to take her happiness away without realizing her worry had done it for her.

'Right, let me get us some pudding. I've got a cake that'll do,' Alma said, piling the plates up. 'Bina, want to help?'

Bina stood up, and headed towards the kitchen, while Alma untucked herself from the sofa, and started to trudge to the front door, her scarf slipping from her neck.

Prem and Maya looked at each other.

'Oi!' Bina called. 'Mad woman – where on earth do you think you're going?'

At the sound of Bina's call, Alma stopped, her hand on the latch. She turned around.

'Bloody hell,' she said, her eyes wide open, as though noticing her friends and the glowing light from the fire for the first time. 'I didn't have the foggiest idea of where I was just then. Maybe *Mr James* is right,' Alma chuckled, a deep, dark laugh. 'Perhaps I am an old bat after all.'

Chapter 23

Bernice

January 2019

SEB RAN STRAIGHT INTO the house when Bernice unlocked the front door, leaving her to carry the bags of presents all by herself. She turned round, glancing at the road. She'd missed it. A fortnight away, and she'd missed Eastbourne Road. She felt comforted by the familiar sounds of the television drifting out of Number 68, the twinkling lights of Number 78 opposite, with little children's drawings of Father Christmas stuck to the front window with Blu Tack. She'd even missed the Nosy Neighbour at Number 80. She hoped he'd given himself the holidays off.

She spotted a discarded, browning Christmas tree, sitting in a puddle of needles. As they'd driven down Clissold Crescent, she'd seen so many trees littering the road. It felt sacrilegious to her. She'd always been resolute about keeping the tree up until 6 January. She couldn't bear to take it down a moment earlier, even when Simon insisted they needed the space back in their apartment.

She wanted to cling to the magic as long as possible.

Her mind returned to one New Year's Day. Simon hadn't come home until the early hours. He'd spent 31 December with colleagues and clients rather than his family, despite the fact that Seb had been asking constantly for Daddy. That night, he'd returned when Seb was fast asleep, saw the Christmas tree was still up and ripped the sparkling fairy lights off. He'd shaken the decorations so they rolled across the floor like marbles. The decorations she and Seb had painstakingly and lovingly put on a few weeks before. Simon then dragged the naked Christmas tree down the stairs to the street below, and left it there, before finally crawling into bed at two in the morning. Stinking of booze and a stress-filled, angry night.

The next morning, beside the discarded tree, Bernice had seen Seb's handmade toilet-roll Angel: gold wings, misshapen face, now soggy from the rain and beyond repair. Simon had simply put the kettle on and made them pancakes.

A little voice cut through the memories.

'Winston!' Seb called through the wall on the staircase. 'Any sign of the parakeets?'

'Shh! Seb, it's nine in the morning – keep your voice down!'

'Winston said he'd keep an eye on the birds.'

'And I'm sure he did, but don't yell at the walls to find out. Go and knock if you really want to know.'

Without wasting a second, Seb bolted down the stairs and through the back door, hammering on his neighbour's kitchen window.

'Oi! Did you hear that?' Seb said to his mum. 'I think I heard him!'

As Bernice prepared to apologize for her son's behaviour, a voice called, 'Up here!'

Stepping back, Bernice saw Winston at the top of his house, head sticking out of the open Velux window.

'Catch!' Winston called, as he showered them with gold-foil chocolate coins.

'Chocolate!' Seb called. Like he hadn't seen the stuff before. Bernice ran inside, hands shielding her head, determined not to start the year by losing an eye because of a bloody chocolate coin.

But Seb kept his eyes on the ground, picking up whatever he could find, relishing the unexpected treasure hunt.

Winston and Seb broke into fits of laughter, like two children, full of glee.

Bernice flicked the kettle on, leaning against the worktop. She'd spent the holiday thinking up excuses to text Winston: *Could you check on the sweet peas in the kitchen for me . . .* or *Has my house alarm gone off?* But there was nothing in flower, the seedlings had barely made an appearance yet. And Winston knew she didn't have a house alarm. He'd made a joke about it when she'd accidentally revealed how much her coffee table cost. She made a mental reminder: *get a house alarm.*

But he seemed okay, didn't he?

As the kettle clicked, she heard the clatter of the letterbox, something thudded onto the doormat. Walking through the hallway, she saw an envelope, stuffed full. *The Lady at Number 77* was written on the front again. She glanced out of the kitchen window. Seb was still running around. Chocolate coins were still raining down. The mystery sender couldn't be Winston. How could it?

She lifted the flap of the envelope and saw two faces – two women – smiling up at her. The words *Alma and Maya – the women who keep the garden going!* above their heads, handwritten in felt-tip pen, photocopied into a dusky grey.

She ran her fingers over the image, searching for a clue. Alma and Maya: who were these women, and what were they trying to tell her?

'Here you go.' Bernice brought out a hot chocolate for Seb, who was tucking into his winnings at the garden table, which was also covered with chocolate oranges and Lindt reindeers. Winston had joined him too, wearing a sparkly 'Happy New Year' jumper.

'A few days late with that, aren't you?' She nodded to Winston.

'Don't people say Happy New Year until like . . . the end of February?' he shrugged, smiling. She couldn't work out his expression. He seemed happy, happier than she'd seen him before she left. But there was still a doleful look; something lost at the back of his eyes, behind the smile and the brightness. 'The chocolate coins – they're from Angela and Sal. I hope that's okay?'

'So kind of them,' Bernice said to Winston. 'But Seb, don't eat them all at once, okay? You'll make yourself sick.'

Seb's eyes darted between the chocolate oranges, the coins, the reindeers and his mum. He nodded, defeated. He handed an orange to Winston, who proceeded to bash it on the table to break it open. It took several attempts and lots of Seb's hot chocolate sloshed over the table before they managed it.

'How was your Christmas?' Winston asked, and Seb began to regale him with tales of his aunt and grandmother, the sloppy kisses from older relatives, the copious presents, the second Christmas with his dad too.

'*Two* whole Christmases,' Winston said, eyes wide.

'Yep, I'm pretty lucky,' Seb said, eyes on his hot chocolate, dipping in a segment of chocolate orange.

'How was yours?' Bernice asked gently, pulling Seb close to her.

'Quiet,' Winston said. 'But all right,' he said hurriedly. 'And that lasagne . . .' he said, looking at Bernice. 'It was delicious.'

'Wait, Winston!' Seb chimed in. 'Any parakeets?'

'Afraid not, pal,' Winston said, shrugging his shoulders and pulling down the sleeves of his Happy New Year jumper to avoid the chill.

Seb looked down, disappointed. 'Oh well, one day,' he said thoughtfully, and picked up his chocolates and empty mug, skipping inside.

'Did Seb have an okay time with Simon?' Winston asked, once Seb had closed the door behind him.

'Definitely, he loves his dad so much. He can . . .' Bernice sighed, not sure where to start, what to say. 'There's a lot of history between me and Simon, and for too long we took out our anger and frustration with our lives on each other. And Seb really felt that. Now there's peace, I think, when we're on our own.'

Winston smiled. Nodding. 'It sounds like you're making it work,' he said. His voice was wistful. 'I've noticed whenever he turns up . . . it's like your mind is somewhere else, constantly worrying. I . . . I'm not great with advice, but I'm here if you want to talk, you know. I'm a good listener at least. Got to be with Sal and Angela as my bosses.'

'Thank you,' she said shyly, not quite able to look him in the eye. 'It's tough, with Seb, trying to make sure he doesn't bear the brunt of the resentment I have for Simon.'

'Well,' Winston leaned on his spade. 'Seb seems to think you're much happier now, and I reckon he's probably cheerier because of it.'

Bernice smiled, a small sliver of light slipping into her mood.

'That's good . . . I . . . Simon made all the decisions, for both of us . . .' she continued, warming up bit by bit.

Winston scoffed. In solidarity, she imagined.

'I never stuck up for myself. For a long time, I felt like it only affected *me*. Until I realized it was affecting Seb too. I always wanted a garden. I thought I was maybe being idealistic, it's almost impossible to get a garden in the city. But then I realized I wanted my son to have a space to play in. Simon only wanted an easy commute to work. I never put my foot down. Somehow he still seems to get his own way, making my life his business.'

'Bernice,' Winston replied softly. 'You're very good at standing up to me, putting your foot down . . . You were proper scary when I first met you! You know, you can have that authority with him too. You just need to believe in it.'

She nodded. He was right, but she didn't know where, or how, to start to change things.

'Have you heard from Lewis?' Bernice asked.

'I . . . I saw him actually. He turned up on New Year's Eve.'

They both watched a robin skip along the fence, not saying anything for a moment, as it flew to the bird feeders, picking up its dinner for the day.

'It was nice to see him. He's gone back to Oxford. I think he's moving into his new house today, in fact. There's still lots to resolve, but I don't hate him right now. I want him to be happy, and . . .' Winston took a slurp of his tea, 'I don't know. There's history between us. He's been there through some of the worst stuff in my life. But who knows?'

She saw Winston's phone flash on the garden table. *Incoming Call. Ruth.*

He pressed the red button hurriedly, and looked up at her to check if she'd seen it.

'I obviously don't know Lewis,' Bernice started, 'but I saw the way he was with you at that Diwali party. He was attentive, caring. In some ways, he's a bit like Simon . . . always at work, busy, doesn't check in often enough. But he's also really different too. Simon had time to work out what he wanted to prioritize, and it was never me. Lewis: I think he's trying to prioritize it all. He just needs to work out what's worth it. And so do you. But he loves you. That's clear as bloody day, Winston.'

Winston nodded, unable to say anything, and Bernice gave his shoulder a squeeze before she stepped back inside her house. She kept watch over him in the kitchen, her fingers running over the photo of the two women, side by side. She wanted to ask him if he knew who these were from. If he knew these women. But, as her eyes lingered on his slumped frame, she knew her questions would have to wait for now.

Chapter 24

Maya

February 1988

'Maybe, if Alma had something to focus on . . . a pet, perhaps, she'd feel more herself?' Maya had said to Prem one day.

According to Bob, Alma had always had pets. 'I've never known her to go longer than a few months without one, let alone years . . .'

And, finally, Alma had agreed she wanted a new cat too. 'But I can't keep up with a kitten again,' Alma said. So the rescue cat Morris was the perfect pick. At five years old, white and ginger with an ever-friendly face, he was the complete opposite of Susie. He was a cuddler; he didn't have the same expression of intrigued disdain Susie had mastered, and he was about twice her size. No one could live up to Susie, and thankfully Morris was so different, he wouldn't even try. He would be loved on his own merits. Not following in Susie's pawprints.

Maya waited by the entrance of the adoption centre. Already on edge, seeing so many cats all in one place. The smell hit her first . . . she'd never be an animal lover, she was sure of that. But it warmed her heart to see Morris introduce himself to Alma, flopping into her arms. She looked forward to him coming home with Alma the next day.

* * *

'You tell your Prem I'll be round for some chess tonight!' Erol said a little later, packing up bags of cat litter behind the counter at the shop. 'You know, since he gave up smoking because of the breathlessness, he told me we'd replace our smoking sessions with chess,' he said, eyebrows raised. 'It was our New Year's resolution . . . and I don't think he's played a single game with me yet . . .'

'Of course, Erol,' Maya replied, checking her watch for the time. 'I'll pass the message on.' It was Friday and she was heading home to spend some time with Prem. Their own New Year's resolution was to make sure they had one morning together – away from the stress of every day. They'd chosen Fridays, because Hiral was out at school and they both had the morning off work. Unlike Erol with the chess, they'd stuck to it so far. Every Friday at eleven, they'd drink a cup of chai in the garden together, taking in the beauty of the world around them. She knew Prem would be waiting for her.

'I think,' Prem had said, when offering up the idea, 'it would start our day off right. I always look forward to you, Maya.'

'But you see me every day, Prem,' she replied, unable to keep the smile from her face.

'I know, and I don't take a single moment for granted.'

Waving goodbye to Alma and the litter bags, Maya unlocked her front door. 'Prem!' she called, pushing the door wide, her shopping by her feet. She stretched her hands to relieve the cramp from the weight of Alma's cat stuff.

'Prem!' she called again. In the kitchen she placed her single bag of shopping on the table. She glanced outside and spotted the back of his head. He was sitting in his chair, basking in the winter sun.

The first thing she noticed were the snowdrops, poking up and flowering underneath the eucalyptus tree, in little clumps by the shed, and dotted around the lawn.

'Prem! The snowdrops,' she said, skipping over to some. The only thing he'd ever asked for in the garden were snowdrops. 'It's what I imagined an English garden to be like,' he'd said. The first day they bloomed each year always felt special. It felt like a small moment to make Prem's dreams come true.

'Prem!' she said again, feeling the silky white bell of the snowdrop with her fingertips.

Then she noticed the silence.

Usually there was a constant buzz of hustle and bustle, of cars and children on bikes from the roads, of birds chatting in the trees.

And Prem. There was no chirrup of 'Good morning' or 'chai time' as was usually her welcome on Fridays.

She turned round to see him, asleep in his chair.

She knew then, didn't she?

She knew the moment she unlocked the door.

The moment she saw the snowdrops.

The moment Prem didn't answer her back.

His cup of chai was resting on the arm of his chair.

'Prem,' her voice was small now. There was a rush of blood in her ears, blocking out the world around her.

Every blade of grass was an obstacle in her way. Every blade of grass was a warning. Don't get any closer. Your life was better there, touching that snowdrop, imagining Prem's eyes lighting up at seeing them emerge.

But when she reached him, knees on the ground, she threw herself in his lap. She picked up his hand, holding it tightly in hers, her finger grazing his wedding ring. The cold of the metal slicing through her.

'Prem,' she said again, praying, hoping to hear his voice. Her brain racked itself for the sound. Had she forgotten already? She'd never thought she'd need to remember.

But she knew there would be no reply. She knew his face in sleep, she'd watched him for so many years falling asleep late at night, or right before he woke first thing in the morning.

Prem wasn't sleeping. His eyes were closed, but his mouth was held open slightly, in an expression he never made.

'No, it's too soon,' she said firmly. As though that might change the course of time.

She was rooted to the spot. She could feel the tsunami of anger and hurt and pain holding itself back for now, just in case he woke up to ask her why she was being so silly.

She looked up then at his face. She thought about the wheeze in his laugh she'd stopped noticing. 'It's nothing to worry about,' he'd said when his chest cramped, forcing him to drop whatever he was holding. 'I'm fine, it's not me you have to worry about,' he always said.

Hadn't she always known? Nothing lasts forever.

She put her face into his chest now. She thought about screaming. But no sound came out.

Maya stayed outside with Prem until the undertakers came, carrying him gently, carefully, but not carefully enough. Maya watched every move, even though Alma told her to come away, to come inside.

But this was her husband, the man she loved, the man she'd raised her daughter with, the man she wanted to spend the rest of her life with, the man she'd imagined beside her at their daughter's wedding. The man she'd imagined her old age with. But they hadn't even had the chance to get there.

She watched because she was still waiting for him to wake up at any moment – to tell her that he had only been sleeping. He'd been so tired recently, work had been so busy, he'd not been looking after himself and needed a lie-down. He rarely got enough sleep.

As Maya watched, Alma was in her kitchen, trying her best to make chai. Only chai would do. The mug that Prem had poured her for their eleven o'clock chai date still sat on the counter – Maya wouldn't touch it. She thought she might keep it forever.

How would she tell Hiral? Prem had walked her to school early that morning. On the way, side by side, she'd have told him about her friends at school, friends changing every day, her favourite lessons, her least favourite teachers, and he would have kissed her goodbye, then crossed the road before they got to the gates. She was at secondary school now, and too grown-up to be seen dropped off at the gates by her dad. And that was it. That was the last she'd ever see of her father.

Neither of them had been able to say goodbye.

Bina arrived that afternoon. Alma sat in the living room as the two sisters drank their chai, bitter but warm. Alma talked – she was the background noise, she didn't expect a response. She filled the silence. She let them tune in and out. Maya's eyes remained rooted to the wall in the living room. Soon a photo of her husband would hang there. A photograph with a garland on it. Telling the world, 'That's my husband. He's dead.'

Her stomach knotted.

Bina tried to laugh at one of Alma's dirty jokes, but she cried instead. Maya watched her. Every muscle was numb. Prem would have laughed his head off.

'I'm so sorry, Maya,' Alma said then, for the first time. Her voice cracked. 'He was the best of them.'

That night, once Maya and Bina had done the impossible job of telling Hiral, they'd both curled up together and fallen asleep in the spare bedroom, with Hiral crying herself to sleep in her mother's arms. In Hiral's face, in her eyes, her tears, Maya saw Prem.

'We have to prepare,' Maya said to Bina the next morning, already dressed in white. 'Thirteen days,' she said.

Prem's spirit remained in the house for thirteen days. They shouldn't wash their hair, they shouldn't cook, they should just pray.

Alma and Bina sent word to neighbours, friends and family – in quiet hushed phone calls, in conversations on the street, in letters and postcards. And at every mealtime, someone would appear on the doorstep with a dish. Erol was the first to arrive, laden with food he'd made. He barely said a word, his eyes red, enflamed, enraged by his broken heart. But he sat with them on the living-room floor. He bowed his head in respect.

'I knew he didn't want to face me over the chessboard,' Erol said eventually, and Maya smiled at the thought.

The next day Ade and Yusuf arrived. 'We'll stay here for as long as you need us,' they said. 'We've taken time off work, so don't worry about us. We don't need to get back yet.' They came almost every day for a week, with a new dish made by Ade's mother Funmi, Isha or Kelly. Their faces were downcast, their eyes red. Every time Maya saw them, she gave them a hug, wishing she could make it all okay again. Wishing Prem was here to do the same.

'It'll be okay,' Alma said, as Maya fell asleep next to her friend, their heads thrown back against the sofa, Morris on Alma's lap. From the moment he'd entered Alma's house, the cat had sensed it was a place of sadness. His cuddly demeanour was subdued. He became a quiet comfort. But how Maya wished she hadn't gone with Alma to the shelter that day. How she wished she'd been with Prem, drinking chai. Maybe she could have saved him.

Could she have called someone before it was too late? A blood clot, they'd said. It had been in his body for a long time, they suspected. Unnoticed. Brushed over. Waiting. Because Prem never complained. Prem just got on with life.

'It'll be okay with time. It won't be okay for a while,' Alma continued. 'It will be a pile of shit until then.' Maya nodded. She squeezed her eyes shut, searching for his face in her memory. *How could you leave me, Prem? This is too soon. Too sudden. We still have so much to do. You have so much life to live.*

On the thirteenth day, after the funeral, Maya sat in the garden and burned a candle. She sat on the lawn, plucking any petals she could find from the plants surrounding her, and she cupped them in her palms. It wasn't the right thing to do, it wasn't the puja she had planned. But it was her own silent ritual to Prem, to let his spirit go.

She looked back towards the houses. Alma was silhouetted in her kitchen window. She hadn't let Maya out of her sight.

'Love,' Alma called through the window eventually. 'Come in. Hiral's having a nap. Let's watch some telly – I'll let you choose. I've made that veggie lasagne too.'

'With seasoning this time?' Maya said, trying to bring a brightness to her face.

'Of course not . . .' Alma replied quietly, gritting her teeth in embarrassment. 'Come on, don't fuss.'

On Alma's kitchen table sat a little cluster of snowdrops in a tiny vase.

'He liked them,' Alma said. 'I picked them for him.'

Chapter 25

Winston

February 2019

'What do you think of these?' Bernice pointed to a selection of hazel trees in one of the gardening books she'd picked up from Stoke Newington Bookshop, recommended by her garden designer friend, Clemmie. 'We could see if B&Q have some? They're really nice in winter and spring, I think.'

Winston glanced over the trees, hmmming noncommittally. His eyes were still on the banana trees in the booklet in front of him.

'Oh, Winston,' Bernice said. 'We can't . . . it would look too out of place.'

'Would it? Loads of people have them,' Winston said, shrugging. 'And it'd look so good from the other side of the wall. It might encourage some people to pop in.'

Bernice gave him a sharp look then. 'This is a *private* garden. We don't want anyone coming in.'

'All right, but I just mean . . . well, maybe if we make it really nice, we could apply for those open garden things. Those are popular, aren't they?'

Bernice gave him an odd look then. Like she was trying to read him. Winston had spent the last few days flicking through a more recent set of leaflets and photographs that had been posted through his door. *Open Garden Drop-In Day – Come Grow with Your Neighbours!* and *Spring Is Upon Us! Time to Get Planting – We Need Your Help!*

The messages felt more and more urgent. He flicked through his stack of letters. There were so many of them. A whole collection of photographs, leaflets, notes. It felt like someone was trying to hurry them up. Get them to open the garden up.

With this latest envelope, Winston had opened up his phone and started learning more about community gardens. There was all sorts of research showing how good they were for people, how gardening aided mindfulness, and gardening in groups reduced loneliness and helped your mental health.

It wasn't what he'd intended . . . but now he could see the garden taking shape, it would be nice to let people in. To share it. His mother's words came to him then: 'Gardens aren't something you can keep all to yourself. It's about enjoying it, in all the big and small ways. Together.'

'Okay . . . we can think about it,' he said to Bernice then, moving the subject on. 'I guess we'd need to run anything past Mr James and maybe my new flatmates, when we finally find out who they might be.'

'No luck yet?'

'People keep finding other places. I met a few people the other week who seemed perfect. When Mr James offered them the room, they'd already found somewhere else. Things are moving so quickly. But Mr James is being really reasonable. I think he wants to give me a bit of space, so he's not forcing anything through yet.'

'That's decent of him.' Bernice's eyebrows were raised, as if to say she wouldn't do the same in his position.

'So,' Winston said, chirpily, wanting to forget the whole flatmate search, 'if we were going to get more hazel trees, where would they go?' He stepped out onto the patio from Bernice's kitchen in his trainers, treading gently over the frosted paving slabs before reaching the lawn, which, he now noticed, was punctuated by a cluster of snowdrops, their little white heads nodding at the ground, wobbling in the wind. The first signs of life!

He could see shoots coming up elsewhere – hints of crocuses and irises to come, but these bright pops of white were the star of the show right now.

'Bernice,' he said, 'did you plant these?'

'Hmm?' came a voice behind him. 'What did you say?'

'Have you seen these?'

Bernice shuffled her boots on and joined him outside.

She looked down at the ground. 'Oh, wow! Snowdrops. Aren't they beautiful?'

'Did you plant them?' Winston asked, bending down to graze his fingers over the soft petals of the flower heads.

'No, didn't you?'

'Not snowdrops.'

'Maybe they were here before,' Bernice said.

'I've never noticed them.'

'Maybe you weren't looking,' she said, and Winston knew she was right. In the depths of winter, these snowdrops had poked their heads through, demanding attention, showing the world they were still going. And it felt like the most obvious, ostentatious display of resilience. But perhaps he'd simply never been looking for such a display before.

Small green stubs and spikes were poking through the earth, hinting at the tulips that might emerge in a few weeks' time, and there were the pots of miniature irises with their spindly leaves like extravagant grasses, biding their time, waiting for their moment to shine.

There was hope here, he just hadn't been searching for it.

'They're beautiful,' Winston whispered. 'I wish I could save them, keep them like this for ever.'

'There'll be more around the corner. Even more,' Bernice said, tapping him on the shoulder, and shuffling back to her kitchen, pulling her scarf around her tightly.

Winston sat himself down in his old wooden chair – *Handmade by Prem* – and simply watched as the heads of the snowdrops bobbed in the late winter breeze.

Part III

SPRING

Wednesday, 20 March 2019

Our favourite season is here. It's been a long, long winter. Although some highlights, of course. On Christmas Day, I got to visit Erol with Jenny, Sal and Angela – Sal's wife. Do you remember her? It was lovely but also reminded me how much has changed . . . I bought him a book from Stoke Newington Bookshop. Do you remember when it first opened? Hiral used to love it in there. It's the first time I've been to a shop in ages (Sal brings me my groceries . . . very kind of him!), but there was so much to choose from and it was lovely to browse again. I kept seeing books, novels mainly, that I'd love to give to you. And there were so many gardening books to choose from! I got Erol a historical mystery – he really likes them. The cover was bright red, but I can't remember the title any more. Erol was pleased though!

When I wake up these days, I hear the birds before I even open my eyes. It always reminds me of the cold yet bright mornings all those years ago, with the sun bursting through the clouds, bringing a warmth we'd long forgotten over the winter months. I used to love watching Susie lounging in the beds of bulbs, sprawled out between the new shoots. We'd be shooing her away so as not to cause any damage. And Prem would be sitting in his chair with his paper and his chai, talking to himself and the birds.

I tend to wander up to Newington Green so I can get a cup of tea from this lovely café, which I think you'd approve of. Sometimes, if I want a longer walk, I go along Albion Road to Clissold Park. I went the other day. On a weekend. I hadn't been for a while, but the man who plays the accordion was there.

He never fails to brighten my day. He's so incredibly talented – he brings such cheer and joy as you wander along Church Street. In the old days, Fraser would have been dragging me on, skipping ahead to chase the pigeons and squirrels in the park. It was one of his favourite things to do. I never minded him chasing the pigeons, as long as he left the ducks alone. There's a tree in the park now with hundreds of shoes hanging by their shoelaces. I don't remember when it started, but there's almost a whole shoe shop up there now. I imagine the sight would have driven Fraser mad – jumping up, trying to catch them.

As I wander through the park, I feel a little out of place. You used to say that, didn't you? Well . . . it's my turn to feel 'old and stale'. Your words, not mine. There are so many youngsters with elegant, long coats, carrying coffee cups in one hand, holding conversations with the other. It's so leisurely. To have so much time. To be so confident and poised at such a young age. When I first arrived here, I was nothing like that. I was constantly frazzled, like I could never keep up. I'd get lost all the time. And I don't really remember a time when there wasn't something *I was rushing to do, especially after Hiral was born.*

It wasn't until I met you properly, and we started becoming friends, and I was meeting everyone around me, that I felt that Prem and I really belonged. The youngsters I see now – it's like they've never doubted it for a moment.

Whenever I'm in Clissold Park, I always think about the plans Prem and I had. We thought we'd travel when Hiral went to uni. Or maybe one day, deep into our old age, we pictured ourselves living by the sea, so we could watch the waves every day, feel the wind in our hair. I wish we hadn't made plans now. Every moment without him feels harder because of all we lost, all I wanted to share with him. Watching Hiral grow up and live her life is the biggest privilege I have, but I so wanted to share it with him. I wish he could see what a wonderful young woman she's become. How wise she is, how thoughtful, just like him.

Anyway . . . I'm sorry. I don't want to be sad, not really.

And I almost forgot to tell you! I bumped into Yusuf the other day: it was wonderful to see his friendly face. I don't see people we used to know very much any more – Jenny, of course, always with her mischievous schemes, she barely leaves me alone – but not many others. It makes home that little bit less homely. I know Jenny feels the same.

Anyway, Yusuf – he was with Emmanuel's baby son. I know! I can barely believe it. Yusuf: a grandfather! He's nearly sixty now! That made me feel practically mummified. He told me that Isha is moving further away still. She's been living in Enfield for the past few years, but Yusuf and Kelly are moving away to Bristol, and she's going to live with them. So, while this is spring, it really does seem that things are coming to an end. But I suppose that's always the way. With each new season, there comes an end to the old, and a start for the new. I'm only wondering where I fit into that cycle.

But the garden, and of course Prem's snowdrops, live on. No matter where we are. I promise you that.

Love always,

Your friend,

Maya x

Chapter 26

Bernice

March 2019

Triiiiing. Triiiing.

What in the hell was this all about? The first ring felt like it was in her dream. The second trill forced her heart to explode out of her chest. Bernice's mind jumped straight to Seb – had something happened? Or was it Simon? Had she overslept?

She looked at the clock on her bedside table. No. It was 7 a.m.

Was her clock wrong?

In her dazed panic, heart pumping with fright, she threw her dressing gown over her pyjamas, and chucked herself down the stairs, holding the banister tight in case her legs ran off without her.

Flinging the front door open, she was met with a '*Hello!*' from the chirpiest man in the greenest outfit – sweatshirt, combat trousers, cap. 'Got a banana here for Mrs Bernice—'

Before he could say her married name, she jumped in with 'Yes, that's me!' She half-expected him to have a banana in his hand, until she spotted the huge box beside him, a silky green leaf curling out of the top of it.

The banana tree.

She'd bought it as a surprise for Winston. She'd instantly felt guilty after shutting down his suggestion, the photographs of his mother's garden flooding her mind. How Winston's face had softened at the memory.

She'd also been haunted – in a good way – by the image of the two women in the mystery post: Alma and Maya. Two neighbours, digging in together. This was her and Winston's *shared* garden. And he deserved to love it as much as she did. Plus, after doing lots of research, and seeing banana trees in other front gardens across the neighbourhood, she realized they really *did* look rather amazing.

Now, looking at the huge box, practically towering over her, she worried whether it was *too* much.

Do you even know how to care for a bloody banana tree? her inner critic (who sounded awfully like Simon) asked.

'God, I hope so,' she muttered out loud to herself, remembering how much she'd spent on it.

The delivery driver looked at her, then at the tree. 'All right if I leave it here?'

She was in her dressing gown, in no state to carry it through to the garden. She could ask him to take it around to the gate, but she didn't want Winston to see it too early. It was meant to be a surprise.

'Mummy?'

Bernice jumped out of her skin.

It was Sebastian, also in his dressing gown, creeping down the stairs towards her. 'Who is it?'

'Sebastian! You scared me!'

'Is it Winston's banana plant?!' His eyes grew wide with delight. 'Wow! It is going to be bea-ooooo-tiful!'

'Shh,' Bernice glanced towards the grinning delivery man. 'Come on, Sebastian. Remember it's a surprise! Winston might hear you through the walls.'

'I'll leave you to it, then, ma'am,' the delivery man said. 'Looks like you've got a good strong chap there to help you out.'

For a second, Bernice's gaze roamed the hallway, in case there was an intruder she hadn't noticed. Nope. He really did mean her ten-year-old son.

Of course . . . flatter the child, but leave me to deal with the massive plant on my own. Wonderful.

'Thank you very much, sir,' Bernice said, her voice flat.

'Have a lovely day!'

Once the delivery driver was well on his way, Bernice started wrestling the plant into her house, with Sebastian pulling at the lower end of the box, uselessly. She heaved it up over the doorstep, wondering how on earth she was going to get it all the way through the house to the garden. As soon as she shut the door behind her, she felt a moment of relief, away from the watchful gaze of Nosy Number 80.

'Sebastian, why don't you go put the kettle on for me? I'll see if I can lift this myself.'

She shuffled the box six inches forward at a time, pushing with each of her slippered feet in turn, her hands keeping the top balanced.

'Mummy,' Sebastian called from the kitchen, as she wriggled the banana tree over the wonky floorboard.

'Yes, darling?' She heard the strain in her own voice, wondering if he noticed it too.

'Don't be grumpy!' he said back.

'Sorry, I'm . . .' she heaved the box once more with a thunk, 'trying to do this.'

'Well, I . . . I don't want to see Daddy today. Can I stay here with you and help with the garden?'

'How come you don't want to see Daddy?' Bernice stood up straight, forgetting the hefty banana plant in front of her.

'No reason,' Sebastian replied. 'I feel like I'm missing out on all the fun bits of the gardening with you. You only do it on Sundays and it's not fair. I did the gardening first. You didn't even *talk* to Winston until *I* started gardening with him!'

'Well, sweetie,' Bernice relaxed, realizing she'd been clamping her jaw shut. 'I only help a little bit really. I like to do some gardening to stop me missing you so much!'

'But if I was here then you could do the gardening and not miss me at all.'

He was leaning against the marble worktop, eyebrows raised, and for a moment she saw the young man he would become.

'How's the tea coming along?' she asked, changing the subject.

'I thought you wanted me to put the kettle on, I didn't realize you wanted me to *make* the tea. Goodness, I have to do everything around here,' he said, with such boldness she could have sworn she'd heard him say the words in her own voice.

Bernice continued to heave the banana tree outside, giving it one final heave over the threshold, feeling the rope of her dressing gown come loose and, in slow motion, her hands flew to her robe. She tied it back up as the banana tree fell to the ground, landing on its side with a splat: THIS WAY UP shouted out at her from the side of the box, judgemental.

'Oh fuck,' she said.

'Mummy!'

'Sorry, Seb,' she picked the box up, but as she did, she noticed Winston in his rotten wooden chair, cigarette in his mouth, baggy T-shirt, jogging bottoms and flip-flops on. A mischievous smile curled his lips.

'Mrs Bernice,' he said. 'Language!' He puffed a plume of smoke out in the opposite direction, before stubbing the cigarette out promptly. 'What's that?' He nodded towards the box.

'How come you're up so early?' she asked accusatorily.

'Someone tried to drop a banana tree at my door . . . I told them they must have the wrong house.' He looked her box up and down.

'Oh shit!' she muttered again. 'Sorry, Seb,' she called behind her automatically.

'Winston,' Seb said firmly, as though embarking on a business transaction.

'Sebastian,' Winston replied, matching his tone.

'*I* want to stay and help with the garden today, but Mum won't let me. She says I've got to go see my dad today.'

'That's all right,' Winston replied. 'You can help with the garden another day. Maybe one evening this week when I'm not working? We can plant something fun. It's spring now so it's going to be busy. We'll still need you looking after it on the other days of the week. Look at all these tulips and irises that need tending to, and the daffodils that need deadheading.' He gestured to the pots around him, overflowing with colours: reds, yellows, purples and blues.

'And someone's got to start planting some of those onions and things, don't they?' Seb said, hopefully.

'Yes, they do. Will that be you?' Winston asked.

'Yes,' Seb said decidedly, allowing his shoulders to drop, finally satisfied with the outcome of his negotiations.

'Bernice, can I see the banana?' Winston's eyes had lit up – and she immediately relaxed.

'Of course. I'll go and get some proper clothes on,' she gestured towards her stupid dressing gown, 'but I'll leave you in peace. You and the banana can have a moment together.'

Winston and Seb started pulling the box apart, gradually revealing the plant underneath. 'Wow!' they said in delighted unison.

'It's so tropical!' Seb said. 'Like the ones in your pictures.'

Winston laughed softly, his face glowing in the spring sunshine.

She'd done the right thing. She'd brought a little bit of Winston's mum, and his first home, into the garden.

'So, where's it going to go?' Winston asked, when they were sitting out in the garden a few hours later, after Simon had picked Seb up. He hadn't stopped stroking the leaves of the banana tree all this time. Reunited with an old friend. Unable to tear himself away.

'By the gate?' she said. She thought Winston would be able to see it there as soon as he looked out of his kitchen window, bringing him a little closer to his mum whenever he was making a morning cup of tea.

'You got a big one, didn't you?' Winston said, eyeing up the monstrous plant once more.

'Yeah, well . . .'

'My mum always used to buy the small ones, they grow so fast. A bit cheaper that way.'

Bernice looked away. This was news to her, but she wasn't about to admit it. 'I wanted to go for something immediately dramatic.'

'Was it expensive?' Winston asked.

'Got it on offer,' she lied. 'Anyway, how are you?'

'Delighted about this,' he said, beaming. 'Thank you so much. I wish Mum was here to see this.'

'I hope she'd approve.'

'She would, I should send a photo to my sister Ruth. She always loved Mum's banana trees.'

Ruth . . .

Bernice remembered those missed calls she'd seen. The name flashing up on his phone. His *sister*, then.

They spent half an hour working out which way they should plant it, admiring it from all angles: from the back of the garden; from the patio; from the gate. In every view, it looked glorious – 'and it's only going to look *more* amazing with time,' Winston said.

When it was settled, they started to dig, pausing every so often to check if the hole was big enough, placing the pot of the banana inside. Every time, it was just a little too shallow, or a little too narrow.

'Oh fucking hell,' Bernice said, frustrated. 'This is never going to end.' She slumped onto Winston's chair for a breather. 'Has Lewis been in touch again?'

Winston stopped. Shrugged. 'He sends me photos of the house every so often, now he's moved in. He wants me to visit.'

'Can I see?'

Winston pulled out his phone, showing her the photos. The front garden, lush and green, invited you in with its fern fronds and tall grasses, pockets of wildflowers here and there. And the cottage looked like something out of a fairy tale. It had a thatched roof, and all the bedrooms had sloping ceilings. The rooms downstairs had big black beams throughout, with a beautiful fireplace in the living room and a staircase that looked like something out of Narnia. There was a summer house in the garden in a ghastly baby blue, and an office, or more accurately a library, with French windows opening onto a back garden crying out for someone to love it.

She could picture Winston there. A few months ago, she wouldn't have been able to see him anywhere other than the rotten wooden chair in the garden, dropping his fag ends into an empty chopped tomato tin resting on the arm. But this house could do with Winston's gardening skills – as fledgling as they were. This place needed someone like him to care for it.

'What's keeping you here? Is it your job?'

'No, I like my job, but I want to be here, in London. I want to be close to Angela and Sal. And, as surprising as Lewis finds it, I'm also kinda happy renting for now.'

'They'd be happy for you, you know? If you moved in with Lewis, I'm sure they'd visit.'

'They never give themselves time off from the shop.' Winston deposited a mound of earth beside his right foot. 'And I don't want the life Lewis wants. I've been thinking about it, properly. Wondering why I stay here. London was never really my dream – it was my dad who wanted me to work in finance in the City – but now I'm here, I can't actually imagine living anywhere else. It gets buried at times – beneath the busyness, the stress, the hustle and bustle – but sometimes I do feel like I belong here. I've thought about Oxford. But there aren't so many people who look like me there. Here, in London, I blend in, I *fit*. I never want to stand out any more than I do.'

'I get it,' she said.

Winston immediately shook his head, not looking at her. 'Bernice, you really, really don't. London is the closest I've felt to belonging since I left home; even there I didn't feel like I could be completely myself. But you . . . *you* can belong anywhere. This world is made for people like you, Bernice. It's not made for people like me.'

'You're right,' Bernice swallowed down her guilt, wondering if this was inadequate too. 'I know I mostly say the wrong things. But I can be a good listener too.' Bernice held her breath but Winston said no more. 'If you need to talk about this stuff ever, I promise I'll listen.'

Winston smiled gently and walked to the other side of the garden. Bernice could hear Radio 4 playing loudly a few doors down, hoots and horns from Stoke Newington Road, and she could smell the smoke of premature barbecues.

Winston was young, he had his whole life ahead of him. She really hoped there'd be a chance for him to fall in love with his life again.

She waited for him to say more, but as he trudged back over to her, his gloved hands caked in a gooey-liquidy-brown gunge, he sloped right over to the banana tree and said: 'Right, is that hole deep enough yet?'

Suddenly there was a cackle, followed by a loud, booming 'Hello!' from the other side of the garden wall.

Bernice shot a quizzical look at Winston. He already had a smile plastered across his features. 'Hey, Jenny!'

'Can I come in?'

'Of course,' Winston leapt forward and pulled the rickety gate open with the newly installed handle, donated by Sal. 'Mind the half-dug hole.'

Bernice grinned awkwardly at this old lady in a fur coat – Jenny – as she shuffled in with her Zimmer frame. She recognized her from the shop, chatting to Sal with such ease.

'Here, let me get you a chair,' Winston said, glancing at the rotten thing and hurrying towards his kitchen, where he dragged out a sturdier Ikea one.

Abandoning her Zimmer frame, Jenny went straight over to the wooden chair with the ease of a swan gliding over a lake. 'Don't worry, Vince – I'll sit in this one. This looks like the one my old friend Prem made. Decades ago. Surprised it's still going.'

Bernice noticed Winston's eyebrows raise in interest. He opened and closed his mouth as if to ask a question, before changing his mind. 'Cup of tea, Jenny?' he said simply.

'Oh, that's okay, dear. My George is expecting me home soon for tea and cake.' Then she turned to Bernice. 'It's his birthday, you see.' Jenny enunciated each syllable carefully, as though Bernice might not understand a word she said otherwise. 'Now,

Vincent, looks like you've been doing a lot of good work on this garden.' She winked at him, as if they were in on a secret together. Bernice's gaze flicked between the two of them . . . 'Looks like you've had a little nudge in the right direction?' Jenny said cheekily, her eyes twinkling.

Curious, thought Bernice. She thought about the mystery post addressed to *The Lady at Number 77*, the pictures of the garden, the hidden message she couldn't quite grasp. Was *Jenny* one of the women?

No . . . she couldn't be. They were called Alma and Maya . . . she was sure of it. But could Jenny have something to do with it?

'You should invite some of your old pals round, you know. Now that it's getting warmer, and you've got this big old garden to show off,' Jenny continued pointedly.

'We'll see, Jenny, it's not in the best state for hosting,' Winston said, looking to Bernice for help.

'Very well, Vince,' Jenny said, a smile wrinkling her face. 'I'll wait for my invite in the post . . . Whenever you're ready.'

She pushed herself up, surprisingly elegantly, and swan-glided back to her Zimmer frame, making her way out of the gate over the upturned earth without looking back.

When Bernice heard Jenny's Zimmer frame wheels turn the corner on to Eastbourne Road, well out of earshot, she allowed herself to breathe a sigh of relief. Winston was already turning some compost into the hole she'd just dug. 'She's a bit forward, isn't she?'

Winston looked up at her. 'Who? Jenny?'

'Yeah. Inviting herself round . . .' She kept her eyes on Winston, searching for any clues.

'She's got to be. To uphold her title of most sociable person in the whole of North London.'

Bernice turned away, unable to explain why she felt odd, out of place suddenly. Like Jenny had looked all the way through her.

She looked back at her house, the Farrow and Ball duck-egg paint in the kitchen catching her eye, the brand-new kitchen island, pristine. Within the walls of that house, though it had taken a while to get used to, she felt at home. But when she was out in the world, out talking to the people who lived on her road, she still wasn't a part of the community, was she? Winston thought she belonged anywhere – but she didn't belong here yet.

And one last question remained. Did Jenny post the envelope through her door? The most sociable person in North London . . . could that mean she was at the centre of it all?

Chapter 27

Winston

March 2019

'Thanks for coming round!' Winston called, closing the door behind the two people he had just interviewed as potential new flatmates: a couple called Darlene and Heidi. As he sat down on the sofa, shutting his eyes, he went over every little moment of the meeting. Wondering if he'd embarrassed himself. If they liked him. If he liked them. Watching them look at each other, appraising the house silently between themselves, had been torture. A secret language held between stares, nudges in the ribs, and squeezed hands walking down corridors.

They'd liked the room at least. He'd refused to show them his. He didn't want them to wonder why he, the single one, had the biggest room. It didn't make sense. Except for the fact Winston wanted to stay. He wanted the room with the Velux window that looked over the gardens. And . . . in all honesty . . . he wanted to live with the memories of a life with Lewis. He wanted to live *here* with Lewis. But it was too late for that now.

'What about the garden?' Heidi had asked. 'It looks lush. Is it shared?'

She'd watched as Seb ran outside blasting bits of fence and wall with a hose as he 'watered' the garden. Thoroughly inefficient. Winston couldn't help but smile.

'Yeah, shared. The neighbours next door are a small family – mother and son. They're lovely. We've been working together to tidy it up,' he said. It wasn't even a lie. After all the altercations they'd had when Bernice first moved in, he never imagined that they'd get to this point. 'It's a huge garden. So we need as much help as we can get. Are you keen gardeners?'

Heidi and Darlene had exchanged a glance with each other. Winston couldn't translate.

'I am,' Darlene said. 'I . . . I'd love to help if we . . . if we get to move in.'

'Sure, sure,' Winston had nodded. He didn't want to give anything away. Mr James was leaving the final decision up to him. It was more power than Winston had ever had. And he had no idea what he wanted. He was still coming to terms with the concept of sharing with anyone.

Now, out of all the viewings, he'd met two singletons and two couples. Did he want the doctor who worked late nights and confessed he hated socializing? Or did he want the overly friendly couple, who would probably invite their friends round all the time, living their shared life in the home that used to be his and Lewis's?

Darlene and Heidi, on the other hand, seemed nice. A good balance. But still . . . they were strangers in his home.

Whatever happened. Things were going to change.

'You know, if you need more hands on deck in the garden, you should open it up as a neighbourhood garden,' Darlene had said. 'There's street access. I've volunteered in a couple in Hackney before – they host workshops, children's gardening mornings. Could be really fun. It's a cool vibe?'

Winston noted the upward inflection at the end of her sentence.

'Maybe,' he'd said. He thought of the mysterious Maya and Alma again. The Bonfire Night party, the huddle of neighbours around the incinerator. The Google searches he'd done, the benefits of community gardens. 'But the neighbour next door – she's got a young kid. She wants it to be a private space.'

'I get that. But it's a shared space now anyway.'

'Yeah, but only with me,' Winston said. He wanted to share the garden with everyone, and a few months ago, he'd have loved the idea of going against Bernice's wishes, but he knew it wasn't his decision alone to make. They were a gardening team now – and their decisions should be made together.

'What were they like?' Bernice asked later that day, as they sat outside with cups of tea in the garden.

'Nice,' Winston nodded.

'Ooof,' Bernice groaned. 'That bad?'

'What do you mean?'

'Nice. Doesn't that mean bland?'

'No,' Winston laughed. 'Sometimes nice means *nice*. And they really do seem it. I just don't know if I want to be living with a couple. Sort of feels like a kick in the teeth.'

'I see your point.' She slurped her hot tea loudly.

'They had ideas about the garden,' he said cautiously. 'They suggested we open it up as a sort of neighbourhood garden. Put it up for a community garden scheme or something. She mentioned children's gardening sessions that they do in other community spaces . . . and open days,' he continued, trying to sound nonchalant. 'I know you really want it to be a private space but . . .' He trailed off there, unsure what to say next.

Since those mysterious letters had started dropping through his door, there seemed to be signs everywhere for them to open up the garden. He needed to start relaying those signs to Bernice too.

'It could be really rewarding,' Winston continued, glancing into the kitchen where Seb was doing his homework at the table, around the trays of sweet peas, almost ready to be planted. 'And Seb could meet people in the neighbourhood, like beyond his school. Get him stuck into the community spirit. He'd love it.'

Bernice's face transformed; she suddenly looked like the Queen of Sheba all over again. 'Seb does things for the community,' she replied sharply. He'd overstepped the mark, hadn't he? He knew Bernice much better now, and while they were friends of sorts . . . she'd never tolerate taking advice from him about her kid. 'I mean . . . his school is hosting an Easter fête soon. That's for the community.'

'I know, I know,' Winston wished he hadn't brought it up at all. 'It wouldn't have to be open all the time. We could start off with one vegetable bed or something that we shared with the community, and people could plant and pick things? Then we could see how it went. You see, Angela was telling me this garden used to be run as a community garden before. By two best friends.'

'Alma and Maya,' Bernice said automatically, her head turning so fast to look at him he was surprised she didn't get whiplash. 'Was it you?'

'What?' Winston looked at her. How did she know? What did she mean?

'Did you put the letters through my door?'

Winston's eyes widened.

'About the garden? The community garden . . . that used to be here . . . you've been trying to convince me to do it for ages, haven't you?'

'Did you say you got letters? Like . . . an envelope of stuff?' he said.

'Yes, exactly that,' Bernice said, putting her tea down, a face of muddled confusion. 'I want a private garden, Winston, you know that. I want a garden that Seb can run around in whenever he wants. So, can you stop with all the secret messages?'

'Bernice, it wasn't me, I promise. But I've been getting them too. And I suppose it's those letters that actually gave *me* the idea about it. If we're putting all this work into it, wouldn't it be great to have other people enjoy it? To create something really special?' He looked at the banana tree, waving in the wind, picturing his mother's face, the look of joy when she showed friends and neighbours around her own garden.

Behind the eucalyptus tree, the thick, ominous clouds hanging in the sky started to part, and the glow of the sun burst through. 'Bernice, you might love it. You'd get to meet more people in the area. I'd love for you to meet some of the characters I see at the shop. They're lovely. There's community here, somewhere in Stoke Newington. We've just got to invite them in if we want to be involved.'

'I don't know.'

'You don't have to mistrust everyone, Bernice. It's a friendly place. People are *nice*.'

'I'm not mistrustful,' Bernice snapped, standing up quickly and grabbing her tea, marching towards the kitchen door.

'Please, think about it, okay?' he said, as a wash of brilliant green flew into his line of vision and landed on one of the yoghurt pots.

A parakeet, like something from another world. Another life.

Chapter 28

Maya

April 1988

'Hello there.' It was the landlord, Mr James, coming through the garden gate. He was dressed head to toe in navy blue, and accompanied by a man Maya didn't recognize, dressed all in brown and smelling of nerves. 'This is Martin,' Mr James said.

Behind her, Maya could hear Hiral and her friend, Iffy, running around the kitchen, causing havoc. Maya allowed Hiral to have her friends round all the time now; she wanted the house to be filled with noise, with life, to cover up the emptiness that permeated every corner. Hiral, her laughter and her tears, had kept Maya breathing these last few months. If it hadn't been for her, she'd have stayed in bed, desperate for the world to swallow her up. But for Hiral, she kept going.

Seeing Mr James there, Maya's mind ran into overdrive: was the house too messy, could he penalize her for that? Should she make him a cup of tea? What was he here for? Was it the rent? He'd been kind for the last few months, allowing Maya to pay what she could. Sanjaykumar and Bina had been helping her out too. But maybe she'd been complacent.

Or was it something worse? *Waiting for the right time to sell.*

'Come in,' she said calmly. 'I'm sorry, my daughter has a friend round, so they're . . . having fun!'

'Never apologize for yourself,' Prem had told her, over and over again, because she had this tendency to say sorry to Mr James, even when she tried really hard not to. 'You never need to apologize for living in your own home.' But whenever Mr James came to visit, Maya was always reminded that this wasn't her house, not really. *He* grew up here. She pictured her parents, and her sister, running around their home in Mombasa, drying out papad on hot summer days on the roof, playing in the garden – she couldn't imagine watching another family living there. It meant that whenever Mr James came round, she wanted to become invisible. A ghost walking the floors, leaving no trace of herself behind.

'All right, Alma?' Mr James said, and Martin gave a polite hello too, as they walked through the garden.

'Oh, look who's here,' Alma said sharply, stepping in their path. 'You do realize how much this family has gone through in the last few months? They don't need you here disrupting everything. What you here for today, *Mr James*? Bringing up the bastard fence again, are you?'

Maya watched from the kitchen doorway, the three figures silhouetted against the late-afternoon sky.

'Martin's here to do a valuation, measure up a few things . . .' he looked at Maya then, cautiously, ' . . .we'll start with our side of the garden. I hoped we could take some photographs too, but the house isn't quite in the best shape. Maybe we can come round next week instead for that? What do you think?'

Maya shrugged, feeling shame and worry spread like pinpricks over her.

'Charlie, what the bloody hell do you think you're doing?' Alma said forcefully.

'We'll have to approximate the boundary, I'm afraid, Martin,' James said. 'And Alma, that fence will need to go up eventually. We don't like that you have the whole bloody neighbourhood round here.'

'Who's *we*? You and your crone of a father? Do you have any opinions of your own or are you just his puppet?'

'Looking forward, we're likely to sell, Alma,' he said brusquely, losing his patience.

'Why?'

'My father, he doesn't want us to have the stress of this place any more . . . He doesn't like us renting to . . .'

'What do you mean?'

Maya tried to tune it out – she knew where this was going. She didn't want to hear it.

'He doesn't want me renting it out to . . .' Mr James started, but looked at the ground. 'He . . . He's anxious we'll lose money.'

'You can't even say it, can you?' Alma snapped at him. 'You don't even believe in your father's bigoted, racist world view, yet you're happy to do his dirty work?'

Mr James looked at Martin, who stared down at the ground.

'This is my decision, Alma. Leave it to me. And thank you, Mrs Bhatt, I'm sorry to disturb you, we won't be too long,' Mr James said, storming through the kitchen door and into the house.

Maya followed him inside, and Martin trailed after. She couldn't turn round – she didn't want to see Alma's face. Alma owned her home. It would always be hers until she decided she didn't want it any longer. She wouldn't understand the fear Maya had always harboured in the pit of her stomach, buried away, so she didn't have to face it every single day. The fear that she and Hiral would one day be forced to move far away from here because rents were only rising.

Now, without Prem, without his way with words, without his salary, without a man to make them seem like a proper 'family', it would be harder. She'd be judged. She'd be treated like a liar, quizzed about how much she earned, how much she could afford. No one cared that she worked hard, that she and Prem had never once been late with their bills. They didn't care that they were clean, they'd treat the place with more care than anyone else imaginable. Maya knew none of that mattered to landlords or estate agents, not once they saw her foreign-sounding name, and the colour of her skin.

When Mr James had finished showing Martin around, she ambushed them both in the hallway.

'Mr James,' she called, as he was letting himself out, turning round to check for Martin. 'Will you give us notice?'

'What do you mean?'

'About selling. Will you give us plenty of notice?'

'Of course, Mrs Bhatt. I . . . It's not certain yet. A valuation . . . That's all for now. I'm sorry, I didn't want you to find out like this. I didn't . . . Alma just . . . She knows how to push my buttons.'

'It's okay,' she said to him, but really nothing about this was okay.

This was the only home Hiral had known. Prem's snowdrops . . . his snowdrops were here, they would come up every year. She couldn't leave them. Leave him. And Prem's chair, which no one had sat in since he'd passed away, it had stayed exactly where it was. She could never move it: she imagined him there, his soul still watching over them all from his favourite spot. 'Please give us time. It's hard . . . to find a home. The market is hard at the moment. And without Prem . . .' Maya stopped herself, before her voice broke. 'Things have been hard,' she said. 'In all sorts of ways.'

He nodded at her then, unable to meet her eye – but all Maya could think about was Alma, and the heartbreak of leaving her behind too. She thought of that Christmas night, with Alma locked outside. If someone else bought the house, would they look after her? Alma had made it very clear she would never leave this place, the eucalyptus tree, the memories of her life with her father, Susie's grave at the far end of the garden too . . . Her whole life was tied up here.

Martin shuffled out, squeezing past Maya.

'Pub then, mate?' Martin said. 'The Londesborough?'

The next morning, Maya unlocked the kitchen door to find a little posy of bluebells tied up with a piece of twine left on her doorstep. Underneath sat a note, in Alma's small caps handwriting.

MAYA – DON'T WORRY. I HAVE A PLAN. A X

Chapter 29

Maya

April 1988

A FEW WEEKS LATER, Mr James was back, under personal invitation from Alma.

'Hello, Miss Hiral,' Mr James said, as she ran past him in the garden. Twenty-six-year-old Ade was weeding the narrow central flower bed, full of spring bulbs. He was bopping along to 'Turn Your Love Around' by George Benson, which was booming out of the cassette tape player perched on Prem's table.

Maya and Alma were digging trenches to plant their early potatoes; it was one of Alma's favourite jobs of the year. One year, however, they'd had nothing but tiny marble-sized ones: all that waiting and hoping and digging over had gone to waste. Erol had seen a recipe in the newspaper, determined to make the best of them, and they'd made patatas bravas. Prem had loved them – he practically inhaled them before anyone else could get a look in.

Mr James cleared his throat to attract their attention, and when they both looked up, his face was tense. 'What can I help you with, Alma?' he asked, his voice formal. Maya could see from the look on Alma's face that she was up to something. She had to stare at her hands, her finger twisting over her wedding ring.

'Good of you to make it, Charlie. How's your dad doing?' Alma said sharply, not looking at him. Maya watched her friend like she was one of the police officers in *The Bill*.

'He's . . . fine, thanks,' he said, glancing round. 'Now, if you could just get to the point and tell me why you called me here.' Bicycle bells ring-a-ling-linged in the background.

Erol and Patrick wandered through the gate, nodding a hello in Alma's direction, before bopping along to George Benson too. They took themselves over to the shed. Erol started rummaging around for secateurs and the two men got to work deadheading their way round the garden. Maya smiled as she noticed Erol wearing the gardening gloves Prem had embroidered for her. Her heart caught, mid-air for a moment, her breath held with it.

'Do you remember how much your mother loved this garden? Always used to help out with the vegetables?' Alma said, her voice softening. 'You know, Charlie, this neighbourhood isn't always as friendly as it was when you and I were growing up. People aren't looked after in the same way. But this garden, the one we all created decades ago – *this* is a safe place. Or at least, we want it to be.' Alma's eyes were focused, a brilliant blue – brighter than Maya had ever seen them before. Her mouth was a thin, straight line.

'You *loved* this garden, Charlie. Don't let your father tell you you didn't,' Alma continued. 'You know it's not just about me, Maya and Hiral. It's important for our neighbours too. We have the space, we should use it. Not everybody is lucky enough to have all this.'

And as if on cue, Jenny walked in with George: seventeen, practically a grown man now. George joined Ade to help with the cut flowers. Jenny headed to Maya, embracing her. 'It'll be all right, Alma's got a plan,' she whispered in Maya's ear.

'This place, it's good for all of us. It gives us a patch to belong, to hang out together,' Alma gestured to the busyness behind her. There was a clunkiness in her delivery, like a speech she hadn't rehearsed.

Mr James shrugged his shoulders, but Maya could sense a shift in his eyes, a softening. 'It's a nice thing you do,' he said, trying to keep a smile on his face as he exchanged a glance with Erol. 'But it's not proper, is it? This is my property. I've had no say in the use of this garden. You can't have strangers here gallivanting around my land.'

'If you lived here, we might have let you have a say. And they're not strangers, they're friends. They're our neighbours,' Alma continued.

'Alma, I know you're upset, but we've been asking you to put up a fence for years. You've never listened to us, and we've given you the chance. Maya is your friend, but . . . but not everyone who lives here will want to share a garden with you. They will want privacy. That is what gardens are for.'

'No, *Mr James*,' Alma scoffed. 'This is not what all gardens are for. Don't you remember when you were a little boy and we dug out this very vegetable bed?' She gestured to the trenches with her shovel. 'Potatoes. We did that to feed ourselves but also our neighbours. Don't you remember? It was for everyone. This garden has always been for everyone.'

Maya saw everyone standing up, eyes on Alma, listening carefully, nodding in agreement.

Mr James looked at the ground as though he were a child being told off by a rather stern schoolteacher.

'And your mother enjoyed getting stuck in too, she loved the shed most of all. That sign,' she pointed in its direction, *The Potting Shed*. 'I've kept it pristine for years. Painted it again and again in the same colours. Prem used to go to the maintenance shop and try to find some similar wood paint. He didn't even know her, but he cared for that sign as if he did. And now he's gone, I maintain it for her memory and for his too. This garden isn't just mine, Charlie, it was once yours, and your mother's, your father's, and it belonged to the people in the community as much then as it does now. Now suddenly everything we've been doing is against your wishes, is it?'

Mr James looked down at his feet, blinking hurriedly, and then at Maya. Softly, he said, 'Maya, I'm very sorry about all of this. We haven't had the valuation back yet—' His eyes washed over *The Potting Shed* sign again, and she watched her landlord, usually so firm and unflappable, bow his head slightly, hiding his eyes from all around.

Still, Maya felt her heart sink. She looked back to see Jenny trying to shepherd Hiral inside, to stop her hearing everything. 'Mum, are we going to be okay?' she'd ask again and again. 'We're not going to have to leave Auntie Alma, are we? Dad wouldn't want us to.'

'Oh, Charlie,' Alma snapped. 'Stop changing the subject! You know I'm right.' She thrust a piece of paper in front of him. 'Here.' She'd circled the note from the council about community gardens three times in pencil. At one point, the sheer force of her passion had caused the pencil to rip through the page, revealing a small, oval-shaped tear in the paper, as though it too was screaming at Mr James to listen. To pay attention.

'I don't want to put pressure on you, but I wouldn't be saying this if I felt this was your decision, Charlie. Your mother? She loved this place, but your crone of a father was always telling her this garden was a waste of time. Has he been telling you the same too? Remember when she came home from work that day, and she saw you picking some tomatoes. You were just seven or so, and sweet back then. She was so proud of you

– *bursting* with it. I know she's gone now and may her soul rest in peace, Charlie, honestly. But if your mother was still here, she'd not let you sell . . . because she loved this garden so much. Don't think I haven't noticed that in the last ten years since she's been gone, your dad has got more and more miserly about this place. But is his way the right way? Or do you want her legacy to live on? It's your choice now. And I think she'd agree that this house and this garden is your history as much as it is hers, whatever your father says.'

Alma let the words hang in the air.

Mr James lifted his head. And very quietly, said, 'I know, I know.' Maya heard the quiver in his voice.

After a moment, Alma cleared her throat, and Maya noticed everyone had stepped closer to her. 'We would like to apply to make this a community garden . . . *officially*.' Alma looked at Mr James firmly.

Hiral clapped her hands with glee and Maya could see Jenny beaming, nodding encouragingly at Alma. Ade and Erol had stopped what they were doing, and George was trying to surreptitiously stub out his cigarette. At that moment, Bob came in with his dog, who ran up to Hiral immediately and began licking her hands.

'It's what we want,' Alma said, nodding towards Maya, who had no idea about any of this. 'Well, not just us.'

'Us too,' Erol said, smiling.

'Keeps me fit!' Patrick said, as though rehearsing for a TV advertisement, a cheesy grin breaking out onto his face.

'Me as well,' Ade said, his face stern.

'Do it, Mr James, you grumpy old git,' Jenny called from the kitchen doorway, covering Hiral's ears.

'I think your ma would be proud of this. I know my pa would be.'

Mr James was looking from face to face, then back down at the piece of paper. Alma cleared her throat and continued, just as Isha walked in holding a trug and some scissors to pick some more flowers. She was wearing an elegant gold hijab, and she looked like she'd made a definite effort: 'I'm not late, am I?' she said, before spotting Mr James, covering her mouth, and quickly finding her position next to Ade's flower bed.

'You're all right, thanks, Isha,' Alma said, nodding. 'We need the consent of both homeowners, and we might have to do some legal things regarding the deeds and public right of way through the garden. The council are looking for spaces that can be used for community gardening schemes, and seeing as that's basically what we already do, why not?'

Mr James ran his eye down the paper, slowly shaking his head.

'No,' he said, but he didn't sound as firm as usual, 'I don't see how that would even work. I wouldn't be able to sell this house if the garden was a community garden. Who'd want to live here then?'

'But Mr James,' Maya said finally, though she knew her voice was barely above a whisper. 'You don't really want to sell it, do you? This was once your home.' She looked at him dead on, feeling brave for the first time today. Everything, her home, her family's security, felt like it hung on this man's one decision.

'Alma, Maya, everyone, thank you for the offer. But this idea . . . it's ridiculous. Alma, I can't imagine even *you* would want to officially register this as a community garden. Your age, your health, it . . . how would you manage it? It'll cause so many problems, complicated legal things, won't it?'

'I'll have you know my health is fine,' Alma said, but Maya sensed a tremor in her voice, a tiny denial. Jenny and Maya exchanged a worried glance.

'It's simple,' Alma said, more boldly. 'We own the land – all we need to do is formalize an agreement to have this space as a community garden, take out some extra liability insurance. It'll mean we can apply for funding to make sure it's up to scratch if we want to, that it's working for the community it serves. But I have one request.'

'Oh, you do, do you? Mr James said with a laugh.

'I want this space to *always* be a shared garden, ideally for the community. Even when the two of us are long gone. I want it in writing. I want whoever owns these two houses to *have* to keep this garden as one, to share it. I don't want everything we've done here to go to waste, forgotten as soon as we're dust.'

'Alma,' Mr James said. 'That's ridiculous.' But, as the words left his mouth, he looked around at the garden, to see the faces of everyone who had found a sanctuary, a home, here: Ade, Erol, Jenny, Patrick, Isha, Bob and George. He opened his mouth to speak again, but Maya watched as the words stuck in his throat. It was hard to tell people who loved a place that they could have it no longer.

'It still feels like a garden for me and Maya, and over the years we've been able to share it with Ade and his friends, and a host of our other neighbours too, whenever we open that gate. It means more because of that. It is a joy and a pleasure. I want this garden to have a legacy long after we're gone. For my parents. For your mother. For Prem. And for us,' she said gently, nodding towards Maya.

There was a beat of silence.

Then a sigh from Mr James.

'Look, I'll take this, all right?' He picked up the newspaper, tucked it under his arm, and let himself out of the gate.

'Well, that went well,' Jenny said sarcastically. 'The grumpy bastard,' she growled.

'Look, let's not write him off yet,' Alma said, hopeful, taking a large gulp of her now cold tea, flopping down onto an old kitchen chair, her hand practically shaking. Her cheeks were flushed with passion. 'He's got a decision to make. Let's hope he's up to the job.'

Chapter 30

Winston

April 2019

Winston unlocked the back door and headed straight to his vegetable beds. The air was warm now, the ground sodden from a recent downpour, but the water was evaporating off leaves as steam, the sun burning brightly. Today he was taking Bernice and Seb to Sal's allotment – it was Sal's idea, he'd been mentioning an outing ever since learning they were doing up the garden. So over the last few days, Winston had begun to draw diagrams of each of the beds in preparation. Now, notebook, measuring tape and pen in hand, Winston analysed his crops. His broad beans and peas seemed to be doing well, climbing up the tipis of tree branches he'd made, and he felt a small pop of pride in his chest.

He'd been putting together something that resembled a planting plan in his muddied, muddled notebook. He'd kept planting things too early or in the wrong conditions – like the potatoes he'd planted in February, when apparently they should be planted on Easter Sunday. He'd put out some nicotiana seedlings, which got frosted early in the season, and he hadn't even bothered to try to 'harden them off', getting the seedlings used to the cold. While he was really enjoying the gardening – the process of planting seeds in soil, pricking out seedlings, digging holes, raking over the earth and aerating new soil – the disappointment when something didn't take was something else. He wasn't only competing with the neighbourhood animals and foxes, who loved to chomp through any new growth, but also with his own impatience and ineptitude. He needed to start thinking strategically. He hoped that Sal's allotment might give him some answers.

Winston would usually be at the shop on a Saturday. But thankfully, the 'new boy', Angela's nephew Nigel, had agreed to cover. Sal didn't seem too keen about leaving Nigel unattended, but Ange had vouched for him. So Winston was free to help or, more precisely, observe and take notes as Angela and Sal planted up their allotment in Tottenham. He also knew that Sal spent a lot of time chatting to the neighbouring gardeners, so Winston hoped that *maybe* it could help to plant a seed with Bernice. Show her that gardening *together*, with your friends and neighbours, wasn't such a bad idea after all.

Once his diagrams were made up, his list of queries and questions for Sal completed, Winston locked up and made his way to Bernice and Seb's front door. 'Come on, we'll be late,' Winston called through Bernice's letterbox, his notebook in hand and a canvas bag hanging from his shoulder.

'We're coming, Winston!' Seb called back, and within seconds, he and Bernice appeared in the doorway wearing matching outfits: shorts and khaki T-shirts. Winston looked down at his outfit: denim jeans and a grubby old moth-eaten T-shirt he mainly wore when he was cleaning the house. 'Looks like you forgot to send me the memo,' Winston groaned.

Seb poked him jovially. 'Get over it,' he said, sticking his tongue out. It was a mischievous face that reminded Winston uncannily of Ruth when she was younger, prone to teasing her little brother. *I must reply to her message*, he thought with a pang of guilt.

'Right, let's go!'

After a ride on the 76 bus, the three of them cut down a path that led to Tottenham Marshes along the canal. Seb swung his arms, the sunshine flickering in his hair. On either side of them, the cow parsley, comfrey and rape plants stood taller than Seb, creating a spring blanket of white, yellow and purple. They wandered down to an orchestra of insects.

'*Bees*,' Seb gasped, as though he'd never seen them before. He took a moment to admire it all.

'It's beautiful here,' Bernice said. 'What's this?' She pointed to the bell-like flowers.

'Comfrey,' Winston replied.

'Isn't that a weed?'

'Depends if you like it or not,' Winston said robotically. His new favourite catchphrase. Bernice rolled her eyes, chuckling.

Here, spring was like summer. There was so much to see.

Winston had only been down here once or twice before, dropping things off for Sal at his allotment, hemmed in by the marshes themselves. It was peaceful, like a secret retreat. Yet in the distance, you could see the cheese grater building, the Shard, signs of the city. When he'd first come, he'd not allowed himself the time to take it all in. But as Seb slowed down, admiring the scene, Winston and Bernice did too. There was the rush of water in the canal, fast from the recent rains, blending in with the sound of distant traffic from the road, the insects flitting around in front of his eyes, weaving in and out of each other. The flowers, bobbing in the breeze. The light greens of new growth. The buds on the trees. It really was beautiful.

'Winston!' Angela called. A hand waved over a green wire fence on their left. 'Come, you'll need to go round the other side for the gate.'

A few minutes later, battling through stinging nettles on the back path, they finally arrived and Angela welcomed them in, her arms and smile wide.

'Hello, darlings. Thank you for coming to help!' she said, bending down to Seb first. She revealed a handful of boiled sweets for him, the same treats she often gave to cute kids at the shop. She couldn't help it. She and Sal had never had children – and Winston had never asked why or even assumed that's what they'd wanted. But she'd be the best grandmother there could be.

'It's a bit selfish, really,' Winston replied. 'We're obviously here to help, but also . . . we need your gardening wisdom.' He looked at Bernice, who nodded in confirmation.

'We're still very much rookie gardeners,' she said. 'I've got all the books, but it feels like *you* probably know how to do the stuff, and what to plant, what works well here. You know?'

Winston smiled. He'd told Bernice flattery went a long way with Angela. And, as expected, Ange beamed, batting the compliments away with her hand. 'Well, in our experience, getting stuck in is the best way to learn. Come. We're over here.' She led them along a small path, surrounded by sunken beds, neatly raked, with shoots and leaves springing up in orderly lines. There were several ramshackle sheds dotted around the space, with old chairs and makeshift tables, created from pallets or old fencing panels. Seb admired the wigwams made from tree branches or canes. Windy, weird and wonderful.

A few plots down they saw a family – a grandson and grandfather, by the looks of it – working away to the sound of their own chatter. The radio in the background ignored. Digging, potting, planting and picking.

'Hello Mrs Angela!' the eldest man called. He must have been about eighty, Winston thought, but he looked good for it, in a yellow fleece and old wellington boots.

'All right, Uncle Patrick!' she called back. 'Careful of your back. Remember what happened last time. You make sure you get your little one to do the hard work.' The 'little one', his grandson, was at least in his mid-twenties – he laughed in response.

'Patrick is an old friend of Erol's, Sal's father,' Angela explained as they got a little closer to Sal. 'In fact, they were both friends with someone who used to live in your house.'

'Oh?' Winston nodded encouragingly.

'What was his name?' Angela said, knitting her brow. 'Prem! That was it. I never got to meet him, he passed away before I was on the scene. But apparently he was lovely. Kind man. Died too young.'

Handmade by Prem. Winston thought of the old chair in the garden – Angela must be talking about the same man?

'All four generations of Patrick's family come here. His grandson now has a little girl, she's three, I think. And already a keen gardener . . . Patrick . . . he's been losing his memory a little recently. Nothing dramatic. Just in the way that can happen when we get a bit older. But whenever he's here . . . he's crystal clear. He remembers everything. The allotment brings him back to himself.'

Winston paused, watching a little girl run out of the shed to pour a packet of seeds into her grandfather's outstretched hand. The old man noticed him watching, and smiled, waving, as though they knew each other, as though they were friends. Winston raised his hand back, smiling and shielding his face from the glare of the spring sunshine.

He skipped ahead to catch Angela, Bernice and Seb weaving down through plots, under arches laden with climbers, and between sheds and flower beds. When they reached Sal's plot, his eyes were immediately drawn to the beautiful white clematis with spiky leaves, and the grape vine winding itself around anything it could get hold of. Its leaves starting to bud: small, sweet, growing around a trellis against their little shed.

Sal was drinking from a flask, perched in a rickety old chair. 'Like that?' he said, nodding towards the clematis. 'My father took it from a cutting in your very garden. Years and years ago now. Probably long gone in your garden, I expect.'

'Actually,' Winston said proudly. 'I think I might have rescued it. It was hidden behind lots of bindweed but seems to be coming back okay.'

Sal stood up and embraced him, resting his face on Winston's shoulder. He didn't let him go for a while – he held on tight. As though they hadn't seen each other every day for the past few years.

'It's lovely to have you here, my son,' Sal said. Then he stepped back, keeping his hands on Winston's arms, inspecting every inch of his face, trying to find answers to questions Winston didn't know, searching his soul. 'Here for some tips, I hear!'

Glancing around, Winston spotted potatoes and tomatoes, both doing well. The potatoes had been earthed up, so looked like large mounds with tiny hints of leaves poking through.

'Your potatoes . . .' Winston said. 'When did you plant them?'

'A couple of weeks ago, so they're starting to sprout. They're earlies, so end of March they went in. They're coming on well. You got some going?' Sal asked.

'Erm,' Winston swallowed. 'The foxes . . . they've been coming in every few days to flatten everything I've earthed up. Like it's a game to them.' It wasn't a lie . . . but it wasn't the sole reason they'd failed. But Winston couldn't bring himself to admit the extent of his potato disaster. 'Stems snapped off, leaves crushed, mounds trampled.'

'We earthed them up today,' Sal said. 'My favourite, potatoes. That and cabbages. Look at the artichokes,' he said, pointing to huge, silvery leaves, overshadowing the plants beneath them.

'Any foxes?' Bernice ventured.

'Look at these fences.' Sal pointed to the green metal fence encircling them. 'No foxes getting in here, I tell you.'

'Should we get something like that?' Bernice asked Winston.

'Oh, it'd be so expensive,' Angela said. 'And isn't sharing your garden with all sorts half the fun?'

Winston looked at Angela, his eyebrow raised. 'Honestly, Ange, have you ever picked up fox shit before? Sorry!' he added hastily, realizing Seb was in earshot.

Sal started to chuckle. 'That garden . . . my dad always used to give Alma, the lady who lived there, chilli flakes to keep them at bay.' Winston caught Bernice's eye. *Alma*. 'Huge bags of it,' Sal continued, oblivious. 'Only ended up giving her cats a funny bum. I think the first cat was Susie. She suffered the most . . . but the foxes kept coming. It's useless trying to keep them out.'

Winston grimaced at the thought of the chillied cat bum.

'Right, enough of that,' Angela swooped in, as Sal wandered into his shed. 'What would you like me to show you?' She rubbed her hands together to shake loose some flecks of soil.

'Everything!' Bernice said, and Angela accepted the task at hand.

'Finally, you come to us for advice,' Sal said, handing a KitKat out to them all, nudging Winston playfully in the ribs, while Angela began to talk them through the vegetables, paying special attention to the mustard greens.

'*So* easy to grow – you can use it instead of spinach,' she exclaimed. 'Here, have a try.' She broke off some leaf for them both. Winston's KitKat-coated taste buds took a while to adjust, until they were flooded with the bitter heat of mustard.

'They really *are* like mustard,' he nodded, wincing slightly as the chocolate made a comeback, creating a strange, though not unpleasant, sensation in his mouth.

'Of course,' Angela said, before moving on to the clematis. 'My pride and joy, this. You'll see, if yours flowers, it should be in bloom for several weeks. Full of bees!'

She told them how to care for it, and Winston whipped out his notebook to keep track. When to cut back. When to leave. Then she drew her attention to her bleeding hearts – huge shrubs with little delicate heart-shaped flowers dangling from the branches. Winston hated them. 'They look like something a grandma might have,' he said.

'Well, Winston,' Angela frowned at him. 'Aren't I old enough to be a grandma?'

He didn't comment for a little while after that. Bernice took over the chatting, ooh-ing and aah-ing at all the right moments.

'Now, sweet peas – we started these indoors along our window-sills early this year,' Angela said.

'Mum!' Seb whispered. 'Isn't that what we've got in our kitchen?'

'It is, sweetie,' Bernice whispered back. 'Not looking quite as strong as these . . .'

That was the understatement of the century, Winston thought. They looked like spindly spiders' legs.

Angela smiled at them both and continued her role of teacher: advising when to pot them out, what to look for in a good strong plant, and when to pick. 'As often as possible, to keep them in flower over the whole summer. And if you start to see any little furry pea pods appearing after it's flowered, pick them off!'

As Angela took herself off to the shed to pack up cuttings for them, Sal beamed at them, standing awkwardly. For once, it seemed he'd run out of conversation. Winston seized the opportunity to probe Sal about the past.

'So, our shared garden . . . you said your father's friends used to look after it?'

Sal suddenly lit up. 'Oh yes!'

'Angela pointed Patrick out when we first arrived,' Winston said encouragingly.

'Oh, lovely Uncle Patrick! He's quite a character. Always been in my life, that man.'

'So who ran the garden? Did they live in our terrace?' Bernice asked.

'Oh, where to start,' Sal said wistfully. 'Yes, so my uncle Prem lived at Number 79, Winston's house, and he passed away many years ago. But Maya, who was Prem's wife, well she's still around, and she used to run the garden with Alma next door, in your house, Bernice. You know her, don't you? Auntie Maya.'

Winston shook his head. He'd never met a Maya.

'I'm sure you must have met her in the shop . . . but I suppose,' Sal went quiet then. 'Yes, I suppose she's not been out as much as she used to. Not since you've been here, perhaps. She seemed to tuck herself away after her dog passed, and then her lovely cat, but that was so many years ago now. She moved out of your house, but she didn't go far, she's a few doors up on the other side of the road from you. Almost like she couldn't bear to leave the past behind,' he said, a little sadly. 'Number 68.'

Winston glanced at Bernice. It was the house with the window open all the time. The TV voices drifting out. She'd been there all that time, and he hadn't known? He tried to bring the Maya of his imagination to the fore. He couldn't imagine her watching TV all day. No company. The window – there weren't even any flowers on the windowsills, were there?

The gardening leaflets, the notes. Could they be from Maya? Someone just across the road, all this time.

'She used to go for regular walks with her dog. She's been quite alone ever since Prem passed and Alma moved away, and her daughter – Hiral – she's living abroad, I think. Never quite the same once she left that garden. I guess, when life moves on . . .' Sal petered off then. 'I do try to get her out and about, but I really must do more,' Sal said, admonishing himself. 'Jenny is an old friend of hers too, she pops round to the flat often. We try to encourage her. And I do go round with shopping for her once a week and we have a little chat. I've really never talked about Auntie Maya to you?'

Winston tried to think. Had he?

'Well, my father signed up for an allotment when they moved out, left the shared garden behind. We've had it years now. He wanted to keep gardening, you see. He was in his mid-sixties by then, and he already had dodgy joints. Didn't have many years of gardening left in him. So, here I am, keeping it going.' Sal looked up to the sky, then glanced over at Patrick, who waved again, wandering over to a water butt with his watering can. 'My dad, Erol . . . If he was well enough, I'd bring him to meet you. To see you doing something with that garden. I never took much interest in it at the time – too interested in . . .' he took a cautious glance at Angela, 'the ladies! . . . But he'd be so proud. He loved that place. Loved the people most of all. He always said the best thing about that garden was the company, creating something with friends.'

'Sal,' Winston said. 'Do you think . . . Well, Bernice and I have received little newspaper clippings, old flyers for community things, and photographs through our letterboxes. We wondered . . . do you think Maya could be behind it?'

Sal shook his head. 'I don't know . . . maybe. But, when I say she keeps herself to herself these days, she really does. I don't know if . . .' he pondered a moment, then shrugged. 'Maybe you could show her the garden? It might be nice. I could mention it to her—'

'No,' Winston said hurriedly, looking at Bernice. 'It's not ready yet.' He recalled the photographs from the past, the beauty of the garden. While the garden was looking better, it wasn't good enough yet. 'I want her to see it when we're happy with it. When it's finished.'

Winston couldn't quite explain it, but the garden held an important legacy. And with the trail leading back to Maya, a *real* person tied up in its history . . . well, he needed to honour it properly.

Sal nodded. 'Okay . . . I won't say a thing for now. But remember, son. A garden is never really finished.'

'Here you go!' Angela said, coming out with two plastic bags full of cuttings, passing one to both Bernice and Winston. Seb, who'd been wandering around all the beds, weaving in and out, hurried back to take a peek in the bag.

'Thank you,' Bernice said. 'I think you've answered lots of questions for us.' She gave Winston a knowing look.

'Come back soon, okay?' Sal said.

'And look out for the apple and cherry blossom!' Angela said. 'It's my favourite at this time of year.'

Waving goodbye to Seb and Bernice back on Eastbourne Road, Winston unlocked his front door, and noticed a missed call on his phone. There was a message from Mr James: *Winston! Darlene and Heidi really liked meeting you. They've been offered a flat somewhere else, but wanted to check where you were. They seem keen! They're looking to move in eight weeks, so some time yet. Let me know by tomorrow, if you can. My daughter's going to sort out the paperwork if you're happy. Hope all okay.*

Winston sighed and glanced down at his feet. There, as if he knew it would be, was another envelope sitting on the mat. *The Young Man at Number 79*. Handwriting he'd come to know so well.

Inside was one leaflet, faded but still legible.

Friend and Neighbour,

You're invited to the opening of Eastbourne Road's official community garden. Come and celebrate with us this Sunday, 1 May, and join the gardening fun!

Alma and Maya x

Maya. She was here after all. And she was sending them a message.

Chapter 31

Maya

May 1988

'Without further ado, we do declare this community garden . . .' Alma paused; there was a whistle from the small crowd, Bob snapped photographs on his Pentax . . . 'OFFICIALLY OPEN! Charlie James, would you do the honours?'

Mr James looked at her quizzically, and she shrugged, gesturing to the ribbon stretched across the gate. He started to hack away uselessly with pink safety scissors to some jovial groans from the crowd and titters of amusement. Eventually, Mr James managed to saw through the final thread, and the two sides fell away with an anticlimactic sigh. But it didn't dampen the cheers of delight.

Maya found herself searching for Prem's face in the crowd, wishing he were here to see this. She imagined his cheeky smile, the glint in his eyes. His ability to always make her feel calm, no matter the circumstances.

Hiral, now twelve but going on twenty-five, was on hand to pass around glasses of punch made by Bina, with one of her dad's novelty aprons wrapped around her waist. One of the less lewd ones. 'So he's here with us, Mum,' she'd said that morning, squeezing her mother's hand.

A few dark clouds rippled in the sky behind them, and Maya hoped the fair weather would hold for long enough. But she remembered Prem's words: 'Rain brings good luck: always hope for rain.' She knew he was right; if only they'd got more robust plates.

'Maya,' Mr James said, as the crowd filtered through the gate into the garden. 'I do want to apologize for all the back and forth, I know how uncertain this has all been for you.'

'No,' Maya shook her head. 'Thank you, Mr James. Thank you for listening to us.'

'Eventually . . . I know I took my time, but it really is clear to see what a lovely space this has become. I've no need to sell right now, and it seems a shame to ruin something so important. Are you pleased? With the party?'

Maya looked around at the garden. 'Yes, I really am.' She'd found herself spending less and less time here since Prem's passing. The breeze brought in memories, and sometimes Maya couldn't cope with them. But she realized she missed it; being here, seeing everyone enjoy it, smelling the flowers and admiring the early roses, spotting the bursts of colour as they emerged from the brown earth, it gave her great pleasure. This was where her family belonged, and she was doing what she could to keep them here, for as long as possible.

Maya spotted Alma setting out paper bowls ready for Hiral's friends to descend on the cake made by Sal's new love interest, Angela. 'Chubby cheeks!' Jenny called to him. 'Your new missus make this?' Sal turned bright red.

As soon as the teenagers grabbed the bowls, Alma's eyes flew to spots in the garden affected by the foxes and she began pushing dislocated soil back into the holes they'd dug, while looking up at the party around her so no one would notice. Spring: the worst time of year for fox destruction, as the newly established shoots were at their most vulnerable.

Maya looked over at Prem's chair; still empty. It seemed no one wanted to sit there, leaving space for the memories. But, a second later, Bob's Golden Retriever puppy, Harold, was running around Maya's feet, all shaggy and smiley. She froze. Maya was certain Bob had only got the dog for Alma's attention. Or to give Maya the fright of her life.

'Maya!' Bob called over, his round face beaming at her. His forehead was licked with sweat from the sunshine, and he dabbed it away with his handkerchief. 'Just give him a tap on the head. S'all he wants! He's saying congratulations to you!'

Maya was standing as still as possible. Harold's tongue, all pink and wet, was flopping out of his mouth.

'Does he know he's terrifying me?' Maya blurted.

'Course he doesn't, Maya,' Bob said. And, right then, the dog leapt into Prem's seat and Maya yelped. Mr James shot round to look at her, worry in his eyes – probably concerned they'd have to use the liability insurance sooner than they'd hoped.

'Look at that!' Alma said, an arm around Kate, who'd travelled specially to celebrate the garden opening. 'No one has sat in Prem's chair in forever. Harold must know how much Bob loved that man.'

Maya smiled, but avoided looking at Harold. Hiral was scruffing the dog affectionately, giggling as he tried to lick her hand. Unlike Hiral, Maya was not a dog person. Cats she could tolerate. They largely kept themselves to themselves. Dogs . . . Dogs were another matter entirely.

Erol then wandered through the gate, declaring 'I'm sorry I'm late!', making a beeline for Mr James, and handing him a cigar. 'Knew you'd prove yourself to be a good 'un, Mr James,' Erol said. Maya rolled her eyes at him, lovingly.

'Come on everyone, once you've had some cake, come get some veggie lasagne,' Alma bellowed. 'I made it!'

'Cake before lasagne?' Maya asked, trying to catch Alma's eye.

'I thought you said there'd be a dosa station,' Bina said, filling up her third or fourth glass of punch.

'That would have been so good!' Hiral said, appearing in front of her and crossing her arms. 'You should have told Mum, Bina Masi.'

'Look,' Maya said tightly, staring at Harold, who was now sprawled at her feet. 'This dog smells my fear. He looks friendly, but I don't want him near me.'

'All right, don't worry,' Bob said, grabbing Harold gently by the collar, his eyes roving for Alma.

'Good boy, you're a good boy, aren't you?' Erol said, instantly becoming the 'dog person' he had never been before.

Maya scowled at him and trotted into the kitchen, where the sight of something special immediately softened her. On the table was a wooden sign: *Eastbourne Road Community Garden*. In an unexpected act of kindness, Mr James had bought the wood and one of his friends had carved the words. 'It seemed only fitting now it's all official. I thought perhaps the community could paint it?' he'd said. Maya noticed he'd still said *community* cautiously, pronouncing each syllable awkwardly, as though it were a person he didn't know very well. 'I reckon my mother would have loved it. Though I'm not as good at making signs as she is.' He'd beamed, chuffed with his handiwork.

'Can you believe all this?' Maya said to Alma, who'd followed her in, closing the kitchen door behind her. 'And it's all down to you! Prem would *adore* all this.' Alma slumped down in the kitchen chair, her eyes unseeing.

'Alma?' Maya said, bending down to the floor immediately, resting her hands on her friend's lap. 'What's the matter?'

'Nothing,' Alma said. 'Nothing, nothing. I . . .' she took a deep breath, her eyes focused on somewhere in the far distance.

'I think I lost my train of thought, is all. Can't remember for the life of me where I put my dad's recipe for this.'

'Recipe for what?'

'That's right,' Alma said, nodding, as though Maya had answered the question. 'You're absolutely right, Maya. But do I usually use squash or beetroot?'

Maya said, 'You've already made the lasagne, Alma. But it's usually squash.'

'But you hate squash, don't you?' Alma said, her face animated – suddenly Alma – again.

'Absolutely I do,' Maya said. 'What happened there, Al?'

'I was about to start chopping the carrots for the lasagne, when I remembered I should sow the courgettes at the end of the month – thought of my dad. He *loved* courgettes – nearly poisoned us once, they got too much heat, turned the courgettes sharp. Horrible. Told me off for leaving my veggies, until he realized. I remember watching him, in this same kitchen. I just got lost in the memories,' Alma said, pulling herself up, as though that explained everything.

Maya loved the sound of Alma's father. 'He was a little like your Prem, actually,' Alma used to say. 'So funny, and cheeky, but kind too. My father would say it was hard to find kind men around. The war had changed them all – scarred by what they'd seen, traumatized, no fault of their own – so my father, he said he did all he could to keep kindness in his heart.'

Erol, Mr James, Bob and Patrick guffawed outside and a loud bark emanated from Harold, terrorizing the children now.

'That dog is a *nightmare*,' Maya said.

'I think Harold's a sweetie,' Alma said, fiddling with a paint-brush, running a finger into the grooves of the lettering on the wooden sign. 'Susie,' Alma called, addressing the space above the kitchen cabinets, Susie's old spot, talking to a cat that wasn't there.

'Why don't you get over yourself and say hello to Harold? Morris at least tolerates the dog.'

Susie had been dead for years, but Alma was acting as though she was still alive, while also talking about Morris, the ginger rescue cat they'd only had for a few months.

Maya looked up at the spot, and pictured what Alma must be seeing. Susie, sitting on top of the cabinets like a little loaf, her eyes brilliantly wide and alert. She imagined her now, wherever she might be, hiding away from the menace that was Harold, and she felt a kinship with the tiny cat.

'Why don't you go out and socialize, Al?' Maya said, unsure how to respond, unable to tell Alma that Susie wasn't here any longer. 'It's such an important day, you've got to be out there chatting away! I'll finish tidying up here.'

'No, I'm all right – too noisy for me out there.'

'I think Bob might be putting his cigarette butts in the asparagus bed,' Maya shrugged.

'Oh, he better not be!' Alma stomped out, outraged.

'That did the trick, didn't it?' Maya said to the imaginary Susie, who she thought would probably be grooming her paws in a pose that resembled an evil genius. She felt a sinking in her heart, imagining Alma pottering around the house talking to a cat that wasn't there.

But then again, when Hiral wasn't around, Maya spoke to Prem all the time, didn't she? She never stopped. Sitting beside his chair, hoping he might talk back one day.

Alone in the room, Maya looked around the kitchen and went over to the half-empty pot of lasagne. She cut herself a sliver of what was left.

'Yuck,' Maya told ghost-Susie. 'The woman forgot seasoning, *again*! Every. Time.'

Maya grabbed the saltshaker she'd bought Alma as a Christmas present a few years ago (her first hint) as well as the 'all in one' seasoning pot she'd popped beside the pot of oil too (her second hint) and took them outside, putting them on the table for anyone who needed a little more flavour.

Later that evening, when the party had quietened down, Maya could hear the laughter of Hiral and her friends echoing up to her bedroom window from the garden. She loved the sound of it, the babble of their carefree joy. She pictured Prem sitting on the bed, reading a book, smiling with her.

She continued folding Hiral's clothes, warm from the sun. One day Hiral would start shopping without her, she'd stop wearing clothes Bina and Maya had made for her, she'd start living a life of her own. Making decisions for herself, building a home for herself . . . Even this wouldn't last forever.

A shout suddenly cut through her thoughts: 'Oi, get out of there!' Loud and sharp.

'Is that Alma?' she asked the house around her, wishing for an answer back from Prem.

'I *SAID* get out of there!' the voice sounded again. The babble stopped, and she could hear a scurrying.

Maya dropped the T-shirt she was folding into a pile in the basket, and trotted down the stairs two at a time, bursting into the garden. She saw Hiral standing alone, surrounded by a circle of empty chairs – the garden gate was open, her friends had gone, a trail of paper cups and plates in their wake.

'Hiral,' Maya muttered. 'Come here, darling.' A few metres away, a pair of yowling cats scarpered too.

Then she spotted Alma. Her face was screwed up in anguish. Maya traced her gaze. Had Alma been shouting at the neighbourhood cats?

No. Her eyes were on Hiral.

Maya felt her heart pounding in her throat. Alma looked like she was holding back tears.

Almost in slow motion, Hiral got up and headed straight to Maya, wrapping herself up in her arms. For a second, she wasn't twelve any more, she was a child who needed her mother.

'Everything okay, Alma?' Maya kept her voice soft, calm. She felt Prem by her side.

Alma shook her head slowly. She wasn't looking at her. She was looking at the newly planted bed with a face of disgust, as though it had been destroyed. It was untouched.

Maya turned away from her friend, and cautiously led her daughter inside. As soon as the kitchen door was shut, Maya sat Hiral on a kitchen stool and knelt to look her in the eye, where she promptly burst into floods of tears.

Maya hugged her close, humming softly under her breath in a bid to calm her. When Hiral eventually managed to find the breath to speak, she said: 'Does Auntie Alma hate me?'

'No, no, beta, she doesn't hate you. She loves you very much.'

'But she screamed at me. We were only being silly,' she said between sobs. 'She said it was okay for us to be out there, I asked her and everything.'

'I know you did, sweetie, please don't worry.' She kissed Hiral on the forehead. 'Will you go upstairs, and I'll join you soon? I just need to check on Alma.'

'Can you come with me?' Hiral said, her voice small. Maya glanced behind her, watching Alma staring at the garden, before grabbing a spade, starting to dig randomly into one of the beds.

She directed Hiral up the stairs. 'Come on, beta,' she said, as her daughter hiccupped and coughed, trying in vain to hold back her tears. 'It's okay.' In Hiral's bedroom, she whispered conspiratorially, 'Do you want to get tucked up in bed and snuggle up warm?'

'Yes,' she said, pulling the silky eiderdown on top of her – a gift from Alma years ago. 'I'm so sorry if I upset Auntie Alma.' Her voice was soft, Maya could barely hear her.

'Oh my beta,' Maya clutched her close. 'You didn't. She knows you didn't mean to.'

'She was so angry . . . because of me and my friends.' Maya noticed the pause, which was certainly for dramatic effect, but it still got to Maya, clawing at the very centre of her heart.

They sat like that for a while, until Maya noticed the steady thump of the spade in the garden had stopped. Hiral had fallen asleep resting her head on Maya's chest, as she had years ago, rocked to sleep in sadness, the day they'd lost Prem.

Maya allowed herself to squeeze out from under her daughter, laying a final soft kiss on her hairline as she left.

Stepping out into the garden, she saw Alma, now planting out tomato plants that they'd left in pots far too long. The leaves were crisp, brown. She noticed tears dropping from Alma's face. Part of her wanted to reach out to her, but she was angry too. And she didn't want to scare Alma, nor did she want to say something she might regret. She knew it wasn't Alma's fault. It wasn't Alma.

Eventually, Alma calmed herself, her eyes became lucid as she patted the tomato plants in place. She pulled herself up and wandered back into her kitchen. Oblivious to Maya's presence.

Maya sat in Prem's chair, looking out at the garden. The sunlight was waning in the garden, the sky beyond the houses turning pink. She loved this sky, the rosy London clouds. She didn't know what caused it – pollution, probably. Something horrible. But it was so beautiful. Like candyfloss suspended in air. Her childhood dreams come true.

Yet here, in adulthood, she was so much more aware of how far away those clouds were. She couldn't simply launch herself up to touch them, catch them in her mouth and feel them melt into a sugary mess on her tongue. So many miles up in the sky, she'd never be able to reach them.

Her eye was drawn to a movement in the garden. A fox, nuzzling her way through the asparagus bed. If it had been yesterday, she might have shooed her away, but she enjoyed watching the pink light bounce off her orange coat, the white-grey fur on her nose turn a baby pink. She enjoyed watching her dig, causing destruction in the most natural kind of way. Was Alma watching too? Was Alma as frustrated with the fox as she had been with Hiral and her friends?

She knew she shouldn't be angry. Prem would tell her not to take it personally. But right now, it felt like she was losing so much and she needed someone to blame. It should have been the happiest of occasions, the garden finally open officially to the community – but Alma hadn't even been there to enjoy it, to take it all in, not really.

As the fox dug and dug and dug, just for the fun of it, Maya watched, feeling nothing for the garden it was destroying, the garden she and Alma had worked so hard for. The garden Alma loved more than anything.

Tomorrow, Maya would need to call Kate. She didn't want to do it all alone. She needed to tell someone what was going on with Alma. It was getting worse.

Chapter 32

Winston

May 2019

Over a month had passed since Bernice and Winston's trip to the allotment, and the thought of Maya living close by seemed to spur them on to make the garden glorious. Bernice was out there every evening. When she wasn't on a site visit, or in a client meeting, she'd opt to work from home to help Winston out during her lunchbreak. They took pride in their work, and as the weather got warmer, the rewards were finally arriving.

Once or twice, Winston had even caught Bernice looking at the old photographs of the garden on her kitchen table, admiring the gatherings, the neighbours congregating to celebrate a harvest, or a party. He wondered if she might be warming to the idea of letting people in . . .

Winston picked up one of the photographs, sticking it onto the shed wall with Blu Tack. He was putting up all the images and little snippets that had come through his door, lining the walls of the potting shed.

'Hey,' Bernice appeared in the doorway. 'Are you hiding out here?' She nodded back to the house. Winston's new flatmates, Darlene and Heidi, were moving in today. Every room, apart from his, was full of boxes. He'd assumed they might not have that much stuff, coming from a large houseshare already, but he was wrong. Very, very wrong.

'Sort of . . . But I want to give them some space, you know. So they can explore and settle in without me nosing around.'

Bernice laughed, sensing the lie. 'It'll be okay you know. It'll be different, but it'll be all right. You might even make *friends*, Winston!'

He smiled. A year ago, that wouldn't have seemed a possibility. A year ago, he hadn't even imagined the option of living with flatmates again.

'Shall I add my mystery mail?'

'What?'

'To your wall,' Bernice said.

Winston nodded. 'Are the photos different?' He'd assumed that perhaps they'd been sent identical packages to set them both on the same path, but Bernice quickly nodded. 'Some are the same . . . most are different though,' she said, her eyes running over the wall.

So, the mystery gardener (although they were now sure it had to be Maya) had sent them different pieces of the same puzzle.

'We'll do it,' she said simply, holding up a wodge of her own leaflets, photographs and newspaper cuttings.

'What?' Winston asked, preoccupied with sticking Blu Tack onto more clippings.

'Well . . . a little garden party. Nothing to the scale they did,' she nodded towards the 'Community Garden Open Day' poster. 'But the garden is looking nicer now, something we can be proud of. So maybe we could invite some of the neighbours round. A garden-warming. Get a sense of whether people might like to be involved. Seb hasn't stopped talking about how much he liked the allotments, everyone in proximity, working together. He said it reminded him of home.' Bernice smiled. 'He meant here.'

Winston pulled Bernice into an awkward, sideways hug then. And they coughed in embarrassment when they broke apart.

'You reckon Simon would have an issue with it?'

'Simon doesn't rule my life,' Bernice said, though the quiver in her voice betrayed her nervousness. 'I think it's a good thing for Seb, and that's what matters. Plus, if Simon hates the idea, it makes me want to do it more.'

Winston snickered. There was truth in that. More truth than even Bernice would care to admit.

'Now, I'm not saying I want people in here every day. It's not going to be a proper community garden. But once a fortnight or something . . . that might be all right. I don't know. Let's just see.' She shrugged, babbling, her hands flicking through the photographs in her hand.

Winston rolled his eyes, a smile on his face. With Bernice, it was a few steps forward, one step back . . . but progress, nonetheless.

'We'll have to talk to Darlene and Heidi to see if they're all right with us hosting a garden party too.'

'I reckon they'll be happy,' Winston said confidently.

'This is what she wants, isn't it?' Bernice asked, doubting herself all of a sudden.

'Who? Darlene?'

'No! Maya . . . If she *is* the one sending the letters. Do you think a party is what she had in mind?'

Winston thought about Sal's words. About how Maya's world had become smaller since she'd left this house, and the garden. Every time he wandered down the road, he wondered what she was doing. Was she watching him? Waiting for him to invite her in?

'I think she might want us to care for the garden. Maybe that's all.' It might have taken Winston years to make a start, it might have taken Maya to nudge him in the right direction . . . but the legacy that Maya and her friend Alma had left behind, had brought these two neighbours together, after all, hadn't it? Two people who couldn't be more different from one another. It might even have made them friends.

'We should ask her,' Bernice said, and in response to Winston's slightly worried look, she added: 'I mean . . . when the garden is ready. We should ask her. Maybe, if we do a garden party, we should invite her ourselves. In person. Maybe Sal could introduce us?'

'I like that idea. But we don't want to ambush her.'

'We won't, we won't. She wants to see this garden looking nice again. We should be excited to show it off to her.'

'Okay,' Winston nodded, his mind wandering to his mother's garden, watching her reading a book in her hammock underneath the banyan tree. His mother had died over four thousand miles away from him. The last time he'd seen her, she was dropping him off at the airport after Diwali beaming at him, her hair pulled up in a neat bun, the chanlo on her forehead matching her purple sari, as always.

He hadn't made it home for the funeral; he hadn't been there for the funeral rites; he hadn't seen her body, adorned with all the tokens, the butter, the spices, the rice, the petals, to make sure she had a safe journey to Akshardham. Going home would only force him to face it all – to face that she wasn't there any more.

'But remember,' he said to Bernice, a tear crowding his eye, 'there might be memories here, memories she's hidden from for quite a while. We should tread gently, and let's not get our hopes up.'

As soon as Bernice mentioned the idea of a party to Seb, he became so excited he hadn't been able to sleep.

'Seb,' Winston overheard Bernice telling him calmly one weekday morning. 'This party isn't going to be until the summer holidays, okay? We've got to make sure to put lots of energy and love into the garden for then. So you better start sleeping or you'll wear yourself out.'

After a week of unpacking and settling in, Darlene and Heidi cooked Winston a delicious 'thank you for letting us live with you' dinner of pea risotto. Sitting with them in the kitchen, watching them cook together, a carefully choreographed culinary dance, he couldn't help but feel content. He missed Lewis, he felt the ache in his core when he saw the natural grazes of hand on forearm, the odd kiss on the cheek when leaning over one another. But he also couldn't help but bask in the warmth of Darlene and Heidi's joy. Their things populated the shelves and cupboards. Winston expected to feel resentment, hurt, to see their stuff slowly erasing his own life. But really, it created a new sense of life for him too.

He wanted to call Lewis, to tell him all about Darlene and Heidi. But he didn't want to hurt him. To make it feel as though he was forgotten. He wanted to tell him that, watching the way they made compromises with one another, it made him think about what he could have done differently – it even made him wonder if it was possible for them once again.

'So,' Winston said, after a few glasses of orange wine, hand selected by Heidi from the organic wine bar she worked in in Hackney. 'My next-door neighbour Bernice and I were thinking of hosting a garden party. To invite the neighbours along. In summer, when the weather is better, when hopefully more flowers will be out. What do you think?'

'I *love* that idea!' Darlene said, and Heidi nodded vigorously.

'I can supply the wine!' Heidi said, taking another gulp from her glass.

'Come, let me show you something.' He stood up and led them down the garden path that had been cleared and laid with gravel to suppress the weeds. He opened the shed door, and turned the torch on his phone on. 'See,' he said, illuminating the wall of photos and leaflets. 'The garden used to be run by two friends. They kept it open for their neighbours, their community. It looked so picturesque.'

'Wow,' Darlene's eyes ran over the faces in the photographs. 'It's amazing. It's like . . . a piece of history.'

'Winston!' Seb came running out of his kitchen door. 'Let me take a photograph of you and Mummy for the invitation.'

Bernice appeared in the doorway. She waved awkwardly to Darlene and Heidi, who waved back, relaxed, at ease. They'd met several times over the last fortnight, but still Bernice seemed a little closed off, self-conscious, whenever they were around. Now Winston knew her better, he could see the difference between relaxed Bernice, and uncomfortable, awkward Bernice. But at least she wasn't bellowing at them, hammering on their door first thing in the morning, or trying to chuck their favourite chair into her dustbin.

'Mate, it's a few weeks away yet. We're not going to have a party until August, right?' He looked at Bernice for confirmation. 'It's only June.'

'We need to get the invites out early!' Seb said. 'People need to put it in their diaries! Let me take a photo. This light is *really* good.'

Winston looked up at the sky, all dark pinks, blending into purples higher up. It looked too dark to take a proper photo, but he didn't want to burst Seb's bubble, his mum's phone clasped in his hands.

'Come on! By the banana plant. By the gate! Arms around each other!' Seb bossed them around.

Getting into position, Winston and Bernice posed. Her arm was hugging him tight. Winston could smell the hairspray, and it was clear Bernice had been forewarned, and done her hair for the occasion. Winston, on the other hand, looked a mess.

'Mum!' Seb said, looking over the top of the phone. 'Stop pulling funny faces.'

'I'm not pulling funny faces!' Bernice chuckled, her tongue sticking out, her eyes crossed.

'You are!' Sebastian stamped his foot. 'Be serious!'

Bernice promptly pulled a grumpy face, and Darlene and Heidi chortled happily.

'Mum!' Seb said again. 'I mean be *happy* but serious. Don't be silly.'

This time Bernice got it right. Seb spent a moment analysing the results on Bernice's phone.

'Wait!' he said eventually, as Winston and Bernice broke apart. 'Do we need a sign for the garden? Like they had back then?'

'No, I'm not sure we do, sweetie. I mean, it's only a garden party. It's not a *community* garden,' Bernice said clearly.

Winston shook his head. Typical Bernice, he thought to himself, but glanced at her fondly.

As he admired the garden in the evening light, summer just a few days away, Winston felt something. Was it pride, or sadness, or a combination of the two?

The alliums, in their fading forms of purple, were like bubbles of bliss dotted through the garden. He'd planted a second lot of potatoes – main crop, this time – and they seemed to be establishing better. A few weeks ago, he'd identified and subsequently rescued the asparagus, which must have been here for years hidden within the most unwieldy, weedy bed. Now it could show off its big, bushy fronds, unobstructed by bindweed and roving roses.

The sunflowers Seb had planted were starting to take shape too, shooting from the ground, eager to show themselves off.

He knew it wouldn't last forever – nothing did.

It would come back next year though, equally bold and beautiful – but would he be here to see it?

He looked over at Darlene and Heidi, now chatting away together, in their own little world. Would this become their home soon? Their garden?

So much had changed in the last few months. As Winston put more and more of his energy into the garden, he could feel the weight of his own pain lifting, easier to carry. But how much had really changed? He'd still barely spoken to Ruth. He'd hardly dug into his emotions, hadn't told her how he'd been feeling. Anxious to keep her at arm's length. And Lewis. Things were still unclear there. They were talking, but what did it mean? What did he want? He wanted to share this world with them both. But was he brave enough to let them in?

He wished he could tell his mother how much he loved her. But in every flower he planted, every branch he pruned, in everything he did, she was with him, in his heart and in his soul.

'Okay, guys,' Seb said, authoritative, bringing Winston back to the garden. 'Leave this with me. I'll get you a nice invitation all designed up in no time! Garden party, here we come!'

Part IV

SUMMER

Friday, 21 June 2019

I have a confession to make. It's been nearly twenty-seven years since I moved out of Number 79. Writing these letters to you, every equinox and solstice, has been my way of pretending that I was still in that house. Holding on to the past. Hoping, and praying, that the garden would be looked after, as I always promised it would be.

I've never been far away. Keeping an eye from a distance. Watching our old home change with time. I've never been back inside, though. And I haven't set foot in that garden either. The gate has been firmly shut ever since I left.

When you were moving out, I couldn't bear to tell you that Hiral and I were going too. At the time, I didn't want to rattle you. I hoped everything would be as smooth as possible. I promised *I'd keep the garden going for everyone we loved, that I'd look after it, but I couldn't, Alma. Not because I didn't want to, but because I no longer had the power. I kept pretending. At first for your sake, and then for my sake too. I've lived in my hopes and dreams for years.*

I'm only able to say this now. To write this down. To admit to myself that I did fail you. Because it feels as though I might not have completely failed you after all.

I've been watching the goings-on of Number 77 and Number 79 ever since I moved in here across the road – into Bob's old flat, actually. Number 68. Like Bob, I always keep the living-room window open a smidge.

Morris liked to sit here and observe in his old age, and Fraser sometimes poked his nose out too. I keep the TV on, to fill the space with sound. It makes me feel a bit less alone. And from that spot, I sit and watch. Having the window open means I generally hear what's going on. I've hidden myself away, a little, Alma. I don't know if you can tell. But this glimpse of the outside world, it's my connection to the community around me. The place that used to be ours.

Well, it was only recently that someone finally moved into your house, Alma. I know Kate's been trying to sell it for years, but things kept falling through, as they do. Do you remember me telling you about the warring neighbours? Well . . . one of them lives in Number 77, the other in 79. I couldn't believe it. Two neighbours, who seemed to despise each other so much. How could they look after the garden?

What came next was Jenny's idea really. She knows the young man. She calls him Vincent, but I've got a feeling his name might be Winston. He works at the shop with our Sal. He seems nice, kind. Sal likes him, anyway. I've seen him before, of course I have. Anyway, Jenny told me if I wanted the garden to be looked after, I might have to do something about it.

I wondered if she meant that I should go and confront them, but the thought of doing that set my hair on end. I couldn't. Not on my own. And then she said that in this day and age, no one would listen to me. They'd think I was mad . . . some weird old lady with a strange attachment to the place. I suppose I am in a way. Jenny said, 'If you want to change it, you've got to make it seem like their idea.' And so, I did what I could. I've sown a few seeds myself.

I posted through little notes, snippets of our life and our garden, to see if it might give them the spark they needed. I worried at one point that they might never get there, when their fighting got so bad. But Jenny, who's been keeping an eye on things for me, popped in a short while ago. She loves the mischief of it all, the mystery. I rather worried she'd give the game away. But she said the garden was looking lovely. Different, but lovely nonetheless. Anyway, every time I go for a wander, I take a walk past the garden wall. This last autumn or winter, I could barely see what was going on. All I have, I hate to admit, is a little glimpse of whatever's brave and bold enough to crawl over the wall. And in the early spring, there still wasn't anything there.

However, last week, as I was wandering past, I didn't see the usual peep of brambles and bindweed trickling over. Alma, I saw the tips of a banana tree . . . a banana tree! I even caught sight of our clematis, planted all those years ago. It was back. Somehow, they rescued it from oblivion.

In that moment, they rescued me too.

That banana tree, it feels like a new era. The banana tree and that clematis, it blends the old and the new. Maybe it also feels like the blending of me and you!

Whenever I wander past now, the wall is a tapestry of hope. And the gate! It was rotting away. But it's back now, with a new handle. And I hoped they might open it up once more.

This is a bit of a ramble, Alma, but I wanted to tell you that it seems as though Jenny and I, and the strangers of course, we kept your promise after all.

I kept asking Jenny if she knew whether I'd be able to see the garden one day, and I could see she was concerned. I think she was anxious that if I did see it, it might break my heart. If it wasn't as we'd kept it.

Today, someone knocked on my door. I don't get uninvited visitors, Alma, so I never open up. Usually it's someone trying to sell me something, and I get worried I might say the wrong thing. Ever since I stopped working over a decade ago, I'm not quite as clued up. I'm seventy-three and although Jenny's eighty, she seems twenty years younger than me. She always jokes that since you guys left, since Hiral moved away, I started my hermit life . . . but it's true. I've never once been busy in the last few years.

Anyway, they knocked a few times, even after I ignored them, and when I looked down, out of the window, I saw it was them. The neighbours. Number 77 and Number 79. I worried that one of them caught a glimpse of me as I twitched at the curtain.

I felt my heart pounding at the speed of light. I hid, Alma. I just hid. I knew it was my chance to talk to them. I realized then they must have known it was me. But I was scared. I'm not sure what of. Maybe it's the fear of talking to someone new. Or maybe it was the worry of speaking to people I'd made up stories about in my own head. And I was ashamed, embarrassed, that the life I used to lead – with you, and Prem – is so far from the life I lead now. I heard the young man say, eventually, 'Let's try again another day,' and I felt my temperature drop. It was a relief. I could breathe again.

When I was certain they'd gone, I wandered down to the front door because I was sure I'd heard them drop something through. And sitting on the doormat was a note, and a flyer. On the flyer was a photograph. Two neighbours, arm in arm, in front of that gate. Ring a bell?

It wasn't us though – it was them! The neighbours!

And they're hosting a garden party for the neighbours of Eastbourne Road and beyond.

It's 26 August. Uncanny, I know. It must be a coincidence. Life is funny that way.

And the note. It was addressed to me. To Maya. They've invited me to see the garden. Before anyone else does. They said it seemed only right that I get to see it first. Now, I might get to keep a promise I made to myself too.

All my love, always,

Your friend,

Maya x

Chapter 33

Bernice

July 2019

With a month to go before the party, Bernice and Winston barely had a chance to focus on life beyond the garden. Sal and Angela were spreading the word to some of the locals they knew. Bernice was anxious about it all. Would people turn up and destroy the garden? Would it turn into some kind of illegal rave?

'You're worrying too much,' Winston kept telling her, but she could sense he was nervous too. Perhaps for different reasons.

'Have you invited Simon?' Winston asked one morning, as they both stared out at the pouring rain. For the last two weeks, they'd had a steady cycle of rain and blistering sunshine, which meant everything had grown massively, including the courgettes and squashes, the sunflowers and the grapevine. It was all a bit out of hand. The weeds that were tiny seedlings a month ago had tripled in size and taken over the garden: brambles were poking out between beds, bindweed had tangled itself around benches and flowerpots and plants, pulling them down to the ground.

Today, after days of psyching themselves up, they'd agreed to get to work in earnest. It had to be sorted, presentable, before the garden party in a few weeks' time. And for Bernice, her most consistent worry was: 'What would Maya think?'

Maya, however, hadn't made contact since they attempted to invite her. Their note and flyer had gone unanswered. And Bernice now found herself holding her breath whenever she passed Number 68.

'Bernice,' Winston repeated, bringing her back to the present. 'Have you spoken to Simon?'

'Yes,' Bernice said, with a sigh. 'He's refusing to come.'

She tried to hide her disappointment. Did all she could to keep her voice flat, unemotional. At first she wasn't sure why it hurt her so much. She'd only mentioned it in passing. She didn't think it would be a big thing. But Simon, who had been in a fairly good mood for once while dropping Seb off, had suddenly gone cold. Sullen. She couldn't read him. Even after all these years, she couldn't read him.

'No, Bernice,' he'd said. 'I'm not spending my weekend with strangers, just so you can rub this all in my face.'

Bernice took a step back then, pleased Seb was out of earshot.

'Simon,' she said quietly. 'That's not what this is about.'

'What else would it be about? You've always wanted this. I could never make you happy. And now you want to show me everything I did wrong? I don't want to spend a *day* with any of your neighbours. Seb was saying you've got two more in that house next door . . . like a conveyer belt of strangers. It's not good for Seb. He needs consistency. How do you really know who you're living next door to? Who knows what they're capable of?'

She could see his conspiracy theories escalating. He was egging himself on, getting more and more angry.

'This isn't about you,' she'd said in response, her tone even. 'But do what you like.'

Now, she wished she'd said something else to him. She wished she'd really told him what was on her mind.

There was a knock at the gate and seconds later, Sal emerged under the arch, pushing a wheelbarrow with a trowel and some green sacks.

'Hey, Sal!' Winston said brightly.

'The little one Seb told me there's lots to do, so I'm here to volunteer!'

'Yeah, we've got *lots* of tidying to get through,' Winston nodded. 'Thanks for helping, mate.' Winston took a final slurp of his coffee, then left his mug on the garden table. Sal looked hopefully between Winston then Bernice who, sensing what he was aiming for, said: 'Would you like a coffee, Sal?'

'Oh yes, please, very kind! Thank you!' When Bernice poured him a cup, he promptly put down his trowel and green sacks, and took the mug from her with both hands.

'You've come to help!' Seb said, wrestling with his wellington boots on the kitchen doorstep. He was all prepared in his gardening clothes – an old Superman T-shirt that was a bit too small and last year's school shorts. 'There are SO many weeds in the garden. Winston let them get out of hand.'

'Eh!' Winston called. 'Not my fault – blame the rain.'

'Now, young man,' Sal said, putting his cup of coffee down, having drunk it all in one go. 'Are you going to show me what needs doing?'

Seb continued wrestling with his boots, his tongue sticking out in concentration.

Winston chipped in: 'Sal, I can show you if you want?'

Sal clapped his hand onto his back, and Winston led the way. He pointed out the weeds that had grown out of control ('Yes, Bernice, these are definitely weeds now – we don't want them') and Sal rolled up his sleeves, ready to get stuck in.

When Seb finally managed to put on his boots, he ran to join them, and Bernice watched happily. She pictured that garden, the idyllic garden she'd wanted – with pools of mud, and grass, and beautiful flowers everywhere, a children's paradise. She'd always imagined it had to be private, only for them. But watching Seb playing with Sal and Winston . . . this was better, wasn't it? Her son was interacting with people he might never have met, he had new figures in his life now to guide him, to show him the way.

What she'd really wanted was space to breathe – a place to call home. And now, that's what they had.

It took them a good few hours of solid work, with Seb quickly finding his way inside, shirking his gardening responsibilities, the novelty having worn off. By the end of the afternoon, they had ten big sacks full of earth and weeds, which they piled up in Bernice's front garden.

'You're sure you're happy to keep them here?' Winston said cheekily. He could tell she hated it.

'Yeah, no problem,' Bernice said through gritted teeth.

Winston's phone, sitting on the garden table, suddenly pinged: a WhatsApp notification. She watched as Winston clocked it, put the phone straight back down and tapped the screen to minimize the app, before wandering off. But Winston hadn't noticed that the incoming voice note had started to play.

Hey little bro, came a woman's voice.

Ruth.

I'm coming to London for work in a couple of weeks and I'm determined to see you, no matter how much you avoid me. So, call me back, okay? I want to plan!

Bernice looked around at Sal, who was sitting in Winston's decrepit chair, with his hat over his face, shielding him from the afternoon sun. Winston was tidying up the tools in the garden. He hadn't heard, had he?

She wandered closer to the phone, which was still unlocked, and she could see a string of messages from Ruth, a few missed video calls too. Winston hadn't replied to much in the last week or so. And the replies he had sent were basic. She asked questions like 'How are you doing? I miss you' and his replies were no more involved than 'Been hectic! How are the kids?' He only seemed to ask questions of her, he never gave anything of himself back.

She looked away quickly, feeling guilt creep through her veins. She shouldn't be looking – this was invading his privacy.

She glanced up. Winston was now putting things back in the potting shed. She took the opportunity. Quickly, she clicked on Ruth's profile photo, taking her through to her number, and snapped a photo with her own phone. She knew she was going behind Winston's back. She shouldn't. She could ruin everything with this. But maybe he needed a push in the right direction.

'Well,' Sal said, pulling himself up from his chair, completely exhausted. His hat skew-whiff, flecks of green dust from the weeds stuck to sweat on his face. 'I better be off – I won't be needed again before the party, will I? I'm happy to help with that but . . . no more intensive gardening for me. I can't cope with this *and* an allotment!' He loped off, walking much slower than before.

'Winston,' Bernice said, sitting at the garden table with a glass of wine that evening.

'Mmm?' he said.

'Do you think you'll invite Lewis to the party? Have you seen much of him lately?'

Winston stopped for a moment. He leaned back in his chair and picked up his beer, rotating it silently in his hands.

'He'd be so proud of everything you were doing. And maybe he'd like to meet Darlene and Heidi too.'

'Bernice,' he said, looking at her. 'How do *you* know he'd be proud?' His gaze was sharp, but his voice had softened.

'Look, it's obvious you miss him. Doesn't he keep saying he wants to see you?'

Winston stopped looking at her, and began to pick at the ring pull of his can instead. 'He's . . . Yeah.'

'And, do you want to see him?'

He shrugged.

'Winston, do you still love him?'

'Of course I do,' he replied, without a moment's hesitation. 'I just don't want to live the life he wants. I want to be here, in London. If he can compromise . . .' He petered off. 'Well . . . I don't see he'll ever do that. Not with his job.'

'Is that a decision you can make for him?' Bernice felt herself going into 'stern parent mode' but she couldn't help herself.

'Bernice . . . he's got a life to live. That's never going to change. He never made time for me.'

Bernice nodded, a lump forming in her throat, a scenario so familiar.

'I know,' she said, eventually. 'But maybe he needed to realize how much he might lose if he didn't. Maybe everything that's gone on between you, could that be his wake-up call? Let's face it, he's barely left your life. He turned up on New Year . . . he's been asking you to visit him ever since.'

'Yeah,' Winston said quietly, eyes looking out on the garden as the sun gradually disappeared behind the rows of houses ahead of them, the sky bright orange. 'But I don't want to push him into anything. I don't want to hold him back.'

'Winston,' Bernice looked him square in the face now. 'Have you told him any of this? Said what *you* want?'

Winston shrugged. 'I don't want him to make any decisions for me,' he said.

'Oh, Winston,' Bernice said, taking a huge glug of her drink. 'It might be that he's willing to do whatever it takes to be with you. You only have to ask.'

At that, Winston pulled his phone towards him, and nodded. 'Yeah . . . maybe you're right.'

'I am,' Bernice said smugly.

'I said *maybe*,' he smiled back coyly, and took a final slurp from his can. 'But the real question, Bernice, is when are you going to give Simon a proper piece of your mind?'

Bernice smiled, caught off guard. He was right. 'Well,' she said, clinking her glass with his. 'All in good time.'

Chapter 34

Maya

June 1990

'We're getting too old for these trips,' Maya huffed, as she and Alma tried to lug three bags of compost into Erol's car.

'Speak for yourself. You're a youngster compared to me and I'm still going strong!' Alma said, standing a few feet away, watching her friend do all the heavy lifting. She was looking around the car park, searching for something. 'Have you seen my niece?'

'What?' Maya sighed, picking up another bag from the trolley.

'Kate – I thought she said she'd be around here?'

Maya's eyes darted immediately to her friend, and for a moment she forgot the weight of the compost cradled in her arms. 'Kate? Alma, Kate doesn't live here.'

'Oh no, silly woman,' Alma snapped grumpily. 'She's visiting friends, I thought she said she'd be here this weekend.'

'What? Here? At the garden centre?'

'No, no, in Canonbury.'

'It's a big place, Alma,' Maya said cautiously. 'She could be anywhere.'

'I know – I thought I'd keep an eye out, that's all,' she said, plonking herself in the passenger seat of Erol's car.

'Erol!' Maya called, as the compost began to slip through her hands. Erol turned towards her, away from the new friends he'd made outside the pub. At the sight of her beetroot face, he said a hasty goodbye and legged it towards the car.

'Maya, Maya, Maya, let me get that,' he wheezed as he approached. Erol was at least ten years her senior, and she wondered whether he was any more capable of lifting the bag than she was, but if it gave her a bit of a break, she was grateful nonetheless. 'These are huge. What's it all for?'

'We're getting some new plants – donated by the Jameses. In memory of Prem, actually,' Alma called back. 'Charlie thought it'd be nice to have a few plants around his chair, so it's more of a "thing", you know. It'd be rather nice, I think, but we need the compost or they'll die.'

'All right, all right, if it's for Prem,' he said. 'That old Mr James really is getting soft, isn't he? From demon landlord, to sentimentalist?' Erol laughed. 'Nice though. Prem would like it.'

In recent years, Mr James had become more of a friend to them all. Alma still didn't agree with everything he said, and Maya remained cautious around him. She still paid him rent, and was conscious he could boot her out whenever he wanted. But, despite her worries, he was kind and thoughtful and those qualities were clearer to see in him these days. He had also proved to be a huge help in the garden when he had the time.

To Maya, it felt like Prem had been here only yesterday, but she also felt like she'd lived a whole life grieving him. She missed his presence in the house, the sight of his face in the morning, trying desperately to stay asleep. She pictured him coming in after work in his suit, his bag by his side, his face lighting up as soon as he saw her or Hiral. She missed his thoughtfulness when it came to Alma and the garden. He'd always have one eye on her, ready to help if she needed it, but silently, unimposing.

Even after all this time, Alma and Maya toasted Prem every Friday evening. Maya tried to see Prem in the little things. She let him live on in her daily kindness to strangers, in her patience with difficult situations, and in the optimism she tried so hard to hold on to, because that's what Prem would have wanted for her. For them all. He saw the good in things. He encouraged her to keep going.

Recently, however, all the days seemed to blur into one. The only markers of the passing of time were Hiral's rigorous school and revision schedules. And the garden, flower buds waking up for the sun, their heads eventually drooping with tiredness, browning with age, seasons changing. And finally, Alma's moments of forgetfulness increasing in frequency, of being lost in her own home, of seeing things, people, pets, who weren't there any more.

Now, without Prem by her side, she had no one to talk her down, no one to help put her worries in check. She knew Hiral sensed her worry, but she couldn't bear to put anything more on her daughter's shoulders. She'd been through so much, she'd already been so brave; braver than she should ever have to be.

Instead, she would look up at the photo of Prem and wish for his wisdom, a calming hand on her shoulder. When no answer came, she would simply step into the garden when the world around her was quiet, and cry, with no one to listen to her but the night air and the foxes, mischievous as ever.

Alma had started speaking to a doctor, after lots of convincing from Kate. She knew that much. But Alma hadn't told Maya what that doctor was saying.

'Patient–doctor confidentiality,' Alma said, when they'd finally had the conversation. They were pruning the roses, cutting off the dead flowers.

'Alma, *you're* allowed to talk about things, it's only the doctor who can't,' Maya reminded her, her eyes on her secateurs, her name embroidered on her gloves.

'Well, my business,' Alma said, trying to put a brave face on.

Prem would have known what to say, wouldn't he? He'd have come up with a funny line, something that made them smile yet still left them with a message. What would he say?

'*What would you say?*' Maya had whispered out loud.

'Erol,' Maya instructed, back at the house, 'help Alma into the garden. She wanted to dig the trenches for the new plants. Can you help her?'

'Help?! Erol?!' Alma guffawed. 'Erol can't be of any help to me, he's too impatient.'

'You're not, are you, Erol?'

Erol shook his head.

'Bob!' Maya called through her house, to where Bob was raking in the garden already. 'Can you bring the wheelbarrow through the gate?' Erol looked relieved that he didn't have to carry the compost. Moments later, Patrick was there too in Prem's ancient, disintegrating wellington boots and holey gardening gloves. Bob was beside him with the wheelbarrow.

'Come on now, get a move on,' she nodded to the three men.

Maya stepped into Alma's kitchen with her friend. Even now, the change surprised her. Usually slightly disordered, thoroughly lived in, Alma's house was spotless. Over the last few months, when Alma had been worrying herself about lost keys, or remote controls, or kitchen utensils, Alma and Maya had painstakingly tidied the whole house and created 'official' places for things. The house still held Alma's essence, but it was at least a little more organized than before, a bit more manageable.

Alma used to keep her keys on the Formica table, thrown over some newspapers. Now the newspapers were in an enamel magazine rack in the same spot, and there was a little enamel dish printed with a photograph of carnations ('Maya, I fucking hate carnations, you know this!') beside the rack for her keys. So far, it seemed to be doing the trick. Or at least it made it easier for Maya, and Kate (who was here more often these days) to assess what was missing and where it had ended up.

'Cup of tea before we start work?' Maya asked Alma as Morris curled himself around Alma's leg.

'Yes, of course – I wonder if Kate will pop round. My niece. She's very nice.'

'Yes, I know Kate,' Maya said quietly.

'She found some things that her dad left behind, she thought I'd like them. Pictures of us out in the garden. Charlie James is there too, actually. Face like a slapped arse. But only because his dad was the one that did the slapping.'

Maya chuckled, and clicked the kettle on. 'Two sugars today? For your energy?'

'Yeah, go on then. You only live once, after all.'

Alma and Maya managed to spend the rest of the afternoon chatting away, making Maya's famous paneer samosas that Alma absolutely loved, providing they weren't too spicy, and letting Erol and Patrick get on with the digging and planting. Bob kept popping over, trying to wriggle his way into conversation with Alma.

Maya glanced outside, watching the two men digging either side of Prem's chair, and she imagined him sitting there, observing his friends doing all the hard work, with a very satisfied smile on his face. She thought he'd also spare a thought for Bob, his love unrequited still, after years of hoping.

Seizing an opportunity to be bossy, with a cup of tea in one hand and a samosa in the other, Alma stepped into the garden and called: 'Patrick! No, make sure you pull the roots apart a little – look how pot-bound that is!'

'Erol! Stop that! You need to keep the plants a foot apart!'

'Manure that now!'

'Bob! That looks great!'

Maya watched, entertained, and grateful to see Alma fully embracing herself. Now, she could put her feet up in Alma's kitchen, the door thrown wide open. Even in the late June warmth, there was a nip in the air – she kept one of Bina's shawls draped over her legs.

Alma shook her head at the men jokingly, walking gingerly back towards the kitchen. Suddenly, Maya watched as her friend's legs gave way, buckling at the knees. Alma collapsed heavily, her head hitting the ground with a thud.

In an instant, Bob rushed forward, kneeling down to Alma, a protective hand on her arm. Erol, Patrick and Maya also hurried over as quickly as they could.

'Alma?' Maya said softly but firmly, panic in her heart. 'Alma, can you hear me?'

Alma's cheek was pressed against the ground, her arms awkwardly positioned under her. Her eyes were closed, unmoving, and Maya watched as a single tear rolled from one of her eyes, when a crack of thunder sounded somewhere overhead, followed by a sudden burst of rain, showering them all.

'Patrick, can you call an ambulance?' Maya said hurriedly, her heart slamming, 'and Erol, will you call Kate? She's staying with a friend. Her number is on my fridge.'

As the two men nodded solemnly, following their instructions without another word, Maya sat beside her friend. She held Bob's hand, as the two of them stayed close by Alma.

'Please, Alma, please be okay,' she whispered, like a prayer, over and over again.

Chapter 35

Winston

August 2019

Lewis, Bernice and I are hosting a garden party for the neighbourhood in a week's time. I—

He typed the words out, lingering on the second sentence, before deleting it all immediately.

Lewis, Bernice and I would love it if—

Delete. Delete. Delete.

Hey, L, he tried again. *Hope all good in Ox. We're hosting a garden party for the neighbours next week. Would love to see you there. Details attached. Love xxx*

His finger lingered over the delete button. Three kisses, was it too much?

Oh for goodness' sake, he told himself. He wasn't a teenager any more. And Lewis wasn't some schoolboy crush. He attached the invitation and sent it over, watching as the single tick became a double.

He stared at the message for a moment, and when *online* appeared below Lewis's name, he quickly clicked out of the chat, checking his other threads. And there was that message from Ruth. The voice note. She'd sent it a couple of weeks ago now. She was coming to London for work. Just her.

And it coincided with the party.

Winston looked up at the photograph of his mum, hanging on the wall. He knew she'd tell him to invite her, to let his sister in, to let his family in. *You've shut yourself away for too long.*

But he couldn't invite her. There was a physical block, something stopping him. He'd replied with a non-committal message: '*So exciting, Ruth! Would love to see you. I'll have to check if I can get some time off. Maybe we could meet for dinner one day? I can come into town, we can do something nice.*' Ruth had replied, '*Of course, lovely brother! Whatever works for you.*'

Somehow he'd sensed her disappointment.

Winston was hiding. He was still hiding his life from her.

But if he brought her here, if she saw that he was sharing a house with strangers, that he was no longer with Lewis – the one part of his life he'd told her about – when he was thirty-three years of age, she'd worry. And the last thing he wanted was for her to worry about him.

A message popped up.

Winston, this is amazing. I'm so proud of you. Your mum would love this so much. Well done. I'll be there. L xx

The message felt like a jolt, a shot of brightness straight into his veins.

But it meant nothing. Lewis was being supportive. They were still on good terms, weren't they?

The mention of his mum allowed Winston to sink back into memories once again. The sight of her working in the garden in the early mornings, admiring the leaves on her banana plant late in the evening to a chorus of crickets.

'No,' Winston shook his head, his mood dropping. Grief could creep up on him in strange ways. Watching a sunset from the top of the house, knowing his mother would never experience that. Laughing at a funny customer at work, knowing he'd never be able to share that memory with her, realizing how much of his life he kept hidden, how many stories had gone untold. And this garden party – he wanted her to be there. But it was impossible.

Maybe, he said to himself, *you should at least invite Ruth. So she can see your life too.*

Winston gulped down his trepidation and opened up the conversation thread. It was a Saturday, maybe she'd be free. But as he started typing out a message, fear overwhelmed him, his heart rate increasing, his chest tight. He wasn't ready. Not yet. There was too much to tell her.

Would he ever be ready?

Ping.

Winston's heart rate increased. Was it Ruth?

Or Lewis again?

No.

It was Bernice. With another link to the Google Doc. In all her stress and control-freakery, worried the garden might not be right for Maya, she'd sent a ginormous list with a huge number of tasks under his name.

Hey, I've added a few more things to the list, the message said.

Tidy up patio

Use extra chairs donated by Sal

Pick up extra food from Sal on the day

Weed flower beds first thing

Find something to prop gate open

Winston sighed and headed out to the back garden, preparing to knock on Bernice's door and tell her she needed to calm down a bit. But before his knuckles rapped the door, he caught a glimpse of Simon. He was leaning casually on the kitchen counter, wearing a sweatshirt. Winston had *never* seen him in a sweatshirt.

Winston crept back, but the sound of their voices travelled over, and he stopped, hovering in his kitchen doorway, unseen.

'Simon,' Bernice said. He recognized her tone. It was one she'd adopted over the last few weeks to boss Winston and Seb around the garden. 'Your son wants you to be there. And that's all that matters.'

'I'm busy, Bernice,' he said, like a petulant child. 'I've got work that weekend, and if I'm picking Seb up on Sunday, I want to make sure I have time for him.'

'Right, that's very noble of you,' her voice was sharp. 'But your son wants you there. This garden is not only the work of me and Winston. You don't need to celebrate that. But your son has put so much energy into it. Your little boy loves this garden, and he's proud of the work he's done. Do you know what might make him doubt that?'

There was silence for a moment, and Winston pictured Simon shrugging, looking at the ground, a schoolboy being told off.

'If *you* don't come. Because that little boy idolizes you, Simon. You're his father, and seeing you proud literally makes his day.' Her voice was cracking, she took a deep breath, letting out a heavy sigh, before continuing. 'I don't want us to argue any more, Simon. We've done enough of that over the past few years. We used to love each other, we used to *care* for each other.'

'I know,' Simon replied softly.

'Do you remember how excited we were when Seb was a baby? And we'd take him to coffee shops in the morning on weekends, and he'd rattle sugar packets around in his hands, and we'd simply laugh. And it felt like we had everything in the world?'

'I remember.'

'We still *have* everything in the world, Simon. That boy, he's our everything, and we need to make sure he knows it. We need to realize we're still a team in this. We're a team for *him*.'

Winston's forehead throbbed, his eyes stinging. He could totally imagine baby Seb, a huge gummy grin, looking up at his parents adoringly while shaking sugar sachets like maracas.

'Bernice, I . . .'

'Simon, if it's going to be another excuse about how you can't make it, I don't want to hear it.'

'I wasn't going to say that,' Simon said eventually. 'I just wanted to say . . . I wanted to say I'm sorry.'

Winston held his breath in disbelief.

Simon was apologizing?

'Hey!'

Winston startled and turned round to see Darlene. He leapt up, pretending he wasn't eavesdropping.

'I'm watching the birds on the feeders,' he said hurriedly, embarrassed. Darlene frowned, looking out of the window. 'Oh, you must have scared them off,' he said, blushing.

'Typical me,' Darlene laughed, her voice full of warmth. 'Wanna join us for breakfast? We're thinking of trying the Good Egg. Fuel us up before we help out in the garden this morning.'

Winston turned back to the window. He couldn't hear Bernice any more.

'All right then,' he said. 'Yeah, that'd be nice.'

'Winston!' There was another call as Bernice poked her head out of her front door ten minutes later. He spotted Simon and Seb wandering down the pavement to the car. 'I've added a couple of things to the garden party list. Did you see?'

'Yes, Bernice! Calm down – we've still got a week to go!' he said. But he wanted to stop and tell her how proud he was of her. For finally speaking her mind to Simon, bringing the Queen of Sheba into action. He even, almost, felt proud of Simon.

'Winston!' Seb called over his shoulder as his dad led him away. 'It's never too soon to get organized! That's what my teacher says. And it better be perfect by the time I get back tomorrow!'

Chapter 36

Maya

July 1990

'Hot, hot, hot,' Kate said, through a mouthful of gözleme.

'You're always so impatient,' Maya chuckled, holding her own in its paper bag by her side. It was worth waiting a minute or two.

Walking past mothers and babies, weaving in and out of tables of fruit and vegetables, cassava and yam, mangoes and pomegranates, they were wandering to Dalston Kingsland to catch the North London Line to pick up Alma from the hospital.

Listening to the bartering, the chatter between shop owners and customers enquiring about elderly mothers, and recipes, and invites for dinner, Maya could almost pretend that when they got a taxi home later, the world wouldn't be different.

Maya finally took a bite of her gözleme, the cheese and onion seeping out, liquid gold. The day was warm for mid-May, almost a heatwave, and the air was sticky with the heat. Maya was wearing her lightest cotton Punjabi dress, and Kate was in a T-shirt, linen trousers, and sandals that 'flip-flopped'. With every bus that passed by, the exhaust fumes lingered in the air a bit, but it didn't dampen the mood. The joy was all around them; a hot day in the city.

'You know,' Maya said, as they arrived at the train station, 'I think we're going to have to broach the topic of her either sorting out the house, so it's more accessible—'

'Which she can't afford,' Kate said.

'Yes, exactly, or . . .' Maya couldn't bear to say it, it felt like an unspeakable future. 'Or, her moving somewhere else.'

Kate and Maya had had the conversation many times, but only as a vague option. It was easier that way. Easier to believe you were simply being 'practical', 'sensible', but that it might never come to pass.

'She's still welcome to come and live with me,' Kate continued. She lived in a bungalow in the Peak District. 'She'd hate it though. I mean, it's bloody beautiful – but you know her, she loves London. She's only ever known the city really. I think the silence might be enough to do her head in.'

Maya couldn't help but chuckle at that.

'Maya,' Kate whispered, as though Alma were listening in. 'I'm always here if you need me. I know it's not going to be easy convincing Alma to live with me, and it might not happen overnight, but if anything feels off, if you need anything, you let me know. I'll be there in a heartbeat.'

Maya nodded. She looked at Kate. They were the same age, but somehow, with the years of worry, Maya wondered if Kate saw her as someone closer to Alma's age. The weight of a lifetime on her shoulders. 'She's lucky she has you, Kate. You're so kind.'

'Maya . . . I think she's been lucky to have you, and Hiral. And Prem. The family she always needed.'

'Be careful, Alma,' Kate said, as Maya held open the garden gate. Alma was sitting in a wheelchair, because the nurses had said she was still a little unsteady on her feet and it would be better to try to encourage her to only walk indoors until she built her confidence up.

'Oh, come on, I'm not some fragile doll!' Alma shouted. 'I just want a cup of tea – the stuff in the hospital tasted all watered down and horrible.'

Kate and Maya exchanged a knowing glance. For the last couple of weeks, while Alma had been kept in the hospital for recovery and lots of tests, she'd constantly complained about the tea. Nothing else. She repeated, persistently, that the nurses were lovely, but the 'tea tasted like piss'.

'I'll bring you a flask of some then,' Kate had promised, but Alma had said: 'Oh don't bother with that, I'll be out of here in no time. I want to get home.' But her progress had been slow, in many senses. And she was shaky on her feet. Bina, Maya and Kate had taken it in turns to visit. Alma was always grateful and happy to hear their voices. But once or twice, she'd got Maya and Bina confused with each other, and Bina had got upset, seeing Alma getting muddled for the first time. But she knew Alma meant no harm. She was trying hard. She was trying to get better.

As soon as Alma made her way into her house, she pushed herself up from her chair confidently, and sat down at the kitchen table. She'd looked so small, inferior, in that hospital bed. Surrounded by machines, large windows, lots of wires, other patients. And here, she still looked tiny. Like she'd lost half of herself on the way. A lesser version of the Alma they knew before the fainting incident in the garden. Maya wondered if Kate noticed it too.

Kate sat next to her aunt as Maya put the kettle on, Morris running in and meowing, wrapping himself around her ankles. While Alma had been in hospital, it had been up to Maya to feed the cat, and seeing him in the empty house, she'd ended up spending more time with him; he'd become a welcome companion, a little life running around Alma's house, keeping it warm while she was away.

'Alma,' Kate said gently.

'What?' Alma said, tapping her fingers impatiently on the Formica table. 'How's that tea coming on, Maya?'

'Alma,' Kate said again, holding her hand. 'Maya and I have been talking and we wondered if . . .' Kate trailed off. Alma was still watching Maya, as though she knew what Kate was about to say.

'Morris, Morris my dear, come here,' she said, putting her free hand towards the cat. On cue, Morris leapt up onto her lap, turning round and round to get strokes from all angles.

'Knock knock!'

The three women turned to look at the kitchen door: it was Bob, holding a bunch of pink and white roses. 'From all of us,' he said, thrusting them at Alma. 'It's lovely to see you back home!'

'Oh, Bob!'

Maya watched as Alma's face lit up – she'd never seen her so happy to see Bob, but she knew that it was probably because he was saving her from a conversation she really didn't want to have.

'Is that the kettle I hear?' Bob said, looking at Maya hopefully.

'Of course, one sugar?'

'You know me,' he said, before sitting down next to Alma.

'So, Bob, tell me everything I've missed.'

'Well . . .' he started. 'I've been down to the south coast quite a bit, to see my sister, recently. It's lovely there. I'd love to take you!'

Kate watched the two old friends fall into easy conversation, and gestured towards Maya that they leave them to it. 'She knows,' Kate said, as Maya settled herself in the living room, 'that she's going to have to listen to us one day.'

'Yes, she does, but she'll keep us waiting.' Maya took a hurried sip of her too-hot tea and looked around the living room at Alma's garish wallpaper, now decades out of date, and her too-low seventies sofas. Everything was impractical, but it was exactly as Alma wanted it.

'Look, sit down, give yourself a break for today,' Maya said as she took in Kate's tense frame and furrowed brow. 'We'll let her settle in. She knows this conversation is coming. The fainting is one thing, but she's getting lost more and more, forgetting things . . . She knows being with you, with family, will be best,' Maya said. Her voice was steady, level, but she could feel her mug shaking.

Would Maya continue to live at Number 79 if Alma wasn't here? Would there be any point? She was living in a house too big for her and Hiral, but a house too full of memories for her to leave.

But without Alma . . . would anything feel the same?

Life, from here on, was about to change. She knew that much. She wished she could rewind, relive their life, relive the days working in the garden, the garden parties, Prem and his friends laughing and joking on the picnic bench while Alma made her signature flavourless veggie lasagne. Hiral crawling about on the lawn, admiring her family around her.

Oh what she would give for that awful veggie lasagne, and an afternoon as her life was all those years before.

What she would give for the old, indomitable, unstoppable Alma.

Chapter 37

Winston

August 2019

Winston couldn't sleep. When five thirty arrived, he took himself out of bed, crept down the stairs, avoiding the creaky ones so he wouldn't wake Darlene and Heidi – one of whom was snoring incredibly loudly – and he settled himself on the sofa. In a few hours, the garden would be open. After all these months of tension and toil with Bernice, they were *actually* throwing a party. He looked at Lewis's message on his phone once again: would he turn up? What if he couldn't make it? What if work got in the way? Winston forced his mind to stop running at a million miles an hour, but the excitement, the anxiety, coursed through his veins.

Today he'd meet neighbours he'd never seen before. He wondered if the nosy parker at Number 80 might turn up. Maybe the family at Number 78 too. But his biggest question was whether Maya would be there. With every knock on the garden gate, every slap of post on the doormat these last few days, he'd hoped it might be her.

Peering out of the window, he looked over to Number 68, wondering what Maya was doing right now. Wondering if she had the leaflets, if she'd read them, if she would turn up. The window boxes along the street were teeming with flowers, and the day was already blinding. Number 80's hedge was perfect as always, and the window at Number 68 was open, once more, but no signs of Maya had poked out just yet.

Winston turned instead to old WhatsApp messages with his mum. Two years after her death, he still checked under her username, imagining one day he'd see the word 'online'. He scrolled through the photos she'd sent years ago. Candids of his dad reading the newspaper, or holding a hand to cover his face if he realized. He pressed play on a video – it was his mum giving a tour of the garden.

He got swept away with the sound of her voice, the characteristic rasp in her laugh. He focused on her face, surrounded by the greens and oranges of the garden, and he watched her move, the way she wrinkled her nose in joy, her eyes scrunching shut soon after, and she leaned back, giggling. In those moments, his mother was young again – she was a teenager, laughing with her sisters, a young woman tickled by her child.

All the muscles in Winston's face went rigid, all the strength in his core was working to keep him watching. If he didn't look away, she was still here. Her laugh, her voice, filling his ears.

He took a deep breath, fighting for air, when the video came to an end.

He scrolled further. Selfies she'd sent him, a reflection of the flash in her eyes, like a sparkle just for him. Pictures of her dinner – mug badh kadhi, his favourite, mithai and prasad on Diwali, hundreds and hundreds of graphics forwarded and forwarded again on WhatsApp, wishing him a good morning, a prosperous year . . . Photos of her beside her banana trees, almost three times her height, her hands clasped in front of her like she was posing for a school picture. She'd sent him pictures that she'd taken of old photographs of him and his sister as little children, the flash from her phone bouncing off the glossy paper, knocking out a baby's head, or emanating from their heart like ET. They were almost always dressed in neat sweaters and shorts, like tiny golfers. And there she was, in a pale peach sari, her hair big and permed, kneeling down to them, her body language as fluid as the chiffon she was wearing.

When he returned to the conversation, he found a photograph that had been sent with a message. Nine years ago. The day after he first travelled to London. There, in that message, were the words he'd never allowed himself to believe. He'd spent so much of his life lying to her. Pretending he was successful, pretending he was making friends, making money, doing her and his father proud, using the education they'd paid for.

Every day, you make me proud, beta, her message said. *The only gift I ask for is that you are happy and that you prioritize your happiness. If you are happy, and healthy, you have all the wealth in the world. Surround yourself with love, and nothing can harm you. I love you, my beta, come home soon xx*

Winston reread those words, over and over again, as he wandered out to the garden. He lifted his gaze up from the screen, to breathe in the air around him, taking in the sounds of an aeroplane thundering in the distance, the whispering of leaves, the sound of birds singing, the grass quivering in the early morning breeze. The sun was fighting through the city haze, warm and orange light bouncing off the leaves, the petals of the roses, misted through the asparagus. The patches of shade still had evidence of the morning dew. Everything in the sun had been burnt off, in this bold, bright day.

He could hear the difference in that message now, couldn't he?

This, the transformation of the garden . . . it had made him happy. And that's all she wanted for him. Only now did he see that. Only now did he feel brave enough to trust her words.

He turned back to his phone. *Ruth*. She was here, in London. After today, when the party was out of the way, he'd call her. He'd tell her everything. How he was feeling, how he could see he was going to be okay. And maybe they'd have the chance to start afresh.

When Winston arrived at Angela and Sal's flat later, they'd already put together four huge foil trays of food. Angela was in charge of the sandwiches, and Sal's contribution was a whole landscape of babaganoush, the oil forming lakes in the dips, coriander luxuriating on the top. It looked delicious. There was homemade hummus as well, seasoned with chilli flakes, and mountains of cheese pies, the filo pastry flaking away.

'This looks *incredible*,' Winston said, eyes wide, mouth watering.

'I always told him he should be a caterer,' Angela nodded to Sal. 'But it's a mission and a half to get him to cook *me* dinner.'

'Let's hope people turn up to enjoy it.'

'If not,' Sal said. 'We get to eat it all ourselves!'

The thought of no one turning up was, of course, Bernice's worst nightmare.

Angela, Sal and Winston headed down to Eastbourne Road with chairs tucked under an arm, and platters of food held in the other. They were grappling and readjusting the chairs outside the mosque when Jenny trotted past them, calling back behind her: 'Vince! Big day today, eh? . . . Remember to save me some food! I might even see if I can get some blasts from the past there. We can share some stories about when little Chubby Cheeks there was practically in nappies.' She nodded towards Sal, whose cheeks had gone bright red. 'Adorable, he was!'

Angela chuckled away, her tray wobbling dangerously.

As they stumbled through the garden gate, after what felt like a marathon journey with several stops on the way, they saw

Bernice and Darlene laying out plates of food. Seb was already digging in. Pyramids of vegetarian sushi, bowls of tapenade and some fresh sourdough bread.

'Stop it, Seb!' Bernice said, batting his fingers away as they aimed straight for the tapenade, her face stressed. 'We've got to save this for later. Ah . . . please could you go and help Sal and Angela?'

Seb, unperturbed by his mother's brusqueness, skipped forward and reached up for Angela's tray.

'Thank you kindly, young man,' Angela said, in a regal tone.

When all the platters were laid out, they got on with the final tidy-up.

And an hour later, they were all standing in different spots in the garden, gazing round awkwardly, not sure what to do with themselves. Hosts, waiting for the first guests to turn up.

'Look,' Bernice said, finally calming down her frantic worrying, as she held up an old photograph to the view in front of them, passing it first to Winston, and then the others. The plants weren't identical, the landscaping differed slightly, it wasn't exactly the same garden as it had been all those years ago, but there were people here, there was friendship. And the flowers and vegetables looked amazing.

'I think we've done a good job,' Winston said to Bernice with a smile.

'I think we have,' Bernice nodded, her face the picture of pride, and as the photo made its way back to her, her thumb brushed the faces of the two best friends. She looked at Winston then. He nodded back.

'She'll come,' he said, knowing what she was thinking. 'I'm sure she will.'

'The mustard's going strong,' Angela cut in from across the garden.

'It's terrific,' Bernice said, tucking the photograph carefully away from all the food. Winston noticed her tap it once more for luck as she placed it on her kitchen counter. 'I've been putting it in almost every dish.' At that, Seb made a disgusted face, but thankfully, neither Bernice nor Angela noticed.

'And those *roses*,' Angela continued, snapping a photo of them on her phone. 'It really is all looking magnificent.'

They all then startled at the sound of the garden gate creaking open.

'Hey . . .' the gate pushed itself open a little wider, and in came Lewis, five or six sunflowers clutched in his hands. His hair had grown and was swept back with gel. He looked different, younger somehow.

Winston darted forward, his heart pounding in his ribcage. His ears burned hot, probably red. Suddenly aware of all the eyes on the back of his neck, watching his every move. 'Lewis,' he said. He heard his voice, as if for the very first time, high and squeaky – not what he'd intended.

'I brought these for you both, to say well done, for all the,' Lewis looked around the garden, waving the flowers at Angela and Sal in greeting, 'all the work you've done on this place. I . . . I grew them,' he said, when Winston took them. 'I thought it was the only appropriate gift. Something grown with love.'

Winston smiled, looking only at the flowers. He could see a few snail-eaten leaves and petals, a cluster of aphids clinging to the thick stem.

'They're so beautiful.'

'Let me put them in some water.' Bernice rushed forward and grabbed them from Winston's hand, and then beckoned the rest of them to a corner, allowing Winston and Lewis a moment to themselves – like something out of a sitcom.

'So, where are your housemates?' Lewis asked.

'Oh, they're out getting some more supplies. They'll be back soon. You'll like them, I promise.'

'I'm sure I will,' Lewis smiled, and Winston detected a sadness behind the curve of his lips. 'Winston, I . . . I wanted to tell you . . . I'm . . . I got promoted the other day.'

Winston smiled weakly. He shouldn't be surprised, Lewis's work always came first. 'That's terrific, congratulations,' he said with a subdued nod.

'I turned it down,' he continued hurriedly. 'I'm still there, I've not packed it all in. But I'm trying, I'm trying really hard to not commit my whole life to the job. I think I can balance things better. I *want* to do that. And . . . I take evenings off now. As much as possible. Not every day, but most days.' Lewis was babbling, his eyes flicking everywhere, nervous. 'I know I've made some mistakes, but I . . . I wondered if maybe next week . . . Could I take you for dinner?'

'What do you mean?'

'I mean that . . . well,' Lewis laughed, letting out a breath he'd been holding tight. Nervous. Like this was their first date. 'I don't expect you to forgive me or for everything to be okay. But I thought if we could spend a little time getting to know each other again. I want to show you how I feel. I didn't do that before, but I think I can now.'

Winston looked behind him, one eye on the gate. 'I'm not going to move in with you, Lewis, I want to stay here. At least for a bit longer.'

'No, no, I know that,' Lewis said, catching sight of Angela, who was making a beeline for them. 'I thought we could take it slow. Start again. Maybe?'

While Winston was still thinking about what to say, Angela nudged him out of the way and swooped in to pull Lewis, almost twice her height, into her arms. Winston raised his eyebrows in surprise.

'Lewis! My dear, come let me give you a guided tour.' By the sound of it, Angela may already have had two or three glasses of alcoholic punch. He'd forgotten to warn her it was lethal . . .

'Ange,' he said, 'I think he knows his way around.'

'It's all right,' Lewis laughed, relaxing. 'Look, I'm really proud of you. This – it all looks amazing, you're so talented with this gardening stuff, Winston. And think about what I said, okay? And get back to your party! I'll be fine.'

Before he could say anything else, Angela swept Lewis away, who cast a mock-terrified glance over his shoulder at Winston, and a few more people trickled in through the gates. First of all, there was Jenny, who waved to everyone like she was the queen, and headed straight towards the snacks, cigarette in her mouth.

After Jenny, there came, to Bernice and Winston's delight, the nosy parker at Number 80. He was actually here. 'Shall I go and say hi?' Bernice asked, gleeful.

'Rather you than me!'

Winston let her lead, and overheard him introducing himself as 'Damian', boldly, confidently, as though he hadn't spied on them for every day of their lives on the road! Winston glanced around the garden, suddenly alive with people. Some he recognized, others he didn't. A couple with a daughter who looked the same age as Seb wandered in, and Seb took his turn to introduce them to the garden. 'Shall I show you round?' he said to the little girl. Ten minutes later, Seb and his new friend were running around, skipping in and out of beds, and Bernice had to call 'Be careful!' out of habit. Winston laughed at Seb's joyful abandon.

Darlene and Heidi were now taking it in turns to give guided tours. Angela and Sal seemed to be doing their best to force-feed people. Simon arrived soon after, causing Seb to abandon his new friend with an 'I'm sorry! I'll catch you in a bit!' before rushing forward screaming 'Daddy!' at the top of his voice.

Winston watched from the safety of the kitchen, filling a jug with water. No longer chatting to Number 80, Bernice headed towards Simon and gave him a hug. Winston couldn't hear what they were saying, but immediately he could see Simon's body language was different. He wasn't standing tall, chest out, as though putting his armour up. He seemed relaxed, calmer, eyes on his son. 'Thank you,' Bernice seemed to say, clasping a hand on Simon's. Seb was yanking at his father's other hand: 'DAD! LET ME SHOW YOU WHAT I'VE BEEN DOING!'

'Yes please!' Simon replied. It looked like he meant it, and Bernice let them go, standing by the gate and watching them, a smile curling the corners of her mouth. Content, Winston thought. She looks content. Not stressed, not worried, not angry or hurt. Simply content.

From the kitchen, Winston saw someone else approach the gate and make their way under the arch. A familiar smile. Hair tied up in a bun. For a moment, Winston was seeing his mother walking between the vegetable patches. He imagined what she'd be saying. 'Tsk, tsk, this needs more water at this time of year,' or 'this is planted a bit too close to the others'. Or would she notice the little titbits of her advice sprinkled around the garden, the fruits of his labour? For that moment, he saw her, wandering through his garden, stroking the silky leaves of the banana plant, the yellow of her kurta top shimmering in the sun, the material flowing over her arm and behind her. It was nothing but a memory, a wish.

But it *was* someone he knew. Wasn't it?

'Ruth?'

Bernice turned around and walked up to embrace his sister. Winston watched the introduction take place silently, until Bernice started searching the garden, one arm on Ruth.

Heart in his throat, he made his way outside. Legs like jelly. Feet tingling. His sister. She was here.

'Winston!' Ruth called, her voice loud and light, and he pictured her then, all those years ago, running ahead of him playing chase, washing the dishes with him, drawing on each other's faces, then getting told off by their dad for hours afterwards. He'd kept her away for so long, and he knew why – she reminded him of everything he'd lost. Every moment he'd missed out on.

'Ruth,' he whispered back, approaching her, disbelieving. She trotted forward, enveloped him. Her perfume took him back to their childhood, to her first years working in Mumbai, coming home every few weeks exhausted after days and days at a desk, curling up on the sofa with her snotty-nosed teenage brother, watching TV, hiding from their parents. Ruth – *she* was home.

'This garden,' she said, pushing herself away, but holding onto his shoulders, as though he might disappear again if she let go. 'I'm so proud of you. Ma would love this so much.' She held a hand to her heart. 'Bernice invited me,' she said, in response to Winston's confused expression. 'I hope it's okay that I'm here. Her message arrived about three weeks before yours did . . .'

'Of course,' he said, and he meant it. He should be angry. Somehow, Bernice had got hold of Ruth's details, gone behind his back, and invited her. Without speaking to him about it once. But in this moment, all he wanted to say was sorry. Sorry for not being there for her, for grieving on his own and for forgetting her, for shutting her out.

'Ruth,' he said, grabbing her by her hand. 'Come, Lewis is here. And I'll introduce you to Angela and Sal . . . I want you to meet them. And my new housemates too!'

Ruth released her hand from his and squeezed her brother's cheeks, palms on either side of his face. She kissed him square on the forehead, forcing him to tilt his head down. 'I'd love that,' she said. 'But first,' she pulled out a rakhi from her handbag, the red string decorated with gold and silver beads. He put his arm out, instinctually, and felt the cold of her fingers as she tied the string around his wrist. He pulled her close when she'd finished. 'Happy Rakshabandhan, brother. Sorry I'm a few weeks late, but better than sending it in the post,' she said to him, smiling. It was the first time she'd been able to tie a rakhi on his arm in five years. 'I'm afraid I don't have all the stuff for the puja,' she said, 'Mum always handled that. But this,' she said, tapping the string on his wrist, 'is for your protection. Like I always promised. I'll protect you.'

Winston couldn't say anything in response, he just held her close, feeling the warmth of her soul next to his. And as he looked around, he felt the joy, the laughter, the chatter, from his neighbours and friends around him, flood his senses.

It was perfect. Everything was perfect.

Later, as they waved goodbye and dusk was setting in, the sky turning that golden pink, Bernice, Winston, Lewis, Ruth, Sal and Angela were tidying up. Simon was putting Seb to bed. He was completely wiped out from chatting non-stop, running around with new friends in the neighbourhood.

As they continued with their tidying, laughter from the last garden partygoers diminished in the distance, sirens blared as usual, cars tooted along the main road. It was the bank holiday weekend. Time for celebration.

'Hold on,' Sal said, breaking the silence. 'I'll be back in a minute.' He slipped out of the garden gate, with a nod to Angela.

'What's got into him?' Winston said as he yawned, eyes watering from the tiredness. 'It's been such a long day,' he said, remembering his unintentional five-thirty start.

He felt a gentle nudge on the arm from Bernice then. 'She didn't come,' she whispered, to no one but Winston. 'She didn't come after all.'

Winston nodded. He'd been thinking the same thing. Focusing on each new person who'd walked through the gate. Not one of them had been her. He continued his tidying, picking up the odd tissue discarded in the garden, folding up the notebook with the 'would you like a garden open day once a fortnight?' questionnaire Seb had hurriedly demanded halfway through the event. They had fifteen names already.

'Hold on,' Angela said, her ears pricking up. Sal then appeared at the gate, poking his head through. He had a cheeky look on his face, the jovial smile that belonged only to a soul like Sal.

Then he stepped aside, and Winston held his breath. Could it be?

'Hello?' A voice came from behind Sal. And he saw her then. Maya.

She looked the same as in the photographs. Her face imprinted in their minds. Though she was older, her hair was still dark, her eyes still bright.

'I'm sorry I am late,' she said tentatively. 'I . . . I've always liked twilight in the garden, and I'm not very good with crowds now. I hope it's okay that I came? Your note . . .' she started. 'It said I was welcome whenever but—'

'No, no,' Bernice said hurriedly, standing up like she was in the presence of royalty. 'Of course you're welcome whenever. We've been so looking forward to meeting you, Mrs Bhatt.'

'Maya,' she said. 'Please call me Maya.'

'Come in,' Winston said, finally finding his voice. 'Welcome home.'

Chapter 38

Maya

August 2019

Sal guided Maya through the gate, squeezing her hand tight as she squeezed back.

Maya held her breath. She was hit by the smell of sweetness; plants in flower mixed with the syrupy smell of food, ice cream, lingering on the breeze. She spotted the asparagus, one of Hiral's favourite things, in all its glory in the corner, exactly where they'd left it. And the beautiful banana tree welcomed them inside. She could see the yellow and orange sunflowers grazing the sky – tall, proud – and beans climbing up tipis made of tree branches. There was the clematis she'd seen poking over the wall, now completely in flower, and trailing along the old potting shed, which had been given a new lick of paint.

'The eucalyptus,' Maya breathed, her mouth an 'o' of awe as she took in its size. 'It's beautiful,' she said, her eyes instantly brightening. 'You've done such an amazing job.' She took in the view of the houses: Alma's at Number 77, which had been almost completely modernized; and her old house, Number 79, which looked like nothing had changed at all. Rather typical of Mr James. He hadn't even replaced the rickety windows.

'Do you want to take a look around?' Sal said softly.

Maya nodded, gripping Sal's hand.

'This was Ade's cut-flower bed,' Maya said, as she placed one foot in front of the other gingerly. And that's when she saw it, propped against the wall. Her heart skipped, her breath caught in her chest.

Prem's chair.

It was old, disintegrating, but it was there. She let go of Sal's hand for a moment, and walked steadily towards it. Spotting her move, the man she thought was Winston leapt forward and immediately pulled it away from the wall to show her the inscription on the back.

'Handmade by Prem,' he said softly, as she studied the words. Clear as day.

She put her hand to her mouth, to hide a sob. It was still here. After all these years.

'You know,' Maya said, 'Prem, my husband,' she looked the man in the eye then, 'he made that. Decades ago now. We'd told him to make a bench, a picnic bench is what we imagined. And he spent over a week making this. Useless for a party! I can't believe his one measly chair almost outlasted us all,' she said, laughing at the memory. She laughed so she wouldn't cry.

'Well, he certainly knew what he was doing,' the man said, and Maya noticed the lady smiling softly out of the corner of her eye. 'It's been my constant companion in this garden – and I'm pretty sure it's the reason Bernice started talking to me. So I guess, in some ways, it set us on our way. As did you, we think . . .'

The lady, Bernice, with hair as red as the sunset, wandered over to her. 'Mrs Bhatt . . . Maya,' she said, shaking her head, correcting herself. Maya kept one hand on Prem's chair, and Sal was only a foot away for moral support.

'Yes,' Maya nodded, shaking her head in disbelief, her cheeks tight with her smile. 'You did it!'

'Well . . . we *think* it's all down to you,' Bernice said, gesturing towards the potting shed. 'Come and see what we've done.'

She led them over, and through the windows, Maya could see a wall of memories covering the inside of the shed. Photos of her and Alma, the newspaper clippings, the leaflets and flyers they'd created. Beside it, she saw more photos. Photographs of the warring neighbours, and a little boy, working away at the garden. And there, underneath, was Hiral's scrawl: *I ♡ Susie*. She reached forward, her fingers tracing the words. Hiral. Her daughter was here too, always. She couldn't wait to tell her. Maybe she could show her one day as well.

'You kept them,' she said, her voice soft. 'The letters, photos. I didn't know if you'd care.'

'Well,' the man said. 'I wasn't sure at first . . . but something in them,' he pointed to the photo of Maya and Alma, their arms around one another, 'something told me this garden was special. I'm Winston, by the way.'

'Winston,' Maya smiled, 'not Vincent then?'

Winston rolled his eyes, theatrically, sunny and smiling. 'Jenny?' he ventured.

'Yes, she's been calling you Vincent for all these years! Are you going to tell her?' Maya asked, chuckling to herself.

'Probably not . . . I imagine Jenny doesn't really like being corrected.'

'Looks like you've got her sussed!'

'And I'm Bernice,' the woman put her hand out, formally, before registering the wad of envelopes clasped between Maya's hands.

'Oh, these,' Maya said, looking down at the bundle of letters. 'I . . . I wrote these for Alma. My friend who— she lived in your house, Bernice. She's the reason this garden was so loved. I've written her a letter at the start of every season. I've been wanting to . . .' she laughed to herself then, realizing how silly it sounded out loud, 'I'd wanted to bring them back here. To the eucalyptus tree. It meant so much to Alma . . . but maybe they're better off with you.'

She held the envelopes out, green ribbon shining up at them.

'No, we couldn't,' Winston shook his head.

'No, you can,' Maya said again, more forcefully. 'They're nothing more than silly ramblings of an old lonely woman . . . but every season, I wrote to her. I made her a promise, you see, that I'd keep this garden going when I knew I'd never be able to. And I wanted to finally fulfil that promise. It was *you* who did it for me. In these letters, it's mainly me going on, pretending, pretending, pretending I was still here. I've lived so much of my life in my mind since I left. I never wanted to let it go you see. In denial, I suppose. My daughter would say that. You see, lots of my friends moved away . . . my sister, who was in Brent, moved back to Kenya for her retirement, and . . . and recently, I've been living my life through you. But with everything you've done, you've fulfilled a promise that I never could. They might bore you silly, but if not, you might at least find some gardening tips,' she said, looking around, as the flowers and plants absorbed the purple glow of the sky.

'And so,' Winston said gently. 'Alma. Your neighbour. What happened to her?'

Maya took a breath, and looked over at the eucalyptus tree. She prepared herself for the final chapter of that story.

Chapter 39

Maya

August 1992

'ALMA! MAYA!' JENNY CHIMED, squeezing her way through the half-opened gate.

'Jenny!' they called back in unison.

'Don't mind me,' Jenny said. 'I'm going to sit down in my favourite chair until the revellers arrive.' She nodded towards Prem's chair, now dusted green with age. 'A bit like me,' Alma would joke, and her laugh was bold but her movements were gentler now, less confident, as she reached for a place to sit.

'Who have you invited again?' Alma asked. 'Will Kate be here?'

Alma had been jittery all day. They'd been shirking around the sadness of this garden party – the last one in this house. The last one with Alma and Maya living side by side. In the last year, Alma had begun to talk about 'life after Stoke Newington'. She called them her twilight days: 'Oh, Maya, you know, when I'm living out my twilight days in some rural abode in the Peak District or something, I'll think about these silly things we did . . .'

Maya and Kate agreed this was a good sign, no matter how heavy it made Maya's heart. Alma was adamant she didn't want to go to a care home, and Maya was grateful Alma had Kate. Her niece would do all she could to keep Alma at home. To keep her safe and happy for as long as she needed. It didn't make it hurt less, though. Knowing that the end of some of the happiest years of her life had arrived. Stubborn Alma was also now pretending that this move to the Peak District with Kate was her idea after all. And once Alma had an idea, nothing could stop her.

A couple of months after Alma returned from hospital, Kate had dropped off a little highland terrier she'd adopted from a shelter. Fraser. He was a present for Alma and Maya. She hadn't known that Maya didn't like animals, seeing how much joy Morris brought her these days. Kate's intention was for Fraser to prove a helpful companion for Alma, to encourage her to get out a little more and go for walks, build up her confidence again, while also looking out for her. 'I saw how much she loved Bob's puppy Harold . . . I thought maybe they could go on walks together,' Kate said. 'Well, Bob said she might like it . . . I thought he could be right.'

But Fraser was a big ball of energy, running in and out of the crops, causing havoc, waking up in the middle of the night, needing to be let out to relieve himself. And because Alma sometimes woke up disorientated, she would ring a bell that was hooked up to Maya's house, and muppet Maya would have to come and unlock Alma's back door for the dog.

'I'm sorry, Maya,' Kate had said a few weeks later when she'd told her what a nightmare it had all been. 'I didn't realize . . . I just thought a dog might help get her out and about.'

'Maya?' Alma asked again now. 'Is Kate coming?'

'Yes, she's driving down now! She shouldn't be long,' Maya said, keeping her voice flat. 'Fraser! Get away from that,' she shooed the puppy away from the corn, and he lopped over to Hiral, who picked him up in her arms. She loved that dog.

Maya didn't want to think about Kate arriving. Because when Kate left, she'd be taking Alma with her. And, with Alma gone,

Maya and Hiral were set to move across the road, to Bob's flat. Kate had said she could live in Alma's house, until they sold it, but Maya couldn't bear the thought. It wouldn't be the same.

Bob had moved in with his sister on the south coast – Eastbourne in fact – two months ago, leaving his flat empty, and he was waiting for someone else to rent it. It felt appropriate, leaving Eastbourne Road for the real thing, he'd said. An old people's village apparently.

He'd asked Alma if she'd wanted to go too and she'd laughed at him. 'No, no, I'll visit though, don't you worry,' she said, and Bob smiled sadly at that.

Bob's place was a smaller flat, one Maya would be able to afford and which she wouldn't rattle around in when Hiral went off to university the following year.

'Mum,' Hiral had said when she found out. 'You don't reckon Bob's left his Alma shrine behind, do you?'

'Oi, you!' Maya had pinched her cheek gently. 'Don't you be cheeky.' But she couldn't help but smile. She was sure Alma missed Bob, her constant admirer.

The garden looked quieter this year. The beds weren't overflowing with flowers as they generally would be in the height of summer. The corn hadn't grown as strong either – the squirrels had nabbed most of the ears and left them abandoned on the other side of the fence, uneaten. It pained Maya to think of the corn left wasted. Hiral loved picking herself some corn at their garden parties, showing off in front of her friends.

'You miss him at this time of year, don't you?' Alma looked over at her friend then. Maya looked back. Alma was completely lucid, completely present in the moment, but her face was thinner, her eyes had a fog of time, of age, in front of them.

'I miss him every day, at every time of the year. But yes, especially now.'

'No wonder the garden has lost a little of its sparkle,' Alma said, considering the plants and shrubs and vegetables before them. The table Prem had built for them was laden with food: Alma's vegetarian sausage rolls; Maya's paneer samosas and her batata nu shaak; and Angela's lamb casserole. Hiral had made a tiramisu – her first attempt.

'Hello?' came a small voice from the gate.

'Kate!' Alma jumped from her seat, more quickly than she could really manage, and she steadied herself using the table for a moment. As Alma made her way over to her niece, gingerly, her muscles not what they were, Maya's heart dropped, realizing that Kate was Alma's family now. Soon, Maya would be only a memory from the past.

Kate slipped in. Fraser ran straight up to her and started nuzzling her knees.

'Hello you!'

Morris, sunning himself among the sunflowers, looked over, rolling onto his back, as casually as anything. Maya thought of Susie – who hid from any kind of dog possible. This young, yappy little white dog gave Morris no trouble at all. She realized that when Alma took Morris, she'd miss him too. She'd miss his little meow as she walked into the garden in the morning. She might even miss Fraser, waking her up in the middle of the night. They both held a piece of Alma's heart, and that's what Maya would miss most of all.

Kate was, in many ways, a spitting image of Alma: watching them side by side, Maya noticed it as if for the first time, seeing them as a unit now – the new unit. The main differences were their build – Alma was broad-shouldered, after so many years of digging and digging and digging, though her strength was fading away, her shoulders hunching as she walked; Kate was slender, and her hair was always tied up in a bun, whereas Alma's was cropped short because she didn't have the time nor energy nor patience to style it in any way, and Maya, who now cut her hair for her, was grateful for it.

'Fraser, have you been looking after Auntie Alma?' Kate chirruped at the dog, as he bounded up to Alma and onto her lap.

'You have, haven't you?' Alma giggled at the dog, her face illuminated, and suddenly Maya caught Hiral smiling at them, a small tear in the corner of her eye. Her daughter had been brave. She hadn't told Maya how she felt about it all, about her life suddenly changing, but she was being brave. She was Maya's rock right now.

Gradually the garden filled up, with all the old and new faces: Erol, Sal and Angela, and some new neighbours who'd moved into Mrs Graham's house – a young couple with a tiny baby. Hiral's boyfriend Jay turned up, smothering Hiral in kisses, which she hastily wiped away, embarrassed, as Alma guffawed at their display. Maya smiled, seeing her daughter's future building already. She wished Prem had been here to share it too. She hoped Alma might stay here, present, long enough this evening for them to have a little debrief over a small shot of brandy. Prem would have loved that.

Then came Patrick, and Isha, Yusuf, Kelly and their family now all so grown up. And Bina and Sanjay, of course, and Ade with his new girlfriend. Ade stared at her with such wholesome admiration, it warmed Maya's heart.

Within an hour, all the food had been demolished, and Yusuf offered to go fetch some more from his mum's. 'Auntie, you know my mum, she's got lots of food ready to go.'

'If you're sure,' Maya nodded, as the yappy dog ran around her heels. She moved as quickly as she could, nearly knocking over the last tray of chicken wings.

'Maya! You better pick them up or they'll attract the foxes!' Alma called from across the garden.

'It's a good turn out,' Yusuf said, when the dog finally bounded away towards Kate. Yusuf wasn't a dog fan either.

'It is . . . they wouldn't miss her last party, now, would they?'

'Nice to properly meet Sal's new lady,' he said, nodding towards Angela.

'You haven't met Angela before?' Maya frowned. 'Really?'

'Yes, really . . . I'm barely around here any more, am I?' Yusuf shrugged.

'That's right . . . I feel like you never left.'

He chuckled as the dog started bounding over again. 'You know, she'll always be a part of this place, Auntie, even when she's living miles away,' Yusuf said, stroking the dog, and Maya nodded, a lump forming in her throat.

'Oh, seriously! Uh-re-ruh!' Maya said, as Fraser jumped onto her lap with his muddy paws. She brushed him off and brushed herself down, before skipping indoors, shutting the kitchen door behind her for a bit of peace and quiet.

'Hey, Mum,' Hiral was sitting at the kitchen table – her spot, between Prem and Maya's chairs. 'You doing okay?'

'Of course, sweetie. Are you?'

'Mum, I'll always be here to look after you,' she said, out of nowhere.

'Hiral! What do you mean? Your life, it's only starting. You've got to go and live it. Don't you worry about me,' she said, pulling out a chair for herself.

'But I mean when I'm at uni, and afterwards . . . I'll always be with you.'

'Hiral, beta, that's so kind of you. But I want you to live your life – I don't want you having to care for me. I'm still young, anyway. Look at me. I'm all right myself.'

'I don't want you to be here on your own when I'm away.'

For a moment, Maya was about to say what she always said when Hiral brought this up: 'I won't be on my own, beta, I'll have your Auntie Alma.' But she knew that very soon, that would no longer be true. Instead, she said: 'I'll ask for help when I need it. I promise.' Knowing, really, that she never would.

Maya turned away from her daughter, and looked out at the garden. She had a feeling, deep in her heart, her bones, that this was the last time her friends and neighbours would congregate like this, in her garden, eating and drinking, commenting on the plants, smelling the cut flowers, remarking on the strength of the asparagus fronds, the funny texture, talking about their lives, their worlds.

'Right, everyone,' they heard Alma call, a glass in her hand. 'Where's Maya? Come out here!'

Hiral, now half a foot taller than Maya, squeezed her mother's shoulder and led her outside to join the rest.

'There they are! My partners in crime.' Alma was standing on the patio, glass raised, with everyone gathered round in a circle in front of her. Even now, with Alma frailer than before, she had a booming presence. All eyes on her. 'I'm going to keep this brief, because no one wants to hear me rattle on. But you should all know, this woman and her family – Prem, God rest his soul, and Hiral – have been the very best family I could have asked for. Hiral, it's been a privilege to watch you grow up into a wonderful young woman. And Maya, thank you for letting me be part of it all.' Maya's hand flew to the locket around her neck; she saw Prem's face in front of her when he handed it to her, the light reflected in his eyes. 'And you, all of you, have made my days here the most memorable and joyful. I couldn't have wished for better friends. You're the best of people – and this place, it's not too bad either. Cheers, to all of you!'

Alma raised her glass, a huge smile on her face, the creases around her mouth more pronounced since the waning of her cheeks. Maya felt a tear fall from her eye landing in her own glass, Hiral's warm hand squeezing her tight. She wondered what Alma's future looked like, and she wished she could be there to see her through all the bumps in the road.

'To you, Alma,' she whispered back.

The next morning, with the remains of the party collected and tidied up and Alma's house packed away in boxes, the world felt like a different place entirely.

'Do you have everything you need?' Maya said to Alma as they stood beside Kate's car. Alma's eyes were completely dry, whereas Maya had had to keep taking herself away to the bathroom, prompting Alma to say, 'Maya, did you eat something funny? It was those courgettes, wasn't it? I knew we'd had too hot a summer for them. Poisoned them, didn't we?'

'No, Al, it's not the courgettes.' Maya shook her head.

She pulled Hiral close to her, holding her tight. Hiral couldn't say a word. Her eyes were red-rimmed.

'Hold on!' Maya gasped, in complete horror. 'Where are Morris and Fraser? You haven't . . . They're not in their crates?'

'Alma!' Kate tutted, looking her aunt straight in the eye. 'You haven't told her?'

'Must have slipped my mind,' Alma winked mischievously. 'I was . . .'

'Alma, be careful what you say here.'

'Maya, now, don't go crazy, okay? I know you're not the *biggest* fan of that little dog . . . but I do know you love Morris. I want you to look after them for me, okay? It won't be forever. I know Hiral bloody loves them both.'

Hiral smiled, a croaked laugh escaping from her throat. Maya looked at Alma, eyes wide.

'Look, hear me out, okay? I don't want you to be alone. I know, I *know* you have Hiral, and millions of friends, and you'll have the garden to keep you busy, but they'll be good companions. They'll take care of you when Hiral is off at university, taking over the world. I didn't want them to leave their home – they love this place. And, as much as you hate it, they love you too. And it'll give me a reason to visit, regularly, won't it?'

Maya, whose heart was already bursting with agony, smiled, her lips pulled tight together over her teeth, trying as hard as she could to keep the tears in. 'Where are they now?' she asked.

'They're in your house – I popped them in the living room, a few hours ago.'

'*A few hours ago!*' Maya yelped, horrified. She exchanged a glance of terror with Hiral. 'What did you go and do that for! They'll . . . the cushions!'

'They'll be *fine*, don't fuss, Maya,' Alma said.

'I'd go check on them quickly if I were you!' Kate whispered to Maya and Hiral. 'I'm sorry, I didn't know she hadn't told you!'

'All right,' Maya said through gritted teeth. 'I'll take them for now, until you get settled . . . Then they're going with you, okay? They can be *my* reason to visit . . .'

'Suit yourself,' Alma chortled.

'Well, Alma, look after yourself and Kate, okay? Don't drive her mad like you have me.' Maya smiled, hoping she could trick her breaking heart into gluing itself back together.

'I'll do my utmost, dear Maya,' Alma smiled, her face soft, the creases around her eyes a reminder of their years of laughter.

'Okay, well, call me when you arrive,' Maya said, keeping her voice practical, trying to keep her mind off the reality of the moment. 'And keep me updated. On everything! Kate, you have my home and work numbers, don't you? And Alma. I'll write – you better write too!'

'Come on, Maya, don't get all soppy on me,' Alma shrugged.

'Okay, I won't,' Maya nodded, tapping the top of the car. She'd seen people do it in films, and it seemed the right thing to do, but as she did, she felt stupid.

'Thank you, Maya,' Alma said. 'For letting me make my own decisions.'

'Alma, you never gave us a choice,' Maya smiled back.

As the car pulled away, Alma called out of the window, 'Hiral, I love you, my girl! You make sure your mum keeps her promise, okay? And whoever buys my house, I'll tell them to only take instructions from you, Maya!'

Hiral croaked 'I love you' back, and Maya simply waved. She hadn't told Alma that she was moving. She couldn't bring herself to.

As quickly as she could, Maya gulped down the rock in her throat, and opened her living-room door, where Morris and Fraser were bounding around the room after one another. Fraser, joyfully, Morris exasperated. And, as she expected, in the corner . . . someone had relieved themself.

'Goodness me, what a leaving present, Alma,' she muttered to the animals. 'Come on you two, go outside!' Hiral ran to open the kitchen door, and Fraser promptly chased Morris outside, right up onto the fence, out of Fraser's reach, and the little dog yapped up at him playfully. Maya and Hiral watched them for a while, arm in arm, imagining their friend watching from her kitchen next door too, on the other side of the wall, with a smile on her lips.

After everything in Maya's life, she knew eras came to an end. But she'd thought this one might last for ever.

Hiral took herself upstairs, kissing her mother on the cheek. 'I'm going to finish packing,' she said. And as she left, Fraser came bounding inside and nestled at Maya's feet. For once, she didn't flinch. She pictured Alma's face, Alma's smile when Fraser raced up to her, nuzzling her, rolling over to be stroked.

Alma had loved everyone Maya loved – Prem, Hiral, Bina – fiercely, as though they were her own. And now, it was Maya's turn to return the favour.

'Come on, you,' Maya said, ruffling the dog's head. 'Let's get you some dinner, you silly dog.'

Chapter 40

Maya

August 1995

Initially, in the years that followed, Maya and Bina visited Alma every two months, spending just a day at Kate's because a weekend was a bit too much for Alma. One day, Alma mistook Maya for a health visitor. It was the first time she hadn't recognized her immediately.

'I'm fine, miss,' she'd said, curt and cold, not wanting to be fussed. Maya had kept a smile on her face, desperate not to unsettle her further. But she'd had to fight hard to stop the tears spilling from her eyes. She'd had to bite down on her tongue to stop herself from crying out. And then she'd simply sat back down, watching as Kate chatted about their routine, the day trips they'd taken. Alma nodded when she needed to, but her eyes looked over Kate's shoulder, out to the garden.

This year, Maya had been to visit three times, once with Hiral, and twice alone. The journeys home on her own were the worst, filled with worry and regret and sadness for her friend, whose life had changed so much. And she was sad for herself, for the years they'd spent together, the happiest of memories now held only by her.

She'd wanted to see her more, but Kate had said Alma was getting tired, and her strength had all but gone. Things were difficult, visitors unsettled her more often than not. So Kate liked to keep things simpler these days, it was easier that way. In lieu of a visit, she'd send Maya a photograph of Alma, smiling, toothy and warm, with one of Kate's cats nestled on her lap. She missed her, oh every day she missed her, but she knew she was looked after. And when Alma had a good day, when Alma remembered, Kate told her everything – how loved she was, by everyone. By Maya too.

Today marked three years since Maya had moved out of her house. That afternoon, she and Morris watched from the window as the family who'd lived in the house since the January of 1993 – a baby girl and a mother and father – moved out of Number 79. The girl was now a toddler. Maya had seen her taking her first steps out of the front door, along the street, a hand in her mother's, toddling up and down the street to delighted squeals of glee from both her parents. Maya couldn't help it. She'd been watching the comings and goings of that house ever since she'd moved out, her heart tugging every time someone walked out of that door. The 'To Let' sign was already up, and in a few days' time, she knew there'd probably be a new set of people living there.

Alma's house, however, remained unsold, uninhabited.

Fraser, previously curled up in his bed, began to bark, blocking out the laughter playing on the television. He had taken to the new flat quite easily, unlike Morris, who had spent days under the bed. The needs of the dog and the cat were the most interesting parts of her day now. Hiral was off at university, studying in Italy for the year, sending postcards, living her life. Whenever she came home for the holidays, there was life again – but when she was gone, everything was quiet. It was like Maya was trapped in a mausoleum of memories; photos littering every surface, every shelf, every cabinet. But still, nothing felt like home, she didn't belong here yet. She wasn't sure she'd ever belong here.

Fraser continued yapping, and Maya brought herself back to the present, away from the window, and she searched for the cause. Her telephone was trilling on her new glass coffee table, a present from Hiral.

Her phone continued to ring.

'Hello?'

'Hi Maya, it's Kate.'

Maya could tell from the tone of her voice. Even Fraser had stopped barking. Maya could sense how muggy her flat was, the heat overpowering, the only sound the over-dramatic conversation on the TV. Her consciousness washed in and out. She was in the garden, watching Alma lying on the grass with baby Hiral on her stomach. She was watching Prem building a bench, Alma a foot away barking instructions. Alma, crying among the vegetable patches, calling for her dad. Alma giving her speech, toasting them, the place they'd created, the life they'd lived. She watched Alma pull Hiral into a hug. She watched as Alma trotted on the Underground with the protest signs, Bina's face of disapproval. She saw Alma, that very first moment she'd set eyes on her. Gruff, frustrated, standoffish. And then that first smile, when she finally began to thaw in the garden. Coffees shared almost every morning. Planting plans drawn up. Lists and notes of Alma's dotted around everywhere.

Her friend's smile. Her laugh. Sitting in her bed, Kate's cat on her lap.

It was gone. It was all gone.

She squeezed her eyes shut, as if the darker her vision became, she might be able to erase it all.

'She asked for you, Maya,' Kate said eventually. 'Last night, she said we should call you in the morning, invite you over. I think she knew.'

Maya nodded, her eyes still closed, her heart frozen.

'I'm sorry, Kate,' Maya said, when she was able to make her voice work. 'I'm so sorry.' And without another word, Maya hung up the phone.

She pulled out a pad of paper. She could barely see. Her eyes scrunched up so tight, so red and raw, but she picked up a pen and she began to scrawl.

The first letter. Just for today. A chance to fulfil a promise.

Saturday, 26 August 1995

Fraser whimpered, resting his nose on Maya's lap as she rocked herself, one hand resting on her face, blocking out everything around her.

Chapter 41

Bernice

August 2019

THERE WAS A SILENCE in the muggy summer air as Maya finished her story. Bernice was the first to speak.

'I'm so sorry, Maya.' She didn't know what else to say, her mind on these two friends she'd imagined for the last few months.

Maya was sitting on Prem's chair, which they'd moved under the eucalyptus tree for her, and from here she admired the garden, looking up at the house she'd once lived in. She shook her head slowly. 'Thank you,' she replied quietly, before adding, louder, 'You both looking after the garden, that's been the loveliest thing for me. Honestly, I prayed for it. I hoped, and didn't dare believe until now.' Her brown eyes glinted then, her hands still clutched around her letters. 'Here,' she passed them to Bernice, who took them gingerly. 'For you.'

'Thank you,' Bernice replied quietly. 'Hold on, we've . . . we've got something for you too.' She looked at Winston then, who shrugged, unsure what she was doing, and she threw herself into her house, rattling through the utensils drawer, searching frantically.

Then she found it. The spare key to the gate.

Coming back outside, she noticed Maya looking around the garden, taking it all in. And Winston – his eyes locked onto Lewis's.

It was a look that told her there was more to Lewis and Winston's story. Maybe this was a new beginning for them too. Their hands sat next to each other on the table, the hair on their arms touching. The unselfconsciousness with which they both conducted themselves, like they'd slipped back into the past, when love was all they thought about. Love was what kept them going.

'Here,' Bernice passed the key to Maya, who held it between both palms. Bernice looked around at the garden, the plants tucking themselves away as the sun finally left the sky, the night casting a blanket over them all. 'It's a key to the garden gate,' she explained. 'You can come whenever you please. You can spend some time here, even when we're not around, so you can have a few moments of peace. This place . . . it holds so much of your history. It'd be lovely for us to share it with you again, because you've shared so much with us. I don't think you even realize what a gift all those leaflets and photographs have been.'

Bernice caught Winston's eye, and he placed a hand on his heart, and bowed his head at her. She'd let someone in.

Maya smiled, nodding, and opened her mouth to speak but she couldn't say a word. She simply looped the key chain round her necklace, a locket, the large key giant in comparison.

'Oh, so silly, I'll find a proper place for it,' she said, more to herself than anyone else, then she looked up at Bernice and Winston, and said: 'Thank you for being so kind to me.'

Twenty minutes later, Sal and Angela walked Maya home, and Winston, Ruth and Lewis were tucked up in their living room. 'Sure you don't want to join us?' Winston had asked Bernice.

'No, no, you have fun, you've got lots of catching up to do, I imagine!' she smiled and waved them off.

She looked towards the eucalyptus tree, haloed by the orange haze of the sky, brushing the edges of the leaves with colour. She pictured the wad of envelopes, sitting on the kitchen table, and she wondered what mysteries and memories lay within. She wondered what lives had been lived in this garden before them.

And as she thought of Lewis, Winston and Ruth, as she pictured Seb snoring upstairs, Simon tucking him in, she wondered what memories lay ahead of them all too.

Chapter 42

Winston

One week later, September 2019

After the party, Ruth stayed at Winston's for a few days before she had to head back home. He'd given her his bed, while he slept in a sleeping bag on the floor. He wouldn't do it for anyone else other than his big sister; having her there with him had been worth it. She'd been a huge hit with Darlene and Heidi too.

Winston had shown Ruth London; the London he knew, and the London he'd forgotten. They spent every afternoon in pub gardens reminiscing, catching up on life, and every night they'd gone out for dinner someplace nice, her treat, followed by cocktails in a variety of bars in Dalston and Shoreditch. Winston had felt alive for the first time in forever.

Today, Lewis drove them both to the airport, and hung back to let them say goodbye.

'I'm proud of you, little Winston,' Ruth whispered in his ear, her hands tight around him. 'Mummy would be so happy. To know the life you've created for yourself. All by yourself,' she said, looking him in the eyes. He'd told her, a couple of days into her visit, that he was no longer in finance. The lie had hung between them for days already, and he knew he needed to say something. And the moment he did, the weight of a secret kept for so many years lifted from his heart, and his sister's smile grew wider.

'You know,' she said. 'I feel prouder of you now than I ever did. I know it's cheesy, but you're living life for *you*. Not what Dad wanted, or even Mum. You're doing something for you. Just make sure you don't stick with what's easy, or convenient. Always follow what you want. However often that changes. You've never been one to do what was easy.'

'You're starting to sound like Mum,' he laughed, his hand fiddling with his rakhi.

'Someone has to!' She kissed his forehead then, and pushed away from him, her hand waving goodbye behind her.

'Send my love to the kids,' Winston called to her. 'Tell them they'll be seeing me at Diwali.'

'I've already told them, they can't wait!'

Winston beamed. For the first time in years, he was excited to fly to Canada to see Ruth's life, to experience the world she lived in, the life she'd built for herself. They'd agreed he'd visit for a week, and then they'd both fly to India to see their father. He knew it'd be difficult, but he wouldn't be doing it alone.

A few days later at home, Winston looked out at the garden: it was dormant, signs of the party the week before almost gone, apart from the trodden-down sundried grass Bernice had been trying to resurrect ever since. Lewis was back in Oxford, Ruth in Canada, Bernice and Seb were out with family, and Darlene and Heidi were at work. But he didn't feel the weight of loneliness in the air now.

That's when he noticed the gate creeping open, and in came Maya, dressed in a cardigan like one his mother might have had years ago. She looked around the garden before making her way to Prem's chair, carefully, but more confidently than last time. No need for Sal's encouraging hand today. She ran her fingers over the sunflowers on her way. Winston noticed the glimmer of a smile on her face.

He turned away, leaving her for a moment to enjoy the space on her own.

Finally, he let himself out of the door, with two cups of tea in his hand.

'Hello,' he said quietly, not wanting to break the peace.

'Hello there,' Maya said, looking up. 'I hope it is okay, me being here?'

'Of course, you're welcome *whenever* you want. That's what the key's for.' It was clasped tightly in her hands. 'I brought you a cup of tea . . . milk and a Canderel. I hope that's okay?'

'Perfect, thank you.'

They stayed like that for a while, listening to the birds, slurping their tea, watching parakeets coming down to feed, with an intake of breath from Maya as they swooped close by overhead.

'I've been thinking,' he said, eventually. 'I bought an album, to put all your photos in. We lined the shed walls with the clippings, but I don't want them to get damp,' he said hurriedly. 'I thought it'd be nice to have something a bit more permanent. Keep all the memories, past and present, in one place. Hold on, let me show you.'

He hurried into the kitchen and brought out his canvas bag of crafting materials – a box of the clippings, carefully taken down from the shed walls, now ordered and tacked in place.

'What do you think?' he said, showing her page by page.

'You know,' she said, looking up at him. 'I've got the originals, they might go a little better!'

'No, no,' he said, 'I can't take your originals.'

'We got loads of copies, don't worry. That's what we did back then, before photo printers! I'll be five minutes, and I can bring them here.'

'It's okay,' he said, apologizing. 'I didn't want to ambush you. We can do it another time.'

'I've got an afternoon free, haven't you?' she said, smiling. 'Make me another tea, and I'll be back in a moment!'

When Maya returned, an armful of Kodak envelopes clutched in her hands, he quickly relieved her of them and laid them out on the garden table.

Winston's eyes roved over the photographs, crisper, clearer, than he'd seen them before.

They worked together, organizing the photographs chronologically, guided by Maya's commentary. 'That's Erol, Sal's dad,' she said, pointing to a tall man with dark hair. Strong cheekbones and eyebrows.

'But he's so tall?' Winston laughed, picturing Sal, who stood a foot shorter than him.

'I know, Sal seemed to miss that gene. But got everything else,' Maya chuckled. 'That's my Prem,' she continued, pointing to a man sitting in a chair Winston knew well. He was wearing a flat cap, a broad smile, cheeks full, nose pointed, a bundle cradled in his arms. So young. And kind, it was clear he was kind, even from here. 'And my little girl Hiral.'

They spent the next few hours sticking the photographs in, and Winston handed Maya the gold pen he'd bought specially to write captions against the black sugar paper. He watched as her hand wrote carefully, slightly shaky, nervous.

Guy Fawkes' Night, 1975

Bina and Alma sporting their protest signs, 1976

Alma and Maya, digging, again, 1978
Erol, Bob, Prem and Patrick enjoying each other's company, 1984
Hiral, Isha and Yusuf, picking veg for lunch, 1986
The first 'official' community garden party, 1988

Until eventually, she wrote the final caption for her photographs: *The last community garden party, 1992*

She passed the book over to Winston then, and he pulled out a glossy photograph of his own, tucked at the back of the pages.

Seb had taken it. He'd spent the day entertaining, and chatting, and hosting, while also running around with his mum's phone, snapping candids of everyone he saw. Bernice had sent them all to Winston and he'd finally discovered this one among the sixty-odd others. A snapshot of the garden. The banana tree in full view, the eucalyptus towering over everyone. Every spot of the garden was full. And in the centre, framed by their neighbours, were Bernice and Winston chatting, clinking their glasses together.

Underneath, in his messier handwriting, Winston wrote: *The second first garden party, 2019*

Then he closed the book, leaving pages and pages to be filled by memories yet to be made.

'What made you want to do it? The book?' Maya asked.

'Well, I thought it'd be nice to have something to keep, for whoever lives here after me. Mr James could keep it for them, or Bernice. A little introduction.' He cleared his throat.

'You don't think you'll be here forever?'

Winston looked at the garden around them.

'I love it here, and I'd really like to be here a while longer, but I don't think I'll be here forever.' He thought of Sal and Angela in the shop, Ruth in Canada, Lewis in Oxford, his dad back in India. He knew his life didn't have to be tied up in one place; it was the people who mattered most.

'I'm just loving being here right now,' he said.

'Cheers to that,' Maya said, and they clinked their mugs of tea together. 'So am I.'

Epilogue

August 1992

'Maya!' Alma called in to the kitchen, as Maya finished washing up. They'd been going over the plans for their final garden party, only a few weeks away, and Hiral, their minute-taker, was zonked out on her mother's bed, exhausted from trying to keep up.

Neither Maya nor Alma could sleep, buzzing with adrenaline, thinking about all that was to come.

'They're at it again,' Alma said. 'Come see, Maya! I thought you'd put some coffee grounds down to keep them out.'

'I think they *like* the coffee,' Maya said, settling into the chair beside Alma, a steaming cup of the stuff in her hand.

'Look at them, trampling everything. Look – our ornamental grasses in that bed, just a mess now – a *nest*. They use it as a nest!'

'Well, you're always talking about getting more wildlife into the garden. And you didn't even like those ornamental grasses.'

'True – too poncy for me,' Alma smiled, admiring the garden in the evening light, the flowers and plants haloed by the pinky-orange glow of the city. 'I spoke to the doctor again today, Maya. He says it might not be long before things become even more unfamiliar.' She kept staring ahead as she said the words, unable to look at Maya, knowing her friend's face would be what broke her. Not what the doctor said to her. Not the fact that in a few months or years, she might not remember her friend she loved at all.

'Alma,' Maya said softly, holding her hand.

'No, Maya, it's fine. I'm fine about it. It's life. A fish-like memory always did run in my family, my father would have forgotten his head if it hadn't been screwed on,' she laughed to herself. 'I wanted to be here forever,' she looked at Maya now, who was squeezing her hand so tight. 'I wanted to be here for the rest of my life.'

'Alma,' Maya said, wanting to say something hopeful, unable to say anything at all.

'No, we don't need to keep going over it. I know me leaving – it's for the best. But, while I'm all here, for tonight at least, I want you to promise me something,' she turned to look at Maya, and suddenly Alma was the same stern fifty-one-year-old she had been when Maya first arrived in this house, when Maya had been shellshocked, unsure of what to expect, hoping Alma could be a mother figure to her. How wrong she'd been.

Maya simply nodded, the warmth of her hand on Alma's telling her that she would promise, of course she would. She would promise the world.

'I want you to keep this garden going. I want this garden to hold the spirit we have created. Will you promise?'

'I will, Alma, of course. This garden will always live on.'

'Good. And also, don't let them ever put me in one of those pink nighties, okay? Wherever I go, at Kate's or after, promise me that too. Pink is not my colour.'

Maya clapped her hands at that, surprised by her own laughter. 'Sure thing, boss,' she said.

'Don't call me boss,' Alma said, in Hiral's little-girl voice. She cleared her throat.

'Alma,' Maya said softly. 'I promise – I promise it all.'

Maya watched Alma, who had turned away and was lost in the sights and sounds of Stoke Newington once more. Lost in the intricacies of the planting. The fronds of the asparagus, long and leggy, she was lost in the hollyhocks, and the self-seeded buddleia, forming a barrier towards the end of the garden. She was lost in the memories of their friends, crowded around this garden, chatting, laughing, for all those years. And there, in the middle of the patio, was Prem's chair. For a moment, Maya saw him sitting there in his linen shirt, a cigarette hanging from his hand, when, in the corner of the garden, she saw a little fox cub sneak its way through the fence into the nest among the ornamental grasses, tucking himself up for the night.

'You know, I've always loved those foxes,' Alma whispered to Maya, finally, like it was their little secret.

Acknowledgements

THOUGH THE FIRST DRAFT of this book was written during lockdown, I had the support of so many wonderful people to keep me going. This book wouldn't exist without them.

Huge thank you to Hayley Steed, the best agent I could ask for. Hayley is the voice of reason and wisdom, and has been a support and a friend when I've needed it. I'm so lucky to have you in my corner! Thank you to the wonderful team at Madeleine Milburn Literary Agency, especially Elinor Davies, Valentina Paulmichl, Liane-Louise Smith, Amanda Carungi, Georgina Simmonds, Giles Milburn and Georgia McVeigh. And a massive thank you to my editor Charlotte Brabbin, who saw the potential in this book from its very first iteration, and whose guidance and creativity kept me excited about it draft after draft after draft. Thank you to the whole team at HarperFiction for all your incredible work on my books. Thank you to Susanna Peden, Olivia French, Alice Gomer, Harriet Williams, Erin White, Lynne Drew, Ellie Game, Sophie Waeland, Laura Daley, Kim Young and Victoria Pullen. Thank you to Jyotirmayee Patra for the most beautiful cover illustration too.

I'm indebted to the brilliant team at William Morrow for their care with my novels. Thank you to my editor Rachel Kahan – it's been a joy working with you – and to the whole team, including Holly Rice, Rachel Berquist, Jennifer Hart, Ariana Sinclair and

Pamela Barricklow. I know my books are in the best hands with you all.

Thank you to the international publishers who've taken my books to readers worldwide – it's been lovely to be in touch with some of you over the past few years, and it will always feel like a dream when readers from all over the world message to tell me they have enjoyed meeting my characters!

To all the wonderful readers, booksellers, librarians and library staff. Your support and love for *The Reading List* gave me such a boost while I was writing this one. It means so much, so thank you! I hope you like spending time with Alma, Maya, Winston and Bernice.

To my colleagues and friends at Hodder Studio, Bea, Harriet, Izzy, Jamie, Kwaku and Myf – I think you had to listen to TOO much of my first draft and editing chat, but thank you for all your wisdom along the way. And to all my authors at Hodder, you made my job as an editor the biggest privilege ever. Working with so many talented writers has been a joy. I'm so proud to call so many of you friends now; you all inspire me constantly. I've always known this, but it has become even clearer recently, I really do have the best friends in the world. Michael, I don't think anyone bought more copies than you did of *The Reading List* – I'm so grateful for your support and love, and I hope your family liked the book . . . and I hope you like this one! Rachael, thank you for being one of my first readers, hearing how much you loved *The Twilight Garden* made my year. Mary, thank you for everything – I'm so honoured to have you as the ultimate cheerleader and friend in my life. Ifey, thank you for so much, but especially for always helping me put things into perspective when my mind runs away with me. Noor, your friendship and encouragement will always mean the world – thank you for being you. Thank you to *all* my friends, especially to those who've been there every step of the way, who've helped calm down my anxiety when things got too much and celebrated the wins too. Christina, Josh, Kitty, Maeve, Radiya and Rosie – I don't know where I'd be without you! Sukh and Callie, thank you both for being not only the best writing pals, but wonderful friends too.

Thank you to all my family. To my auntie, for taking every opportunity to shout about my book and sharing it with everyone she knows! And, in particular, to my parents – I hope you never forget that I write because of you, because you encouraged me when I was younger, because you've been so supportive from the very beginning. Thank you for helping me make my dreams come true. Every story I write is for you.

And finally, to Will. I'll always think of this book as *our* book, because of all the little snippets and details from our life in Stoke Newington, and for how often you've had to listen to me talk about these characters, and for all your gardening wisdom too, of course. I'm so grateful for you being so patient and kind with every little worry I have, for listening to me repeat the same things over and over again (yes, I said the same thing in the last acknowledgements, but it continues to be true). And thank you for reading this book multiple times, in every iteration. Thank you, always.